THE GREAT AMERICAN NOVEL

PHILIP ROTH

THE
GREAT
AMERICAN
NOVEL

JONATHAN CAPE
THIRTY BEDFORD SQUARE LONDON

First published in Great Britain 1973
Copyright © 1973 by Philip Roth

Jonathan Cape Ltd
30 Bedford Square, London WCI

ISBN 0 224 00953 2

Portions of this book have appeared, in slightly different
form, in *Sports Illustrated* and *Esquire*

Printed in Great Britain
by Lowe and Brydone (Printers) Ltd
Thetford, Norfolk
Bound by W and J Mackay Ltd, Chatham

... the Great American Novel is not extinct
like the Dodo, but mythical like the Hippogriff ...

Frank Norris, *The Responsibilities
of the Novelist*

To Barbara Sproul

ACKNOWLEDGMENTS

The baseball strategy credited to Isaac Ellis in chapters five, six, and seven is borrowed in large part from *Percentage Baseball* by Earnshaw Cook (M.I.T. Press, 1966).

The curve-ball formula in chapter five was devised by Igor Sikorsky and can be found in "The Hell It Doesn't Curve," by Joseph F. Drury, Sr. (see *Fireside Book of Baseball*, Simon and Schuster, 1956, pp. 98–101).

The tape-recorded recollections of professional baseball players that are deposited at the Library of the Hall of Fame in Cooperstown, New York, and are quoted in Lawrence Ritter's *The Glory of Their Times* (Macmillan, 1966) have been a source of inspiration to me while writing this book, and some of the most appealing locutions of these old-time players have been absorbed into the dialogue.

I also wish to thank Jack Redding, director of the Hall of Fame Library, and Peter Clark, curator of the Hall of Fame Museum, for their kindness to me during my visits to Cooperstown.

P. R.

CONTENTS

THE GREAT AMERICAN
NOVEL

PROLOGUE

CALL ME SMITTY. That's what everybody else called me—the
ballplayers, the bankers, the bareback riders, the baritones, the
bartenders, the bastards, the best-selling writers (excepting
Hem, who dubbed me Frederico), the bicyclists, the big game
hunters (Hem the exception again), the billiards champs, the
bishops, the blacklisted (myself included), the black marke-
teers, the blonds, the bloodsuckers, the bluebloods, the bookies,
the Bolsheviks (some of my best friends, Mr. Chairman—what
of it!), the bombardiers, the bootblacks, the bootlicks, the
bosses, the boxers, the Brahmins, the brass hats, the British
(*Sir* Smitty as of '36), the broads, the broadcasters, the bronco-
busters, the brunettes, the black bucks down in Barbados
(*Meestah* Smitty), the Buddhist monks in Burma, one Bulk-
ington, the bullfighters, the bullthrowers, the burlesque comics
and the burlesque stars, the bushmen, the bums, and the but-
lers. And that's only the letter B, fans, only *one* of the Big
Twenty-Six!

Why, I could write a whole book just on the types beginning with X who have called out in anguish to yours truly—
make it an encyclopedia, given that mob you come across in
one lifetime who like to tell you they are quits with the past.
Smitty, I've got to talk to somebody. Smitty, I've got a story
for you. Smitty, there is something you ought to know. Smitty,
you've got to come right over. Smitty, you won't believe it but.
Smitty, you don't know me but. Smitty, I'm doing something
I'm ashamed of. Smitty, I'm doing something I'm proud of.
Smitty, I'm not doing anything—what should I do, Smit? In

transcontinental buses, lowdown bars, high-class brothels
(for a change of scenery, let's move on to C), in cabarets,
cabanas, cabins, cabooses, cabbage patches, cable cars, cabri-
olets (you can look it up), Cadillacs, cafés, caissons, calashes
(under the moon, a' course), in Calcutta, California, at Cal-
gary, not to be confused with Calvary (where in '38 'a voice
called "Smitty!"—and Smitty, no fool, kneeled), in campa-
niles, around campfires, in the Canal Zone, in candlelight (see
B for blonds and brunettes), in catacombs, rounding the Cape
of Good Hope, in captivity, in caravans, at card games, on
cargo ships, in the Caribbean, on carousels, in Casablanca (the
place *and* the movie, wherein, to amuse Bogey, I played a
walk-on role), in the Casbah, in casinos, castaway off coasts,
in castles (some in air, some not), in Catalonia (with Orwell),
Catania, catatonia, in catastrophes, in catboats, in cathedrals,
in the Catskills (knaidlach and kreplach with Jenny G.—I taste
them yet!), in the Caucasus (Comrade Smitty—and proud of
it, Mr. Chairman!), in caves, in cellars, in Central America, in
Chad, in a chaise longue (see under B burlesque stars), in
chalets, in chambers, in chancery, in a charnel house (a disem-
bodied voice again), in Chattanooga (on Johnny's very choo-
choo), in checkrooms, in Cherokee country, in Chicago—look,
let's call it quits at Christendom, let's say *there*, that's been
Smitty's beat! Father confessor, marital adviser, confidant,
straight man, Solomon, stooge, psychiatrist, sucker, sage, go-
between, medicine man, whipping boy, sob sister, debunker,
legal counselor, loan service, all-night eardrum, and sober
friend—you name it, pick a guise, any guise, starting with
each and every one of the Big Twenty-Six, and rest assured,
Smitty's worn that hat on one or two thousand nights in his
four score and seven on this billion-year-old planet in this
trillion-year-old solar system in this zillion-year-old galaxy
that we have the audacity to call "ours"!

   O what a race we are, fans! What a radiant, raffish,
raggedy, rakish, rambunctious, rampaging, ranting, rapacious,
rare, rash, raucous, raunchy, ravaged, ravenous, realistic, reasonable, rebellious, receptive, reckless, redeemable, refined,
reflective, refreshing, regal, regimented, regrettable, relentless, reliable, religious, remarkable, remiss, remorseful, re-
pellent, repentant, repetitious (!!!!), reprehensible, repressed,

reproductive, reptilian, repugnant, repulsive, reputable, resentful, reserved, resigned, resilient, resistant, resistible, resourceful, respectable, restless, resplendent, responsible, responsive, restrained, retarded, revengeful, reverential, revolting, rhapsodical, rhythmical, ribald, rickety, ridiculous, righteous, rigorous, riotous, risible, ritualistic, robustious (*adj. Archaic or Humorous* [pick 'em], meaning "rough, rude or boisterous," according to N.W.), roguish, rollicking, romantic, rompish, rotten, rough-and-ready, rough-and-tumble, roughhousing, rowdyish, rude, rueful, rugged, ruined, rummy (*chiefly Brit.* don'cha know. *Slang* odd; queer), rundown, runty, ruthless race!

A' course that's just one man's opinion. Fella name a' Smith; first name a' Word.

And just who *is* Word Smith? Fair enough. Short-winded, short-tempered, short-sighted as he may be, stiff-jointed, soft-bellied, weak-bladdered, and so on down to his slippers, anemic, arthritic, diabetic, dyspeptic, sclerotic, in dire need of a laxative, as he will admit to the first doctor or nurse who passes his pillow, *and in perpetual pain* (that's the last you'll hear about that), he's not cracked quite yet: if his life depended on it, the man in the street could not name three presidents beginning with the letter J, or tell you whether the Pope before this one wore glasses or not, so surely he is not about to remember Word Smith, though it so happened old W.S. cracked a new pack of Bicycles with more than one Chief Exec, one night nearly brought down the republic by cleaning out the entire cabinet, so that at morn—pink peeking over the Potomac, you might say—the Secretary of the Treasury had to be restrained by the Secretary of the Interior from dipping his mitt in the national till to save his own shirt at stud, in a manner of speaking.

Then there are the Popes. Of course no poker, stud, straight, *or* draw, with Pontiffs, other than penny ante, but rest assured, Smitty here in his heyday, kneepans down on terra firma, has kissed his share of rings, and if no longer up to the kneeling-down, still has starch enough left in these half-palsied lips for tasting the papal seal and (if there should be

any takers) touching somewhat tumescent flesh to the peachier
parts of the softer sex, afore he climbs aboard that sleeper
bound for Oblivion. Chucklin': "George, what time she due at
Pearly Gates?" Shufflin': "Don' you worry none, Mistuh
Smitty, I call ya' in time fo' you to shave up and eat a good
heffy breakfass' fo' we gets dere." "*If* we gets there, George.
Conductor says we may all be on a through train, from what
he hears." "Tru'? To where, Mistuh Smitty? De end of de
line?" (Chorus behind, ahummin' and astrummin', "Tru'
train, tru' train, choo-choo on tru', I wanna choo-choo on home
widout delay!") "Seems there isn't any 'end' to this line,
George." Scratchin' his woolly head: "Well, suh, day don'
say nuttin' 'bout dat in de schedule." "Sure they do, old
George, down in the fine print there: 'Stops only to receive
passengers.' " "Which tru' train dat, Mistuh Smitty?"
"Through train bound for Oblivion, George." " 'Oblivion'?
Dat don't sound lak no stop—dat de name of a little girl!"
("Tru' train, tru' train, lem-me choo-choo on home!")

Smitty! Prophet to porters, padre to pagans, peacemaker
for polygamists, provider for panhandlers, probation officer
to pickpockets, pappy to parricides, parent to prostitutes,
"Pops" to pinups, Paul to pricks, plaintalker to pretenders,
parson to Peeping Toms, protector to pansies, practical nurse
to paranoids—pal, you might say, to pariahs and pests of
every stripe, spot, stigma, and stain, or maybe just putty in
the paws of personae non gratae, patsy in short to pythons.
Not a bad title that, for Smitty's autobio.

Or how's about *Poet to Presidents*? For 'twasn't all billiards on the Biggest Boss's baize, sagas of sport and the
rarest of rums, capped off with a capricious predawn plunge
in the Prez's pool. Oh no. Contract bridge, cribbage, canasta,
and casino crony, sure; blackjack bluffer and poker-table personality, a' course, a' course; practiced my pinochle, took 'em
on, one and all, at twenty-one; suffered stonily (and snoozed
secretly) through six-hour sieges of solitaire, rising to pun
when they caught me napping, "Run out of patience, Mr. P.?";
listen, I played lotto on the White House lawn, cut a First
Child for Old Maid in the Oval Office on the eve of national
disaster . . . but that doesn't explain what I was there for.
Guessed yet how I came to be the intimate of four American

presidents? Figured me out? Respectful of their piteous portion of privacy, I call them henceforth ABC, DEF, GHI, and JKL, but as their words are public record, who in fact these four were the reader with a little history will quickly surmise. My capital concern?

I polished their prose.

GHI, tomb who I was closer than any, would always make a point to have me in especially to meet the foreign dignitaries; and his are the speeches and addresses upon which my influence is most ineradicably inked. "Prime Minister," he would say—or Premier, or Chairman, or Chancellor, or General, or Generalissimo, or Colonel, or Commodore, or Commander, or Your Excellency, or Your Highness, or Your Majesty—"I want you to meet the outstanding scribbler in America. I do not doubt that you have a great language too, but I want you to hear just what can be done with this wonderful tongue of ours by a fellow with the immortal gift of gab. Smitty, what do you call that stuff where all the words begin with the same letter?" "Alliteration, Mr. President." "Go ahead then. Gimme some alliteration for the Prime Minister." Of course it was not so easy as GHI thought, even for me, to alliterate under pressure, but when GHI said "Gimme" you gam, get me? "The reason they call that 'elimination,' Prime Minister, is on account of you leave out all the other letters but the one. Right, Smit?" "Well, yes, Mr. President, if they did call it that, that would be why." "And how about a list for the Prime Minister, while you're at it?" "A list of what, Mr. President?" "Prime Minister, what is your pleasure? This fella here knows the names of just about everything there is, so take your choice. He is a walking dictionary. Fish, fruits, or flimflam? Well now, I believe I just did some myself, didn't I?" "Yes, you did, Mr. President. Alliteration." "Now you go ahead, Smitty, you give the Prime Minister an example of one of your lists, and then a little balance, why don't you? Why, I think I love that balance more than I love my wife. Neither-nor, Smitty, give him neither-nor, give him we cannot-we shall not-we must not, and then finish him off with perversion." "Perversion, sir, or inversion?" "Let's leave that to the guest of honor. Which is your preference, Your Honor? Smitty here is a specialist in both."

Do not conclude, dear fans, from this or any GHI anecdote that he was buffoon, clown, fool, illiterate, sadist, vulgarian only; he also knew what he was doing. "Smitty," he would say to me when he came in the morning to unlock the door of the safe in the White House basement where I had passed the night in an agony of alphabetizing and alliterating, "Smitty," he would say, studying the State of the Union address whose inverted phrases and balanced clauses seemed at that moment to have cost me my sanity, "I envy you, you know that, locked away down here in blessed solitude behind six feet of sound-proof blast-proof steel, while just over your head the phone is ringing all night long with one international catastrophe after another. Know something, my boy? If I had it to do all over again—and I say this to you in all sincerity, even if I do not have the God-given gift to say it backwards and inside out—if I had it to do all over again, I'd rather be a writer than President."

Waybackwhen, in my heyday (d.), when "One Man's Opinion" counted for something in this country—being syndicated as it was on the sports page of the Finest Family Newspapers (d.)—back when the American and the National Baseball Leagues existed in harmonious competition with the Patriot League (d.) and I traveled around that circuit for the Finest Family, whose *Morning Star* (the whole constellation, d.) was the daily tabloid in the seven Patriot League cities (I see now they are putting Sports Quizzes on cocktail napkins; how about this then, napkineers—*Query:* Which were the seven cities of the old P. League? What drunk has the guts to re-member?), back before teams, towns, trusting readership simply vanished without a trace in the wake of the frauds and the madness, back before I was reduced to composing captions for sex-and-slander sheets (not unlike a Jap haiku genius working for the fortune cookie crumbs—in my prime, remember, I was master of that most disparaged of poetic forms, the head-line), back before they slandered, jailed, blacklisted, and forgot me, back before the Baseball Writers' Association of America (to name a name, Mr. Chairman!) hired a plainclothesgoon to prevent me from casting my vote for Luke Gofannon at the Hall of Fame elections held every January just one hundred miles from this upstate Home of the D. (sixty-three home runs for the Ruppert Mundys in 1928, and yet Luke ''the Loner'' is ''ineligible,'' I am told—just as I am archaic in my own century, a humorous relic in my own native land, d. as a doornail while still drawing breath!), back before years became decades and decades centuries, when I was Smitty to America and America was still a home to me, oh, about eleven, twelve thousand days ago, I used to get letters from young admirers around the country, expressing somewhat the same sentiment as the President of the United States, only instead of sardonic, sweet: O *so* sweet!

> Dear Smitty, I am ten and want to grow up to be a sports righter two. It is the dream of my life. How can I make my dream come true? Is spelling important as my teacher say? Isn good ideas more important and loving baseball? How did you become so great? Were you born with it? Or did you have good luck? Please send me any pamphlets on being like you as I am making a booklit on you for school.

O sad! Too sad! The sight of my own scratchings makes me weep! How like those schoolchildren who idolized me I now must labor o'er the page! Sometimes I must pause in the midst of a *letter* to permit the pain to subside, in the end producing what looks like something scratched on a cave wall anyway, before the invention of invention. I could not earn passage into the first grade with this second childhood penmanship—how ever will I win the Pulitzer Prize? But then Mount Rushmore was not carved in a day—neither will the Great American Novel be written without suffering. Besides, I think maybe the pain is good for the style: when just setting out on a letter like the lower case w is as tedious and treacherous as any zigzag mountain journey where you must turn on a dime to avoid the abyss, you tend not to waste words with w's in them, fans. And likewise through the alphabet.

The alphabet! That dear old friend! Is there a one of the Big Twenty-Six that does not carry with it a thousand keen memories for an archaic and humorous, outmoded and out-

dated and oblivion-bound sports-scribe like me? To hell with
the waste! Tomorrow's a holiday anyway—Election Day at
the Hall of F. Off to Cooperstown to try yet again. My heart
may give out by nightfall, but then a' course the fingers will
get their rest, won't they? So what do you say, fans, a trip
with Smitty down Memory Lane?

aA
bB
cC
dD
eE
fF
gG
hH
iI
jJ
kK
lL
mM
nN
oO
pP
qQ
rR
sS
tT
uU
vV
wW
xX
yY
zZ

O thank God there are only twenty-six! Imagine a hundred! Why, it is already like drowning to go beyond capital F!
G as in Gofannon! M as in Mundy! P as in Patriot! And what
about I as in I? O for those golden days of mine and yore!
O why must there be d for deceased! Deceit, defeat, decay,
deterioration, bad enough—but d as in dead? It's too damn
tragic, this dying business! I tell you, I'd go without daiquiris,

daisies, damsels, Danish, deck chairs, Decoration Day double-headers, decorum, delicatessen, Demerol, democratic processes, deodorants, Derbys, desire, desserts, dial telephones, dictionaries, dignity, discounts, disinfectants, distilleries, ditto marks, doubletalk, dreams, drive-ins, dry cleaning, duck au montmorency, a dwelling I could call my own—why, I would go without *daylight,* if only I did not have to die. O fans, it is so horrible just being defunct, imagine, as I do, day in and day out

D E A T H

Ten days have elapsed, four in an oxygen tent, where I awoke from unconsciousness believing I was a premature infant again. Not only a whole life ahead of me, but two months thrown in for good measure! I imagined momentarily that it was four score and seven years ago, that I had just been brought forth from my mother; but no—instead of being a premature babe I am practically a posthumous unpublished novelist, ten days of my remaining God only knows how few gone, *and not a word written.*

And worse, our philistine physician has issued an injunction: give up alliteration if you want to live to be four score and eight.

"Smitty, it's as simple as this—you cannot continue to write like a boy and expect to get away with it."

"But it's all I've got left! I refuse!"

"Come now, no tears. It's not the end of the world. You still have your lists, after all, you still have your balance—"

Between sobs I say, "But you don't understand! Alliteration is at the foundation of English literature. Any primer will tell you that much. It goes back to the very beginnings of written language. I've made a study of it—it's true! There would have been no poetry without it! No human speech as we know it!"

"Well, they don't teach us the fundamentals of poetry in medical school, I admit, but they do manage to get something through our heads having to do with the care of the sick and the aged. Alliteration may be very pretty to the ear, and fun to use, I'm sure, but it is simply too much of a stimulant and a strain for an eighty-seven-year-old man, and you are going to have either to control yourself, or take the consequences. Now blow your nose—''

"But I *can't* give it up! No one can! Not even *you,* who is a literary ignoramus by his own admission. 'Stimulant and strain.' 'To control yourself or take the consequences.' Don't you see, if it's in every other sentence even *you* utter, how can I possibly abstain? You've got to take away something else!''

The doctor looks at me as if to say, "Gladly, only what else is left?" Yes, it is my last real pleasure, he is right . . .

"Smitty, it's simply a matter of not being so fancy. Isn't that all really, when you come down to it?''

"My God, *no!* It's just the opposite—it's as natural as breathing. It's the homiest most unaffected thing a language can do. It's the ornamentation of ordinary speech—''

"Now, now.''

"Listen to me for once! Use your ears instead of that stethoscope—listen to the English language, damn it! Bed and board, sticks and stones, kith and kin, time and tide, weep and wail, rough and ready, now or—''

"Okay, that's enough, now. You are working yourself into another attack, and one that you may not recover from. If you do not calm down this instant, I am going to order that your fountain pen and dictionary be taken away.''

I snarled in response, and let him in on a secret. "I could still alliterate in my head. What do you think I did for four days in the oxygen tent?''

"Well, if so, you are deceiving no one but yourself. Smitty, you must use common sense. Obviously I am not suggesting that you abstain from ever having two neighboring words in a sentence begin with the same sound. That would be absurd. Why, next time I come to visit, I would be overjoyed to hear you tell me, 'Feelin' fit as a fiddle'—if it happens to be true. It is not the ordinary and inevitable accidents of alliteration that occur in conversation that wear down a man of your age, or even the occasional alliterative phrase used intentionally for heightened rhetorical effect. It's overindulgent, intemperate, unrestrained excursions into alliteration that would leave a writer half your age trembling with excitement. Smitty, while you were comatose I took the liberty of reading what you've been writing here—I had no choice, given your condition. My friend, the orgy of alliteration that I find on the very first page of your book is just outright ridiculous in a man of your age—it is tantamount to suicide. Frankly I have to tell you that the feeling I come away with after reading the first few thousand words here is of a man making a spectacle of himself. It strikes me as wildly excessive, Smitty, and just a little desperate. I wish I could tell you otherwise, but there's no sense pulling punches with an eighty-seven-year-old man."

"Well, Doctor, much as I welcome your medical school version of literary criticism, you have to admit that you are not exactly the Pulitzer Prize Committee. Besides, it is only the prologue. I was only opening the tap, to get the waters running."

"Well, it still seems needlessly ostentatious to me. And a terrible drain on the heart. And, my friend, you cannot write a note to the milkman, let alone the Great American Novel, without one of them pumping the blood to your brain." He took my hand as I began to whimper again—he claims to have read "One Man's Opinion" as a boy in Aceldama. "Here, here, it's only for your good I tell you this . . ."

"And—and how's about reading alliteration, if I can't write it?"

"For the time being, I'm going to ask you to stay off it entirely."

"Or?"

"Or you'll be a goner. That'll be the ballgame, Smitty."

"If that's the case, I'd *rather* be dead!" I bawled, the foulest lie ever uttered by man.

Than longen folk to goon on pilgrimages.

So said Chaucer back in my high school days, and a' course it is as true now as then.

> And specially, from every shires ende
> Of Engelond, to Caunterbury they wende,
> The holy blisful martir for to seke,
> That hem hath holpen, whan that they were seke.

That is copied directly (and laboriously I assure you) from the famous Prologue to his immortal (and as some will always say, immoral) *Canterbury Tales*. I had to copy it only so as to get the old-fashioned spelling correct. I can still recite the forty-odd lines, up to "A Knight ther was," as perfectly as I did in tenth grade. In fact, in the intervening million years—not since Chaucer penned it, but since I memorized it—I have conquered insomnia many a night reciting those dead words to myself, aloud if I happened to be alone, under my breath (as was the better part of wisdom) if some slit was snoring beside me. Only imagine one of them bimbos overhearing Smitty whaning-that-Aprille in the middle of the night! Waking to find herself in the dark with a guy who sounds five hundred years old! Especially if she happened to think of herself as "particular"! Why, say to one of those slits —in the original accent—"The droghte of Marche hath perced to the rote," and she'd kick you right in the keester. "There are some things a girl won't do, Mr. Word Smith, not even for dough! Good*bye*!" On the other hand, to do women justice, there is one I remember, a compassionate femme with knockers to match, who if you said to her, "So priketh hem nature in hir corages," she'd tell you, "Sure I blow guys in garages. They're human too, you know."

But this is not a book about tough cunts. Nat Hawthorne wrote that one long ago. This is a book about what America did to the Ruppert Mundys (and to me). As for *The Canterbury Tales* by Geoffrey Chaucer, I admit that I have by now forgot what it all meant, if ever I knew. I'm not just talking about the parts that were verboten either. I take it from the copy that I have before me, borrowed on my card from the Valhalla Public Library, that those "parts" are still taboo for schoolkids. Must be—they are the only ratty-looking pages in an otherwise untouched book. Reading with the help of magnifying glass and footnotes, I see (at nearly ninety) that it is mostly stuff about farting. Little devils. They have even decorated the margin with symbols of their glee. Appears to be a drawing of a fart. Pretty good one too. Kids love farts, don't they? Even today, with all the drugs and sex and violence you hear about on TV, they still get a kick, such as we used to, out of a fart. Maybe the world hasn't changed so much after all. It would be nice to think there were still a few eternal verities around. I hate to think of the day when you say to an American kid, "Hey, want to smell a great fart?" and he looks at you as though you're crazy. "A great what?" "Fart. Don't you even know what a fart is?" "Sure it's a game—you throw one at a target. You get points." "That's a dart, dope. A *fart*. A bunch of kids sit around in a crowded place and they fart. Break wind. Sure, you can make it into a game and give points. So much for a wet fart, so much for a series, and so on. And penalties if you draw mud, as we called it in those days. But the great thing was, you could do it just for the fun of it. By God, we could fart for hours when we were boys! Somebody's front porch on a warm summer night, in the road, on our way to school. Why, we could sit around a blacksmith's shop on a rainy day doing nothing but farting, and be perfectly content. No movies in those days. No television. No nothin'. I don't believe the whole bunch of us taken together ever had more than a nickel at any time, and yet we were never bored, never had to go around looking for excitement or getting into trouble. Best thing was you could do it yourself too. Yessir, boy knew how to make use of his leisure time in those days."

Surprising, given the impact of the fart on the life of the American boy, how little you still hear about it; from all appearances it is still something they'd rather skip over in *The Canterbury Tales* at Valhalla High. On the other hand, that may be a blessing in disguise; this way at least no moneyman or politician has gotten it into his head yet to cash in on its nostalgic appeal. Because when that happens, you can kiss the fart goodbye. They will cheapen and degrade it until it is on a level with Mom's apple pie and our flag. Mark my words: as soon as some scoundrel discovers there is a profit to be made off of the American kid's love of the fart, they will be selling artificial farts in balloons at the circus. And you can just imagine what they'll smell like too. Like *everything* artificial.

Yes, fans, as the proverb has it, verily there is nothing like a case of fecal impaction to make an old man wax poetic about the fart. Forgive the sentimental meandering.

And specially, from every shires ende
Of AMERICA to COOPERSTOWN they wende
The holy BASEBALL HEROES for to seke,
That hem hath holpen whan that they were SIX.*

For the ambulatory among my fellow geriatrics here our
annual trip to Cooperstown is something very like the kind of
pilgrimage Chaucer must have been writing about. I won't go
into the cast of characters, as he does, except to say that as I
understand it, his "nine and twenty" were not so knowledge-
able in matters of religion as you might at first expect pilgrims
to be who are off to worship at a holy shrine. Well, so too
for the six and ten it was my misfortune to be cooped up
with on the road to Cooperstown, and then all afternoon long
at the Baseball Museum and Hall of Fame. Ninety-nine per
cent of their baseball "memories," ninety-nine per cent of
the anecdotes and stories they recollect and repeat are pure
hogwash, tiny morsels of the truth so coated over with dis-
credited legend and senile malarkey, so impacted, you might
say, in the turds of time, as to rival the tales out of ancient mythology. What the aged can do with the past is enough
to make your hairs stand on end. But then look at the delusions
that ordinary people have about the day before yesterday.

*A "shire" is a county. Thus the word "sheriff"—he is the reeve ("an
administrative officer of a town or a district") of a shire. I am using "holpen"
to mean "inspired": the baseball players who inspired them when they were
six years old. I realize of course from reading the footnotes that it does not
mean inspired any more than it means "helped." But it will if you want it to,
and I want it to. A writer can take certain liberties. Besides, the word "inspired" appears just twelve lines earlier (line six): "Inspired hath in every
holt and heeth." I will not go into what it means there or how it is pronounced—though I do hope you will note hath,.holt, and heeth, Doctor!—but
the point is I didn't just pull "inspired" out of left field. On the other hand,
if you want to understand the line as G. Chaucer (1340–1400) intended, with
"holpen" meaning "cured," then change the last word to "sixty." Something
like: the baseball players whom they would like to have cure them of being
sixty. Not bad. But then you lose the rhyme. And the truth is that these boys
are over sixty. Though I suppose you could insert the word "over" in there.
I recognize, of course, that "six" does not exactly rhyme with "seke" either,
but that is the only word I could think of to get my meaning across. Writing
is an art, not a science, and admittedly I am no Chaucer. Though that's only
one man's opinion.

Of course, in the way of old men—correction: in the way of all men—they more or less swallow one another's biggest lies whole and save their caviling for the tiniest picayune points. How they love to nitpick over nonsense and cavil over crap all the while those brains of theirs, resembling nothing so much as pickles by this time, soak on in their brine of fantasy and fabrication. No wonder Hitler was such a hit. Why, he might still be at it, if only he'd had the sense to ply his trade in the Land of Opportunity. These are three homo sapiens, descendants of Diogenes, seeking the Truth: "I tell you, there was so a Ernie Cooper, what pitched four innings in one game for the Cincinnatis in 1905. Give up seven hits. Seen it myself." "Afraid you are thinking of Jesse Cooper of the White Sox. And the year was 1911. And he pitched himself something more than four innings." "You boys are both wrong. Cooper's name was Bock. And he come from right around these parts too." "Boggs? Boggs is the feller what pitched one year for the Bees. Lefty Boggs!" Yes, Boggs was a Bee, all right, but the Cooper they are talking about happened to be named Baker. Only know what they say when I tell them as much? "Who asked you? Keep your brainstorms for your 'book'! We are talking fact not fiction!" "But you're the ones who've got it wrong," I say. "Oh sure, *we* got it wrong! Ho-ho-ho! That's a good one! Get out of here, Shakespeare! Go write the Great American Novel, you crazy old coot!"

Well, fans, I suppose there are those who called Geoffrey Chaucer (*and* William Shakespeare, with whom I share initials) a crazy coot, and immoral, and so on down the line. Tell them what they do not wish to hear, tell them that they have got it wrong, and the first thing out of their mouths, "You're off your nut!" Understanding this as I do should make me calm and philosophical, I know. Wise, sagacious, and so forth. Only it doesn't work that way, especially when they do what they did to me ten days ago at Cooperstown.

First off, as everyone knows, the Baseball Hall of Fame at Cooperstown was founded on a falsehood. No more than little George Washington said to his father, "Dad, it is I, etc.," did Major Abner Doubleday invent the game of baseball on that

sacred spot. The only thing Major Doubleday started was the
Civil War, when he answered the Confederate Beauregard by
firing the first shot from Fort Sumter. Yet, to this day, shout
such "heresy" in the bleachers at a Sunday doubleheader, and
not only will three out of four patrons call you crazy, but some
self-styled authority on the subject (probably a Dad with his
Boy—I know the type) will threaten your life for saying something so awful in front of innocent kids.

My quarrel with Cooperstown, however, is over nothing
so inconsequential as who invented the game and where. I
only draw attention to the longevity of this lie to reveal how
without conscience even the highest authorities are when it
comes to perpetuating a comforting, mindless myth everyone
has grown used to, and how reluctant the ordinary believer, or
fan, is to surrender one. When both the rulers and the subjects
of the Holy Baseball Empire can sanctify a blatant falsehood
with something supposedly so hallowed as a "Hall of Fame,"
there is no reason to be astonished (I try to tell myself) at the
colossal crime against the truth that has been perpetrated by
America's powers-that-be ever since 1946. I am speaking of
what no one in this country dares even to mention any longer.
I am speaking of a chapter of our past that has been torn from
the record books without so much as a peep of protest, *except
by me.* I am speaking of a rewriting of our history as heinous as
any ordered by a tyrant dictator abroad. Not thousand-year-
old history either, but something that only came to an end
twenty-odd years ago. Yes, I am speaking of the annihilation
of the Patriot League. Not merely wiped out of business, *but
willfully erased from the national memory.* Ask a Little
Leaguer, as I did only this past summer. When I approached,
he was swinging a little bat in the on-deck circle, ironically
enough, resembling no one so much as Bob Yamm of the Kakoola Reapers (d.). "How many big leagues are there, sonny?"
I asked. "Two," he said, "the National and the American."
"And how many did there used to be?" "Two." "Are you
sure of that now?" "Positive." "What about the Patriot
League?" "No such thing." "Oh no? Never heard of the Tri-
City Tycoons? Never heard of the Ruppert Mundys?" "Nope."
"You never heard of Kakoola, Aceldama, Asylum?" "What
are those?" "Cities, boy! Those were big league towns!"

"Who played for 'em, Mister?" he asked, stepping away from me and edging toward the bench. "Luke Gofannon played for them. Two thousand two hundred and forty-two games he played for them. Never heard his name?" Here a man took me by the arm, simultaneously saying to the boy, "He means Luke Appling, Billy, who played for the White Sox." "Who are you?" I asked, as if I didn't know. "I'm his Dad." "Well, then, tell him the truth. Raise the boy on the truth! You know it as well as I do. I do not mean Luke Appling and I do not mean Luke 'Hot Potato' Hamlin. I mean Luke Gofannon of the Ruppert Mundys!" And what does the Dad do? He puts a finger to his temple to indicate to this little brainwashed American tyke (one of tens of millions!) that *I* am the one that is cracked. Is it any wonder that I raised my cane?

You can look in vain in the papers of Friday, January 22, 1971, for a mention of the vote I cast the previous day at the annual balloting for baseball's Hall of Fame. But the fact of the matter is that I handed it personally to Mr. Bowie Kuhn, so-called Commissioner of Baseball, and he assured me that it would be tabulated along with the rest by the secretary-treasurer of the Baseball Writers' Association of America. WELL, MR. BOWIE KUHN IS A LIAR AND THE HALL OF FAME SHOULD BE NAMED THE HALL OF SHAME.

Of course, the plainclothesgoon they hire especially to keep an eye on me during these annual election day visits greeted our contingent at the Museum door pretending to want to do no more than make us gentlemen at home. "*Well*, if it isn't the senior citizens from over Valhalla way. Welcome, boys."

Oh yes, we are treated like royalty at Cooperstown! How they love "the elderly" when they behave like *boys! Choir*-boys. So long as the only questions we ask have to do with Bock Baker and Lefty Boggs, everything is, as they say over there, "hunky-dory."

"Greetings, Smitty. Remember me?"

"I remember everything," I said.

"How you feeling this year?"

"The same."

"Well," he asked of the pilgrims in my party, "who you boys rooting for?"

"Kiner!"

"Keller!"

"Berra!"

"Wynn!"

"How about you, Mr. Smith?"

"Gofannon."

"Uh-huh," said he, without blinking an eye. "What did he bat again lifetime? I seem to have forgotten since you told me last year."

"Batted .372. Five points more than Cobb. You know that as well as I do. Two thousand two hundred and forty-two regular season games and twenty-seven more in the World Series. Three thousand one hundred and eighty hits. Four hundred and ninety home runs. Sixty-three in 1928. Just go down where you have buried the Patriot League records and you can look it up."

"Don't mind Shakespeare," chortled one of my choirboy companions, "he was born that way. Figment lodged in his imagination. Too deep to operate."

Haw-haw all around.

Here the p.c. goon starts to humor me again. He sure does pride himself on his finesse with crackpots. He wonders if perhaps—oh, ain't that considerate, that perhaps—if *peut-être* I am confusing Luke Gofannon of the—what team is that again?

"The Ruppert Mundys."

—Of the Ruppert Mundys with Lou Gehrig of the New York Yankees. As I can see from the plaque just down the way a hundred feet, the great first-sacker is already a member of the Hall of Fame and has been since his retirement in 1939.

"Look," says I, "we went through this song-and-dance last time round. I know Gofannon from Gehrig, and I know Gofannon from Gehringer, and I know Gofannon from Goose Goslin, too. What I want to know is just why do you people persist in this? Why must you bury the truth about the history of this game—*of this country?* Have you no honor? Have you no conscience? Can you just take the past and flush it away, like so much shit?"

"Is this," asked those two droopy tits known as our nurse, "is this being 'a good boy,' Smitty? Didn't you promise this year you'd mind your manners, if we let you come along? *Didn't you?*" Meanwhile, she and the bus driver had spun me around on my cane, so that I was no longer addressing the goon, but the glove worn by Neal Ball when he made his unassisted triple play in 1909.

"Hands off, you lousy smiling slit."

"Here here, old-timer," said the pimply little genius who drives our bus, "is that any way to talk to a lady?"

"To some ladies it is the *only* way to talk! That is the way half the Hall of Famers whose kissers you see hanging up in bronze here talked to ladies, you upstate ignoramus! Hands off of me!"

"Smitty," said the slit, still smiling, "why don't you act your age?"

"And what the hell does that mean?"

"You know what it means. That you can't always have what you want."

"Suppose what I want is for them to admit THE TRUTH!"

"Well, what may seem like the truth to you," said the seventeen-year-old bus driver and part-time philosopher, "may not, of course, seem like the truth to the other fella, you know."

"THEN THE OTHER FELLOW IS WRONG, IDIOT!"

"Smitty," said the slit, who last year they gave an award and a special dinner for being the best at Valhalla at handling tantrums and rages, "what difference does it make anyway? Suppose they *don't* know it's the truth. Well, they're the ones who are missing out, not you. Actually, you ought to think of yourself as fortunate and take pride in the fact that where others are mistaken, you are correct. If I were you, I wouldn't be angry with them; I would feel *sorry* for them."

"Well, you ain't me! Besides, they know the truth as well as I do. They are only pretending not to."

"But, Smitty, *why?* Now you can be a reasonable and intelligent man, at least when you want to. Why would they want to do a thing like that?"

"Because the truth to them has no meaning! The real

human past has no importance! They distort and falsify to
suit themselves! They feed the American public fairy tales
and lies! Out of arrogance! Out of shame! Out of their terrible guilty conscience!''

"Now, now," says the slit, "you don't really think people
are like that, do you? How can you, with your wonderful love
of baseball, say such things while standing here in the Hall
of Fame?"

I would have told her—and anybody else who wants to
know—if I had not at that moment seen coming toward me down
the stairway from the Babe Ruth Wing, the Commissioner
himself, Mr. Bowie Kuhn, and his entourage. Looking for all
the world like the President of General Motors. And she asks
me why they feed the people lies. Same reason General Motors
does. The profit motive, Mr. Chairman! To fleece the public!

"Commissioner! Commissioner Kuhn!"

"Yes, sir," he replies.

"No, no!" says the slit, but I free myself from her grasp
by rapping her one on the bunions.

"How do you do, Commissioner. I would like to introduce
myself, in case you have forgotten. I am Word Smith, used to
write the 'One Man's Opinion' column for the Finest Family
Newspapers back in the days of the Patriot League."

"Smitty!"

"I see," said Kuhn, nodding.

"I used to be a member of the Baseball Writers' Association of America myself, and until 1946 voted annually in
these Hall of Fame elections. Then, as you may recall, I was
slandered and jailed. Cast my vote in the very first election
for Mr. Ty Cobb."

"I see. For Cobb. Good choice."

By now a crowd of geezers, gaffers, and codgers, including the six and ten puerile Methuselahs of my own party,
are all pushing close to get a look at the Commissioner and
the crackpot.

"And I am here," I tell him, "to cast another vote today."
Here I extracted from my vest the small white envelope I had
prepared the previous day and handed it to Mr. Bowie Kuhn.

To my astonishment, he not only accepted it, but behind
those businessman's spectacles, *his eyes welled up with tears*.

Well, fans, so did mine. So do they now, remembering.

"Thank you, Mr. Smith," he said.

"Why, you're welcome, Commissioner."

I could have burst right through my million wrinkles, I was so happy, and Kuhn, he couldn't tear himself away. "Where are you living these days?" he asked.

I smiled. "State Home for the Aged, the Infirm, the Despondent, the Neglected, the Decrepit, the Incontinent, the Senile, and the Just About Scared to Death. Life creeps in its petty pace, Commissioner."

"Don't mind him, Mr. Kuhn," someone volunteered from the crowd, "he was born that way."

"Bats in the belfry, Commissioner. Too deep to operate."

Haw-haw all around.

"Well," said Kuhn, looking down at my envelope, "have a good day, Mr. Smith."

"You too, Mr. Commissioner."

And that was it. That was how easy it was to trick me into thinking that at long last the lying had come to an end! Shameful! At eighty-seven years of age, to be so gullible, so innocent! I might as well have been back mewling and puking, to think the world was going to right its ways because I got smiled at by the man in charge! And they call me embittered! Why, take me seriously for twenty seconds at a stretch, and I roll over like a puppy, my balls and bellyhairs all yours.

"My, my," said the slit to the plainclothesgoon, "just give in a little to someone's d-e-l-u-s-i-o-n-s o-f g-r-a-n-d-e-u-r, and he's a changed person, isn't he?"

Well, sad to say, the slit spoke the truth. You don't often hear the truth introduced by "my, my" but there it is. Wonders never cease.

Also, in my own behalf, I think it is fair to say that after twenty years of struggling I had come to be something of a victim of exhaustion. When they are ranged against you, *every living soul*, then you might as well be down in the coal mines hacking at the walls with your teeth and your toenails, for all the impression that you make. There is nothing so wearing in all of human life as burning with a truth that everyone else denies. You don't know suffering, fans, until you know that.

Still and all, Kuhn took me in.

What follows is the list of players who, *according to* the BBWAA, received votes that day for the Hall of Fame.

Yogi Berra	242	Johnny Sain	11
Early Wynn	240	Harvey Haddix	10
Ralph Kiner	212	Richie Ashburn	10
Gil Hodges	180	Ted Kluszewski	9
Enos Slaughter	165	Don Newcombe	8
Johnny Mize	157	Harry Brecheen	7
Pee Wee Reese	127	Walker Cooper	7
Marty Marion	123	Wally Moses	7
Red Schoendienst	123	Billy Pierce	7
Allie Reynolds	110	Carl Furillo	5
George Kell	105	Bobby Shantz	5
Johnny Vander Meer	98	Bobby Thomson	4
Hal Newhouser	94	Roy Sievers	4
Phil Rizzuto	92	Gil McDougald	4
Bob Lemon	90	Ed Lopat	4
Duke Snider	89	Carl Erskine	3
Phil Cavarretta	83	Dutch Leonard	3
Bobby Doerr	78	Preacher Roe	3
Alvin Dark	54	Vic Wertz	2
Nelson Fox	39	Vic Power	2
Bobo Newsom	17	Vic Raschi	2
Dom DiMaggio	15	Wally Moon	2
Charley Keller	14	Jackie Jensen	2
Mickey Vernon	12	Billy Bruton	1

In that to be elected requires mention on 75 per cent of the ballots, or 271 of the 361 cast (including my own, that is; according to the BBWAA it required only 270 out of 360), the electors issued this statement at about two in the afternoon: "Despite the heaviest vote in the history of the Hall of Fame balloting, the Baseball Writers' Association of America was unable to elect a candidate for enshrinement next summer."

Oh, that set 'em to quacking! You should have heard those fools! How could they keep out Berra when back in '55 they'd let in Gabby Hartnett who was never half the catcher Yogi was! Wasn't half? Why he was twice't! Was! Wasn't! Same for Early Wynn: whoever heard of a three hundred game winner failing to be mentioned by one hundred and twenty electors

(excluding me) when right over there is a plaque to Dazzy
Vance who in all his career won less than *two* hundred. Next
thing you know they will be keeping out Koufax and Spahn
when they are eligible! Well, it took Rogers Hornsby six years
to make it, didn't it—with a lifetime of .358! And Bill Terry
and Harry Heilmann *eleven years apiece!* Meanwhile they
are also arguing over Marion and Reese, which was better
than the other and whether both weren't a darn sight better
than Hall of Famer Rabbit Maranville. Oh what controversy!
Tempers raging, statistics flying, and with it all *not a word
from anyone about a single player who played for the Patriot
League in their fifty years as a major league. Not a mention
in the BBWAA's phony tabulations of my vote for Luke
Gofannon.*

Billy Bruton! Jackie Jensen! Wally Moon! Outfielders
who did not even bat .300 lifetime, who would have had to *pay*
their way into Mundy Park in the days of the great Gofannon,
and there they are with five votes between them for the Hall of
Fame! I was near to insanity.

What was it put me over the top? Why did I hurl my cane
and collapse in a heap on the floor? Why had they to hammer
on my heart to get it going again? Why have I been bedridden
all these days and ordered off alliteration for the remainder
of my life? Why wasn't I calm and philosophical as befits a
man of my experience with human treachery and deceit? Why
did I curse and thunder when I know that writing the Great
American Novel requires every last ounce of my strength and
my cunning? Tell me something (I am addressing only men
of principle) : *What would you have done?*

Here's what happened: Commissioner Kuhn appeared,
and when reporters, photographers, and cameramen (plus
geezers) gathered round to hear his words of wisdom, know
what he said? No, not what this sentimental, decomposing,
worn-out wishful thinker was pleading with his eyes for Kuhn
to say—no, not that the BBWAA was a cheat and a fraud and
disgrace for having failed to announce the vote submitted for
Luke Gofannon of the extinguished Patriot League. Oh no—
wrongs aren't righted that way, fans, except in dreams and
daytime serials. "The fact that nobody was elected," said the
Commissioner, "points up the integrity of the institution."

And if you don't believe me because I'm considered cracked,
it's on TV film for all to see. Just look at your newspaper for
January 22, 1971—before they destroy that too. *The integrity
of the institution.* Next they will be talking about the mag-
nanimity of the Mafia and the blessing of the Bomb. They will
use alliteration for anything these days, but most of all for
lies.

After fighting a sail for forty-five minutes off the Florida
coast and finally bringing it in close enough for the fifteen-
year-old Cuban kid who was our mate to grab the bill with his
gloved hands, pull it in over the rail, and send it off to sailfish
heaven with the business end of a sawed-off Hillerich and
Bradsby signed "Luke Gofannon," my old friend (and
enemy) Ernest Hemingway said to me—the year is 1936, the
month is March—"Frederico"—that was the hard-boiled way
Hem had of showing his affection, calling me by a name that
wasn't my own—"Frederico, you know the son of a bitch who
is going to write the Great American Novel?"
     "No, Hem. Who?"
     "You."
     They were running the white pennant up now, number five
for Papa in four hours. This was the first morning the boats
had been out for a week, and from the look of things everybody
was having a good day, though nobody was having as good a
day as Papa. When he was having a good day they didn't
make them any more generous or sweet-tempered, but when
he was having a bad day, well, he could be the biggest prick in
all of literature. "You're the biggest prick in all of literature,"
I remember telling him one morning when we were looking
down into the fire pit of Halemaumau, Hawaii's smoldering
volcano. "I ought to give you to the goddess for that one,"
said Hem, pointing into the cauldron. "That wouldn't make
you any less of a prick, Hem," I said. "Lay off my prick,
Frederico." "I call 'em like I see 'em, Papa." "Just lay off
my prick," he said.
     But that day in March of '36, our cruiser flying five white
pennants, one for each sail Hem had landed, and Hem watching with pleasure the mullet dragging on his line, waiting for

number six, it seemed you could have said anything in the
world you wanted to Papa about his prick, and he would have
got a kick out of it. That's what it's like when a great writer
is having a good day.

It had squalled for a week in Florida. The managers were
bawling to the Chamber of Commerce that next year they
would train in the Southwest and the players were growing
fat on beer and lean on poker and the wives were complaining
because they would go North without a sunburn and at night
it got so cold that year that I slept in my famous hound's-tooth
raglan-sleeve overcoat, the one they called "a Smitty" in the
twenties, after a fella name a', I believe. My slit was a waitress at a Clearwater hotel with a degree in Literatoor from
Vassar. All the waitresses that year had degrees in Literatoor from Vassar. They'd come South to learn about Real
Life. "I've never slept in bed before with a fifty-two-year-
old sportswriter in a hound's-tooth raglan-sleeve overcoat,"
my Vassar slit informed me. I said, "That is because you have
never been in Florida before during spring training in a year
when the temperature dropped." "Oh," she said, and wrote
it in her diary, I suppose.

Now she was measuring Hem's sail. "It's a big one," she
called over to us. "Seven foot eight inches."

"Throw it back," said Hem and the Vassar slit laughed
and so did the Cuban kid who was our mate that year.

"For a waitress with a degree in Literatoor," Hem said,
"she has a sense of humor. She will be all right."

Then he took up the subject of the Great American Novel
again, joking that it would probably be me of all the sons of
bitches in the world who could spell cat who was going to write
it. "Isn't that what you sportswriters think, Frederico? That
some day you're going to get off into a little cabin somewhere and write the G.A.N.? Could do it now, couldn't you,
Frederico, if only you had the Time."

During that week of squall in March of that year Hem
would talk till dawn about which son of a bitch who could
spell cat was going to write the G.A.N. By the end of the week
he had narrowed it down to a barber in the basement of the
Palmer House in Chicago who knew how to shave with the
grain.

"No hot towels. No lotion. Just shaves with the grain and washes it off with witch hazel."

"Any man can do that, can write the Great American Novel," I said.

"Yes," said Hem, filling my glass, "he is the one."

"How is he on the light trim?" I asked.

"Not bad for Chicago," Hem said, giving the barber his due.

"Yes," I said, "it is a rough town for a light trim where there are a lot of Polacks."

"In the National League," said Hem, "so is Pittsburgh."

"Yes," I said, "but you cannot beat the dining room in the Schenley Hotel for good eats."

"There is Jimmy Shevlin's in Cincinnati," Hem said.

"What about Ruby Foo's chop suey joint in Boston?"

"Give me Lew Tendler's place in Philadelphia," said Hem.

"The best omelette is the Western," I said.

"The best dressing is the Russian," Hem said.

"Guys who drink Manhattans give me the creeps."

"Liverwurst on a seeded roll with mustard is my favorite sandwich."

"I don't trust a dame who wears those gold sandals."

"Give me a girl who goes in swimming without a bathing cap if a slit has to hold my money."

"I'd rather kill an hour in a newsreel theater than a whorehouse."

Yes, over a case of cognac we could manage to touch upon just about every subject that men talk about when they're alone, from homburgs to hookers to Henry Armstrong . . . But always that year the conversation came around to the G.A.N. Hem had it on his brain. One night he would tell me that the hero should be an aviator; the next night an industrialist; then a surgeon; then a cowboy. One time it would be a book about booze, the next broads, the next Mother Nature. "And to think," he said, on the last night of that seven-day squall, "some dago barber sucking on Tums in the basement of the Palmer House is going to write it." I thought he was kidding me again about the barber until he threw his glass into the window that looked onto the bay.

Now he was telling me that I was going to write it. It seemed to me a good compliment to ease out from under.

"Gladly, Hem," I said, thinking to needle him a little in the process, "but I understand that they wrote it already."

"Who is this they, Frederico?"

"The slit says Herman Melville wrote it. And some other guys, besides. It's been done, Papa. Otherwise I'd oblige."

"Hey, Vassar," he called, "get over here."

Of course the slit was very impressed with herself to be out sailfishing with Hem. She liked to hear him calling her "Vassar." She liked me calling her "Slit." It was a change from what they called her at home which was "Muffin." The first time she'd burst into tears but I told her they both meant the same thing anyway, only mine was the more accurate description. The truth is I never knew a girl worth her salt who did not like being called a slit in the end. It's only whores and housewives you have to call "m'lady."

"What's this I heard," said Hem, "that Herman Melville wrote the Great American Novel? Who's Herman Melville?"

The slit turned and twisted on her long storky legs like a little kid who had to go. Finally she got it out. "The author of *Moby Dick.*"

"Oh," said Hem, "I read that one. Book about catching a whale."

"Well, it's not *about* that," the slit said, and flushed, pure American Beauty rose.

Hem laughed. "Well, you got the degree in Literatoor, Vassar—tell me, what is it about?"

She told him that it was about Good and Evil. She told him the white whale was not just a white whale, it was a symbol. That amused Hem.

"Vassar, *Moby Dick* is a book about blubber, with a madman thrown in for excitement. Five hundred pages of blubber, one hundred pages of madman, and about twenty pages on how good niggers are with the harpoon."

Here the pole jerked. Hem came off his chair and the little Cuban kid who was our mate that year started in shouting the only English word he knew—"Sail! Sail!"

After the sixth white pennant was raised and the slit had measured Hem's sail at eight feet, he resumed quizzing her about the name of the G.A.N. "And no more blubber, Vassar, you hear?"

"*Huckleberry Finn*," the slit said gamely—and flushing of course, "by Mark Twain."

"Book for boys, Vassar," said Hem. "Book about a boy and a slave trying to run away from home. About the drunks and thieves and lunatics they meet up with. Adventure story for kids."

Oh, no, says the slit, this one is about Good and Evil too.

"Vassar, it is just a book by a fellow who is thinking how nice it would be to be a youngster again. Back when the nuts and lushes and thieves was still the other guy and not you. Kid stuff, Kid. Pretending you're a girl or your own best friend. Sleeping all day and swimming naked at night. Cooking over a fire. Your old wino dad getting rubbed out without having to do the job yourself. The Great American Daydream, Vassar. Drunks don't die so conveniently for the relatives anymore. Right, Frederico?"

Hem had to stop here to catch another sailfish.

According to the slit this one measured only five feet eleven inches. She shouldn't have said "only."

Trying to joke it off, Hem said, "Never be a basketball star, will he?" but it was clear he was not happy with himself. You might even have thought that seventh sail was a symbol of something if you were a professor of Literatoor.

I sat with Hem and we drank, while the Cuban kid fiddled with the fish and the slit wondered what she had said that was wrong. When it was clear the fishing was ruined for the day the kid took in the lines and we started home, the terns and the gulls giving us the business overhead.

"The slit wasn't thinking," I said.

"Oh, the slit was thinking all right. Slits are always thinking in their way."

"She's just a kid, Hem."

"So was Joan of Arc," he said.

"You're taking it too hard," I said. "Try not to think about it."

"Sure. Sure. I'll try not to think about it."

"She didn't mean 'only,' Hem."

"Sure. I know. She meant 'merely.' Hey, Vassar."

"She's a kid, Hem," I warned him.

"So was Clytemnestra when she started out. But once they get going they don't leave you anything. You can count on that. Hey, Vassar."

"What are you going to do, Hem?"

"Sharks like fresh slit as much as the next carnivore, Frederico."

"Don't be a prick, Hem."

"Lay off my prick, Frederico. Or you'll go too. Ever see a shark take after a raglan-sleeve coat with a sportswriter in it? That's the way the Indians used to get them to charge the beach, by waving a swatch of Broadway hound's-tooth at them."

The slit from Vassar who had come South that year to be a waitress and learn about Real Life was showing gooseflesh on her storky legs when she approached the great writer to ask what he wanted. In all that they had taught her about great writers at Vassar they had apparently neglected to mention what pricks they can be.

Hem said, "Tell me some more about the Great American Novel, Vassar. You don't meet a twenty-one-year-old every day who is an authority on fiction and fishing both, especially from your sex."

"But I'm *not,*" she said, as pale a slit now as you might ever see.

"You go around judging the size of sailfish, don't you? You have a degree in Literatoor, don't you? Name me another Great American Novel. I want to hear just who us punks are up against."

"I didn't say you were up against—"

"No!" roared Hem. "I did!" And the gulls flew off as though a cannon had been fired.

"Name me another!"

But when she stood there mute with terror, Hem reached out with a hand and smacked her face. I thought of Stanley Ketchel when she went down.

She looked up from where Hem had "decked" her. *"The Scarlet Letter,"* she whimpered, "by Nathaniel Hawthorne."

"Good one, Vassar. That's the book where the only one

who has got any balls on him is the heroine. No wonder you like it so much. Frankly, Vassar, I don't think Mr. Hawthorne even knew where to put it. I believe he thought A stood for arsehole. Maybe that's what all the fuss is about."

"Henry James!" she howled.

"Tell me another, Vassar!"

"*The Ambassadors! The Golden Bowl!*"

"Polychromatic crap, honey! Five hundred words where one would do! Come on, Vassar, name me another!"

"Oh please, Mr. Hemingway, please," she wept, "I don't know anymore, I swear I don't—"

"Sure you do!" he roared. "What about *Red Badge of Courage!* What about *Winesburg, Ohio! The Last of the Mohicans! Sister Carrie! McTeague! My Antonia! The Rise of Silas Lapham! Two Years Before the Mast! Ethan Frome! Barren Ground!* What about Booth Tarkington and Sarah Orne Jewett, while you're at it? What about our minor poet Francis Scott Fitzwhat'shisname? What about Wolfe and Dos and Faulkner? What about *The Sound and the Fury,* Vassar! A tale told by an idiot, signifying nothing—how's that for the Great American Novel!"

"I never read it," she whimpered.

"Of course you haven't! You can't! It's unreadable unless you're some God damn professor! You know why you can't name the Great American Novel, Vassar?"

"No," she moaned.

"Because it hasn't been written yet! Because when it is it'll be Papa who writes it and not some rummy sportswriter in his cute little cottage by the lake in the woods!"

Whereupon a large fierce gull swooped down, its broad wings fluttering, and opened its hungry beak to cry at Ernest Hemingway, "*Nevermore!*"

Or so he claimed afterwards; I myself didn't know what he was carrying on about when he shouted up at the bird, "You can't quoth that to me and get away with it, you sea gull son of a bitch!"

"*Nevermore!*" the gull repeated, to hear Hem tell it later. "*Nevermore!*"

Hem raced down to the cabin but when he returned with his pistol the gull was gone.

"I ought to use it on myself," said Papa. "And if that bastard sea gull is right, I will."

Here he stumbled wildly over the deck, stepping blindly across the slit, and leaned over the side to watch his shadow in the water . . . "Frederico," he called.

"Hem."

"Oh, Frederico; it is a mild, mild wind, and a mild looking sky. On such a day—very much such a sweetness as this—I wrote my first story—a boy-reporter of nineteen! Eighteen—eighteen—eighteen years ago!—ago! Eighteen years of continual writing! eighteen years of privation, and peril, and stormtime! eighteen years on the pitiless sea! for eighteen years has Papa forsaken the peaceful land, for eighteen years to make war on the horrors of the deep! When I think of this life I have led; the desolation of solitude it has been; the masoned, walled-town of a novelist's exclusiveness, which admits but small entrance to any sympathy from the green country without—oh, weariness! heaviness! Guinea-coast slavery of solitary command!—when I think of all this; only half-suspected . . . I feel deadly faint, bowed, and humped, as though I were Adam, staggering beneath the piled centuries since Paradise! God! God! God!—crack my heart—stave my brain!—mockery! mockery! Close! Stand close to me, Frederico; let me look into a human eye. The Great American Novel. Why should Hemingway give chase to the Great American Novel?"

"Good question, Papa. Keep it up and it's going to drive you nuts."

"What is it, Frederico, what nameless, inscrutable, unearthly thing is it; what cozening, hidden lord and master, and cruel, remorseless emperor commands me; that against all natural lovings and longings, I so keep pushing, and crowding, and jamming myself on all the time; recklessly making me ready to do what in my own proper, natural heart, I durst not so much as dare? Is Papa, Papa? Is it I, God, or who, that lifts this writing arm?" he asked, raising the pistol to his head.

"All right, Hem, that's enough now," I said. "You don't even sound like yourself. A book is a book, no more. Who would want to kill himself over a novel?"

"What then?" said Papa, and turned to look at the decked slit. It was to her he said sardonically, "A whale? A woman?"

Only it wasn't the same kid who had boarded with us at dawn that morning who answered him. A few hours with a man like Hem had changed her forever, as it changed us all. That's what a great writer can do to people.

"Wouldn't it be pretty to think so?" snorted the slit.

End of story, nearly. As I did not want to let him out of my sight in that murderous mood, I brought Hem along with me to see the Mundys take their first workout in a week. John Baal, the big bad first-baseman the sentimentalists used to try to dignify by calling him "Rabelaisian"—the first two syllables would have sufficed—was in the cage, lofting long fly balls out toward a flock of pelicans who were cruising in deep center. "I'm going to get me one of them big-mouthed cocksuckers yet," said John, and sure enough, after fifteen minutes of trying, he did. Pelican must have mistaken the baseball for something good to eat, a flying fish I suppose, because he went soaring straight up after one John had hit like a shot and hauled it in while it was still on the rise. When I went to the telegraph office that night to file my story, Papa was still with me, muttering and miserable. The slit had already packed her diary and boarded the first train back to Poughkeepsie. I was not in such good spirits myself.

"Big John Baal of the Mundys," my story began, "was robbed of a four-bagger during batting practice this afternoon in Clearwater. Credit a pelican with the put-out.

"He looked at first glance like any other pelican. He was wearing the grayish-silvery home uniform of his species, with the white velvety neck feathers and the fully webbed toes. The bird was of average size, I am told, weighing in at eight pounds and with a wing spread of seven and a half feet. On close inspection there seemed nothing unusual about the large blackish pouch suspended from the lower half of his bill, except that when they pried the bill open, the pouch was found to contain, along with four sardines and a baby pompano, a baseball bearing the signature of the President of the Patriot League. The pelican was still soaring upwards and to his left when he turned his long graceful neck, opened his bill, and with the nonchalance of a Luke Gofannon, snared Big John's mighty blast.

"We had pigeons when I was a boy. My old man kept them in a chicken-wire coop on the roof. My old man was a pug with a potent right hand who trained in the saloons and bet himself empty on the horses before he evaporated into thin air when I was fifteen. He loved those pigeons so much he fed them just as good as he did us—bread crumbs and a fresh tin of water every day. A boy's illusions about his father are notorious. I thought he was something very like a god when he stood on the roof with a long pole, shaking and waving it in the air to control the pigeons in their flight. And the next thing I knew he had evaporated into the air.

"The press and the players are calling the pelican's catch an 'omen,' but of what they can't agree. As many say a first division finish as a second. That is the range of some people's thinking. Of course there are the jokers, as there always are when the utterly incomprehensible happens. 'Forgive them Father,' begged the suffering man on the cross one Friday long ago, and the smart Roman punk betting even money the shooter wouldn't make an eight in two rolls looked up and said in Latin, 'Listen who's trying to cut the game.'

"The learned Christian gentleman who manages the Mundys is not happy about what Big John Baal is going to do with the dead pelican, but then he has never been overjoyed with Big John's sense of propriety. Mister Fairsmith, a missionary in the off-season, tried to bring baseball to the Africans one winter. They disappointed him too. They learned the principles of the game all right but then one night the two local teams held a ceremony in which they boiled their gloves and ate them. 'The pelican represented as piercing her breast is called "the pelican vulning herself" or "the pelican in her piety," ' Mister Fairsmith reminded Big John. 'She then symbolizes Christ redeeming the world with His blood.' But Big John is still going to have the phenomenal bird stuffed and mounted over the bar of his favorite Port Ruppert saloon.

"I loved my old man and because of that I never understood how he could disappear on me, or play the ponies on me, or train in taverns on me. But he must have had his reasons. I suppose that pelican who made the put-out here in Clearwater today had his reasons too. But I don't pretend to be able to read a bird's brain anymore than I could my own dad's. All I know is that if the Mundys plan on breaking even this year somebody better tell Big John Baal to start pulling the ball to right, where the pasture is fenced in.

"But that's only one man's opinion. Fella name a' Smith; first name a' Word."

Nursing Ernest all day, I had been forced to compose the story in bits and half-bits, which accounts for why it is so weak on alliteration. As it says over the door to the Famous Writers' School in Connecticut: A Sullen Drunk Packing A Gat Is Not The Best Company For An Artist Finicky About His Style.

I read the story aloud to the telegraph operator, so I could balance up the sentences as I went along, writing the last paragraph right there on my feet in the Western Union office.

Then I turned to see Hem pointing the pistol at my belt.

"You stole that from me."

"Stole what, Hem?"

"First you steal it and then what's worse you fuck it up."

"Fuck what up, Hem?"

"My prose style. You bastards have stolen my prose style. Every shithead sportswriter in America has stolen my style and then gone and fucked it up so bad that I can't even use it anymore without becoming sick to my stomach."

"Put down the pistol, Papa. I've been writing that way all my life and you know it."

"I suppose I stole it from you then, Frederico."

"That isn't what I said."

"Hear that, bright boy?" Hem said to the baby-faced telegraph operator, who had his hands over his head. "That isn't what he said. Tell the bright boy who I steal my ideas from, Frederico."

"Nobody, Hem."

"Don't I steal them from a syndicated sportswriter in a hound's-tooth overcoat? Fella name a' Frederico?"

"No, Hem."

"Maybe I steal them from the slit, Frederico. Maybe I steal them from a Vassar slit with a degree in High Literatoor."

"They're your own, Hem. Your ideas are your own."

"How about my characters. Tell bright boy here who I steal them from. Go ahead. Tell him."

"He doesn't steal them from anybody," I said to the kid. "They're his own."

"Hear that, bright boy?" Hem asked. "My characters are my own."

"Yes, sir," said the telegraph operator.

"Now tell bright boy," Hem said to me, "who is going to write the Great American Novel, Frederico? You? Or Papa?"

"Papa," I said.

"Yes, sir," said the telegraph operator, his hands still up in the air.

"So you think that's right?" Hem asked him.

"Sure," the telegraph operator said.

"You're a pretty bright boy, aren't you?"

"If you say so, sir."

"You know what I say, bright boy? If I have a message, I send it Western Union."

The telegraph operator forced a smile. "Uh-huh," he said.

"Sit down, bright boy."

"Yes, sir." And did as he was told.

Hem walked up and held the pistol to the telegrapher's jawbone. "To Messrs. Hawthorne, Melville, Twain, and James, in care of the Department of Literatoor, Vassar College, New York. Dear Illustrious Dead: The Great American Novelist, *c'est moi*. Signed, Papa."

He waited for the last letter to be tapped out, then he turned and went out the door. Through the window I watched him pass under the arc-light and cross the street. Then because I am something of a prick too, I asked how much the telegram would cost, paid, and went on back to my slitless hotel room, never to see Ernest again.

Every once in a while I would get a Christmas card from Hem, sometimes from Africa, sometimes from Switzerland or Idaho, written in his cups obviously, saying more or less the same thing each time: use my style one more time, Frederico,

and I'll kill you. But of course in the end the guy Hem killed
for using his style was himself.

MY PRECURSORS, MY KINSMEN

1. *The Scarlet Letter,* by Nathaniel Hawthorne

Well, I tend to agree with Hem—having now done my homework—that the men Miss Hester Prynne got herself mixed up
with do not reflect admirably upon the bearded sex. But then
make me out a list of a hundred who do? I count it a miracle
that the lady didn't latch onto a lushhead as well. And yet,
standard stuff as it may seem to a slum kid like myself to
hear tell of a sweet young thing throwing away her life on a
lout, there is something suspicious about a beautiful, brave,
voluptuous, and level-headed slit such as Hester marrying a
misshapen dryasdust prof easily three times her age (who
undoubtedly had her posing in all sorts of postures in her petti-
coats in order for him to get it up, if up it would even go) and
from him moving on to a "passionate" affair with that puny
parson. Ten to one when they saddled up in the woods, it was
Hester mounted the minister and not t'other way about. I
admire the girl for her guts but have my doubts about any slit
who savors sex with sadists and sissies. I only regret that this
big black-eyed dish did not reside in the Boston area in the era
of the Red Sox and Bees. I might have showed her something.
　Students of Literatoor (as Hem was wont to mispronounce
it) will have recognized the debt that I owe to Mr. Hawthorne
of Massachusetts. Yes, this prologue partly derives from reading that lengthy intro to his novel wherein he tells who he is
and how he comes to be writing a great book. Before embark-
ing on my own I thought it wouldn't hurt to study up on the
boys Hem took to be the competition—for if they were his then
they are mine now. Actually I did not get overly excited about
the author's adventures as boss of a deadbeat Salem Custom-
House as he ramblingly relates them in that intro, but surely I
was struck by the fact that like my own, his novel is based
upon real life, the story of Hester Prynne being drawn from
records that he discovered in a junk heap in a corner of the
Custom-House attic. In that the Prynne-Dimmesdale scandal

had broken two hundred years earlier, Hawthorne admits he had to "dress up the tale"—nice pun that, Nat—imagining the setting, the motives and such. "What I contend for," Hawthorne says, "is the authenticity of the outline." Well, what *I* contend for is the authenticity of the whole thing!

Fans, nary a line is spoken in the upcoming epic, that either I heard it myself—was *there,* in dugout, bleachers, clubhouse, barroom, diner, pressbox, bus, and limousine—or had it confided to me by reliable informants, as often as not the parties in pain themselves. Then there are busybodies, blabbermouths, gossips, stoolies, and such to assist in rounding out reality. With all due respect to Hawthorne's "imaginative faculty," as he calls it, I think he could have done with a better pair of ears on him. Only *listen,* Nathaniel, and Americans will write the Great American Novel for you. You cannot imagine all I have heard standing in suspenders in a hotel bathroom, with the water running in the tub so nobody in the next room could tune in with a glass to the wall, and my guest pouring out to Smitty the dark, clammy secrets of the hard-on and the heart. Beats the Custom-House grabbag any day. Oh, I grant you that a fellow in a fix did not speak in Hester's Boston as he did in Shoeless Joe's Chicago—where the heinous hurler Eddie Cicotte said to me of the World Series game he threw, "I did it for my wife and kiddies"—but I wonder if times have changed as much as Nathaniel Hawthorne would lead you to believe.

A more spectacular similarity between Hawthorne's book and my own than the fact that each has a windy autobiographical intro that "seizes the public by the button" is the importance in both of *a scarlet letter* identifying the wearer as an outcast from America. Hawthorne recounts how he found "this rag of scarlet cloth," frayed and moth-eaten, amidst the rubbish heaped up in the Custom-House attic. The mysterious meaning of the scarlet letter is then revealed to him in the old documents he uncovers. "On the breast of her gown," writes Hawthorne of Hester, with admirable alliteration too, "in fine red cloth, surrounded with an elaborate embroidery and fantastic flourishes of gold thread, appeared the letter A." A for "Adulteress," at the outset; by the end of her life, says the author, many came to think it stood for "Able; so strong was Hester Prynne, with a woman's strength."

Well, so too did a red cloth letter, this one of felt, appear on the breast of the off-white woolen warm-up jackets worn by the Mundys of the Patriot League—only their fateful letter was R. At the outset R for Ruppert, the team's home; in the end, as many would have it, for "Rootless," for "Ridiculous," for "Refugee." Fact is I could not but think of the Mundys, and how they wandered the league after their expulsion from Port Ruppert, when I heard my precursor's description of himself at the conclusion to his intro. "I am," wrote Hawthorne, "a citizen of somewhere else." My precursor, and my kinsman too.

2. *The Adventures of Huckleberry Finn,* by Mark Twain

Listening to Huckleberry Finn ramble on is like listening to nine-tenths of the baseball players who ever lived talk about what they do in the off season down home. The ballplayers are two and three times Huck's age, and contrary to popular belief, most are not sired in the South like Huck, but hail from Pennsylvania—yet none of this means they care any the less for setting up housekeeping in the thick woods first chance they get, cooking their catch for breakfast and dinner, otherwise just being carried with the current in a comfy canoe, their sole female companion Mother N. Boys would be big leaguers, as everybody knows, but so would big leaguers be boys. Why, when a manager walks out to the mound to calm a pitcher in trouble, what do you imagine he tells him? "Give him the old dipsy-do"—? Not if he has any brains he doesn't. If the pitcher could get the old dipsy to do he'd be doing it without being told. Know what the manager says? "How many quail did you say you shot when you were hunting last fall, Al?" And if you think I am making that one up so as to link my tale to Twain's (as I have already shown it to be linked to Hawthorne's) if you think I am—as Huck Finn would have it—telling "stretchers" to falsify my literary credentials and my family tree, then I strongly advise you to read *Pitching in a Pinch* by Christy Mathewson, wherein the great Matty, as truthful in life as he was tricky on the hill, quotes the famous

Giant manager and Hall of Famer John Joseph McGraw—as have I. How many quail did you say you shot when you were hunting last fall, Al? Yes, that is the strategy they talk on the mound—same kind they talk on a raft!

And since, admittedly, we are seeking out similitudes of all sorts twixt Twain's microcosm and mine, what about Huck Finn's sidekick, the runaway slave Nigger Jim? Who do you think he grew up to be anyway? Let me tell you if you haven't guessed: none other than the first Negro leaguer (according to today's paper) to be welcomed to the Hall of Fame, albeit in the bleacher section of the venerable, villainous institution: Leroy Robert (Satchel) Paige (see papers 2/11/71). In that Satchel Paige was born in Mobile, Alabama, approximately four years before Sam Clemens died in Hartford, Connecticut, it is doubtful that the eminent humorist ever saw him pitch, except maybe with some barnstorming pickaninny team; what's more to the point, he did not live to hear Satch speechify. If he had it would surely have delighted him (as it does Smitty in Sam's behalf) to discover that the indestructible Negro pitcher who is said to have won two thousand of the two thousand and five hundred games he pitched in twenty-two years in the Negro leagues, is Huck's Jim transmogrified.

Just listen to this, fans, for sheer prophecy: "Jim had a hairball as big as your fist, which had been took out of the fourth stomach of an ox, and he used to do magic with it. He said there was a spirit inside of it, and it knowed everything." And this: "Strange niggers would stand with their mouths open, and look him all over, same as if he was a wonder . . . and he was more looked up to than any nigger in that country." With his hairball Jim could perform magic and tell fortunes—with his fastball, Satch once struck out Rogers Hornsby *five times* in a single exhibition game! But the proof of the pudding is the talking. Listen now to Satch, offering to humankind his six precepts on how to stay young and strong. Students of Literatoor, professors, and small boys who recall Jim's comical lingo will not be fooled just because Satch has dispensed with the thick dialect he used for speaking in Mr. Twain's book. Back then he was a slave and had to talk that way. It was expected of him. Satchel Paige's recipe for eternal youth:

1. Avoid fried meats which angry up the blood.

2. If your stomach disputes you, lie down and pacify it with cool thoughts.

3. Keep the juices flowing by jangling around gently as you move.

4. Go very light on the vices, such as carrying on in society. The social ramble ain't restful.

5. Avoid running at all times.

6. Don't look back. Something might be gaining on you.

Now if this is not the hairball oracle who floated down the Mississippi with Huckleberry Finn, then someone is doing a pretty good imitation.

Colored players started coming into the majors just when Smitty and the P. League were being escorted out the door, so I do not know firsthand how the white boys have managed living alongside them. I suppose there were those like pricky little Tom Sawyer, America's first fraternity boy, who took childish delight in tormenting the colored however they could, and others, like Huck, more or less good-natured kids, who were confused as hell suddenly to be sharing dugout, locker room, and hotel bath with the dusky likes of Nigger Jim. Do you remember, students of L., when Huck tricks Jim into believing the crackup of their raft had occurred only in Jim's dreams? And how heartbroken old Jim was when he discovered otherwise? "It was fifteen minutes," says Huck, "before I could work myself up to go and humble myself to a nigger; but I done it, and I warn't ever sorry for it afterward, neither. I didn't do him no more mean tricks, and I wouldn't done that one if I'd 'a' knowed it would make him feel that way." It figures that more than a few ballplayers have by this time come around to Huck's way of thinking, as he expresses it so sweetly here. But I expect, given what I know of that lot, that the leagues have still got their share of Tom Sawyers, who even under the guise of doing Jim good had himself the time of his sadistic little small-town life heaping every sort of abuse and punishment he could think of upon that shackled black yearning to be free of Miss Watson. Of course as of 2/11/71 the shackles are off poor Jim and he is not only free but in the Hall of Shame. That just leaves Gofannon in shackles, don't it? The Patriot League, America, those are your niggers now, *for when you are blackballed from baseball, then verily, you are the untouchables in these United States.*

Students of L. and fans, the story I have to tell—prefigured as it is in the wanderings of Huckleberry Finn and Nigger Jim, and the adventures in ostracism of Hester Prynne, the Puritans' pariah—is of the once-mighty Mundys, how they were cast out of their home ball park in Port Ruppert, their year of humiliation on the road, and the shameful catastrophe that destroyed them (and me) forever. Little did the seven other teams in the league realize—little did any of us realize, fella name a' included—that the seemingly comical misfortunes of the last-place Mundys constituted the prelude to oblivion for us all. But that, fans, is the tyrannical law of our lives: today euphoria, tomorrow the whirlwind.

Bringing us to our blood brother.

3. *Moby Dick,* by Herman Melville

Moby Dick is to the old whaling industry (d.) what the Hall of Fame and Museum was *supposed* to have been to baseball: the ultimate and indisputable authority on the subject—repository of records, storehouse of statisticians, the Louvre of Leviathans. Who is Moby Dick if not the terrifying Ty Cobb of his species? Who is Captain Ahab if not the unappeasable Dodger manager Durocher, or the steadfast Giant John McGraw? Who are Flask, Starbuck, and Stubb, Ahab's trio of first mates, if not the Tinker, Evers, and Chance of the *Pequod*'s crew? Better, call them the d.p. combination of the Ruppert Mundys —d.p. standing here for displaced person as well as double play—say they are Frenchy Astarte, Nickname Damur, and Big John Baal, for where is the infield (and the outfield, the starters and relievers, the coaches, catchers, pinch-runners and pinch-hitters) of that peripatetic Patriot League team today, but down with the bones and the timbers of the Moby Dick-demolished *Pequod,* beneath "the great shroud of the sea." Their remote Nantucket? Ruppert. Their crazed and vengeful Ahab? Manager Gil Gamesh. And their Ishmael? Yes, one did survive the wreck to tell the tale—an indestructible old truth-teller called me!

Gentle fans, if you were to have bound together into a

single volume every number ever published of the baseball
weekly known as *The Sporting News,* as well as every manual,
guide, and handbook important to an understanding of the
game; if you were to assemble encyclopedic articles describing
the size, weight, consistency, color, texture, resiliency, and
liveliness of the baseball itself, from the early days when the
modern Moby Dick-colored ball was not even mandatory and
some teams preferred using balls colored red (yes, Mr. Chairman, not white but *red!*), to the days of the "putting-out system" of piece labor, wherein baseballs were hand sewn by
women in their homes, then through to the 1910's when A.G.
Spalding introduced the first cork-centered baseball (thus
ending the "deadball" era) and on to 1926, when the three
leagues adopted the "cushion cork center" and with it the
modern slug-away style of play; if you were to describe the
cork forests of Spain, the rubber plantations of Malaysia, and
the sheep farms of the American West where the Spalding
baseball is born, if you were to differentiate between the three
kinds of yarn in which the rubber that encases the cork is
wrapped, and remark upon the relative hardness of that wrap-
ping over the decades and how it has determined batting vs.
slugging averages; if you were to devote a chapter to "The
Tightness of the Stitching," explaining scientifically the
aerodynamics of the curveball, or any such breaking pitch,
how it is affected by the relative smoothness of the ball's
seams and the number of seams that meet the wind as it ro-
tates on its axis; and then if from this discussion of the ball,
you were to take a turn, as it were, with the bat, noting first the
eccentric nineteenth-century variations such as the flattened
bat that Wright designed to facilitate bunting, and the curved-
barrel bat in the shape of a question mark invented by Emile
Kinst to put a deceptive spin upon the struck ball (enterpris-
ing Emile! cunning Kinst!), and thence moved on to describe
the manufacture out of hickory logs of the classic bat shaped
by Hillerich and Bradsby, the first model of which was turned
in his shop by Bud Hillerich himself in 1884—the bat that
came to be known to the world of men and boys as "the Louisville Slugger"; if you were by way of a digression to write a
chapter on the most famous bats in baseball history, Heinie
Groh's "bottle bat," Ed Delehanty's "Big Betsy," Luke

Gofannon's "Magic Wand," and those bats of his that Ty Cobb would hone with a steer bone hour upon hour, much as Queequeg, Tashtego, and Dagoo would care lovingly for their harpoons; if then you were to write a chapter on the history of the baseball glove, recounting how the gloves of fielder, first-baseman, and catcher have evolved from the days when the game was played bare-handed, first into something resembling an ordinary dress glove, then into the "heavily-padded mitten," of the 1890's, the small webbed glove of the twenties, and finally in our own era of giantism, into the bushel-basket; if you were to describe the process by which Rawlings manufactures baseball shoes out of kangaroo hide, commencing with the birth of a single fleet-footed kangaroo in the wilds of Western Australia and following it through to its first stolen base in the majors; if you were to recount the evolutionary history of the All-Star game, beanballs, broadcasting, the canvas base, the catcher's mask, chewing tobacco, contracts, doubleheaders, double plays, fans, farm systems, fixes, foul balls, gate receipts, home runs, home plate, ladies day, minor leagues, night games, picture cards, player organizations, salaries, scandals, stadiums, the strike zone, sportscasters, sportswriters, Sunday ball, trading, travel, the World Series, and umpires, you would not in the end have a compendium of American baseball any more thorough than the one that Herman Melville has assembled in *Moby Dick* on the American enterprise of catching the whale. I would not be surprised to learn that his book ran first as a series in *Mechanix Illustrated,* if such existed in Melville's day, so clear and methodical is he in elucidating just what it took in the way of bats, balls, and gloves to set yourself up for chasing the pennant in those leagues. Today some clever publisher would probably bring out *Moby Dick* as one of those "How To Do It" books, providing he left off the catastrophic conclusion, or appended it under the title, "And How Not To."

Only today who cares about how to catch a whale in the old-fashioned, time-honored, and traditional way? Or about anything "traditional" for that matter? Today they just drop bombs down the spouts to blow the blubber out, or haul the leviathans in with a hook, belly-up, those who've been dumb enough to drink from the chamberpot that once was Melville's

"wild and distant sea." How's that for a horror, Brother
Melville? Not only is your indestructible Moby Dick now an
inch from extinction *but so is the vast salt sea itself*. The sea
is no longer a fit place for habitation—just ask the tunas in the
cans. Two-thirds of the globe, the Mother of us all, and according to today's paper, *the place is poisoned*. Yes, even the *fish*
have been given their eviction notice, and must pack up their
scales and go fannon—which is just baseball's way of saying get lost. Only there is no elsewhere as far as I can see for
these aquatic vertebrates to go fann *or* fin in. The fate that
befell the Ruppert Mundys has now befallen the fish, and who,
dear dispensable fans, is to follow?

Let me prophesy. What began in '46 with the obliteration
of the Patriot League will not end until the planet itself has
gone the way of the Tri-City Tycoons, the Tri-City Greenbacks, the Kakoola Reapers, the Terra Incognita Rustlers,
the Asylum Keepers, the Aceldama Butchers, the Ruppert
Mundys, and me; until each and every one of you is gone like
the sperm whale and the great Luke Gofannon, gone without
leaving a trace! Only read your daily paper, fans—every day
news of another stream, another town, another species biting
the dust. Wait, very soon now whole continents will be can-
celed out like stamps. Whonk, Africa! Whonk, Asia! Whonk,
Europa! Whonk, North, whonk, South, America! And, oh,
don't try hiding, Antarctica—*whonk* you too! And that will
be it, fans, as far as the landmass goes. A brand new ballgame.
Only where is it going to be played? Under the lights on
the dark side of the Moon? Will Walter O'Malley with his feel
for the future really move the Dodgers to Mars? There is no
doubt, Mr. O'M., that you cannot beat that planet for parking,
but tell me, has your accountant consulted your astrophysicist
yet? Are you sure there are curves on Mars? Will pitchers on
Venus work in regular rotation in temperatures of five hundred degrees? And fly balls hit into Saturn's rings—ground-
rule doubles or cheap home runs? And what of the historic
Fall Classic and the pieties thereof—plan to rechristen it
the Solar System Series, or do you figure eventually to go
intergalactic? Only when you get beyond the Milky Way, sir,
do they even *have* October? Better check. And hurry, hurry—
there is much scheming and bullshitting and stock-splitting to

be done, if you are to be ready in time for the coming cataclysm. For make no mistake, you sharp-eyed, fast-talking, money-making O'Malleys of America, you proprietors, promoters, expropriators, and entrepreneurs: *the coming cataclysm is coming.* The cushy long-term lease has just about run out on this Los Angeles of a franchise called Earth—and yes, like the dinosaur, like the whale, like hundreds upon hundreds of species whose bones and poems we never even knew, you too will be out on your dispossessed ass, Mr. and Mrs. Roaring Success! Henceforth all *your* games will be played away, too. Away! Away! Far far away! So then, farewell, fugitives! Pleasant journey, pilgrims! *Auf Wiedersehen,* evacuees! *A demain,* d.p.s! *Adios,* drifters! So long, scapegoats! *Hasta mañana,* émigrés! *Pax vobiscum,* pariahs! Happy landing, hobos! *Aloha,* outcasts! *Shalom, shalom,* shelterless, shipwrecked, shucked, shunted, and shuttled humankind! Or, as we say so succinctly in America, to the unfit, the failed, the floundering and forgotten, HIT THE ROAD, YA BUMS!

1

HOME SWEET HOME

*Containing as much of the history of the Patriot League as is
necessary to acquaint the reader with its precarious condition
at the beginning of the Second World War. The character
of General Oakhart—soldier, patriot, and President of the
League. His great love for the rules of the game. His am-
bitions. By way of a contrast, the character of Gil Gamesh,
the most sensational rookie pitcher of all time. His attitude
toward authority and mankind in general. The wisdom and
suffering of Mike "the Mouth" Masterson, the umpire who is
caught in between. The expulsion from baseball of the law-
breaker Gamesh. In which Mike the Mouth becomes baseball's Lear and the nation's Fool. A brief history of the Ruppert Mundys, in which the decline from greatness is traced,
including short sketches of their heroic center-fielder Luke
Gofannon, and the esteemed manager and Christian gentleman Ulysses S. Fairsmith. The chapter is concluded
with a dialogue between General Oakhart and
Mister Fairsmith, containing a few
surprises and disappointments
for the General.*

W HY THE RUPPERT MUNDYS had been chosen to become
the homeless team of baseball was explained to the Port
Ruppert fans with that inspirational phrase of yesteryear,
"to help save the world for democracy." Because of the
proximity of beautiful Mundy Park to the Port Ruppert harbor
and dock facilities, the War Department had labeled it an
ideal embarkation camp and the government had arranged to
lease the site from the owners for the duration of the struggle.
A city of two-story barracks was to be constructed on the playing field to house the soldiers in transit, and the ivy-covered
brick structure that in the Mundy heyday used to hold a happy
Sunday crowd of thirty-five thousand was to furnish headquarters facilities for those who would be shipping a million
American boys and their weapons across the Atlantic to liber-
ate Europe from the tyrant Hitler. In the years to come (the

local fans were told), schoolchildren in France, in Belgium, in Holland, in far-off Denmark and Norway would be asked in their history classes to find the city of Port Ruppert, New Jersey, on the map of the world and to mark it with a star; and among English-speaking peoples, Port Ruppert would be honored forever after—along with Runnymede in England, where the Magna Charta had been signed by King John, and Philadelphia, Pennsylvania, where John Hancock had affixed his signature to the Declaration of Independence—as a Birth-Place of Freedom . . . Then there was the psychological lift that Mundy Park would afford the young draftees departing the ballfield for the battlefront. To spend their last weeks on American soil as "the home team" in the stadium made famous by the incomparable Mundys of '28, '29, and '30, could not but provide "a shot in the arm" to the morale of these American soldiers, most of whom had been hero-worshipping schoolkids back when the Mundys, powered by the immortal Luke Gofannon, had won three hundred and thirty-five games in three seasons, and three consecutive World Series without losing a single game. Yes, what the hallowed playing fields of Eton had been to the British officers of long, long ago, Mundy Park would be to G.I. Joe of World War Two.

As it turned out, bracing sentiments such as these, passionately pronounced from a flag-draped platform in downtown Port Ruppert by notables ranging from Secretary of War Stimson and Governor Edison to the Mayor of Port Ruppert, Boss Stuvwxyz, did work to quash the outcry that the Mundy management and the U.S. government had feared from a citizenry renowned for its devotion to "the Rupe-its" (as the team was called in the local patois). Why, feeling for the Mundys ran so high in that town, that according to Bob Hope, one young fellow called up by the Port Ruppert draft board had written "the Mundys" where the questionnaire had asked his religion; as the comedian told the servicemen at the hundreds of Army bases he toured that year, there was another fellow back there, who when asked his occupation by the recruiting sergeant, replied with a straight face, "A Rupe-it roota and a plumma." The soldiers roared—as audiences would if a comic said no more than, "There was this baseball fan in Port Ruppert—" but Hope had only to add, "Seriously

now, the whole nation is really indebted to those people out
there—'' for the soldiers and sailors to be up on their feet,
whistling through their teeth in tribute to the East Coast
metropolis whose fans and public officials had bid farewell to
their beloved ball club in order to make the world safe for
democracy.

As if the Mundys' fans had anything to say about it,
one way or another! As if Boss Stuvwxyz would object to con-
signing the ball club to Hell, so long as his pockets had been
lined with gold!

The rationale offered "Rupe-it rootas" by the press and the
powers-that-be did not begin to answer General Oakhart's
objections to the fate that had befallen the Mundys. What infuriated the General wasn't simply that a decision of such
magnitude had been reached behind his back—as though he
whose division had broken through the Hindenburg Line in the
fall of 1918 was in actuality an agent of the Huns!—but that
by this extraordinary maneuver, severe damage had been inflicted upon the reputation of the league of which he was president. As it was, having been sullied by scandal in the early
thirties and plagued ever since by falling attendance, the
Patriot League could no longer safely rely upon its pres-
tigious past in the competition for the better ball players,
managers, and umpires. This new inroad into league morale
and cohesiveness would only serve to encourage the schemers
in the two rival leagues whose fondest wish was to drive the
eight Patriot League teams into bankruptcy (or the minors—
either would do), and thus leave the American and National
the only authorized "big" leagues in the country. The troops
laughed uproariously when Bob Hope referred to the P.
League—now with seven home teams, instead of eight—as
"the short circuit," but General Oakhart found the epithet
more ominous than amusing.

Even more ominous was this: by sanctioning an arrange-
ment wherein twenty-three major league teams played at least
half of their games at home, while the Mundys alone played
all one hundred and fifty-four games on the road, Organized
Baseball had compromised the very principles of Fair Play in

which the sport was grounded; they had consented to tamper with what was dearer even to General Oakhart than the survival of his league: the Rules and the Regulations.

Now every Massachusetts schoolchild who had ever gone off with his class to visit the General's office at P. League headquarters in Tri-City knew about General Oakhart and his Rules and Regulations. During the school year, busloads of little children were regularly ushered through the hallways painted with murals twelve and fifteen feet high of the great Patriot League heroes of the past—Base Baal, Luke Gofannon, Mike Mazda, Smoky Woden—and into General Oakhart's paneled office to hear him deliver his lecture on the national pastime. In order to bring home to the youngsters the central importance of the Rules and Regulations, he would draw their attention to the model of a baseball diamond on his desk, explaining to them that if the distance between the bases were to be shortened by as little as one inch, you might just as well change the name of the game, for by so doing you would have altered fundamentally the existing relationship between the diamond "as we have always known it" and the physical effort and skill required to play the game upon a field of those dimensions. Into their solemn and awed little faces he would thrust his heavily decorated chest (for he dressed in a soldier's uniform till the day he died) and he would say: "Now I am not telling you that somebody won't come along tomorrow and *try* to change that distance on us. The streets are full of people with harebrained schemes, out to make a dollar, out to make confusion, out to make the world over because it doesn't happen to suit their taste. I am only telling you that ninety feet is how far from one another the bases have been for a hundred years now, and as far as I am concerned, how far from one another they shall remain until the end of time. I happen to think that the great man whose picture you see hanging above my desk knew what he was doing when he invented the game of baseball. I happen to think that when it came to the geometry of the diamond, he was a genius on a par with Copernicus and Sir Isaac Newton, who I am sure you have read about in your schoolbooks. I happen to think that ninety feet was *precisely* the length necessary to make this game the hard, exciting, and suspenseful struggle that it is. And that is why I would impress upon your young minds a belief in following to the letter, the Rules and the Regulations, as they have been laid down by thoughtful and serious men before you or I were ever born, and as they have survived in baseball for a hundred years now, and in human life since the dawn of civilization. Boys and girls, take away the Rules and the Regulations, and you don't *have* civilized life as we know and revere it. If I have any advice for you today, it's this—don't try to shorten the base paths in order to reach home plate faster and score. All you will have accomplished by that technique is to cheapen the value of a run. I hope you will ponder that on the bus ride back to school. Now, go on out and stroll around the corridors all you want. Those great paintings are there for your enjoyment. Good day, and good luck to you.''

General Oakhart became President of the Patriot League in 1933, though as early as the winter of 1919–1920, he was being plugged for the commissionership of baseball, along with his friend and colleague General John "Blackjack" Pershing and the former President of the United States William Howard Taft. At that time it had seemed to him an excellent stepping-stone to high political office, and he had been surprised and saddened when the owners had selected a popinjay like Judge Kenesaw Mountain Landis over a man of principle like himself. In his estimation Landis was nothing more than a show-boat judge—as could be proved by the fact that every time he made one of his "historic decisions," it was subsequently reversed by a higher court. In 1907 as a federal judge he fined the Standard Oil Company twenty-nine million dollars in a rebate case—headlines all over the place—then, overruled by the U.S. Supreme Court. During the war, the same hollow theatrics: seven socialists up before him for impeding the war effort; scathing denunciations from Judge Landis, hefty jail sentences all around, including one to a Red congressman from Milwaukee, big headlines—and then the verdict thrown out the window by a higher court. That was the man they had chosen over him—the same man who now told General Oakhart that it was "an honor" for the Mundys to have been chosen to make this sacrifice for their country, that actually it would be *good* for the game for a major league team to be seen giving their all to the war effort day in and day out. Oh, and did he get on his high horse when the General suggested that the Commissioner might go to Washington to ask President Roosevelt to intervene in the Mundys' behalf. "In this office, General, the Patriot League is just another league, and the Ruppert Mundys are just another ball club, and if either one of them expects preferential treatment from Kenesaw Mountain Landis they have another guess coming. Baseball does not intend to ask for special favors in a time of national crisis. And that's that!"

Back in the summer of 1920, having already lost out to Landis for the commissioner's job, General Oakhart suffered a second stunning setback when the movement to make him Harding's running-mate died in the smoke-filled rooms. No one (went the argument against him) wanted to be reminded of all the boys buried under crosses in France to whom General Oakhart had been "Father, Brother, and Buddy too." Nor—he thought bitterly, when the Teapot Dome scandal broke in '23, when one after another of Harding's cronies was indicted, convicted, and jailed for the most vile sort of political corruption —nor did they want a man of integrity around, either. When Harding died (of shame and humiliation, one would hope) and Coolidge took the oath of office—Coolidge, that hack they had chosen instead of him!—the General came near to weeping for the nation's loss of himself. But, alas, the American people didn't seem to care any more than the politicians did for a man who lived by and for the Rules and Regulations.

Sure enough, when the call went out for General Oakhart, the country was suffering just such panic and despair as he had predicted years ago, if the ship of state were to be steered for long by unprincipled leaders. It was not, however, to the White House or even the State House that the General was summoned, but to Tri-City, Mass., to be President of a baseball league in trouble. With five of its eight teams in hock to the bank, and fear growing among the owners that the Depression had made their players susceptible to the gambling mob, the P. League proprietors had paid a visit to General Oakhart in his quarters at the War College, where he was director of Military Studies, and pleaded with him not to sit sulking in an ivory tower. It was Spenser Trust, the billionaire Tycoon owner, and nobody's fool, who spoke the words that appeared to win the General's heart: he reminded him that it was not just their floundering league that was casting about for a strong man to lead them back to greatness, but the nation as well. An outstanding Republican who rose to national prominence in '33 might well find himself elected the thirty-third President of the United States in '36.

Now as luck would have it—or so it seemed to the General at the outset—the very year he agreed to retire from the military to become President of the P. League, the nineteen-year-old Gil Gamesh came up to pitch for the Tycoons' crosstown rival, the Tri-City Greenbacks. Gamesh, throwing six consecutive shutouts in his first six starts, was an immediate sensation, and with his "I can beat anybody" motto, captured the country's heart as no player had since the Babe began swatting them out of the ballpark in 1920. Only the previous year, in the middle of the most dismal summer of his life, the great Luke Gofannon had called it quits and retired to his farm in the Jersey flats, so that it had looked at the opening of the '33 season as though the Patriot League would be without an Olympian of the Ruth-Cobb variety. Then, from nowhere—or, to be exact, from Babylonia, by way of his mother and father— came the youngster the General aptly labeled "the Talk of the World," and nothing Hubbell did over in the National League or Lefty Grove in the American was remotely comparable. The tall, slim, dark-haired left-hander was just what the doctor had ordered for a nation bewildered and frightened by a ruinous Depression—here was a kid who just would not lose, and he made no bones about it either. Nothing shy, nothing sweet, nothing humble about this young fellow. He could be ten runs on top in the bottom of the ninth, two men out, the bases empty, a count of 0 and 2 on the opposing team's weakest hitter, and if the umpire gave him a bad call he would be down off that mound breathing fire. "You blind robber—it's a strike!" However, if and when the *batter* should dare to put up a beef on a call, Gamesh would laugh like mad and call out to the ump, "Come on now, you can't tell anything by him—he never even seen it. He'd be the last guy in the *world* to know."

And the fans just ate it up: nineteen years old and he had the courage and confidence of a Walter Johnson, and the competitive spirit of the Georgia Peach himself. The stronger the batter the better Gil liked it. Rubbing the ball around in those enormous paws that hung down practically to his knees, he would glare defiantly at the man striding up to the plate (some of them stars when he was still in the cradle) and announce out loud his own personal opinion of the fellow's abilities. "You couldn't lick a stamp. You couldn't beat a drum. Get your belly button in there, bud, you're what I call duck soup." Then, sneering away, he would lean way back, kick that right leg up sky-high like a chorus girl, and that long left arm would start coming around by way of Biloxi—and next thing you knew it was strike one. He would burn them in just as beautiful and nonchalant as that, three in a row, and then exactly like a barber, call out, "Next!" He did not waste a pitch, unless it was to throw a ball at a batter's head, and he did not consider that a waste. He knew a hundred ways to humiliate the opposition, such as late in the game deliberately walking the other pitcher, then setting the ball down on the ground to wave him from first on to second. "Go on, go on, you ain't gonna get there no other way, that's for sure." With the surprised base runner safely ensconced at second, Gil would kick the ball up into his glove with the instep of his shoe—"Okay, just stand there on the bag, bud," he would tell the opposing pitcher, "and watch these fellas try and hit me. You might learn somethin', though I doubt it."

Gamesh was seen to shed a tear only once in his career: when his seventh major league start was rained out. Some reports had it that he even took the Lord's name in vain, blaming Him of all people for the washout. Gil announced afterward that had he been able to work in his regular rotation that afternoon, he would have extended his shutout streak through those nine innings *and on to the very end of the season.* An outrageous claim, on the face of it, and yet there were those in the newsrooms, living rooms, and barrooms around this nation who believed him. As it was, even lacking his "fine edge," as he called it, he gave up only one run the next day, and never more than two in any game that year.

Around the league, at the start of that season, they would

invariably begin to boo the headstrong nineteen-year-old when he stepped out of the Greenback dugout, but it did not appear to affect him any. "I never expect they are going to be very happy to see me heading out to the mound," he told reporters. "I wouldn't be, if I was them." Yet once the game was over, it invariably required a police escort to get Gamesh back to the hotel, for the crowd that had hated him nine innings earlier for being so cocksure of himself, was now in the streets calling his name—adults screaming right along with kids—as though it was the Savior about to emerge from the visiting team clubhouse in a spiffy yellow linen suit and two-toned perforated shoes.

It surely seemed to the General that he could not have turned up in the league president's box back of first at Greenback Stadium at a more felicitous moment. In 1933 just about everybody appeared to have become a Greenback fan, and the Patriot League pennant battle between the two Tri-City teams, the impeccably professional Tycoons, and the rough-and-tumble Greenbacks, made headlines East *and* West, and constituted just about the only news that didn't make you want to slit your throat over the barren dinner table. Men out of work —and there were fifteen million of them across the land, men sick and tired of defeat and dying for a taste of victory, rich men who had become paupers overnight—would somehow scrape two bits together to come out and watch from the bleachers as a big unbeatable boy named Gil Gamesh did his stuff on the mound. And to the little kids of America, whose dads were on the dole, whose uncles were on the booze, and whose older brothers were on the bum, he was a living, breathing example of that hero of American heroes, the he-man, a combination of Lindbergh, Tarzan, and (with his long, girlish lashes and brilliantined black hair) Rudolph Valentino: brave, brutish, and a lady-killer, and in possession of a sidearm fastball that according to Ripley's "Believe It or Not" could pass clear through a batter's chest, come out his back, and still be traveling at "major league speed."

What cooled the General's enthusiasm for the boy wonder was the feud that erupted in the second month of the season between young Gil and Mike Masterson, and that ended in tragedy on the last day of the season. The grand old man of

umpiring had been assigned by General Oakhart to follow the
Greenbacks around the country, after it became evident that
Gamesh was just too much for the other officials in the circuit
to handle. The boy could be rough when the call didn't go his
way, and games had been held up for five and ten minutes at
a time while Gamesh told the ump in question just what he
thought of his probity, eyesight, physiognomy, parentage, and
place of national origin. Because of the rookie's enormous popularity, because of the records he was breaking in game after
game, because many in the crowd had laid out their last quarter
to see Gamesh pitch (and because they were just plain intimidated), the umps tended to tolerate from Gamesh what would
have been inexcusable in a more mature, or less spectacular,
player. This of course was creating a most dangerous prece-
dent vis-à-vis the Rules and the Regulations, and in order to
prevent the situation from getting completely out of hand,
General Oakhart turned to the finest judge of a fastball in the
majors, in his estimate the toughest, fairest official who ever
wore blue, the man whose booming voice had earned him the
monicker ''the Mouth.''

''I have been umpiring in the Patriot League since Dewey
took Manila,'' Mike the Mouth liked to tell them on the annual
banquet circuit, after the World Series was over. ''I have ren-
dered more than a million and a half decisions in that time,
and let me tell you, in all those years I have never called one
wrong, at least not in my heart. In my apprentice days down
in the minors I was bombarded with projectiles from the
stands, I was threatened with switchblades by coaches, and
once a misguided manager fired upon me with a gun. This
three-inch scar here on my forehead was inflicted by the mask
of a catcher who believed himself wronged by me, and on my
shoulders and my back I bear sixty-four wounds inflicted during those 'years of trial' by bottles of soda pop. I have been
mobbed by fans so perturbed that when I arrived in the dressing room I discovered all the buttons had been torn from my
clothing, and rotten vegetables had been stuffed into my
trousers and my shirt. But harassed and hounded as I have
been, I am proud to say that I have never so much as changed
the call on a close one out of fear of the consequences to my
life, my limbs, or my loved ones.''

This last was an allusion to the kidnapping and murder of Mike the Mouth's only child, back in 1898, his first year up with the P. League. The kidnappers had entered Mike's Wisconsin home as he was about to leave for the ball park to umpire a game between the Reapers and the visiting Rustlers, who were battling that season for the flag. Placing a gun to his little girl's blond curls, the intruders told the young umpire that if the Reapers lost that afternoon, Mary Jane would be back in her high chair for dinner, unharmed. If however the Reapers should win for any reason, then Masterson could hold himself responsible for his darling child's fate . . . Well, that game, as everyone knows, went on and on and on, before the Reapers put together two walks and a scratch hit in the bottom of the seventeenth to break the 3–3 tie and win by a run. In subsequent weeks, pieces of little Mary Jane Masterson were found in every park in the Patriot League.

It did not take but one pitch, of course, for Mike the Mouth to become the lifelong enemy of Gil Gamesh. Huge crowd, sunny day, flags snapping in the breeze, Gil winds up, kicks, and here comes that long left arm, America, around by way of the tropical Equator.

"That's a ball," thundered Mike, throwing his own left arm into the air (as if anybody in the ball park needed a sign when the Mouth was back of the plate).

"A ball?" cried Gamesh, hurling his glove twenty-five feet in the air. "Why, I couldn't put a strike more perfect across the plate! That was right in there, you blind robber!"

Mike raised one meaty hand to stop the game and stepped out in front of the plate with his whisk broom. He swept the dust away meticulously, allowing the youth as much time as he required to remember where he was and whom he was talking to. Then he turned to the mound and said—in tones exceeding courteous—"Young fellow, it looks like you'll be in the league for quite a while. That sort of language will get you nothing. Why don't you give it up?" And he stepped back into position behind the catcher. "Play!" he roared.

On the second pitch, Mike's left arm shot up again. "That's two." And Gamesh was rushing him.

"You cheat! You crook! You thief! You overage, overstuffed—"

"Son, don't say anymore."

"And what if I do, you pickpocket?"

"I will give you the thumb right now, and we will get on with the game of baseball that these people have paid good money to come out here today to see."

"They didn't come out to see no baseball game, you idiot —they come out to see *me!*"

"I will run you out of here just the same."

"Try it!" laughed Gil, waving toward the stands where the Greenback fans were already on their feet, whooping like a tribe of Red Indians for Mike the Mouth's scalp. And how could it be otherwise? The rookie had a record of fourteen wins and no losses, and it was not yet July. "Go ahead and try it," said Gil. "They'd mob you, Masterson. They'd pull you apart."

"I would as soon be killed on a baseball field," replied Mike the Mouth (who in the end got his wish), "as anywhere else. Now why don't you go out there and pitch. That's what they pay you to do."

Smiling, Gil said, "And why don't you go shit in your shoes."

Mike looked as though his best friend had died; sadly he shook his head. "No, son, no, that won't do, not in the Big Time." And up went the right thumb, an appendage about the size and shape of a nice pickle. Up it went and up it stayed, though for a moment it looked as though Gamesh, whose mouth had fallen open, was considering biting it off—it wasn't but an inch from his teeth.

"Leave the field, son. And leave it now."

"Oh sure," chuckled Gil, recovering his composure, "oh sure, leave the field in the middle of pitchin' to the first batter," and he started back out to the mound, loping nonchalantly like a big boy in an open meadow, while the crowd roared their love right into his face. "Oh sure," he said, laughing like mad.

"Son, either you go," Mike called after him, "or I forfeit this game to the other side."

"And ruin my perfect record?" he asked, his hands on his hips in disbelief. "Oh sure," he laughed. Then he got back to business: sanding down the ball in his big calloused palms, he called to the batsman on whom he had a two

ball count, "Okay, get in there, bud, and let's see if you can
get that gun off your shoulder."

But the batter had hardly done as Gil had told him to
when he was lifted out of the box by Mike the Mouth. Seventy-
one years old, and a lifetime of being banged around, and still
he just picked him up and set him aside like a paperweight.
Then, with his own feet dug in, one on either side of home
plate, he made his startling announcement to the sixty thousand fans in Greenback Stadium—the voice of Enrico Caruso
could not have carried any more clearly to the corners of the
outfield bleachers.

"Because Greenback pitcher Gilbert Gamesh has failed
to obey the order of the umpire-in-chief that he remove himself from the field of play, this game is deemed forfeited by a
score of 9 to 0 to the opposing team, under rule 4.15 of the
Official Baseball Rules that govern the playing of baseball
games by the professional teams of the Patriot League of Professional Baseball Clubs."

And jaw raised, arms folded, and legs astride home plate
—according to Smitty's column the next day, very like that
Colossus at Rhodes—Mike the Mouth remained planted where
he was, even as wave upon wave of wild men washed over the
fences and onto the field.

And Gil Gamesh, his lips white with froth and his eagle
eyes spinning in his skull, stood a mere sixty feet and six
inches away, holding a lethal weapon in his hand.

The next morning. A black-and-white perforated shoe kicks
open the door to General Oakhart's office and with a wad of
newspapers in his notorious left hand, enter Gil Gamesh,
shrieking. "My record is not 14 and 1! It's 14 and 0! Only now
they got me down here for a *loss!* Which is impossible! *And
you two done it!"*

"You 'done' it, young man," said General Oakhart, while
in a double-breasted blue suit the same deep shade as his umpire togs, Mike the Mouth Masterson silently filled a chair by
the trophy cabinet.

"Youse!"

"You."

"Youse!"

"You."

"Stop saying 'you' when I say 'youse'—it *was* youse, and the whole country knows it too! You and that thief! Sittin' there free as a bird, when he oughtta be in Sing Sing!"

Now the General's decorations flashed into view as he raised himself from behind the desk. Wearing the ribbons and stars of a courageous lifetime, he was impressive as a ship's figurehead—and of course he was still a powerfully built man, with a chest on him that might have been hooped around like a barrel. Indeed, the three men gathered together in the room looked as though they could have held their own against a team of horses, if they'd had to draw a brewery truck through the streets of Tri-City. No wonder that the day before, the mob that had pressed right up to his chin had fallen back from Mike the Mouth as he stood astride home plate like the Eighth Wonder of the World. Of course, ever since the murder of his child, not even the biggest numskull had dared to throw so much as a peanut shell at him from the stands; but neither did his bulk encourage a man to tread upon his toes.

"Gamesh," said the General, swelling with righteousness, "no umpire in the history of this league has ever been found guilty of a single act of dishonesty or corruption. Or even charged with one. Remember that!"

"But—my perfect record! He ruined it—forever! Now I'll go down in the history books as someone who once *lost!* And I didn't! I couldn't! I can't!"

"And why can't you, may I ask?"

"Because I'm Gil Gamesh! I'm an immortal!"

"I don't care if you are Jesus Christ!" barked the General. "There are Rules and Regulations in this world and you will follow them just like anybody else!"

"And who made the rules?" sneered Gamesh. "You? Or Scarface over there?"

"Neither of us, young man. *But we are here to see that they are carried out.*"

"And suppose I say the hell with you!"

"Then you will be what is known as an outlaw."

"And? So? Jesse James was an outlaw. And he's world-famous."

"True. But he did not pitch in the major leagues."

"He didn't want to," sneered the young star.

"But you do," replied General Oakhart, and, bewildered, Gamesh collapsed into a chair. It wasn't just *what* he wanted to, it was *all* he wanted to do. It was what he was *made* to do.

"But," he whimpered, "my perfect record."

"The umpire, in case it hasn't occurred to you, has a record too. A record," the General informed him, "that must remain untainted by charges of favoritism or falsification. Otherwise there would not even be major league baseball contests in which young men like yourself could excel."

"But there ain't no young men like myself," Gamesh whined. "There's me, and that's it."

"Gil . . ." It was Mike the Mouth speaking. Off the playing field he had a voice like a songbird's, so gentle and mellifluous that it could soothe a baby to sleep. And alas, it had, years and years ago . . . "Son, listen to me. I don't expect that you are going to love me. I don't expect that anybody in a ball park is going to care if I live or die. Why should they? I'm not the star. You are. The fans don't go out to the ball park to see the Rules and the Regulations upheld, they go out to see the home team win. The whole world loves a winner, you know that better than anybody, but when it comes to an umpire, there's not a soul in the ball park who's for him. He hasn't got a fan in the place. What's more, he cannot sit down, he cannot go to the bathroom, he cannot get a drink of water, unless he visits the dugout, and that is something that any umpire worth his salt does not ever want to do. He cannot have anything to do with the players. He cannot fool with them or kid with them, even though he may be a man who in his heart likes a little horseplay and a joke from time to time. If he so much as sees a ballplayer coming down the street, he will cross over or turn around and walk the other way, so it will not look to passersby that anything is up between them. In strange towns, when the visiting players all buddy up in a hotel lobby and go out together for a meal in a friendly restaurant, he finds a room in a boarding house and eats his evening pork chop in a diner all alone. Oh, it's a lonesome thing, being an umpire. There are men who won't talk to you for the rest of your life. Some will even stoop to vengeance. But that is not your lookout, my boy. Nobody is twisting Masterson's arm, saying, 'Mike, it's a dog's life, but you are stuck with it.' No, it's just this, Gil: somebody in this world has got to run the game. Otherwise, you see, it wouldn't be baseball, it would be chaos. We would be right back where we were in the Ice Ages.''

"The Ice Ages?" said Gil, reflectively.

"Exactly," replied Mike the Mouth.

"Back when they was livin' in caves? Back when they carried clubs and ate raw flesh and didn't wear no clothes?"

"Correct!" said General Oakhart.

"Well," cried Gil, "maybe we'd be better off!" And kicking aside the newspapers with which he'd strewn the General's carpet, he made his exit. Whatever it was he said to the General's elderly spinster secretary out in the anteroom—instead of just saying "Good day"—caused her to keel over unconscious.

That very afternoon, refusing to heed the advice of his wise manager to take in a picture show, Gamesh turned up at Greenback Stadium just as the game was getting underway, and still buttoning up his uniform shirt, ran out and yanked the baseball from the hand of the Greenback pitcher who was preparing to pitch to the first Aceldama hitter of the day—and nobody tried to stop him. The regularly scheduled pitcher just walked off the field like a good fellow (cursing under his breath) and the Old Philosopher, as they called the Greenback manager of that era, pulled his tired old bones out of the dugout and ambled over to the umpire back of home plate. In his early years, the Old Philosopher had worn his seat out sliding up and down the bench, but after a lifetime of managing in the majors, he wasn't about to be riled by anything.

"Change in the line-up, Mike. That big apple knocker out there on the mound is batting ninth now on my card."

To which Mike Masterson, master of scruple and decorum, replied, "Name?"

"Boy named Gamesh," he shouted, to make himself heard above the pandemonium rising from the stands.

"Spell it."

"Awww come on now, Michael."

"Spell it."

"G-a-m-e-s-h."

"First name?"

"Gil. G as in Gorgeous. I as in Illustrious. L as in Larger-than-life."

"Thank you, sir," said Mike the Mouth, and donning his mask, called, "Play!"

("In the beginning was the word, and the word was 'Play!'" Thus began the tribute to Mike Masterson, written the day the season ended in tragedy, in the column called "One Man's Opinion.")

The first Aceldama batsman stepped in. Without even taking the time to insult him, to mock him, to tease and to taunt him, without so much as half a snarl or the crooked smile, Gamesh pitched the ball, which was what they paid him to do.

"Strike-ah-one!" roared Mike.

The catcher returned the ball to Gamesh, and again, impersonal as a machine and noiseless as a snake, Gamesh did his chorus girl kick, and in no time at all the second pitch passed through what might have been a tunnel drilled for it by the first.

"Strike-ah-two!"

On the third pitch, the batter (who appeared to have no more idea where the ball might be than some fellow who wasn't even at the ball park) swung and wound up on his face in the dust. "Musta dropped," he told the worms.

"Strike-ah-three—you're-out!"

"Next!" Gamesh called, and the second man in a Butcher uniform stepped up.

"Strike-ah-one!"

"Strike-ah-two!"

"Strike-ah-three—you're out!"

So life went—cruelly, but swiftly—for the Aceldama hitters for eight full innings. "Next!" called Gamesh, and gave each the fastest shave and haircut on record. Then with a man out on strikes in the top of the ninth, and 0 and 2 on the hitter—and the fans so delirious that after each Aceldama batter left the chair, they gave off an otherworldly, practically celestial sound, as though together they constituted a human harp that had just been plucked—Gamesh threw the ball too low. Or so said the umpire behind the plate, who supposedly was in a position to know.

"That's one!"

Yes, Gil Gamesh was alleged by Mike the Mouth Masterson to have thrown a ball—after seventy-seven consecutive strikes.

"Well," sighed the Old Philosopher, down in the Greenback dugout, "here comes the end of the world." He pulled out his pocket watch, seemingly taking some comfort in its precision. "Yep, at 2:59 P.M. on Wednesday, June 16, 1933. Right on time."

Out on the diamond, Gil Gamesh was fifteen feet forward from the rubber, still in the ape-like crouch with which he completed his big sidearm motion. In their seats the fans surged upwards as though in anticipation of Gil's bounding into the air and landing in one enormous leap on Mike the Mouth's blue back. Instead, he straightened up like a man—a million years of primate evolution passing instantaneously before their eyes—and there was that smile, that famous crooked smile. "Okay," he called down to his catcher, Pineapple Tawhaki, "throw it here."

"But—holy aloha!" cried Pineapple, who hailed from Honolulu, "he call ball, Gilly!"

Gamesh spat high and far and watched the tobacco juice raise the white dust on the first-base foul line. He could hit anything with anything, that boy. "Was a ball."

"*Was?*" Pineapple cried.

"Yep. Low by the hair off a little girl's slit, but low." And spat again, this time raising chalk along third. "Done it on purpose, Pineapple. Done it deliberate."

"Holy aloha!" the mystified catcher groaned—and fired the ball back to Gil. "How-why-ee?"

"So's to make sure," said Gil, his voice rising to a piercing pitch, "so's to make sure the old geezer standin' behind you hadn't fell asleep at the switch! JUST TO KEEP THE OLD SON OF A BITCH HONEST!"

"One and two," Mike roared. "Play!"

"JUST SO AS TO MAKE CLEAR ALL THE REST WAS EARNED!"

"*Play!*"

"BECAUSE I DON'T WANT NOTHIN' FOR NOTHIN'
FROM YOUSE! I DON'T NEED IT! I'M GIL GAMESH!
I'M AN IMMORTAL, WHETHER YOU LIKE IT OR
NOT!"

"PLAY BAWWWWWWWWWW!"

Had he ever been more heroic? More gloriously contemptuous of the powers-that-be? Not to those fans of his he
hadn't. They loved him even more for that bad pitch, deliberately thrown a fraction of a fraction of an inch too low, than
for the seventy-seven dazzling strikes that had preceded it.
The wickedly accurate pitching machine wasn't a machine at
all—no, he was a human being, made of piss and vinegar, like
other human beings. The arm of a god, but the disposition of
the Common Man: petty, grudging, vengeful, gloating, selfish,
narrow, and mean. How could they *not* adore him?

His next pitch was smacked three hundred and sixty-five
feet off the wall in left-center field for a double.

Much as he hated to move his rheumatism to and fro like
this, the Old Philosopher figured it was in the interest of the
United States of America, of which he had been a lifelong
citizen, for him to trek out to the mound and offer his con-
dolences to the boy.

"Those things happen, lad; settle down."

"That robber! That thief! That pickpocket!"

"Mike Masterson didn't hit it off you—you just dished
up a fat pitch. It could happen to anyone."

"But not to me! It was on account of my rhythm bein'
broke! On account of my fine edge bein' off!"

"That wasn't his doin' either, boy. Throwin' that low
one was your own smart idea. See this fella comin' up? He
can strong-back that pelota right outta here. I want for you to
put him on."

"No!"

"Now do like I tell you, Gil. Put him on. It'll calm you
down, for one, and set up the d.p. for two. Let's get out of this
inning the smart way."

But when the Old Philosopher departed the mound, and
Pineapple stepped to the side of the plate to give Gamesh a
target for the intentional pass, the rookie sensation growled,
"Get back where you belong, you Hawaiian hick."

"But," warned the burly catcher, running halfway to the mound, "he say put him on, Gilly!"

"Don't you worry, Oahu, I'll put him on all right."

"*How?*"

Gil grinned.

The first pitch was a fastball aimed right at the batter's mandible. In the stands, a woman screamed—"He's a goner!" but down went the Aceldama player just in the nick of time.

"That's one!" roared Mike.

The second pitch was a second fastball aimed at the occipital. "My God," screamed the woman, "it killed him!" But miracle of miracles, the batter in the dust was seen to move.

"That's two!" roared Mike, and calling time, came around to do some tidying up around home plate. And to chat awhile. "Ball get away from you?" he asked Gamesh, while sweeping away with his broom.

Gamesh spat high in the air back over his shoulder, a wad that landed smack in the middle of second base, right between the feet of the Aceldama runner standing up on the bag. "Nope."

"Then, if you don't mind my asking, how do you explain nearly taking this man's head off two times in a row?"

"Ain't you never heard of the intentional pass?"

"Oh no. Oh no, not that way, son," said Mike the Mouth. "Not in the Big Time, I'm afraid."

"Play!" screeched Gamesh, mocking the umpire's foghorn, and motioned him back behind the plate where he belonged. "Ump, Masterson, that's what they pay you to do."

"Now listen to me, Gil," said Mike. "If you want to put this man on intentionally, then pitch out to him, in the time-honored manner. But don't make him go down again. We're not barbarians in this league. We're men, trying to get along."

"Speak for yourself, Mouth. I'm me."

The crowd shrieked as at a horror movie when the third pitch left Gil's hand, earmarked for the zygomatic arch. And Mike the Mouth, even before making his call, rushed to kneel beside the man spread across the plate, to touch his wrist and see if he was still alive. Barely, barely.

"That's three!" Mike roared to the stands. And to Gamesh—"And that's it!"

"*What's* it?" howled Gamesh. "He ducked, didn't he? He got out of the way, didn't he? You can't give me the thumb— I didn't even *nick* him!"

"Thanks to his own superhuman effort. His pulse is just about beating. It's a wonder he isn't lying there dead."

"Well," answered Gamesh, with a grin, "that's his look-out."

"No, son, no, it is mine."

"Yeah—and what about line drives back at the pitcher! More pitchers get hit in the head with liners than batters get beaned in the noggin—and do you throw out the guy what hit the line drive? No! Never! And the reason why is because they ain't Gil Gamesh! Because they ain't me!"

"Son," asked Mike the Mouth, grimacing as though in pain, "just what in the world do you think I have against you?"

"I'm too great, that's what!"

Donning his protective mask, Mike the Mouth replied, "We are only human beings, Gamesh, trying to get along. That's the last time I'll remind you."

"Boy, I sure hope so," muttered Gil, and then to the batter, he called, "All right, bud, let's try to stay up on our feet this time. All that fallin' down in there, people gonna think you're pickled."

With such speed did that fourth pitch travel the sixty feet and six inches to the plate, that the batsman, had he been Man o'War himself, could still not have moved from its path in time. He never had a chance . . . Aimed, however, just above the nasal bone, the fastball clipped the bill of his blue and gray Aceldama cap and spun it completely around on his head. Gamesh's idea of a joke, to see the smile he was sporting way down there in that crouch.

"That's no good," thundered Mike, "take your base!"

"If he can," commented Gil, watching the shell-shocked hitter trying to collect himself enough to figure out which way to go, up the third- or the first-base line.

"And you," said Mike softly, "can take off too, son."

And here he hiked that gnarled pickle of a thumb into the air, and announced, "You're out of the game!"

The pitcher's glove went skyward; as though Mike had hit his jackpot, the green eyes began spinning in Gil's head. "No!"

"Yes, oh yes. Or I forfeit this one too. I'll give you to the letter C for Chastised, son. A. B. . . . ."

"NO!" screamed Gil, but before Mike could bring down the guillotine, he was into the Greenback dugout, headed straight on to the showers, for that he should be credited with a *second* loss was more than the nineteen-year-old immortal could endure.

And thereafter, through that sizzling July and August, and down through the dog days of September, he behaved himself. No improvement in his disposition, of course, but it wasn't to turn him into Little Boy Blue that General Oakhart had put Mike the Mouth on his tail—it was to make him obedient to the Rules and the Regulations, and that Mike did. On his third outing with Mike behind the plate, Gamesh pitched a nineteen-inning three-hitter, and the only time he was anywhere near being ejected from the game, he restrained himself by sinking his prominent incisors into his glove, rather than into Mike's ear, which was actually closer at that moment to his teeth.

The General was in the stands that day, and immediately after the last out went around to the umpires' dressing room to congratulate his iron-willed arbiter. He found him teetering on a bench before his locker, his blue shirt so soaked with perspiration that it looked as though it would have to be removed from his massive torso by a surgeon. He seemed barely to have strength enough to suck his soda pop up through the straw in the bottle.

General Oakhart clapped him on the shoulder—and felt it give beneath him. "Congratulations, Mike. You have done it. You have civilized the boy. Baseball will be eternally grateful."

Mike blinked his eyes to bring the General's face into focus. "No. Not civilized. Never will be. Too great. He's right."

"Speak up, Mike, I can't hear you."

"I said—"

"Sip some soda, Mike. Your voice is a little gone."

He sipped, he sighed, he began to hiccup. "I oop said he's oop too great."

"Meaning what?"

"It's like looking in oop to a steel furnace. It's like being a tiny oop farm oop boy again, when the trans oop con oop tinental train oop goes by. It's like being trampled oop trampled oop under a herd of wild oop oop. Elephants. After an inning the ball doesn't even look like a oop anymore. Sometimes it seems to be coming in end oop over end oop. And thin as an ice oop pick. Or it comes in bent and ee oop long oop ated like a boomerang oop. Or it flattens out like an aspirin oop tab oop let. Even his oop change-up oop hisses. He throws with every muscle in his body, and yet at oop the end of nineteen oop nineteen oop innings like today, he is fresh oop as oop a daisy. General, if he gets any faster, I oop don't know if even the best eyes in the business will be able to determine the close oop ones. And close oop ones are all he throws oop."

"You sound tired, Mike."

"I'll oop survive," he said, closing his eyes and swaying.

But the General had to wonder. He might have been looking at a raw young ump up from the minors, worried sick about making a mistake his first game in the Big Time, instead of Mike the Mouth, on the way to his two millionth major league decision.

He had to rap Mike on the shoulder now to rouse him. "I have every confidence in you, Mike. I always have. I always will. I know you won't let the league down. You won't now, will you, Michael?"

"Oop."

"Good!"

What a year Gil went on to have (and Mike with him)! Coming into the last game of the year, the rookie had not only tied the record for the most wins in a single season (41), but had broken the record for the most strike-outs (349) set by Rube Waddell in 1904, the record for the most shutouts (16) set by Grover Alexander in 1916, and had only to give up less than six runs to come in below the earned run average of 1.01

set by Dutch Leonard the year he was born. As for Patriot
League records, he had thrown more complete games than
any other pitcher in the league's history, had allowed the fewest walks, the fewest hits, and gotten the most strike-outs per
nine innings. Any wonder then, that after the rookie's late September no-hitter against Independence (his fortieth victory
as against the one 9–0 loss), Mike the Mouth fell into some
sort of insentient fit in the dressing room from which he could
not be roused for nearly twenty-four hours. He stared like a
blind man, he drooled like a fool. "Stunned," said the doctor, and threw cold water at him. Following the second no-
hitter—which came four days after the first—Mike was able
to make it just inside the dressing room with his dignity intact,
before he began the howling that did not completely subside
for the better part of two days and two nights. He did not eat,
sleep, or drink: just raised his lips to the ceiling and hourly
bayed to the other wolves. "Something definitely the matter
here," said the doctor. "When the season's over, you better
have him checked."

The Greenbacks went into the final day of the year only
half a game out in front of the Tycoons; whichever Tri-City
team should win the game, would win the flag. And Gamesh, by
winning his forty-second, would have won more games in a
season than any other pitcher in history. And of course there
was the chance that the nineteen-year-old kid would pitch his
third consecutive no-hitter . . .

Well, what happened was more incredible even than that.
The first twenty-six Tycoons he faced went down on strikes:
seventy-eight strikes in a row. There had not even been a foul
tip—either the strike was called, or in desperation they swung
at the ozone. Then, two out in the ninth and two strikes on the
batter (thus was it ever, with Gilbert Gamesh) the left-hander
fired into the catcher's mitt what seemed not only to the sixty-
two thousand three hundred and forty-two ecstatic fans packed
into Greenback Stadium, but to the helpless batter himself—
who turned from the plate without a whimper and started back
to his home in Wilkes-Barre, Pa.—the last pitch of the '33 Patriot League season. Strike-out number twenty-seven. Victory
number forty-two. Consecutive no-hitter number three. The
most perfect game ever pitched in the major leagues, or con-

ceived of by the mind of man. The Greenbacks had won the pennant, and how! Bring on the Senators and the Giants!

Or so it had seemed, until Mike the Mouth Masterson got word through to the two managers that the final out did not count, because at the moment of the pitch, *his back had been turned to the plate.*

In order for the game to be resumed, tens of thousands of spectators who had poured out onto the field when little Joe Iviri, the Tycoon hitter, had turned away in defeat, had now to be forced back up through the gates into the stands; wisely, General Oakhart had arranged beforehand for the Tri-City mounted constabulary to be at the ready, under the stands, in the event of just such an uprising as this, and so it was that a hundred whinnying horses, drawn up like a cavalry company and charging into the manswarm for a full fifteen minutes, drove the enraged fans from the field. But not even policemen with drawn pistols could force them to take their seats. With arms upraised they roared at Mike the Mouth as though he were their Fuehrer, only it was not devotion they were promising him.

General Oakhart himself took the microphone and attemped to address the raging mob. "This is General Douglas D. Oakhart, President of the Patriot League. Due to circumstances beyond his control, umpire-in-chief Mike Masterson was unable to make a call on the last pitch because his back was turned to the plate at that moment."

"KILL THE MOUTH! MURDER THE BUM!"

"According to rule 9.4, section e, of the Official—"

"BANISH THE BLIND BASTARD! CUT OFF HIS WHATSIS!"

"—game shall be resumed prior to that pitch. Thank you."

"BOOOOOOOOOOOOOOOOOOOOOOOOOOOOO!"

In the end it was necessary for the General to step out onto the field of play (as once he had stepped onto the field of battle), followed behind by the Tri-City Symphony Orchestra; by his order, the musicians (more terrified than any army he had ever seen, French, British, American, or Hun) assembled for the second time that day in center field, and with two down in the ninth, and two strikes on the batter, proceeded to play the National Anthem again.

"'O say can you see,'" sang the General.

Through his teeth, he addressed Mike Masterson, who stood beside him at home plate, with his cap over his chest protector. "What happened?"

Mike said, "I—I saw him."

Agitated as he was, he nonetheless remained at rigid attention, smartly saluting the broad stripes and bright stars. "Who? When?"

"The one," said Mike.

"The one *what?*"

"Who I've been looking for. There! Headed for the exit back of the Tycoon dugout. I recognized him by his ears and the set of his chin," and a sob rose in his throat. "Him. The kidnapper. The masked man who killed my little girl."

"Mike!" snapped the General. "Mike, you were seeing things! You were imagining it!"

"It was *him!*"

"Mike, that was thirty-five years ago. You could not recognize a man after all that time, not by his ears, for God's sake!"

"Why not?" Mike wept. "I've seen him every night, in my sleep, since 12 September 1898."

"'O say does that Star-Spangled Banner yet wave/O'er the land of the free, and the home—'"

"Play ball!" the fans were shouting, "Play the God damn game!"

It had worked. The General had turned sixty-two thousand savages back into baseball fans with the playing of the National Anthem! Now—if only he could step in behind the plate and call the last pitch! Or bring the field umpire in to take Mike's place on balls and strikes! But the first was beyond what he was empowered to do under the Rules and the Regulations; and the second would forever cast doubt upon the twenty-six strike-outs already recorded in the history books by Gamesh, and on the forty-one victories before that. Indeed, the field umpire had wisely pretended that he had not seen the last Gamesh pitch either, so as not to compromise the greatest umpire in the game by rendering the call himself. What could the General do then but depart the field?

On the pitcher's mound, Gil Gamesh had pulled his cap

so low on his brow that he was in shadows to his chin. He had
not even removed it for "The Star-Spangled Banner"—as
thousands began to realize with a deepening sense of uneasi-
ness and alarm. He had been there on the field since the last
pitch thrown to Iviri—except for the ten minutes when he had
been above it, bobbing on a sea of uplifted arms, rolling in the
embrace of ten thousand fans. And when the last pack of
celebrants had fled before the flying hooves, they had deposited
him back on the mound, from whence they had plucked him—
and run for their lives. And so there he stood, immobile, his
eyes and mouth invisible to one and all. What was he thinking?
What was going through Gil's mind?

Scrappy little Joe Iviri, a little pecking hitter, and the
best lead-off man in the country at that time, came up out of
the Tycoon dugout, sporting a little grin as though he had just
been raised from the dead, and from the stands came an
angry Vesuvian roar.

Down in the Greenback dugout, the Old Philosopher considered going out to the mound to peek under the boy's cap
and see what was up. But what could he do about anything
anyway? "Whatever happens," he philosophized, "it's going
to happen anyway, especially with a prima donna like that one."

"Play!"

Iviri stepped in, twitching his little behind.

Gamesh pitched.

It was a curve that would have shamed a ten-year-old
boy—or girl, for that matter. While it hung in the clear September light, deciding whether to break a little or not, there was
time enough for the catcher to gasp, "Holy aloha!"

And then the baseball was ricocheting around in the tricky
right-field corner, to which it had been dispatched at the same
height at which it had been struck. A stand-up triple for Iviri.

From the silence in Greenback Stadium, you would have
thought that winter had come and the field lay under three feet
of snow. You would have thought that the ballplayers were
all down home watching haircuts at the barber shop, or boast-
ing over a beer to the boys in the local saloon. And all sixty-
two thousand fans might have been in hibernation with the
bears.

Pineapple Tawhaki moved in a daze out to the mound to

hand a new ball to Gamesh. Immediately after the game, at the investigation conducted in General Oakhart's office, Tawhaki —weeping profusely—maintained that when he had come out to the mound after the triple was hit, Gamesh had hissed at him, "Stay down! Stay low! On your knees, Pineapple, if you know what's good for you!" "So," said Pineapple in his own defense, "I do what he say, sir. That all. I figger Gil want to throw drop-drop. Okay to me. Gil pitch, Pineapple catch. I stay down. Wait for drop-drop. That all, sir, that all in world!" Nonetheless, General Oakhart suspended the Hawaiian for two years—as an "accomplice" to the heinous crime—hoping that he might disappear for good in the interim. Which he did—only instead of heading home to pick pineapples, he wound up a derelict on Tattoo Street, the Skid Row of Tri-City. Well, better he destroy himself with drink, than by his presence on a Patriot League diamond keep alive in the nation's memory what came to be characterized by the General as "the second deplorable exception to the Patriot League's honorable record."

It was clear from the moment the ball left Gil's hand that it wasn't any drop-drop he'd had in mind to throw. Tawhaki stayed low—even as the pitch took off like something the Wright Brothers had invented. The batter testified at the hearing that it was still picking up speed when it passed him, and scientists interviewed by reporters later that day estimated that at the moment it struck Mike Masterson in the throat, Gamesh's rising fastball was probably traveling between one hundred and twenty and one hundred and thirty miles per hour. In his vain attempt to turn from the ball, Mike had caught it just between the face mask and the chest protector, a perfect pitch, if you believed, as the General did, that Masterson's blue bow tie was the bull's-eye for which Gamesh had been aiming.

The calamity-sized black headline MOUTH DEAD; GIL BANISHED proved to be premature. To be sure, even before the sun went down, the Patriot League President, with the Commissioner's approval, had expelled the record-breaking rookie sensation from the game of baseball forever. But the indestructible ump rallied from his coma in the early hours of the morning, and though he did not live to tell the tale—he was a mute thereafter—at least he lived.

The fans never forgave the General for banishing their hero. To hear them tell it, a boy destined to be the greatest pitcher of all time had been expelled from the game just for throwing a wild pitch. Rattled by a senile old umpire who had been catching a few Zs back of home plate, the great rookie throws *one bad one,* and that's it, for life! Oh no, it ain't Oakhart's favorite ump who's to blame for standin' in the way of the damn thing—it's Gil!

Nor did the General's favorite ump forgive him either. The very day they had unswathed the bandages and released him from the hospital, Mike Masterson was down at the league office, demanding what he called "justice." Despite the rule forbidding it, he was wearing his blue uniform off the field—in the big pockets once heavy with P. League baseballs, he carried an old rag and a box of chalk; and when he entered the office, there was a blackboard and an easel strapped to his back. Poor Mike had lost not only his voice. He wanted Gamesh to be indicted and tried by the Tri-City D.A.'s office for attempted murder.

"Mike, I must say that it comes as a profound shock to me that a man of your great wisdom should wish to take vengeance in that way."

STUFF MY WISDOM (wrote Mike the Mouth on the blackboard he had set before the General's desk) I WANT THAT BOY BEHIND BARS!

"But this is not like you at all. Besides, the boy has been punished plenty."

SAYS WHO?

"Now use your head, man. He is a brilliant young pitcher —and he will never pitch again."

AND I CAN'T TALK AGAIN! OR EVEN WHISPER! I CAN'T CALL A STRIKE! I CAN'T CALL A BALL! I HAVE BEEN SILENCED FOREVER AT SEVENTY-ONE!

"And will seeing him in jail give you your voice back, at seventy-one?"

NO! NOTHING WILL! IT WON'T BRING MY MARY

JANE BACK EITHER! IT WON'T MAKE UP FOR THE
SCAR ON MY FOREHEAD OR THE GLASS STILL
FLOATING IN MY BACK! IT WON'T MAKE UP (here
he had to stop to wipe the board clean with his rag, so that he
would have room to proceed) FOR THE ABUSE I HAVE
TAKEN DAY IN AND DAY OUT FOR FIFTY YEARS!
    "Then what on earth is the use of it?"
    JUSTICE!
    "Mike, listen to reason—what kind of justice is it that
will destroy the reputation of our league?"
    STUFF OUR LEAGUE!
    "Mike, it would blacken forever the name of baseball."
    STUFF BASEBALL!
    Here General Oakhart rose in anger—"It is a man who
has lost his sense of values entirely, who could write those two
words on a blackboard! Put that boy in jail, and, I promise
you, you will have another Sacco and Vanzetti on your
hands. You will make a martyr of Gamesh, and in the process
ruin the very thing we all love."
    HATE! wrote Mike, HATE! And on and on, filling the
board with the four-letter word, then rubbing it clean with his
rag, then filling it to the edges, again and again.
    On and on and on.
    Fortunately the crazed Masterson got nowhere with the
D.A.—General Oakhart saw to that, as did the owners of the
Greenbacks and the Tycoons. All they needed was Gil Gamesh
tried for attempted murder in Tri-City, for baseball to be
killed for good in that town. Sooner or later, Gamesh would be
forgotten, and the Patriot League would return to normal . . .
    Wishful thinking. Gamesh, behind the wheel of his Pack-
ard, and still in his baseball togs, disappeared from sight only
minutes after leaving the postgame investigation in the General's office. To the reporters who clung to the running board,
begging him to make a statement about his banishment, about
Oakhart, about baseball, about anything, he had but five words
to say, one of which could not even be printed in the papers:
"I'll be back, you ———!" and the Packard roared away.
But the next morning, on a back road near Binghamton, New
York, the car was found overturned and burned out—and no
rookie sensation to be seen anywhere. Either the charred

body had been snatched by ghoulish fans, or he had walked away from the wreck intact.

GIL KILLED? the headlines asked, even as the stories came in from people claiming to have seen Gamesh riding the rails in Indiana, selling apples in Oklahoma City, or waiting in a soup line in L.A. A sign appeared in a saloon in Orlando, Florida, that read GIL TENDING BAR HERE, and hanging beside it in the window was a white uniform with a green numeral, 19—purportedly Gil's very own baseball suit. For a day and a night the place did a bang-up business, and then the sallow, sullen, skinny boy who called himself Gil Gamesh took off with the contents of the register. Within the month, every bar in the South had one of those signs printed up and one of those uniforms, with 19 sewed on it, hanging up beside it in the window for a gag. Outside opera houses, kids scrawled, GIL SINGING GRAND OPERA HERE TONIGHT. On trolley cars it was GIL TAKING TICKETS INSIDE. On barn doors, on school buildings, in rest rooms around the nation, the broken-hearted and the raffish wrote, I'LL BE BACK, G.G. His name, his initials, his number were everywhere.

Adolf Hitler, Franklin Roosevelt, Gil Gamesh. In the winter of '33–'34, men and women and even little children, worried for the future of America, were talking about one or another, if not all three. What was the world coming to? What catastrophe would befall our country next?

The second deplorable exception to the honorable record of the Patriot League was followed by the third in the summer of 1934, when it was discovered that the keystone combination that had played so flawlessly behind Gamesh the year before had been receiving free sex from Tattoo Street prostitutes all season long, in exchange for bobbling grounders, giving up on liners, and throwing wide of the first-base bag. Olaf and Foresti, both married men with children, and one of the smoothest double-play duos in the business, were caught one night in a hotel room performing what at first glance looked like a trapeze act with four floozies—caught by the Old Philosopher himself—and the whole sordid story was there for all to read in the morning papers. They hadn't even taken money from the gamblers, money that at least could have bought shoes for their kiddies; no, they took their payoff in raw sex, which was of use to nobody in the world but their own selfish selves. How low could you get! By comparison the corrupt Black Sox of 1919 fame looked like choirboys. Inevitably the Greenbacks became known as "the Whore House Gang" and fell from third on the Fourth of July to last in the league by Labor Day.

And whom did the fans blame? The whoremongers themselves? Oh no, it was the General's fault. Banishing Gil Gamesh, he had broken the morale of Olaf and Foresti! Apparently he was supposed to go ask their forgiveness, instead of doing as he did, and sending the profligates to the showers for life.

And that wasn't the end of it: panic-stricken, the Greenback owners instantly put the franchise on the market, and sold it for a song to the only buyer they could find—a fat little Jew with an accent you could cut with a knife. And, to hear the fans tell it, that was General Oakhart's fault too!

And Mike the Mouth? He went from bad to worse and eventually took to traveling the league with a blackboard on his back, setting himself up at the entrance to the bleachers to plead his hopeless cause with the fans. Kids either teased him, or looked on in awe at the ghostly ump, powdered white from the dozen sticks of chalk that he would grind to dust in a single day. Most adults ignored him, either fearing or pitying the madman, but those who remembered Gil Gamesh—and they were legion, particularly in the bleachers—told the once-great umpire to go jump in a lake, and worse.

BUT I COULD NOT CALL WHAT I DID NOT SEE!

"You couldn't a-seed it anyway, you blind bat!"

NONSENSE! I WAS TWENTY-TWENTY IN BOTH EYES ALL MY LIFE! I HAD THE BEST VISION IN BASEBALL!

"You had it in for the kid, Masterson—you persecuted him to death right from the start!"

TO THE CONTRARY, HE PERSECUTED ME!

"You desoived it!"

HOW DARE YOU! WHY DID I OF ALL UMPIRES DESERVE SUCH INSULT AND ABUSE?

"Because you wuz a lousy ump, Mike. You wuz a busher all your life."

WHERE IS YOUR EVIDENCE FOR THAT SLAN-
DEROUS REMARK?

"Common knowledge is my evidence. The whole world
knows. Even my little boy, who don't know nothin', knows
that. Hey, Johnny, come here—who is the worst ump who ever
lived? Tell this creep."

"Mike the Mouth! Mike the Mouth!"

NONSENSE! SLANDER! LIES! I DEMAND JUS-
TICE, ONCE AND FOR ALL!

"Well, you're gettin' it, slow but sure. See ya, Mouth."

When General Oakhart was advised in January of '43 that the
Mundy brothers had reached an agreement with the War Department to lease their ball park to the government as an
embarkation camp, he knew right off that it was not an over-
flow of patriotic emotion that had drawn those boys into the
deal. They were getting out while the getting was good—
while the getting was *phenomenal*. After all, if the fortunes of
the Patriot League had been on the wane ever since the expulsion of Gamesh, they surely couldn't be expected to improve with a world war on. In the year since Pearl Harbor,
the draft had cut deep into the player rosters, and by the time
the '43 season began, the quality of major league baseball was
bound to be at its all-time low. With untried youngsters and
decrepit old-timers struggling through nine innings on the
diamond, attendance would fall even further than it had in
the previous decade, with the result that two or even three
P. League teams might just have to shut down for the duration. And with that, who was to say whether the whole enterprise might not collapse? . . . So, it was to guard against
this disastrous contingency (and convert it into a bonanza)
that the Mundy brothers had leased their beautiful old ball
park to the federal government to the tune of fifty thousand
dollars a month, twelve months a year.

The Mundy brothers had inherited the Port Ruppert
franchise from their illustrious dad, the legendary Glorious
Mundy, without inheriting any of that titan's profound reverence for the game. Right down to the old man's ninety-second
year, sportswriters who in his opinion hadn't sufficient love

and loyalty for the sport were wise to keep their distance, for
Glorious Mundy was known on occasion to take a swing at a
man for treating baseball as less than the national religion.
He was a big man, with bushy black eyebrows that the cartoonists adored, and he could just glare you into agreement,
if not downright obedience. When he died, they buried him
according to his own instructions in deep center field, four
hundred eighty-five feet from home plate, beneath a simple
headstone whose inscription gave silent testimony to the
humility of a man whose eyebrows alone would have earned
him the reputation of a giant.

GLORIOUS MUNDY

1839–1931

He had something to do with
changing Luke Gofannon from
a pitcher into a center-fielder

It was clear from the outset that to his heirs baseball was
a business, to be run like the Mundy confectionary plant, the
Mundy peanut plantations, the Mundy cattle ranches, and the
Mundy citrus farms, all of which had been their domain while
Glorious was living and devoting himself entirely in his later
years to the baseball team. The very morning after their
father had died of old age in his box behind first, the two sons
began to sell off, one after another, the great stars of the championship teams of the late twenties—for straight cash, like so
many slaves, to the highest bidder. The Depression, don't you
know . . . they were feeling the pinch, don't you know . . .
between excursions with their socialite wives to Palm Beach
and Biarritz!
    In 1932, when they took one hundred thousand dollars
from the Terra Incognita Rustlers for the greatest Mundy of
them all, Luke "the Loner" Gofannon, a tide of anger and resentment swept through Port Ruppert that culminated in a
march all the way down Broad Street by thousands of schoolkids wearing black armbands that had been issued to them at
City Hall. The parade was led by Boss Stuvwxyz (and or-

ganized by his henchmen), but somewhere around Choco-Chew
Street (named for the Mundy candy bar), somebody remembered to give Stuvwxyz his cut, and so he was not present when
the police broke up the rally just before it reached the ball
park.

Luke the Loner—gone! The iron man who came up in
1916 as a kid pitcher, and then played over two thousand
games in center field for the Ruppert club, scored close to
fifteen hundred runs for them, and owned a lifetime batting
average of .372—the fella who *was* the Mundys to three gen-
erations of Rupe-it rootas! Unlike Cobb or Ruth, Luke was a
silent, colorless man as far as personality went, but that did
not make him less of a hero to his fans. They argued that actually he could beat you more ways than Ruth, because he
could run and steal as well as hit the long one; and he could
beat you more ways than Cobb, because he could hit the long
one as well as drive you crazy on the base paths and race
around that center-field pasture as though it weren't any bigger
than a shoebox. Oh, he was fast! And what a sight at bat! In
his prime, they'd give him a hand just for striking out, that's
how beautiful he was, and how revered. Luke kept a book on
every pitcher in the business and he studied it religiously at
night before putting out his light at 9 P.M. And as he said—on
one of the few occasions in his career that he said anything—
he loved the game so much, he'd have played without pay.
Surprising thing was that the Mundy brothers didn't take
him up on that, instead of selling his carcass for a mere hundred grand.

In their defense, the Mundy boys claimed that they were
only getting the best possible price for players who hadn't
more than another good season or two left in their bones anyway; they were clearing out dead wood, said they, to make
way for a new Golden Era. Well, as it turned out, not a single
one of the seven former Mundy greats for whom old Glorious's
heirs collected a cool half a million ever did amount to much
once they left Port Ruppert, but whether it was due to advancing age, as the Mundy brothers maintained, or to the
shock of being turned out of the park to which they had
brought such fame and glory, is a matter of opinion.

Luke the Loner didn't even make it through one whole season as a Rustler. By August of '32 he already had broken the league record for strike-outs—strike-outs they weren't applauding him for either—and he who was reputed never to have thrown to a wrong base in his life, had the infielders scratching their heads because of his bizarre pegs from center. It seemed that shy, silent Luke, whom everybody had thought didn't need much company outside of his thirty-eight-ounce bat, "the Magic Wand," was just lost out there in the arid southwest, hopelessly homesick for the seaside park where he had played two thousand games in the Ruppert scarlet and white. Inevitably, the fans began to ride him—"Hey, Strike-out King! Hey, Hundred Thousand Dollar Dodo!" As the season wore on they called him just about everything under the sun—and the sun itself is no joke in Wyoming—and though he plugged along like the great iron man that he was, his average finally slipped to an even .100. "A thousand bucks a point, Gofannon—not bad for two hours a day!" He was on his way to the plate—in danger of slipping to a two-figure batting average—when the Rustler manager, believing that enough suffering was enough, and that the time had come to cut everybody's losses, stepped to the foot of the dugout, and called in a voice more compassionate than any Luke had heard all year, "What do you say, old-timer, come on out and take a rest," and a pinch-hitter was sent up in his place.

A week later he was back in New Jersey on his cranberry farm. The legislature of the state, in special session, voted him New Jersey license plate 372 in commemoration of his lifetime batting average. People would look for that license plate coming along the road down there in Jersey, and they'd just applaud when it came by. And Luke would tip his hat. And that's how he died that winter. To acknowledge the cheers from an oncoming school bus—boys and girls hanging from every window, screaming, "It's him! It's Luke!"—the sweetest, shyest ballplayer who ever hit a homer, momentarily took his famous hands from the wheel and his famous eyes from the road, and shot off the slick highway into the Raritan River. That so modest a man should die because of his fame was only one of the dozens of tragic ironies that the sportswriters pointed up in the mishap that took Luke's life at the age of thirty-six.

The Mundys A.G. (after Gofannon) promptly dropped from the first division, and for the remaining prewar years labored to finish as high as fifth. If the fans continued to fill the stands almost as faithfully as they had in happier days, it was because a Rupe-it roota was a Rupe-it roota, and because in the Mundy dugout sat their esteemed manager, Ulysses S. Fairsmith, "Mister Fairsmith" as they called him always, whether "they" roasted in the bleachers, or lorded it over the entire game in the big magistrate's chair of the Commissioner's desk in Chicago. Even the Mundy brothers, who ran the franchise with as much nostalgia as a pair of cobras, were careful to call him Mister (to the world), though they considered him a relic about ready for the junk heap, and when they sold seven of their help for a five-pound bag of thousand dollar bills, kept him on the payroll so as to indicate their reverence for Port Ruppert's Periclean past.

And the cheap, cynical trick worked: seated in his rocking chair ("Fairsmith's throne") in the dugout, wearing his starched white shirt, silk bow tie, white linen suit, Panama hat, and that aristocratic profile off a postage stamp, and moving the defense around with the gold tip of his bamboo cane, the Christian gentleman and scholar of the game was enough to convince the rootas of that rabid baseball town that this heavy-footed, butterfingered nine had something to do with the Ruppert Mundys of a few years back, those clubs now known as "the wondrous teams of yore."

Till the day he died, Mister Fairsmith never set foot inside a ball park on a Sunday. Instead he handed over the reins to one of his trusted coaches so that he might keep the promise he had made to his mother back in 1888, when he went off as a youngster to catch for the Hartford team of the old National League. "Sundays," his mother had said, "were not made for doubleheaders. You may catch six days a week, but on the seventh you shall rest." From his rocking chair in the Mundy dugout, Mister Fairsmith often made pronouncements to the press that one would not have been surprised to hear from the pulpit. "If the Lord ever permitted birth to a natural switch-hitter," he would say, for instance, in a characteristic locution, "it was Luke Gofannon." In his early years as a manager, the pregame prayer was practiced in the Mundy clubhouse before the team took the field for the day. It was eventually discontinued when Mister Fairsmith discovered that the content of the prayers being offered up to God was nothing like what he had in mind when he instituted the ritual: mostly they were squalid little requests for extra-base hits, and pitchers asking the King of Kings to help them keep the fastball down. "Give me my legs, Lord," went the prayer of one aging outfielder, "and the rest'll take care of itself." Still, he was kindly to the players, despite their frailties and follies, and never criticized a man in public for a mistake he had made on the field of play. Rather, he waited a day or two until the wound had healed a little, and then he took the fellow for dinner to a nice hotel, and at a table where they would not be observed, and in that gentle way he was revered for, he would say, "Now what about that play? Do you think you did that right?" If a pitcher had to be removed from the mound, Mister Fairsmith would always have a polite word to say to him, as he headed through the dugout to the showers; it did not matter if the fellow had just given up a grand-slam home run, or walked six men in a row, Mister Fairsmith would call him over to the rocker, and pressing the pitcher's hand in his own strong, manly grip, say to him, "Thank you very much for the effort. I'm deeply grateful to you."

General Oakhart, of course, believed that the Mundy brothers' plan to lease their ball park to the government was just the kind of preposterous innovation that the Ruppert manager could be counted on to oppose wholeheartedly. Vain though his plea had been, Mister Fairsmith had spoken so eloquently five years earlier against the introduction of nighttime baseball into the Patriot League schedule, that at the conclusion of the meeting of league owners to whom the address had been delivered, General Oakhart had released the text to the newspapers. The following day selections appeared on editorial pages all around the country, and the Port Rupert *Star* ran it in its entirety in the rotogravure section on

Sunday, laid out on a page of its own to resemble the Declaration of Independence. What particularly moved people to clip it out and hang it framed over the mantel, was the strength of his belief in "the Almighty Creator, Whose presence," Mister Fairsmith revealed, "I do feel in every park around the league, on those golden days of sweet, cheerful spring, hot plenteous summer, and bountiful and benevolent autumn, when physically strong and morally sound young men do sport in seriousness beneath the sun, as did the two in Eden, before the Serpent and the Fall. Daytime baseball is nothing less than a reminder of Eden in the time of innocence and joy; and too, an intimation of that which is yet to come. For what is a ball park, but that place wherein Americans may gather to worship the beauty of God's earth, the skill and strength of His children, and the holiness of His commandment to order and obedience. For such are the twin rocks upon which all sport is founded. And woe unto him, I say, who would assemble our players and our fans beneath the feeble, artificial light of godless science! For in the end as in the beginning, in the Paradise to come as in the Eden we have lost, it is not by the faint wattage of the electric light bulb that ye shall be judged, but rather in the unblinking eye of the Lord, wherein we are all as bareheaded fans in the open bleachers and tiny players prancing beneath the vault of His Heaven."

Several of the owners present were heard by the General to whisper "Amen," at the conclusion to this speech; among them was the new owner of the Kakoola Reapers, whiskey magnate Frank Mazuma, whose plan to install floodlights in Reaper Field had been the occasion for Mister Fairsmith's address. As it happened, not only did the amen-ing Mazuma go ahead to initiate nighttime baseball that very season in Kakoola—with the result that his club led the league that year in strike-outs, errors, and injuries—but in defiance of an anti-radio ban signed by all the Patriot League owners, including Mazuma's predecessor, began to broadcast the Reaper home games on the local station, which he also bought up with his bootleg billions and christened KALE. And, to the surprise of those who had drafted the antiradio ban in great panic some years earlier, Mazuma's broadcasts, rather than cutting further into dwindling gate receipts, seemed, like those bizarre night games, to increase local interest in the Reapers, so that the following season attendance went up a full fifteen per cent, even though the team continued to occupy seventh place one day and eighth the next.

To General Oakhart, needless to say, the idea that people could sit in their living rooms or in their cars listening to an announcer describe a game being played miles and miles away was positively infuriating. Why, the game might just as well not be happening, for all they knew! The whole thing might even be a hoax, a joke, something managed with some clever sound effects and a little imagination and an actor who was good at pretending to be excited. What was there to stop radio stations in towns without ball clubs from making up their own teams, and even their own leagues, and getting people at home all riled up, telling them home runs were being knocked out of the park and records being broken, when all the while there was nothing going on but somebody telling a story? Who was to say it might not come to that, and worse, if there promised to be a profit in it for the Frank Mazumas of this profit-mad world?

Furthermore, you could not begin to communicate through *words,* either printed or spoken, what this game was all about —not even words as poetical and inspirational as those Mister Fairsmith was so good at. As the General said, the beauty and meaning of baseball resided in the fixed geometry of the diamond and the test it provided of agility, strength, and timing. Baseball was a game that looked different from every single seat in the ball park, and consequently could never be represented accurately unless one were able to put together into one picture what every single spectator in the park had seen simultaneously moment by moment throughout an entire afternoon; and that included those moments that in fact accounted for half the playing time if not more, when there was no action whatsoever, those moments of waiting and hesitation, of readiness and recovery, moments in which everything ceased, including the noise of the crowd, but which were as inherent to the appeal of the game as the few climactic seconds when a batted ball sailed over the wall. You might as well put an announcer up in the woods in October and have him do a "live" broadcast of the fall, as describe a baseball game on the radio.

"Well, now, folks, the maples are turning red, and there goes a birch getting yellow," and so on. Can you imagine nature-lovers sitting all huddled around a dial, following that? No, all radio would do would be to reduce the game to what the gamblers cared about: who scored, how much, and when. As for the rest—the playing field with its straight white foul lines and smooth dirt basepaths and wide green band of outfield, the nine uniformed athletes strategically scattered upon it, their muscles strung invisibly together, so that when one moved the rest swung with him into motion . . . well, what *about* all that, which, to the General, was just about everything? Sure you could work up interest even in a bunch of duffers like the Kakoola Reapers by reporting their games "live" over the radio, but it might as well be one team of fleas playing another team of fleas, for all such a broadcast had to do with the poetry of the great game itself.

The General's meeting with Mister Fairsmith reminded him of nothing so much as his tragic interview nearly ten years earlier with Mike the Mouth Masterson, after the great umpire had lost his sense of reality. Where, oh where would it end? The best of the men he knew, the men of principle upon whom he had counted for aid and support—either dead, or gone mad. Would no one of sanity and integrity survive to carry on the great traditions of the league? Would he have to war alone against the vulgarians and profiteers and ignoramuses dedicated to devouring the league, the game, the country—the world? Glorious Mundy, Luke Gofannon, Spenser Trust, all in the grave; and from last report (a news item in a Texas paper) Mike Masterson still traversing the country with a blackboard on his back, hanging around the sidelines at sandlot baseball games demanding "justice." Oh, the times were dark! A Jew the owner of the Greenbacks! Spenser Trust's eccentric widow owner of the Tycoons! A bootlegger gone "straight" the owner of the Reapers! And now Ulysses S. Fairsmith, clear out of his mind!

To be sure, the devout and pious ways of Mister Fairsmith had always struck the General as somewhat excessive (if useful), and frankly he had even considered him somewhat "touched" twenty years back, when he circumnavigated the globe, bringing baseball to the black and yellow people of the world, many of whom had never even worn long pants before, let alone a suit with a number on the back. This excess of zeal (and paucity of common sense) had very nearly cost him his life in the Congo, where he rubbed a tribe of cannibals the wrong way and missed the pot by about an inch. On the other hand, no one could fail to be impressed by the job of conversion he had done in Japan. Single-handedly, he had made that previously backward nation into the second greatest baseball-playing country in the world, and after his 1922 visit to Tokyo, had returned every fall with two teams of American all-stars to play in Japanese cities, large and small, and teach the little yellow youngsters along the way the fine points of the game. They loved him in Japan. The beautiful Hiroshima ball park was called "Fairsmith Stadium"—in Japanese of course—and when he appeared at a major league game in Japan, everyone there, players as well as fans, bowed down and accorded him the respect of a member of the imperial family. Hirohito himself had entertained Mister Fairsmith in his palace as recently as October of 1941—giving no indication, of course, that only two months later, on a quiet Sunday morning, while Christian America was at its prayers, he was going to deal the Mundy manager the most stunning blow of his life by attacking the American fleet anchored at Hawaii. And how could he? For a year now the Mundy manager had suffered an agony of bewilderment and doubt: how could Hirohito do this to Mister Fairsmith, after all he had done for the youngsters of Japan?

"If it is the will of the Lord," said Mister Fairsmith, haggard and wispy from his year of despair, yet with bold blue eyes made radiant by the pure line of malarkey he had sold himself, "if such is the will of the Lord, to send forth the Mundys into the wilderness until the conflagration is ended, who am I to stand opposed?"

"Now, Mister Fairsmith," said the General, suppressing a desire to give the old gent a good shake and tell him to come to his senses, "now, that is of course a very catchy way to put it, Mister F.—'wander in the wilderness.' But if I may take exception, it looks to me more like an endless road trip that is being proposed for these boys. And to my way of thinking, that is far from a good thing for anyone. Such an injustice would test the morale of even the best of teams. And let's face the facts, unpleasant as they may be: despite your managerial expertise"—such as it used to be, said the General, sadly, to himself—"this is no longer a first division club. To speak bluntly, they look to me to be pretty good candidates for the cellar as it is. Wayne Heket, John Baal, Frenchy Astarte, Cholly Tuminikar—they are no longer what they were, and have not been for some time now."

"Which is why the Lord has chosen them."

"How's that? You had better explain the Lord's reasoning to me, sir. On the basis of the logic I studied at the academy forty years back, I can't seem to make head nor tail of it."

"They are to be restored to their former greatness."

"Wayne Heket is? He can't even bend down to tie his shoelaces as it is. Tell me, how is he going to be made great again?"

"Through trial and tribulation. Through suffering," said Mister Fairsmith, ignoring the General's predictable secularist sarcasm, "they shall find their purpose and their strength."

"And then again maybe not. With all due respect to the Lord and yourself, I think that as President of the league I have to prepare myself for that possibility as well. Sir, in my humble opinion, this is just about the worst thing that has happened to this league since the expulsion of Gil Gamesh. I tell you, Ford Frick and Will Harridge couldn't be happier. They have been eyeing our best players for years—they have been waiting for close to a decade for this league to collapse, so they could just sign up our stars and divide this baseball-loving country between themselves. Nothing could please them more than for the players coming home from the war to have just two major leagues they can play for instead of three. Look, you have got an inside pipeline to the Lord, Mister Fairsmith: maybe you can tell me what it is He has against the Patriot League, if He is the one behind sending the Mundys on the road. Why didn't the Lord choose Boston, and make the Bees or the Red Sox homeless? Why didn't he choose Philadelphia, and send the Phillies or the A's into the wonderful wilderness?"

"Because," replied the venerable Mundy manager, "the Lord is not concerned with the Phillies or the A's."

"Boy, aren't they unlucky! They've just got the Devil looking after them—so they get to stay where they are, poor bastards! Pardon my Shakespeare, sir, but why Port Ruppert instead of Brooklyn? They have got a deep water harbor there too, you know. Almighty God could have cleared the Dodgers out of Ebbets Field to make way for the Army—why in hell didn't He! Why were the Mundys chosen!"

"They have been chosen . . ."

"Yes?"

"Because they have been chosen."

"They have been chosen because Glorious Mundy is dead and his heirs are scoundrels! Mammon, Mister Fairsmith, that is who is behind this move! The love of money! The worship of money! And what is more disgusting, they cloak their greed in the stars and stripes! They make a financial killing and call it a patriotic act! And where is God in all this, Mister Fairsmith? Where is He when we need Him!"

"He works in mysterious ways, General."

"*Maybe*, sir, *maybe—but not this mysterious.* That He should stoop to the Mundy brothers to do His business for Him is something even I am reluctant to accept—and I have never hidden the fact that I am not a particularly devout person. Frankly I think you do a serious disservice to God's good name with this kind of irresponsible talk about mysterious ways. And since I've come this far, I want to go further. I want you to straighten me out on something, just so we know where we stand. Are you actually sitting there, without blinking an eye, and suggesting to me that there is some sort of similarity between the Mundys of Port Ruppert, New Jersey, and the ancient Hebrews of the Bible?"

Mister Fairsmith said, "In the words of our great friend, Glorious Mundy, 'Baseball is this country's religion.'"

"True, that was Glory's splendid way of putting it. But surely it is going a little overboard to start comparing a sorry second division club like yours to the people of Israel. And yourself, if I am following this analogy correctly, yourself here to Moses, leading them out of Egypt. Really, Mister Fairsmith, a proper respect for your own achievement is one thing, but does this make sense to you? Now I realize all you have been through in the last year. I have the greatest sympathy with what you have had to endure over the last decade from the Mundy brothers. I have the deepest sympathy for the way you have been treated by the Emperor of Japan. I hate the son of a bitch, and I didn't even know him. But frankly, even taking all of that into consideration, I cannot let you get away with spouting religious hogwash that is going to destroy this league!"

Mister Fairsmith only looked more beatific; the trial and tribulation in which he put so much stock was getting off to an excellent start.

Wearily, the General said, "Look, it's as simple as this, skipper: no good can come of a big league ball club playing one hundred and fifty-four games a year on the road. And I am going to do everything within my power to prevent it."

To which the Mundy manager, hell-bent on deliverance, replied, "General Oakhart, let my players go."

2

THE VISITORS' LINE-UP

THE '43 MUNDYS

SS	Frenchy Astarte
2B	Nickname Damur
1B	John Baal
C	Hothead Ptah
LF	Mike Rama
3B	Wayne Heket
RF	Bud Parusha
CF	Roland Agni
P	Jolly Cholly Tuminikar
P	Deacon Demeter
P	Bobo Buchis
P	Rocky Volos
P	Howie Pollux
P	Catfish Mertzeger
P	Chico Mecoatl
UT	Specs Skirnir
UT	Wally Omara
UT	Mule Mokos
UT	Applejack Terminus
UT	Carl Khovaki
UT	Harry Hunaman
UT	Joe Garuda
UT	Swede Gudmund
UT	Ike Tvashtri
UT	Red Kronos

❧ 2 ❦

A distressing chapter wherein the reader is introduced to each member of the 1943 Mundy starting line-up as he steps up to the plate, and comes thus to understand why Americans have conspired to remove all reminders of such a team from the history books; their records recounted more fully than on the back of the bubble gum cards. Containing much matter to vex the ordinary fan and strain his credulity, which is as it must be, in that real life is always running away with itself, whereas imagination is shackled by innocence, delusion, hope, ignorance, obedience, fear, sweetness, et cetera.

Containing that which will move the compassionate to tears, the just to indignation, and the cruel to laughter.

"BATTING FIRST and playing shortstop, No. 1: FRENCHY ASTARTE. ASTARTE."

Jean-Paul Astarte (TR, BR, 5′10″, 172 lbs.), French-Canadian, acquired in unusual deal late in 1941 from Tokyo team of Japan in association with Imperial Japanese Government—the only player ever traded out of his own hemisphere (and the only player ever traded back). Began career in twenties, down in Georgia, thence to Havana in the Cuban League, Santiago in the Dominican League, finally Caracas. It began to look as though the French-speaking boy out of the freezing North was destined in the end to play for the Equator—but no, misery is never so orderly in its progression; it wouldn't be real misery if it was. Early in the thirties, when baseball boomed in Japan, he was traded to Tokyo by way of the Panama Canal; there he played shortstop for nearly a decade, dreaming day in and day out of his father's dairy farm in the Gaspé. When news reached him in the fall of '41 that he was to be traded once again, he just somehow assumed it would be to Calcutta; he did not understand a word his Japanese owner was telling him (anymore than he had understood his Spanish owner or his American owner when they had called him in to say *au revoir*) and actually started in weeping at the prospect of playing ball next with a bunch of guys talking it up in Hindi and running around the bases in bedsheets. Oh, how he cursed the day he had donned a leather mitt and tried to pretend he was something other, something *more,* than a French-Canadian farmboy! Why wasn't what was good enough for the father good enough for the son? At sixteen years of age, with those powerful wrists of his, he could do a two-gallon milking in five minutes—wasn't that accomplishment enough in one life? Instead he had had dreams (what Canadian doesn't?) of the great stadiums to the south, dreams of American fame and American dollars . . . He boarded the boat with the Japanese ticket in one hand and his bag full of old bats and berets in the other, fully expecting to come ashore in a land of brown men in white dresses, and wound up instead (such was Frenchy's fate) being greeted at the dock by something he could never have expected. "Welcome, *Monsieur!* Welcome to Port Ruppert!" The famous Ulysses S. Fairsmith, the greatest manager in the game! *Mon Dieu!* It was not India he had reached, but America; like Columbus before him, he was a big leaguer at last.

How come? Simple. The Mundy brothers, into whose laps a million tons of scrap metal had dropped, had traded directly with Hirohito, a penny a pound, and (shrewd afterthought) a shortstop to fill the hole that would be left in the Mundy infield when the war started up in December. Yes, there was literally nothing the Mundy brothers didn't have the inside dope on, including the bombing of Pearl Harbor. That's what made them so successful. "Tell you what," they were reported to have said to the eager Emperor of Japan, "throw in the shortstop from the Tokyo club, and you got yourself a deal, Hirohito." Thus did they kill two birds with one stone, and God only knows how many hundreds of American soldiers.

Unfortunately the Most Valuable Player in the Far East found the majors rather different from what he had been imagining during his years of exile. For one thing, he was now thirty-nine, a fact of some consequence when you were hitting against carnivorous two hundred pounders instead of little rice-eaters about the size of your nephew Billy. It was weeks before he got his first Patriot League hit: seven, to be exact. Then there was that throw to first. How come they kept beating out for hits what used to be outs back in Asia? How come the fans booed and hooted when he came to the plate— when they used to cry *"Caramba!"* in Venezuela and *"Banzai!"* in the Land of the Rising Sun? Why, here in the Big American leagues of his dreams, he was even more of a foreigner than he had been in Tokyo, Japan! There he was an all-star shortstop, white as Honus Wagner and Rabbit Maranville—white as them and *great* as them. But here in the P. League he was "Frenchy" the freak.

In '42 he batted .200 for the Mundys, just about half what he'd batted halfway around the globe, and he led the shortstops in the three leagues in errors. His specialty was dropping high infield flies. The higher the ball was hit, the longer it gave him to wait beneath it, thinking about Japan and the day he would return to Tokyo and stardom.

It was Frenchy's error in the last game of the '42 season (and the last game ever played in Mundy Park), that sent two Rustler runners scampering home in the ninth, and knocked the Mundys into last. At the time, finishing half a game out of the cellar or right down in it didn't make much difference to his teammates—by the end of that first wartime season, all those old-timers wanted from life was not to have to push their bones around a baseball field for the next six months. And Frenchy too was able to live with the error by thinking of it as a mere one seventy-fifth of the mistakes he had made out on the field that year—until, that is, word reached him in snowbound Gaspé (as strange to him now as steamy Havana once had been, for his father was dead, as were all the cows he used to know there as a boy) that the last-place Mundys had been booted out of Mundy Park and henceforth would be homeless.

Unlucky Astarte! Because of my error, he thought, that made us come in last! Because at that moment, his mind hadn't been on Ruppert finishing seventh in the P. League, but Japan finishing first in the war! Yes, Japan victorious über alles . . . Japan conquering America, conquering Yankee Stadium, Wrigley Field, Mundy Park . . . Yes, waiting beneath what was to have been the last fly ball of the '42 season, he had been envisioning opening day of 1943—Hirohito throwing out the first pitch to a Ruppert team of tiny Orientals, with the exception of himself, the Most Valuable Player in an Imperial Japanese world . . .

Oh, if ever there was a player without a country, it was the Mundy lead-off man, who forever afterwards believed himself and his traitorous thoughts to have caused the expulsion from Port Ruppert. Was Frenchy the loneliest and unhappiest Mundy of them all? A matter of debate, fans. In the end, he was their only suicide, though not the only Mundy regular to meet his Maker on the road.

"Batting second and playing second base, No. 29: NICK-NAME DAMUR. DAMUR."

Nickname Damur (TR, BR, 5′, 92 lbs.) could run the ninety feet from home to first in 3.4 seconds, and that was about it. At fourteen he was the youngest player in the majors, as well as the skinniest. The joke was (or was it a joke?) that the Mundy brothers were paying him by the pound; not that the boy cared anything about money anyway—no, all he seemed to think about from the moment he joined the team in spring training, was making a nickname for himself. "How about Hank?" he asked his new teammates his very first day in the scarlet and white, "don't I look like a Hank to you guys?" He was so green they had to sit him down and *explain* to him that Hank was the nickname for Henry. "Is that your name, boy— Henry?" "Nope. It's worse . . . Hey, how about Dutch? Dutch Damur. It rhymes!" "Dutch is for Dutchmen, knucklehead." "Chief?" "For Injuns." "Whitey?" "For blonds." "How about Ohio then, where I'm from?" "That ain't a name." "Hey—how about Happy? Which I sure am, bein' here with you all!" "Don't worry, you won't be for long." "Well then," he said shyly, "given my incredible speed and all, how about Twinkletoes? Or Lightning? Or Flash!" "Don't boast, it ain't becomin'. We wuz all fast once't. So was everybody in the world. That don't make you special one bit." "Hey! How about Dusty? That rhymes too!"

But even when he himself had settled upon the nickname he wouldn't have minded seeing printed beneath his picture on a bubble gum card, or hearing announced over the loud

speaker when he stepped up to bat, his teammates refused to
address him by it. Mostly, in the beginning, they did not address him at all if they could help it, but just sort of pushed
him aside to get where they were going, or walked right through
him as though he weren't there. A fourteen-year-old kid
weighing ninety-two pounds playing in their infield! "What
next?" they said, spitting on the dugout steps in disgust, "a
reindeer or a slit?" In the meantime, Damur began tugging at
his cap every two minutes, hoping they would notice and start
calling him Cappy; he took to talking as though he had been
born on a farm, saying "hoss" for horse and calling the infield
"the pea patch," expecting they would shortly start calling
him Rube; suddenly he began running out to his position in
the oddest damn way—"What the hell you doin', boy?" they
asked. "That's just the way I walk," he replied, "like a
duck." But no one took the hint and called him Ducky or
Goose. Nor when he chattered encouragement to the pitcher
did they think to nickname him Gabby. "Shut up with that
noise, willya?" cried the pitcher—"You're drivin' me batty,"
and so that was the end of that. Finally, in desperation, he
whined, "Jee-zuz! What about *Kid* at least?" "We already
got a Kid on this club. Two's confusin'." "But he's fifty years
old and losin' his teeth!" cried Damur. "I'm only fourteen.
I *am* a kid." "Tough. He wuz here before you wuz even
born."

It was Jolly Cholly Tuminikar, the Mundy peacemaker
and Sunday manager, who christened him Nickname. Not that
Damur was happy about it, as he surely would have been,
dubbed Happy. " 'Nickname' isn't a nickname, it's the *name*
for a nickname. Hey—how about Nick? *That's* the nickname
for nickname! Call me Nick, guys!" "Nick? That's for Greeks.
You ain't Greek." "But whoever heard of a baseball player
called *Nickname Damur?*" "And whoever heard a' one that
weighed ninety-two pounds and could not endorse a razor
blade if they even asked him to?"

Indeed, so slight was he, that on the opening day of the
'43 season, a base runner barreling into second knocked Nickname so high and so far that the center-fielder, Roland Agni,
came charging in to make a sensational diving two-handed
catch of the boy. "Out!" roared the field umpire, until he re-

membered that of course it is the ball not the player that has
to be caught, and instantly reversed his decision. The fans,
however, got a kick out of seeing Nickname flying this way
and that, and when he came to bat would playfully call out to
him, "How about Tarzan? How about Gargantua?" and the
opposing team had their fun too, needling him from the bench
—"How about Powerhouse? How about Hurricane? How
about Hercules, Nickname?" At last the diminutive second-
sacker couldn't take any more. "Stop it," he cried, "stop,
please," and with tears running down his face, pleaded with
his tormentors, "My name is Oliver!" But, alas, it was too
late for that.

Nickname, obviously, had no business in the majors, not
even as a pinch-runner. Oh, he was swift enough, but hardly
man enough, and if it was not for the wartime emergency, and
the irresponsibility of the Mundy brothers, he would have
been home where he belonged, with his long division and his
Mom. "How about Homesick?" the sportswriter Smitty whispered into the boy's ear, a month after the '43 season began,
and Nickname, black and blue by now and batting less than his
own weight, threw himself in a rage upon the famous columnist. But what began with a flurry of fists ended with the boy
sobbing in Smitty's lap, in a wing chair in a corner of the
lobby of the Grand Kakoola Hotel. The next day, Smitty's
column began, "A big league player wept yesterday, cried his
heart out like a kid, but only a fool would call him a sissy . . ."

Thereafter the fans left off teasing Nickname about his
size and his age and his name, and for a while (until the catastrophe at Kakoola) he became something like a mascot to the
crowds. Of course, being babied was the last thing he wanted
(so he thought) and so under the professional guidance of Big
John Baal, he took to the booze, and, soon enough, to consort-
ing with whores. *They* called him whatever he wanted them to.
In sleazy cathouses around the league they called him just
about every famous ballplayer's nickname under the sun—all
he had to do was ask, and pay. They called him Babe, Nap,
Christy, Shoeless, Dizzy, Heinie, Tony, Home Run, Cap, Rip,
Kiki, Luke, Pepper, and Irish; they called him Cracker and
Country and King Kong and Pie; they even called him Lefty,
skinny little fourteen-year-old second baseman that he was.

Why not? It only cost an extra buck, and it made him feel like somebody important.

"Batting in third position, the first baseman, No. 11, JOHN BAAL. BAAL."

Big John (TR, BL, 6'4", 230 lbs.), said never to have hit a homer sober in his life, had played for just about every club in the league, including the Mundys, before returning to them in '42, paroled into the custody of their benevolent manager. Baal joined the club after serving two years on a five-year gambling rap—he'd shot craps after the World Series with the rookie of the year, and wiped the boy out with a pair of loaded dice. Not the first time John had walked off with somebody else's World Series earnings, only the first time they caught him with the shaved ivories. In prison Big John had had the two best seasons of his life, earning the ironic appellation (coined, of course, by Smitty) "the Babe Ruth of the Big House." With Big John in the line-up, Sing Sing beat every major prison team in the country, including the powerful Leavenworth club, and went on to capture the criminal baseball championship of America two consecutive seasons after nearly a decade of losing to the big federal pens stocked with hard-hitting bootleggers. Inside the prison walls a Johnny Baal didn't have to put up with the rules and regulations that had so hampered him throughout his big league career, particularly the commandment against taking the field under the influence of alcohol. If a slugger had a thirst around game time, then his warden saw that it was satisfied (along with any other appetite a robust man might develop), because the warden wanted to *win*. But out in society, you couldn't get past the dugout steps without some little old biddy in a baseball uniform sniffing you all over for fear that if you blew on their ball with your sour mash breath, you might pop open the stitching and unravel the yarn. Consequently, aside from his criminal record, the only record Big John held outside of prison was for the longest outs hit in a single season. Christ, he clouted that ball so high that at its zenith it passed clear out of sight— but as for distance, he just could not get it to go all the way, unless he was pickled.

Now, every ballplayer has his weakness, and that was Big John's. If he didn't drink, if he didn't gamble, if he didn't whore and cheat and curse, if he wasn't a roughneck, a glutton and a brawler, why he just wasn't himself, and his whole damn game went to pot, hitting *and* fielding. But when he had fifteen drinks under his belt, there was nobody like him on first base. Giant that he was, he could still bounce around that infield like a kangaroo when he was good and drunk. And could he hit! "Why, one time in that jail up there," Big John told Smitty upon his release from the prison, "I had me a lunch of a case of beer and a bottle of bourbon and got nine for nine in a doubleheader. Yep, everytime I come up, I just poked her into the outside world. But this rule they got out here—why it's disgustin'! It ain't for men, it's for lollipops and cupcakes! It's a damn joke what they done to this game—and that there Hall of *Fame* they got, why, that's a bigger joke! Why, if they ever asked me to come up there and gave me one of them poems or whatever it is they give, why I'd just laugh in their face! I'd say take your poem and wipe your assholes with it, you bunch a' powder puffs!"

Big John's contempt for the Hall of Fame (and his anti-social conduct generally) seemed to stem from grievances against Organized Baseball that had been implanted in him by his notorious father, who, in turn, had inherited from *his* notorious father a downright Neanderthal attitude toward the game. John's grandfather was, as everyone knows, *the* Baal, the legendary "Base," who is still mistakenly credited with the idea of substituting sand-filled bags, or bases, for the posts used to mark off the infield in baseball's infancy; in actuality he earned the nickname early in his career because of his behavior on the playing field. If we are to believe the stories, Base Baal played on just about every cornfield and meadow in America before the first leagues were organized, before stadiums were built and men earned a living as players. Like many American boys, he learned the fundamentals in the Army camps of the Civil War. The game in that era consisted of several variants, all of which would be as foreign to the American baseball fan of today as jai alai or lacrosse. This was long before pitchers began to throw overhand, back when the bat was a stick that was narrow at both ends, if it was not a fence post or a barrel stave, back when there would be as many as twenty or thirty players on a team, and when the umpire, chosen from the crowd of spectators, might well be punched in the nose and run off the field if his judgment did not accord with everyone else's. The ball was a bit larger, something like today's softball, and "plugging" or "soaking" was the order of the day—to get the runner out, you had only to "plug" him (that is, hit him with the ball while he was between two bases), for him to be retired (as often as not, howling in pain). Frequently a fielder, or "scout" as he was called in some parts of the country, would wait for the runner to come right up to him, before "plugging" him in the ribs, much to the pleasure of the onlookers. And that was Base's stock in trade. In fact, when the old fellow finally broke into the newly formed four-club Patriot League in the eighties—by which time the game had taken on many of its modern, more civilized characteristics —he apparently "forgot" himself one day and "plugged" a runner heading home from third right in that vulnerable part of a man's anatomy for which he always aimed. He was instantly mobbed and nearly beaten to death by the other team— a bearded giant of a man, close to sixty now—all the while crying out, "But that's out where I come from!"

Base's son, and Big John's father, was the infamous pitcher, Spit, who in the years before wetting down the ball was declared illegal, would serve up a pitch so juicy that by the end of an inning the catcher had to shake himself off like a dog come in from romping in the rain. The trouble with Spit's spitball was, simply, that nobody could hit it out of the infield, if they could even follow the erratic path of that dripping sphere so as to get any wood on it at all. Once it left Spit's hand, carrying its cargo of liquid, not even he was sure exactly what turns and twists it would take before it landed with a wet thud in the catcher's glove, or up against his padded body. As opposition mounted to this spitter that Baal had perfected—it was unnatural, unsanitary, uncouth, it was ruining the competitive element in the game—he only shrugged and said, "How am I supposed to do, let 'em hit it out their-selves?" On hot afternoons, when his salivary glands and his strong right arm were really working, Spit used to like to taunt the opposition a little by motioning for his outfielders to sit back on their haunches and take a chew, while he struck out—or, as he put it, "drownded"—the other side. Angry batsmen would snarl at the ump, "Game called on accounta rain!" after the first of Spit's spitters did a somersault out in front of the plate and then sort of curled in for a strike at the knees. But Spit himself would pooh-pooh the whole thing, calling down to them, "Come on now, a little wet ain't gonna hurt you." "It ain't the wet, Baal, it's the stringy stuff. It turns a white man's stomach." "Ah, ain't nothin'—just got me a little head cold. Get in there now, and if you cain't swim, float."

In the beginning, various conservative proposals were offered to transform the spitter back into what it had been before Spit came on the scene. The citrus fruit growers of America suggested that a spitball pitcher should have to suck on half a lemon in order to inhibit his flow of saliva—fulfilling his daily nutritional requirement of vitamin C in the process. They tried to work up public interest in a pitch they called "the sourball," but when the pitchers themselves balked, as it were, complaining there was not any room for a lemon what with teeth, tongue, and chewing tobacco in there already, the proposal, mercifully, was dropped. A more serious suggestion had to do with allowing a pitcher to use all the saliva he wanted, but outlawing mucus and phlegm. The theory was that what the ballplayers euphemistically called "the stringy stuff" was precisely what made Baal's pitch dance the way it did. A committee of managers assigned to study his motion maintained that Spit was very much like a puppeteer yanking on a web of strings, and that the rules had only to be rewritten to forbid a pitcher blowing his nose on the ball, or bringing anything up from back of the last molar for the problem to be solved, not only for the batsman, but for those fans who happened to be sitting in its path when it was fouled into the stands. It might even bring more of the ladies out to see a game, for as it stood now, you could not even get a suffragette into the bleachers on a day Baal was pitching, so repugnant was his technique to the fair sex. Even the heartiest of male fans showed signs of squeamishness pocketing a foul tip to bring home as a souvenir to the kiddies. But Spit himself only chuckled (he was a mild, mild man, until they destroyed him).

"When I go to a tea party, I will be all good manners and curtsy goodbye at the door, I can assure you of that. But as I am facin' two hundred pounds of gristle wavin' a stick what wants to drive the ball back down my gullet, why then, I will use the wax out of my ears, if I has to."

It was not a remark designed to placate his enemies. In fact, the discovery that he *had* used earwax on a ball in the 1902 World Series caused the controversy to spread beyond the baseball world; owners who had come to consider wetting the ball a part of the game—and Spit a gifted eccentric who would have his day and pass into obscurity soon enough— became alarmed by the outrage of a public that had seemed on the brink of accepting baseball as *the* American sport, now that it had grown away from the brutish game, marked by maiming and fisticuffs, played by Spit's Daddy. The editorialists warned, "If baseball cannot cleanse itself at once of odious and distasteful ways that reek of the barnyard and the back alley, the American people may well look elsewhere—perhaps to the game of tennis, long favored by the French—for a national pastime." From all sides the pressure mounted, until at the winter meeting of the Patriot League owners in Tri-City, following the World Series of 1902 in which Baal, by his own admission, had waxed a few pitches with some stuff he'd hooked out of his head, the following resolution was passed: "No player shall anoint the ball with any bodily secretions for any purpose whatsoever. Inevitable as it is that droplets of perspiration will adhere to a ball in the course of a game, every effort shall be made by the players and the umpire, to keep the ball dry and free of foreign substances at all times." And with these words baseball entered its maturity, and became the game to which an entire people would give its heart and soul.

Spit's career ended abruptly on the opening day of the 1903 season, when he scandalized the country by an act in such flagrant violation of the laws of human decency, let alone the new resolution passed in Tri-City the previous winter, that he became the first player ever to be banished from baseball— the first deplorable exception to the Patriot League's honorable record. What happened was this: throwing nothing but bone dry pitches, Spit was tagged for eight hits and five runs by a jeering, caustic Independence team even before he had anyone out in the first inning. The crowd was booing, his own team-mates were moaning, and Spit was in a rage. They had ruined him, those dryball bastards! They had passed a law whose purpose was the destruction of no one in the world but him-self! A law against him!

And so before twenty thousand shocked customers—in-cluding innocent children—and his own wide-eyed teammates, the once great pitcher, who was washed up anyway, did the unthinkable, the unpardonable, the inexpiable: he dropped the flannel trousers of his uniform to his knees, and proceeded to urinate on the ball, turning it slowly in his hands so as to dampen the entire surface. Then he hitched his trousers back up, and in the way of pitchers, kicked at the ground around the mound with his spikes, churning up, then smoothing down the dirt where he had inadvertently dribbled upon it. To the batter, as frozen in his position as anyone in that ball park, he called, "Here comes the pissball, shithead—get ready!"

For years afterward they talked about the route that ball took before it passed over the plate. Not only did it make the hairpin turns and somersaults expected of a Baal spitter, but legend has it that it shifted gears *four* times, halving, then doubling its velocity each fifteen feet it traveled. And in the end, the catcher, in his squat, did not even have to move his glove from where it too was frozen as a target. Gagging, he caught the ball with a *squish,* right in the center of the strike zone.

"Stree-*ike!*" Baal called down to the voiceless umpire, and then he turned and walked off the mound and through the dugout and right on out of the park. They banished him only minutes afterward, but (not unlike the great Gamesh thirty years later) he was already on the streetcar by then, still wearing his uniform and spikes, and by nightfall he was asleep in a boxcar headed for the Rio Grande, his old stinking glove his pillow and his only pal. When he finally jumped from the train he was in Central America.

There he founded that aboriginal ancestor of Latin Ameri-can baseball, the hapless Mosquito Coast League of Nicaragua —if you could call it a league, where the players drifted from one club to another for no reason other than whim, and entire teams were known to disappear from a town between games of a doubleheader, never to be seen again. The Nicaraguan youths that Spit Baal recruited for his league had no local games of their own comparable in complexity and duration, and few were ever really able to maintain concentration through an afternoon of play in that heat. But they accepted without question that you could rub anything you wanted on a ball before pitching it, and in fact took to the spitball much the way American children take to the garden hose in summertime. Down in the Mosquito Coast League, Spit's native boys played just the sort of disgusting, slimy, unhygienic game that his own countrymen had so wholeheartedly rejected by passing the resolution against a wet or a waxed baseball. The few Americans who drifted to Nicaragua to play were sailors who had jumped ship, and assorted nuts and desperadoes in flight from a sane and decent society; occasionally an unemployed spitballer would come crawling out of the jungle swamp and onto the playing field, in search of a home. Carried from village to village on mules, sleeping in filth with the hogs and the chickens, or in hovels with toothless Indians, these men quickly lost whatever dignity they may once have had as ballplayers and human beings; and then, to further compromise themselves and the great game of baseball, they took to drinking a wretched sort of raisin wine between innings, which altered the pace of the game immeasurably. But the water tasted of rats and algae, and center field in the dry season in Guatemala is as hot as center field must be in Hell—catch nine innings in Nicaragua in the summer, and you'll drink anything that isn't out-and-out poison. Which is just what the water was. They used it only to bathe their burning feet. Indian women hung around the foul lines, and for a penny in the local currency could be hired for an afternoon to wash a player's toes and pour a bucketful of the fetid stuff over his head when he stepped up to bat. Eventually these waterwomen came to share the benches with the players, who fondled and squeezed them practically at will, and it was not unusual for such a woman to attach herself to a team, and travel with them for a whole season.

Because the pitchers—whose life was no bed of roses down there—rinsed their mouths with raisin wine even while out on the mound, going to the jug as often as a civilized pitcher goes to the resin bag, in a matter of innings the ball came to look as though it had been dipped in blood; the bat too would turn a deep scarlet from contact with the discolored ball and the sticky, sopping uniforms—numeraled serapes, really—of the players. The clean white stitched ball that is the very emblem of the game as played in our major leagues, was replaced in the Mosquito Coast League with a ball so darkly stained that if you were on the sidelines peering through the shimmering waves of the heat, you might have thought the two teams were playing with a wad of tar or a turd.

Into this life Big John Baal was born, the bastard offspring of the only pitcher ever to dare to throw a pissball in a major league ball park, and a half-breed who earned a few coins from the players in the on-deck circle by pouring Central American water over their ears and their ankles. By the time Juanito was two or three seasons old, his father no longer even remembered which of the dozens of waterwomen around the league had mothered his little son—to him they all looked the same, dirty, dark, and dumb, but at least they were a step up from the livestock with whom his battery-mate found happiness. A major leaguer had to draw the line somewhere, and Spit drew it at goats. When the child asked him "Mamma? Madre?" Spit wouldn't even bother to wrack his brain (in that heat wracking your brain could bring on the vertigo) but pointed to whichever one happened to be rolling in the dust with the reliever down in the bullpen (where, on some days, there was even a young snarling bull). By the age of eighteen months, John was already big and strong enough to hold a green banana in his ten fat fingers and swing at the pebbles that the native-born players liked to throw at the manager's little boy when his father happened not to be around; and when a few years later he was able to swing a regulation bat, the child was taught by his father the secret to hitting the spitter. John shortly became so adept at connecting with the scarlet spitball (or spicball, as the disillusioned and drunken expatriates sneeringly called it among themselves) that by the time he was old enough to leave Nicaragua to go out and take his vengeance on the world, it was like nothing for him to lay into a ball that was both white and dry. Oh, what an immortal he might have been, if only he did not have the morals of someone raised in the primordial slime! Oh, if only he had not come North with a heartful of contempt for the league that had banished his dad, and the republic for which it stood!

"Batting fourth for the Mundys, the catcher, No. 37, HOT PTAH. PTAH."

Hothead, or Hot (for short) Ptah (TR, BR, 5'10", 180 lbs.), far and away the most irritating player in baseball, and the Mundy most despised by the other teams, despite the physical handicap which might otherwise have enlisted their sympathies. Probably his disposition had to do with his not having one of his legs, though his mother back in Kansas maintained that he had always been crabby, even when he'd had both. To the wartime fans, Hot was more a source of amusement than anything else, and they probably got more of a kick out of his angry outbursts than from the foibles and eccentricities of any other Mundy. However, those who had to stand at the plate and listen to that one-legged chatterbox curse and insult them, didn't take to it too well, try as they might. "Okay, Hot, so you ain't got all your legs, that ain't my fault." But he would just keep buzzing like a fly on a windowpane—until all at once the batter would whirl around to the umpire, his eyes welling with tears. "Do you hear that! Did you hear what he just said! Why don't you do something about it!" "*O*-kay, what'd he say now?" the ump would ask, for Hot had a way of pouring the venom directly into the hitter's ear, leaving the umpire out of it entirely. "What'd he *say?* A lot of unkind words about my mother bein' intimate with niggers down in the south, that's what!" "Now you listen here, Ptah—" But by this time Hot would have ripped off his mask and started in pounding it on the plate, till you expected one or the other to be smashed to smithereens—or else he would just hammer with his hand and his glove on his chest protector, like a gorilla in a baseball suit, howling all the while about his "freedom of speech." Hot could go into the craziest song and dance ever seen on a ball field (or anywhere, including the Supreme Court of the United States) about the Constitution, the Bill of Rights, the Declaration of Independence, the Monroe Doctrine, the Emancipation

Proclamation, even the League of Nations, in order to defend his right to say what he did into some poor southern boy's ear. "I know you," Hot would whisper to the batter, starting off low and slow, "and your whole damn family and I know your mother . . ." And then he had the gall to defend himself with the First Amendment. And a hundred more things that most umpires had never even heard of, but that. Hot had studied up on in the legal books that he lugged around with him in his suitcase from one hotel to the next. He *slept* with those damn books . . . but then what else could he sleep with, poor gimp that he was? "The Wagner Act! The Sherman Anti-trust Act! Carter versus Carter Coal! Gompers versus Buck Stove! The Federal Reserve Act, damn it! And what about the Dred Scott decision? Don't that count for nothing in this country no more? Gosh *damn!*" And here, having baffled and confused everyone involved, having set the fans to roaring with laughter in the stands (which only burned him up more) he would go hobbling back behind the plate, and the umpire would call for play to be resumed. After all, not being lawyers by profession, the umpires could not be expected to know if what Hot was saying made any sense, and so rather than get into a legal harangue that might end up in the courtroom with a litigious catcher like this son of a bitch, they preferred to respect his so-called freedom of speech, rather than send him to the showers. And besides, if he didn't catch for the Mundys, who would—a guy with *no* legs?

To Hot's credit, it should be said that he had as good a throwing arm as any catcher in the league in '43, and he could drill the ball up against the left-field fence when you needed a run driven in; however, having that leg made out of wood caused him to lurch like something on a pogo stick when he came charging after a bunt, and he was not exactly death on fly balls popped back to the screen behind home plate. His doubles and triples were plentiful, only he was never able to get far-ther than first on them; and his singles, of course, were outs, the right-fielder, or the center-fielder, or the left-fielder to the first-baseman. (If you're scoring, that's 9 to 3, 8 to 3, or 7 to 3.)

Now obviously, in peacetime a one-legged catcher, like a one-armed outfielder (such as the Mundys had roaming right), would have been at the most a curiosity somewhere down in the dingiest town in the minors—precisely where Hot had played during the many years that the nations of the world lived in harmony. But it is one of life's grisly ironies that what is a catastrophe for most of mankind, invariably works to the advantage of a few who live on the fringes of the human community. On the other hand, it is a grisly irony to live on the fringes of the human community.

"Batting fifth and playing left field, No. 13, MIKE RAMA. RAMA."

Even before the Mundys had to play day in and day out on the other fellow's terrain, Mike "the Ghost" Rama (TL, BL, 6′1″, 183 lbs.) had his troubles with the outfield wall. Just so long as there was one of them behind him, whether it was in Mundy Park or on the road, sooner or later the Ghost went crashing up against it in do-or-die pursuit of a well-tagged ball. In '41, his rookie year, he had on five different occasions to be removed on a stretcher from the field in Port Ruppert. The fans, of course, were deeply moved by a brilliant youngster so dedicated to victory as to be utterly heedless of his own welfare. It rent their hearts to hear the *konk* resound throughout the ball park when Mike's head made contact with the stadium wall—was he dead this time? and, damn it, had he dropped the ball? But miraculously neither was the case. The umpire who rushed to the outfield to call the play (before calling the hospital) invariably found the baseball lodged snugly in the pocket of the unconscious left-fielder's glove. "Out!" he would shout, and without irony, for he was describing only the status of the batter. Hurray, cried the fans—whereupon the bullpen catcher and the batboy would come dashing onto the field to lift the crumpled hero from the grass on to the stretcher, and thence to the ambulance that could already be heard wailing across Port Ruppert to the stadium. And how that sound sobered and saddened the crowd . . .

Once the solemnity of the moment had passed the fans did have to wonder if perhaps Mike wasn't a little short on brainpower to be knocking himself out like this every couple of weeks; for it wasn't as though he misjudged the proximity

of the wall in his effort to catch the ball, but rather that he
seemed completely to forget that such things as walls even
existed. He just could not seem to get the idea of a barrier into
his head, even after bringing the two into forceful conjunction.
Why they came to call him the Ghost was because he appeared
to think—if that is the word for it—that what was impenetrable
to the rest of us would be as nothing to him: either he did not
believe that walls were really walls, or flesh only flesh, or he
just was never going to get over having been born and raised
in Texas. For down there, where he had been a great high
school star, it seemed they did not bother to fence the field
in . . . just laid out the bases and let the boys roam like the
longhorns.

In Mike's rookie year, Mister Fairsmith would make it his
business to be at the hospital first thing in the morning to
fetch the Mundy left-fielder once the doctors had put the pieces
back together and proclaimed him ready to have another go at
life. They would drive directly from the hospital to Mundy
Park, where the two would walk out across the manicured
diamond on to the outfield grass. With only the groundskeepers looking up from their rakes to watch the oddly touching
scene, Mister Fairsmith would lead the rookie all the way
from the left-field corner to Glorious Mundy's headstone in
furthest center, and then back again. They might walk to and
fro like this for half an hour at a stretch, Mike, under Mister
Fairsmith's direction, running the tips of his fingers along
the wall so as to prove to himself that it was no figment of
anybody's imagination.

"Michael," Mister Fairsmith would say, "can you tell
me what is going on in your mind when you act like this? Do
you have any idea?"

"Sure. Nothin'. I'm thankin' about catchin' the ball, that's
all. I ain't havin' no sex thoughts or nothin', Mister Fairsmith,
I swear."

"Michael, I am cognizant of the fact that there were no
walls surrounding the ball fields in the part of the world where
you grew up, but surely, lad, you had walls in your house when
you were a boy down there. Or am I mistaken?"

"Oh sure we had walls. We wuz poor, but we wuzn't that
poor."

"And did you, as a child, go running into the walls in your house?"

"Nope, nope. But then a' course I wasn't chasin' nothin' then."

"Son, you are going to be held together by clothesline and baling wire before you are even twenty-one, if you do not change your ways. Keep this up and your next fly ball may be your last."

"Gee, I sure hope not, Mister Fairsmith. I live for baseball. I eat, drink, and sleep baseball. It's just about the only thang I ever thank about, is baseball. I see pop flies in my dreams. I can't even sleep sometimes, imaginin' all the different kinds of line drives there are to catch. Baseball is my whole life, I swear."

"And your death too, lad, if you don't start in this minute thinking about *the reality of the wall.*"

But nothing anyone could say was able to implant in Mike Rama a healthy respect for the immovable and the unyielding. To the contrary, as some men are drawn to wine and some to women, so Mike Rama was drawn to that left-field wall. If he could be said to have had a temptress, that was it. "Why, I'll tell you what I think," said Johnny Baal to Smitty, "if that there wall had titties on it, Mike 'ud marry her."

"Batting sixth and playing third base, No. 2, WAYNE HEKET. HEKET."

Kid Heket (TR, BR, 6', 172 lbs.), the oldest Mundy of them all, the oldest major leaguer of them all, a rookie in 1909 and a utility infielder and pinch-runner thereafter, he had become a regular only after the Mundy brothers had sold everybody of value on the great championship team, and just about everything else that was any good in the dugout "exceptin'," as the Kid told it, "me and the water cooler." Of course he was no longer "so fleet afeet," as he'd been in his pinch-running days, but then, as the aging third-sacker asked, "Who is?" Were his reflexes gone, would he say? "I sure would," replied the Kid. And his eyesight? "Dim durin' the day, practically nil at night. Nope, don't see very good at all no more." His strength? He sighed: "Oh, gone with the wind,

Smitty. Call me broken down and I won't argue." Why did he stay on in baseball then? "What else is there? This here is just about all that I am fit to do now, and, as you see, I ain't fit for it."

Fortunately, playing for the wartime Mundys was not really as taxing physically as a job on a farm or a factory might have been for a man of fifty-two. And, during the winter months the Kid could just sit around down home resting up in the barber shop, enjoying the smell of the witch hazel, the warmth of the stove, and the pictures in the old magazines. During the season itself, in order to conserve what little energy he had, he just played as close as he could to the third-base line, hoping in this way to cut down the extra-base hits, but otherwise granting to the opposition whatever they could poke between him and the shortstop. "The way I see it now, if a feller hits it to my left, he got hisself a single and more power to him. If a' course the Frenchman wants to try and get it, well, that's his business and I don't propose to interfere. His ways is his ways and mine is mine. As I gets older I find myself gettin' more philosophical. I got to ask myself, you see, who am I to say what should be a base hit and what shouldn't, a feller with but four years of schoolin' in his whole life. No, some old folks may do otherwise, but I don't propose to set Wayne Heket up as some kind of judge of others at this late stage of the game." By which he meant the game of life, clearly, for even if it was only the bottom of the first, he paid no mind to what was hit between third and short. "At my age you just got to cut down, no question about it. You just got to give up somethin', so I give up goin' to my left. Let's be honest, Smitty, my runnin' days is over, and there ain't no sense in actin' like they ain't."

When the Mundys came to bat, the Kid always made it his business to catch a quick nap—no sooner did his seat hit the bench but he was out like a light. "That's what I credit my long baseball life to, you know. Them naps. So long as I can catch me some shuteye in that dugout there, there is no doubt that I am a better man for it back on the playing field. A' course, as you can imagine, nobody cherishes more than me them times that we get a little rally goin', and I can really slip off into dreamland. There is no doubt about it—and I tole

Mister Fairsmith, right out, too—if we was a better hittin' team, I would be gettin' more sleep. The worst for me is when the fellers start swingin' at them first pitches. What in hell's the hurry, I ask 'em, where's the fire anyhoo? Sometimes my stiff ol' bones has barely stopped throbbin' with pain, when they are shakin' my shoulder, tellin' me it's time to go back on out to the field. Best of all was the other day in Aceldama. It was top of the eighth and I was near to droppin', let me tell you. I was up first, struck out lookin'—or not lookin', I suppose—come back to the bench, expectin' that of the old forty winks I'd be gettin' myself maybe four, if I was lucky. Well, what happens, but that whole darn bunch of hitless wonders catches fire and we don't go out until they have batted all the way around to me. What a snooze I had! Like a top! Unfortunately, the Butchers, they come back with seven in their half of the inning to beat us—but if I had not had that good long nap while we was up, I tell you, I might not have made it all the way through them seven runs of theirs on my feet. As it was, I dozed off a couple times in the field, but then I usually does, when we is changin' pitchers. Tell you the truth, I thought they had scored only four and we was still ahead by one. I didn't find out till the next mornin' when I seen it in the paper down in the lobby that we lost. Must be then that I was out on my feet for three of them runs—not that it makes much difference. You been around as long as me, you seen one run, you seen 'em all. That afternoon, when I run into some of the Butchers on the streetcar goin' out to the ball park, I asked them how come they didn't wake me up in the eighth yesterday when they was roundin' third. You don't find that kind of consideration every day, you know, especially from the other team, which is usually tryin' to hair-ass you, one way or another. I joked 'em—I said, 'What ever got in to you boys, bein' so quiet and all comin' round the bag? Don't want to rouse the sleepin' beast or somethin'?' And you know what they tole me? I couldn't believe it. They tole me they come *whoopin'* round that bag, each and ever one of 'em, squawkin' their heads off like a bunch of crows, and I didn't budge one inch. Well, that'll give you a idea of just how tired a feller can get bein' in baseball all his life. Maybe that is what it is like bein' in anything all your life, but I can only speak for myself, you know. And I'm just shot. Why, if this here terrible war goes on too long, and I keep playin' in the regular line-up like this, why, I wouldn't be surprised if one afternoon I will just drop off, you know, and that's that. The other fellers'll come runnin' back in to the bench when the innin' is over and it's our turn to bat, but not me. I'll just be left stooped over out there, with my hands on my knees and a jaw full of tobacco juice, waitin' for the next pitch, only I'll be dead. Well, I only hope it don't happen while the game is in progress, 'cause if the other team finds out, they sure as hell will start droppin' them bunts in down the third-base line. Now, even alive I ain't hardly the man with a bunt I was back before the First World War. But with me dead with rigor mortis, and Hothead havin' only one leg, they could just about bunt us crazy, don't you think? If they was smart, that is.''

"Batting seventh and playing right field, No. 17, BUD PA-RUSHA. PARUSHA.''

Bud Parusha (TR, BR, 6′3″, 215 lbs.) was the youngest of the Parusha brothers, two of whom, Angelo and Tony, were all-star outfielders for the Tri-City Tycoons, and until they entered the service boasted the two strongest throwing arms in the majors. A throwing arm no less powerful and accurate was said to belong to the third brother, who surely would have been a Tycoon outfielder too, if it weren't that the throwing arm was the only arm he'd been born with. It was as though Mother Nature—or, to be realistic about it, Mother Parusha—having lavished such gifts upon Angelo and Tony, had run out of steam by the time she got to Bud, and when it came to finishing him off, could not deliver up anything whatsoever, not even a stump, where the mate to the throwing arm should have been. Consequently, when Angelo and Tony went off to the majors, Bud was left to work as best he could as a waiter in his father's restaurant in Bayonne. Then came the war. Angelo and Tony were commissioned and placed in charge of the hand grenade training program for the entire United States Marine Corps, and Bud found himself elevated to the big leagues, not up to the Tycoons of course—they were the P. League champs after all—but across the Jersey marshes, to the team that seemed rapidly to be becoming a haven for the handicapped. Bud moved in with Hothead Ptah, whose averages in the minors he had followed for years in the back pages of *The Sporting News,* and rumor had it that the two would shortly be joined by a one-eyed pitcher from the Blues, a Jewish fellow called Seymour Clops, nicknamed inevitably, "Sy." "What about a sword-swallower and a tattooed man, while they're at it!" cried Hothead, who did not at all cotton to the idea of being a freak in a freakshow. "And what about dwarfs! There must be some of them around! Oh, I just can't wait to get up some morning and look over and find I am rooming with a left-handed dwarf, all curled up and sleepin' in my mitt. And a Jew on top of it!" The dwarf, of course, when he came, would be right-handed and a Christian, the pitcher O.K. Ockatur.

For those who never saw Bud Parusha in action during the war years—and after him, Pete Gray, the one-armed out-fielder who played for the St. Louis Browns—it will be necessary to explain in some little detail, how, and to what degree, he was able to overcome his handicap on the field.

First off, to catch an ordinary fly ball was no more problem for Bud than for any fielder of major league caliber; however, in that he wore his glove on the end of his throwing arm, it did require an unorthodox maneuver for him to return the ball to the infield. Unlike Gray of the Brownies, who had a stump of a left arm under which he could tuck his glove while he extracted the ball from the pocket, Bud (with no left arm at all) had to use his mouth. He was lucky to have a large one —"that old law of compensation," said the sports announcers—and a strong bite which he had further developed over the years by five minutes of chewing on a tennis ball before going to sleep each night. After fielding a ball, he was able instantly to remove it from his glove with his teeth, and hold it clamped between them while he shook the glove from his hand; then he extracted the ball from his mouth with his bare right hand, and hurled it with Parusha-like speed and accuracy to the infield. All this he accomplished in one fluid, unbroken motion and with such efficiency and even grace, that you would have thought that this was the way the outfield was supposed to be played.

In the beginning the fans did not know quite what to make of Bud's singular fielding technique and there were those who laughed at the man in the Mundy outfield who looked from a distance to be giving birth to something through the orifice in his head. There were even those in the bleachers—there always are—who like children popping out of closets would shout "Boo!", hoping in that way to startle Bud and cause him to swallow the baseball. Unfortunately there were occasions when in his anxiety not to drop the ball out of his mouth while flinging off his glove, he would take it too far back between his molars, and find himself unable to extricate it unassisted. It happened infrequently, but always in the same tense situation: with the bases loaded. And each time with the same disastrous result: an inside-the-mouth grand-slam home run. Roland Agni would race over from center and Nickname would tear out from second to try to save the day, but not even those two together, performing the play as they had practiced it— Agni kneeling on Bud's chest, forcing open his jaws like a fellow about to stick his head into the mouth of a crocodile, and young Damur, with those quick hands of his, yanking and jiggling at the ball for all he was worth—were able to prevent the four runs from scoring.

Despite his difficulties—and, in part, because of them— kindly, uncomplaining Bud became popular as Hothead, who had been there first, had never even tried to be. While the sluggers and fancy dans were paid to endorse razor blades and hair oil, Bud's beautifully formed signature soon came to adorn the pages of medical magazines, where he was pictured in his gray road uniform with the scarlet piping and insignia, sitting in a wheelchair, or balancing himself on a crutch. Where it was feasible, he would always test a product before giving it his endorsement—more than most of his colleagues bothered to do for items far less compromising to a ballplayer's prestige than oxygen tents and artificial limbs. And when the Mundys had a free day on the road, he never failed to go off to visit the local veterans hospital, where he would promise one of the amputees to get a base hit for him the next time they threw him anything good. He could not dedicate home runs to them, because big as he was he really could not be expected to hit home runs with only one arm, but every six or seven times at bat, he managed to smack a single, and then from the loud speaker there would be the announcement that Bud's hit had been "for" so-and-so in such-and-such a hospital, and the fans would smile and clap.

Around the league he began to build a real following among the handicapped of all ages; sometimes as many as forty or fifty of them would be out there in the stands along the right-field line when the Mundys and Bud came to town. The public address system had only to announce Bud's number for them to begin banging on the railings with their canes and crutches. "Parusha's Clinic" Smitty dubbed the right-field stands, and in Kakoola and Tri-City they even set up ramps out there to make things easier for the handicapped who turned out to see Bud perform. In their excitement some of his supporters occasionally went too far and would try, for instance, to touch him with the tip of a crutch as he came near the stands to field a foul, endangering his three remaining limbs, not to mention his eyesight. Once a woman in a wheelchair attempted to lean forward to pluck Bud's cap off for a souvenir and tumbled out of the stands onto his back. But mostly they were content to just sit there and take heart from the courage and ingenuity that Bud displayed; in Kakoola, in fact, one fan was so inspired by Bud's example that after ten years in a wheelchair, he found himself up on his feet cheering wildly as Buddy made a diving shoestring catch in the bottom of the ninth. It was in a column about this very fellow that Smitty coined the name "Parusha's Clinic." "I'm walking!" the man suddenly cried out, even as Bud was extracting the ball from his mouth to fire it to first to double off the Reaper runner and end the game.

CRIPPLE CURED AS RUPPERTS ROMP

the Kakoola evening paper reported to its readers that night—but then could not resist the sardonic subhead—

TWO MIRACLES IN ONE DAY

"Batting eighth for the Mundys, and playing center field, No. 6, ROLAND AGNI. AGNI."

Roland Agni (TL, BL, 6'2", 190 lbs.), in '43 a kid of eighteen tapering like the V for Victory from his broad shoulders and well-muscled arms down to ankles as elegantly turned as Betty Grable's—swift on his feet as Nickname Damur, strong as a Johnny Baal, as mad for baseball as Mike Rama, and in his own baby-blue eyes destined to be the most spectacular rookie since Joltin' Joe. One difference: the Yankee Clipper, aside from being four years older than Agni when he entered the majors, had also played a few seasons down in the minors; what was so amazing about Roland, Roland thought, was that he was leaping right from high school to the big time.

Only there was a catch. Upon his graduation the previous June, Roland had turned down forty athletic scholarships in four sports from colleges all around the nation, and offers from twenty-three major league clubs in order to be signed up by his father with the Ruppert Mundys, the only team in the three leagues that had not even bothered to scout him. It was precisely their indifference that had convinced Mr. Agni that the Mundys were the major league team for his son, if major league team there had to be. Not that Mr. Agni, like some fathers, had any objection to baseball as a career; the problem was Roland's pride, which, in a word, was overweening. The boy had been hearing applause in his ears ever since he had hurled a perfect sandlot game at age six, with the result that over the years he had become, in his father's opinion, contemptuous of everything and everyone around him, above all of his family and the values of humility and self-sacrifice that they had tried, in vain, to instill in him. When his father dared to criticize him for his superior attitudes, Roland would invariably storm away from the dinner table, screaming in his high-pitched adolescent voice that he couldn't help it, he *was* superior. "But," asked his mother, using psychology, "do you want the girls to go around whispering that Roland Agni is stuck on himself?" "They can whisper whatever they want— they'd be stuck on themselves too, if they was me!" "But nobody likes a self-centered person, darling, who thinks only of himself." "Oh don't they? What about the forty colleges begging me to enroll there? What about the twenty-three major league teams pleading with me to play ball for them?"

"Oh but they don't want you for your character, Roland, *or* for your mind—they want you only for your body." "Well, they *should,* because that's what's so great about me! That's what makes me so phenomenal!" "Roland!" "But it's true! I got the greatest physique of any boy my age in America! Maybe in the whole world!" "Go to your room, Roland! You are just as conceited as all the girls say! What are we going to do with you to make you realize that you are *not* God's gift to the world?" "But I am—to the baseball world that's just exactly what I am! That's just what the scout said from the St. Louis Cardinals! Them very words!" "Well, shame on him, flattering you that way just so they could sign you up! As if you aren't conceited enough! Oh," cried Mrs. Agni, turning to her husband, "what is going to happen to him out in the real world? How will he ever survive the hardships and cruelty of life with such an attitude? Roland, tell me, whatever made you think you were such a hero at seventeen years of age?" "MY BATTING AVERAGE!" screamed the star, his voice echoing off the dozens of tropies in his room.

Roland's father listened politely to the twenty-three fast-talking major league scouts as each tried to outbid the other for his son's services, and then telephoned the Mundy front office in Port Ruppert to announce that the father of the phenomenal Roland Agni was on the line. "Come again?" said the voice at the other end—"the phenomenal who?" No response could have been more heartening to the boy wonder's dad. He gave the Mundy front office a brief account of Roland's high school career: in four years of varsity play he had batted .732 and regularly hurled shutouts when he wasn't in the outfield robbing the other team of extra-base hits. However, Mr. Agni rushed to say, if hired to play for the Ruppert Mundys, his son was to receive no more than the lowest paid member of the team, was to bat eighth in the line-up in his first year, and to rise no more than one notch in the batting order in each succeeding year. It would be more than enough for a boy as self-centered as Roland to leap from high school directly to the majors without making him rich, or clean-up hitter, in the bargain. These, said Mr. Agni, were his only conditions.

"Look," laughed the Mundys' man in Port Ruppert,

"what about if we go you one better and don't pay him at all."

Mr. Agni leaped at the suggestion. "In other words, I would just continue to give him his allowance—?"

"Right. And of course his room, board, and supplies."

"In other words, he'd be playing for a professional team but still have his amateur status."

"Correct. Of course, we'd need a deposit from you right off, so's we can keep the eighth slot in the batting order open for him. And room and board we'd have to have in advance. You can understand that."

"Fine. Fine."

"All right, you're on. Now what's that name again? Angry?"

"*Ag*ni."

"First name?"

"Roland."

"Okey-dokey. Spring training begins March 1, Asbury Park, New Jersey—on account of the war. Be cheaper for you anyway than Florida. We'll hold the eighth spot for him until noon that day."

"Thank you. Thank you very much."

"Well, thank *you*, Mr. Angry, and thanks for calling the Mundys," said the fellow, with a chuckle, and hung up, believing that he had just indulged a practical joker, or perhaps a sportswriter having some fun at the expense of the Mundy front office. Maybe even a fella name a' Smitty.

To find himself in the P. League with the Ruppert Mundys, and batting eighth in their line-up—and not even getting paid for it—had something like the humbling effect upon their boy that the Agnis had hoped for. Still, crushed and bewildered as he was by this bizarre turn of events, Roland Agni led the league in batting that year with .362, in hits with 188, in home runs with 39, and in doubles with 44. Of course with the pitcher batting behind him, he hardly scored, unless he hit the ball out of the park, or stole second, third, and then home; after getting on with a hit he was generally cut down at second on a d.p. or left stranded as the pitcher went out on strikes. And given the eight who batted before him he had no chance of doing much of anything in the r.b.i. department.

In the middle of the season he was called for his Army

physical and found unfit for service. First the Mundys, now 4F!

It took a team of physicians a whole morning to study his marvelous V-shaped physique, whispering all the while among themselves—in admiration, thought the innocent center-fielder —before arriving at their decision. "Okay, Roland," they asked, slumping wearily to the floor of the examination room after the three-hour ordeal, "what is it? Trick knee? Bad ticker? Night sweats? Nosebleeds? Sciatica?" "What do you mean?" "What's wrong with you, Roland, that you're too ashamed to say?" "Wrong with *me?* Nothin'! Just look," he cried, standing to show himself off in the nude, "I'm perfect." "Listen, Roland," said the doctors, "there's a war on, in case you haven't heard. A *world* war. What happens to be at stake isn't eighth place in the Patriot League but the future of civilization itself. We're doctors, Roland, and we have a responsibility. We don't want somebody going into a battle that may turn the tide of history, suddenly coming down with a sick headache and just lying down on the job in the trench. We don't want the lives of an entire platoon endangered just because somebody like you has to stop to scratch his pruritus ani." "But I don't get sick headaches, or the other thing either." "How do you know you don't get 'the other thing,'" they asked suspiciously, "if you don't even know what it is?" "Because I don't get *anything*—I have never even had a cavity, or a pimple. Smell my breath—it's like fresh-cut hay!" But when he blew his sweet odor into their nostrils, it only further infuriated the doctors. "Look here, Agni—we want to know what the hell is wrong with you, and we want to know now. Constipation? Sinusitis? Double vision? Get the shakes, do you? Hot flushes? Or is it the chills, Roland? How about epilepsy, does that ring a bell?" they asked, slamming him up against the white tile wall to have another go at him with their stethoscopes. "No! No! I tell you, I never been sick in my life! Sometimes I even think I am impregnable! And that ain't a boast—it's a fact!" "Oh it is, is it? Then how come according to our records here you are the only unpaid professional athlete in the business? How come your old man is paying them to keep you on the team, rather than the other way around? How come an impregnable boy like you isn't up with the Tycoons,

Roland?'' ''That's what *I* want to know!'' cried Agni, and collapsed onto the examination stool, where he sat weeping into his hands. They let him sob until it appeared he had no more resistance left in him. Then they stole upon him where he sat unclothed and gorgeous, and softly stroking his golden curls, whispered into his ear, ''Wet the bed? Sleep with a night light? How come a big strong handsome boy like you, leading the league in base hits and doubles, is still batting eighth for Ruppert, Roland? Don't you like girls?''

''Daddy,'' Roland shouted into the phone when he was dressed again and back out in the world, ''I am unfit for the service now too! I am 4F—ONLY THERE IS NOTHING WRONG WITH ME!''

''Well, there is that pride again, Rollie.''

''BUT THE DOCTORS COULDN'T FIND ANYTHING, NOT EVEN THE THREE OF THEM TOGETHER!''

''Well, doctors aren't perfect, anymore than the rest of us. That's the very point I am trying to make to you.''

''But I should be 1A, not 4F! And not a Ruppert Mundy, either! Oh, Daddy, what am I doing on that team, where everybody is some kind of crackpot, thinking all the time about his name, or running into the walls, or having to have me sit on his chest to pull the darn baseball out of his *mouth!*''

''In other words, what you are telling me, Roland, is that you are too good for them.''

''It ain't sayin' you are too good if you just happen to have all your arms and can stay awake for nine innings!''

''In other words then, you're just 'better' than everybody else.''

''On this team, who wouldn't be!''

''And it doesn't occur to you that perhaps your teammates have had hardships in their lives about which you know nothing. Do you ever think that perhaps why you're 'better' is because you were fortunate enough to have all the opportunities in life that they were denied?''

''Sure I think about it! I thank my lucky stars about it! And that's why I don't belong with them, even if I was batting first and gettin' a million dollars!''

''Oh, son, what are we going to do with you, and this unquenchable thirst for fame and glory?''

"Trade me! Trade me away from these freaks and these oddballs! Daddy, they ain't even got a home park that's their own—what kind of major league ball club is that?"

"You mean for the great Roland Agni to be playing with?"

"For *anybody* to be playin' with—but me especially! Daddy, I am leading the league in batting in my rookie year! There's been nobody like me since Joe DiMaggio, and he was twenty-two!"

"And yet you're 4F. Doesn't that mean anything to you at all?"

"No! No! Nothin' means *nothin'* anymore!"

"Batting in ninth position and pitching for the Ruppert Mundys . . ."

The Mundy council of elders: starters Tuminikar, Buchis, Volos, and Demeter; relievers Pollux, Mertzeger, and the tiny Mexican right-hander, Chico Mecoatl—every last one of them flabby in the middle, arthritic in the shoulder, bald on the top. "The hairless wonders," said Jolly Cholly Tuminikar, who had discovered the fine art of self-effacement following the tragedy that destroyed his confidence and his career, "and a good thing too. Ain't a one of us could raise his arm to comb his hairs if he had any. Why, if I go three innings on a windy day, I got to use my other hand the next morning to wipe myself. Don't print that, Smitty, but it's the truth." Yes, has-beens, might-have-beens, should-have-beens, would-have-beens, never-weres and never-will-bes, Tuminikar and his venerable cohorts managed nonetheless to somehow get the ball the sixty feet and six inches to the plate, which was all the rule book required of them. The ball, to be sure, occasionally arrived on a bounce, or moved so slowly and with so little English on it that the patrons back of home plate would pretend to be reading General Oakhart's signature off the horsehide all the while the pitch was in transit. "What time you say she's due in?" they'd ask, holding up their pocket watches, and on and on, comically, in that vein. There was even one of them, Chico Mecoatl, who on occasion tossed the ball in *underhand*. "How about if he fungoes 'em, Chico, then you won't have to throw at all!" the sadistic hecklers called, heedless of the pain that caused Chico to resort sometimes to a style of pitching that had not been the custom now in baseball since the days of the buffalo and the Indian.

The fans who needled the wretched Mexican were not so plentiful actually as their vociferousness might make it appear. Most people seemed to find it eerie, rather than amusing or irritating, to watch him work in relief. Invariably it was dusk when Chico, the last bald man in the bullpen, would trudge across the darkening field to pitch for the Mundys, already brutally beaten with an inning or two of punishment still to come. By this hour, the hometown fans, filled to the gills on all the slugging they'd seen, would have begun to leave their seats, tugging their collars up against the cool breeze and smiling when they peered for a final time out at the scoreboard to what looked now like the score of a football game. Two, three touchdowns for the home team; a field goal for the visitors, if that . . . So, they would converge upon the exits, a swarm of big two-fisted creatures as drowsy with contentment as the babe whose face has dropped in bloated bliss from the sugary nipple. Ah, victory. Ah, triumph. How it does mellow the bearded sex! What are the consolations of philosophy or the affirmations of religion beside an afternoon's rich meal of doubles, triples, and home runs? . . . But then came Chico out to the mound, and made that little yelp of his as he tossed his single warm-up pitch in the general direction of Hothead's mitt, that little bleat of pain that passed from between his lips whenever he had to raise his arm above his waist to throw the ball. The fans, clustered now in the dark apertures that opened on to the ramps leading down to the city streets, would swing around upon hearing Chico's bleat, one head craning above the other, to try to catch a glimpse of the pitcher with the sorest arm in the game. For there was no one who had a motion quite like Chico's: in order to release the ball with a minimal amount of suffering, he did not so much throw it as push it, with a wiggling sort of straight-arm motion. It looked as though he might be trying to pass his hand through a hoop of flames without getting it burned—and it sounded as though he wasn't quite able to make it. "Eeeep!" he would cry, and there would be the ball, floating softly through the dusk at its own sweet pace, and then the solid retort of the bat, and all the base runners scampering for home.

Probably the fans themselves could not have explained what exactly it was that held them there sometimes five and ten minutes on end watching Chico suffer so. It was not pity—Chico could quit and go back to Mexico if he wanted, and do down there whatever it was Mexicans did. Nor was it affection; he was, after all, a spic, closer even to a nigger than the Frenchman, Astarte. Nor was it amusement, for after three hours of watching the Mundys on what even for them was an off day, you didn't have the strength to laugh anymore. It would seem rather that they were transfixed, perhaps for the first time in their lives, by the strangeness of things, the wondrous strangeness of things, by all that is beyond the pale and just does not seem to belong in this otherwise cozy and familiar world of ours. With the sun all but down and the far corners of the stadium vanishing, that noise he made might have originated in the swaying jungle foliage or in some dark pocket of the moon for the sense of fear and wonder that it awakened in men who only a moment earlier had been anticipating their slippers and their favorite chair, a bottle of beer and the lovely memories they would have forever after of all those runners they'd seen galloping around third that afternoon. "Hear it?" a father whispered to his young son. "Uh-huh," said the little boy, shifting on his little stick legs. "Hear that? It can give you the goose bumps. Chico Mecoatl—you can tell your grandchildren you heard him make that noise. *Hear* it?" "Oh, Poppy, let's go."

So home they went (home, to their homes!), leaving Chico, who hardly ever got anybody out anymore, to fill the bases two times over, and the relentless home team to clear them two times over, before; mercifully, the sun set, the field disappeared, and the disaster being played out now for the sake of no one, was called on account of darkness.

3

IN THE WILDERNESS

❦

FINAL STANDINGS 1943

	W	L	PCT	GB
Tri-City Tycoons	90	64	.584	
Aceldama Butchers	89	65	.578	1
Independence Blues	88	66	.571	2
Terra Incognita Rustlers	82	72	.532	8
Tri-City Greenbacks	79	75	.513	11
Asylum Keepers	77	77	.500	13
Kakoola Reapers	77	77	.500	13
Ruppert Mundys	34	120	.221	56

Containing a description of how it is to have your home away
from home instead of having it at home like everybody else.
Mister Fairsmith informs the team of the moral and spirit-
ual benefits that can accrue from wretchedness. With predict-
able cynicism, Big John elucidates the advantages of homeless-
ness. Frenchy forgets where he is. An insinuating incident in
which a man dressed like a woman takes the field against the
Mundys. A lively digression on the Negro Patriot League, the
famous owner of the league, and a brief description of some
fans, containing a scene which will surprise many who believe
Branch Rickey the first major league owner courageous enough
to invite colored players into organized baseball. The Mundys
arouse the maternal instinct in three Kakoola spinsters and
succumb to their wiles with no fight at all. Big John and Nick-
name visit the pink-'n-blue-light district, wherein Nickname
gets what he is looking for, thus concluding the visit to Ka-
koola, in which city the Mundys will suffer more than the hu-
miliation of their manliness before the downfall is complete.
The Mundys are followed on a swing around the league and the
particular manner in which they are intimidated in each of the
league cities is described, including the train ride in and out of
Port Ruppert, which, though short, may draw tears from
some eyes. A victory for the Mundys in Asylum turns into
another defeat, containing, for the curious, a somewhat detailed
account of baseball as it is played by the mad. In this
chapter the fortunate reader who has never felt
himself a stranger in his own land,
may pick up some idea
of what it is like.

SWINGING AROUND THE LEAGUE for the first time in 1943, the
Mundys were honored on the day of their arrival in each of the
six P. League cities with a parade down the main commercial
thoroughfare and a pregame ceremony welcoming them to the
ball park. Because of war shortages, the vehicle which picked
them up at the train station was, as often as not, borrowed for

the hour from the municipal sanitation department. The twenty-five Mundys, having changed into their gray "away" uniforms on the train, and carrying their street clothes in suitcases or paper bags, would climb aboard to be driven from the station down the boulevard to their hotel, while over the loudspeaker fixed to the truck came the voice and guitar of Gene Autry doing his rendition of "Home on the Range." The record had been selected by General Oakhart's secretary, not only because the words to the song seemed to her appropriate to the occasion, but because it was reputed to be President Roosevelt's very own favorite, and would thus strengthen the idea that the fate of the Mundys and of the republic were inextricably bound together. Weary to death of the whole sordid affair, General Oakhart consented, for all that he would have been happier with something time-honored and to the point like "Take Me Out to the Ballgame."

Though it had been hoped that people in the streets would join in singing, most of the pedestrians did not even seem to realize what was going on when a city garbage truck drove past bearing the team that had finished last in the league the previous year. Of course, the tots out shopping with their mothers grew excited at the sound of approaching music, expecting, in their innocence, that they were about to see Santa or the Easter bunny; but excitement quickly faded and in some instances even turned to fear when the truck appeared, jammed full of men, most of them old and bald, waving their baseball caps around in the air, and singing, each in his own fashion—

> Oh, give me a home where the buffalo roam,
> Where the deer and the antelope play,
> Where seldom is heard a discouraging word,
> And the skies are not cloudy all day.

Judging from the racket they made, it couldn't be said that the Mundys were unwilling to give it the old college try, at least at the outset. Obviously a refuse van (as Mister Fairsmith preferred to call it) was not their idea of splendor anymore than it is yours or mine; still, scrubbed clean, more or less, and tricked up with red, white, and blue bunting, it was not really as bad as Hothead could make it sound when he started in, as per usual,

being outraged. "Why, it looks to me like they are carting us
off to the city dump! It looks to me as if they are about to
flush us down the bowl!" cried Hot. "It looks to me like a
violation of the worst sort there is of our inalienable human
rights such as are guaranteed in the Declaration of Independence to all men *including Ruppert Mundys!*"

Yet, as the Mundys knew better than anyone in the game,
there was a war on, and you had to make do with the makeshift
for a while. It just did not help to complain. And hopefully,
said Jolly Cholly T., hopefully the more they sacrificed, the
sooner the war would be over and they would be home—and
not home on the range either, but back in New Jersey, where
they had been beloved and where they belonged.

Around the league the city officials were of course free to
welcome the Mundys with a speech of their own composition;
invariably, however, they chose to follow to the letter the text
that had been composed for the pregame ceremony by General
Oakhart's office, which also supplied the papier-mâché "key
to the city" that was awarded at home plate to Mister Fairsmith, in behalf of the local fans. "Welcome Ruppert Mundys,"
the speech began, "welcome to ———, your home away from
home!" Here the word "PAUSE" appeared in the prepared
speech, capitalized and tucked between parentheses. Though
the officials always correctly inserted the name of their fair
city in the blank provided, they repeatedly read into the microphone at home plate the parenthetical direction intended to
allow time for the fans to rise to their feet to applaud, if they
should be so inclined. Fortunately nobody in the ball park ever
seemed to notice this error; either they took the word for an
electronic vibration coming over the p.a. system, or they
weren't paying that much attention to the dronings of the
nameless functionary in a double-breasted suit and pointed
black shoes who had been dispatched by the mayor to take his
place at the ceremonies. All the fans cared about was the ball
game, and seeing the Mundys clobbered by the hometown
boys. The Mundys, on the other hand, had become so accustomed to the ritual, that when, midway through the first road
trip, a Kakoola city official neglected to make "PAUSE" the
twelfth word in his welcoming speech, a contingent of disgruntled Mundys, led by Hot Ptah, accused the city of Ka-

koola of deliberately treating them as inferiors because they
happened to be a homeless team. In point of fact, by actually
pausing in his speech rather than just saying "PAUSE,"
Bridge and Tunnel Commissioner Vincent J. Efghi (brother
to Boss Efghi, the mayor), had managed to evoke a ripple of
applause from the crowd; nothing thunderous, mind you, but
at least a response somewhat more sympathetic than the
Mundys had received in those cities where the address was
delivered by the local ward heeler, parenthetical instructions
and all.

After the game that day, with Hot and his disciples still
riled up, Mister Fairsmith decided to hold a meeting in the
Mundy locker room, and give the team their first sermon of
the season on the subject of suffering; for the first time since
they had hit the road, he attempted to instruct them in the
Larger Meaning of the experience that had befallen them, and
to place their travail within the context of human history and
divine intention. He began by reminding them that even as
they were playing their baseball games on the road, American
boys were bleeding to death in jungles halfway around the
globe, and being blown to bits in the vast, uninhabited skies. He
told them of the agony of those who had been crushed beneath
the boot heel of the enemy, those millions upon millions who had
lost not just a home in the world, but all freedom, all dignity,
all hope. He told them of the volcanic eruptions that had
drowned entire cities in rivers of fire in ancient times, and
described to them earthquakes that had opened up beneath
the world, delivering everything and everyone there was, like
so much mail, into the churning bowels of the earth; then he
reminded them of the sufferings of Our Lord. By comparison
to such misery as mankind had known since the beginnings of
time, what did it matter if the Bridge and Tunnel Commissioner of bridgeless and tunnelless Kakoola had neglected to
read even *half* the welcoming speech to the Mundys? Solemn
as he could be—and as he daily grew more venerable, that was
very solemn indeed—Mister Fairsmith asked what was to
become of them in the long hot months ahead, if they could not
bear up beneath the tiny burden that they had had to shoulder
thus far? What if they should have to partake of such sufferings as was the daily bread of the wretched of the wretched of

the earth? "Gentlemen, if it is the Lord's will," he told them, "that you should wander homeless through this league, then I say leave off disputing with the Lord, and instead seize the opportunity He has thrust upon you to be strong, to be steadfast—to be saved."

"Horse *shit!*" snorted Hothead, after Mister Fairsmith had passed from the locker room in meaningful silence.

"Ah, forget it, Gimp," said Big John Baal. "It is only a word they left out of that speech there, you know. I mean it ain't exactly a sawbuck, or even two bits. If it was dough, that would *mean* somethin'. But a word, why it don't mean a thing that I could ever see. A whole speech is just a bunch of words from beginning to end, you know, that didn't fool nobody yet what's got half a brain in his head. Ain't that right, Damur?" he said, tossing his jock in the face of the fourteen-year-old whose guardian and protector he'd become. "A nose by any other name would smell as much sweat, ain't that so, *niño?* You fellers care too much about what folks say. Don't listen is my advice."

"You don't get it, Baal," snarled Hot. "You never do. Sure it starts with only a word. But how it ends is with them doin' whatever they damn well please, and kicking all your dreams down the drain."

"Hot," said John, leering suggestively, "maybe you is dreamin' about the wrong sort of things."

"Is justice the wrong thing? Is gettin' your rights like last licks the wrong thing?"

"Aww," said Big John, "it's only a game, for Christ's sake. I'm tellin' ya : it don't *mean* nothin'."

"To you nothin' means nothin'."

"Worryin' over shit like 'justice' don't, I'll tell you that much. I just do like I want anyway."

"Justice ain't shit!" Hot told him. "What they are doin' to us ain't *fair!*"

"Well, like Ulysses S. tole you boys, that's *good* for you that it ain't fair. That's gonna make champs out of you, if not in this here season, then in the next. Wait'll next year, boys! Haw! Haw!" Here he took a slug out of the liniment bottle that sat at the bottom of his locker. "You want me to tell you boys somethin'? This bein' homeless is just about the best thing that has ever happened to you, if you only had the sense to know it. What do you care that you don't have a home and the hometown fans that go with it? What the hell is home-town fans but a bunch of dodos who all live in the same place and think that if we win that's good for 'em and if we lose it ain't? And then we ain't none of us from that there town to begin with—why, it could just as easy say PORT SHITHOLE across your uniform as the name of the place you only happen to be in by accident anyway. Ain't that so? Why, I even used to pretend like that's what it did say, years ago, instead of RUPPERT. I'd look down at my shirt and I'd say to myself, 'Hey, Jawn, ain't you lucky to be playin' for PORT SHIT-HOLE and the glory of the SHITHOLE fans. Boy, Jawn, you sure do want to do your best and try real hard so you can bring honor to the SHITHOLE name.' You damn fools," he said, "*you* ain't from Rupe-it! You never was and you never would be, not if you played there a million years. You are just a bunch of baseball players whose asses got bought up by one place instead of the other. Come on, use your damn heads, boys—you were visitors there just like you are visitors here. You are makin' there be a difference where there ain't."

The Mundys went off to the shower in a silence that be-spoke much confusion. First there had been Hothead to tell them that the word dropped from the welcoming speech was only the overture to the slights, insults, and humiliations that were to be visited upon them in the months to come. Then there was Mister Fairsmith to warn them that slights and insults weren't the half of it—they were shortly to begin to partake of the suffering that was the daily bread not just of the wretched of the earth, but of the *wretched* of the wretched. And now Big John informing them that the Rupe-it rootas, for whom they had all begun to long with a feeling more intense than any was even willing to admit, had been some sort of mirage or delusion. Of course, that the son of Spit and the grandson of Base should speak with such contempt for their old hometown hardly came as a surprise to any of his team-mates; having been raised in the sordid netherworld of Nica-raguan baseball, he no more knew the meaning of "loyalty" than of "justice" or "pride" or "fair play." Still, on the heels of Hothead's warning and Mister Fairsmith's apocalyp-

tic prophecy, it was not reassuring to be told that the place to
which you longed to return had never been "yours" to begin
with.

"Well," cried Mike Rama, over the noise of the shower,
"if we ain't never been from Rupe-it, then the Reapers ain't
from Kakoola, either. Or the Rustlers from Terra Inc. Or the
Blues from Independence. Or nobody from nowhere!"

"Right!" cried Nickname. "They's as worse off as we
is!"

"Only then how come," said old Kid Heket, toweling himself down, "how come the Kakoolas is here in Kakoola and
we ain't there in Rupe-it, or goin' back there all season long?
How come instead of headin' back to Jersey, we are off to
Independence and then all around the league to here again,
and so on and so forth for a hundred and fifty-four games?"

"But what's the difference, Wayne," said Nickname,
who was continually torn between parroting Big John, whose
blasphemous nature had a strong hold upon a fourteen-year-
old away from home for the first time in his life, and siding as
any rookie would with the rest of the players *against* the
Mundy renegade—"so what if we ain't goin' back there? It's
more fun this way anyway. Stayin' in all them hotels, eatin'
hamburgers whenever you want—winkin' at them girls in the
lobby! And all them waitresses in them tight white un-ee-
forms—wheee!"

"Nickname my lad, soon you will discover that it ain't
'fun' either way," said the old-timer, "it's only less confusin',
that's all, wakin' up and knowin' where you are instead of
where you ain't."

So, not much happier than when they went off to the
shower, they returned to the locker room, there to be con-
fronted by Frenchy, standing fully dressed before his locker,
though not in his baggy brown suit and beret. No, the Frenchman was off in never-never land again. Half a dozen times
already this season, one or another of the Mundys had come
upon Frenchy making faces at himself in the washroom mirror, a grown man in need of a shave doing what little kids do
when they want to look like something out of Charlie Chan—
jutting his upper teeth out over his lower lip and holding back
the flesh at the corner of either eye with an index finger.

"Hey!" his teammate would shout, to wake him out of the trance he was in. "Hey, number one son!" and, caught in the traitorous act, Frenchy would run to hide in a toilet stall. What a character! Them foreigners!

But now it was not funny faces he was making in the mirror; no, nothing funny about this at all. There was Frenchy, dressed in the creamy white flannel uniform that none of them had worn all year, the Mundy home uniform, with the faint red chalk stripe and RUPPERT scrawled in scarlet across the chest, the final "t" ending in a flourish nearly as grand as John Hancock's. And what was so sad about it was how splendid he looked. The Mundys were stunned—so accustomed had they become to seeing one another in the drab gray "away" uniforms, they had nearly forgotten how stylish they used to be. No wonder they were beloved by the Rupe-it rootas, even in the worst of times. Just look how they'd looked only the season before!

"Hey, whatcha doin', Frenchman," asked Jolly Cholly, "kel sort of joke is this anyway, chair ol' pal? Ain't today been rough enough? Aw Christ, somebody, what's the French for knock it off?"

"Geem," replied Frenchy, whose English was incomprehensible to his teammates, except occasionally to Chico, who would pass on to Big John, the other Spanish-speaking Mundy, what he believed to be the general drift of Frenchy's zees and zoes—"geem zee wan, ooh zee was zow, zen ah geem zee, ah zee ull!" And he began to beat his skull against the door of his locker.

As best anyone could figure, coming back into the empty locker room from the shower, Frenchy had momentarily forgotten where he was, and begun to dress as though for the second game of a doubleheader back in Ruppert . . . "Crazy Canadian Frog," said Big John, "he still thinks it's on account of him not catchin' that pop-up that they give us the old heave-ho. Hey, Ass-start, don't lose your head over it," chuckled Big John while Cholly and Bud Parusha struggled to keep the shortstop from destroying himself, "look what they done to my daddy. And he didn't go around beatin' his brains out. Hell, he just figured it all out—and then passed it on to me. The wisdom of the ages, Ass-start: it's all shit. You jerk-offs take it too serious."

Here there was a noise at the clubhouse door, the timid peck of a tender knuckle, and then the quivering voice of a little lady inquiring as to whether the Mundys were "decent" . . .

But before narrating what next took place in Kakoola on May 5, 1943—a day that seems in retrospect to stand as the dividing line between the Mundy past and the Mundy future, between the Patriot League as it once had been and the Patriot League as it was to become in the two seasons before its dissolution—it is necessary to point out that Frank Mazuma, the innovative owner of the Reapers, had declared that afternoon "Ladies Day," hoping thus to beef up the skimpy crowd that would otherwise turn out to see the two lowliest P. League teams falling all over each other in their effort to lose. Play, in fact, had been interrupted in the top of the fifth when it was discovered that one of the ladies who had been admitted free of charge was in actuality a man. In a close-fitting dress of flamboyant design, all dolled up in a blond Hollywood wig, and swinging a gaudy handbag and hips, she had given herself away by making a brilliant one-handed stab on a near-miss home run lifted foul into the left-field seats by Big John, who, being perfectly sober, had swung late. At first the crowd got a bang out of the remarkable feat performed by the sexy gal, and stamped and hollered like a crowd at the burlesque show; then, in the next instant, realizing that no woman, no matter how proudly pronged her chest, could ever make a catch like that bare-handed, they began to converge upon the blond bombshell, piercing wolf whistles mixed with obscene threats. When police whistles joined in, the blond rushed down to the edge of the stands and with her dress parachuting up to her pink garters, leaped to the grass. Quickly she disposed of Rudra, the Kakoola left-fielder, with a stiff-arm block that sent him sprawling, and started for second. The Mundys, convinced by now that this was some sort of "half-time" entertainment cooked up by Frank Mazuma, had to join in laughing with the crowd when she sidestepped the charging Kakoola keystone combination (who wound up in one another's arms) and made for the pitcher's mound in those high-heeled, toeless shoes. Big John was still at the plate with his 0 and 2 count when the blond, swinging her purse at the Kakoola pitcher's head, drove him from the hill with his arms around his ears.

Then, the purse still in her right hand, and the foul ball she had caught still in her left, she reared back—whew-whew! those garters again!—and threw the Mundy power hitter the biggest damn curve he'd seen in a decade. Christ, did John get a boot out of that! "A big-titted slit in a little-bitty dress, and she just struck me out! Haw! Haw! With stuff like that, just think what the rest of her looks like!" Next the blond broke for the Mundy dugout, throwing the boys big kisses as she headed their way. Oh brother. The visiting players were shrugging and grinning at one another and so hardly took seriously the cops charging after her, shouting, "Mundys, stop her! She ain't no lady! Stop her, boys—she's under arrest for pretending to be what she ain't!" Even when the police yanked their pistols from their holsters and drew a bead on the blond's behind, the Mundys just shook their heads, and, pretending to be stroking their whiskers, hid their titters behind their hands. Then *smack!* The blond had planted a kisseroo on Mister Fairsmith's mouth—and was down through the dugout and gone. They could hear her heels ringing on the concrete runway to the clubhouse. "Stop!" cried the cops, dashing right on after her. Then *bang!* Oh my God. They had opened fire on her fanny.

No one (except maybe Mazuma) knew what next to expect. Would the blond come back on out to take a bow, waving her wig at the crowd? Or would the cops come up out of the clubhouse dragging her "corpse" behind them? And what about her blood, would it be ketchup or real?

But all that happened next was that the game was resumed, an 0 and 2 count on Johnny Baal and the Mundys down by six . . . and the folks in the stands feverish with speculation. You should have heard the ideas they came up with. Some even began to wonder if maybe a real live homo hadn't got loose on the ball field. "Yep," said the old-timers out in the center-field bleachers, the boys with the green eyeshades who had been predicting the downfall of the game ever since the introduction of the lively ball, "I tole you—you start in foolin' with this here thing, and you start in foolin' with that one, and next thing you know, you got the cupcakes on your hands. You wait, you see—'Ladies Day' is only the beginnin'. They'll be havin' 'Fairy Day' around the league before this thing is over.

*Yes*sir, every la-dee-da window-dresser in town will be out here in his girdle, and they'll be givin' away free nail polish to them fellers, so-called, at the door. Oh, it's acomin', don't worry about that. It's all acomin', every last damn thing you can think of that's rotten and dumb, on accounta they just could not leave the damn ball alone like it was!''

Among the sportswriters, speculation took a less pessimistic if no less bizarre turn; but then they were dealing with Frank Mazuma, who could out-bizarre you any day of the week. Those who had gotten a good look at the blond's sidearm delivery, and followed closely the course of that cruel curve, swore that the "lady" on the mound had been none other than Gil Gamesh done up in falsies and a dress—that's right, the big bad boy of yore, hired for the day as a female impersonator by Frank M. But Frank, who wore a black eyepatch (over the right eye one day, over the left the next) so as to look even more like the pirate he was, only clapped himself on the knee and said, ''Hell, now why didn't I think of that!'' ''You mean, Frank, you are asking us to believe that you had nothing to do with those shameful shenanigans out there today?'' ''Smitty, I only wish I had. Whoever could stage a spectacle like that is just the kind of crowd-pleasing genius I would like to grow up to be. But in all honesty, I have to tell you that I think what happened there in the top of the fifth was something staged by the greatest crowd-pleaser of 'em all: fella name a' God.''

Oh, there was little that Frank Mazuma would not say, or worse, do. Only the season before he had gotten the bright idea of turning the Reapers into the first colored team in Organized Baseball—yes, selling off all the white boys and bringing niggers in to replace them! As things stood in those days—days which must now seem as remote as the age of the Pharaohs to those who search in vain for a white face on the diamond when All-Star time comes around—the bigwigs of the national pastime understood that it was in the best interests of the game—and if of the game, the country; and if of the country, mankind itself—for the big leagues to be composed entirely of white men, with an occasional Indian, or Hawaiian, or Jew thrown in for the sake of color. Furthermore, the darkies had teams of their own, hundreds of them barnstorming around the country wherever colored folk were looking for

a little Sunday entertainment; they even had their own
"major" leagues, the Negro National, the Negro American,
and the Negro Patriot League, composed of teams who made
their homes in the real major league cities, and who were
allowed to play in the big league parks when the white teams
were out of town. Oftentimes these colored teams performed
for Sunday crowds substantially larger than those that paid
to see the white major league team play ball, and that, of
course, was what most intrigued Frank Mazuma, and encouraged him to think along the lines of becoming the Abe Lincoln
of big league ball.

What fans those colored boys had! Why, they would travel
hundreds of miles, make overnight journeys in wagons drawn
by mules and nags, to get to the ball park for a Sunday doubleheader between the Kakoola Boll Weevils and their first division rivals, the Ruppert Rastuses, or the champs playing out
of Aceldama, known affectionately as the Shiftless Nine. In
patched overalls and no shoes, they'd just come straight on
out of the fields Saturday at quitting time, along the dusty
country roads and on to the highways, walking all night long
so as to reach the bubbling asphalt of the city by high noon of
the next day. Batting practice was usually just getting underway, when they emerged at last into those great coliseums
raised by white men and white money and white might. Beneath their feet the cool concrete of the stadium runways was
like soothing waters. (Yeah!) And that green pasture was
greener than anything they knew, this side of the fields of
heaven. (Yeah!) Oh, up, up went the sky-high stadium, up so
high that those pennants seemed to be snappin' around God's
very throne. (Yeah!) Oh them colorful flags, they might have
been the fringes of His Robe! Yes suh, de Big Leagues! (Or,
to be precise, a Negro facsimile of same.)

The owner of all eight teams in the Negro P. League was
of course known to Americans primarily because of her picture on the flapjack box. With the fortune Aunt Jemima had
amassed from the use of her name and her face on the pancake
mix, she had managed to buy up one colored team after another
in P. League towns, until she had organized the circuit and
made it equal in status to the other two Negro "major"
leagues. Of course, everywhere she went, she had that big

smile full of white teeth shining out of her face, and she waxed her skin so it shone just as it did in her portrait on the box, and she was never without that checkered bandanna that made her look so cheery and sweet—but when it came to a business deal, she was a match for Mazuma himself; her name notwithstanding, she was nobody's aunt.

Aunt Jemima was always up in Kakoola on Sundays to watch her favorites, the Boll Weevils, take on whichever colored club was visiting with them that week; invariably she was accompanied by her brother, the famed valet of radio and motion picture fame, Washington Deesey, who year in and year out tap-danced the National Anthem from atop a bass drum set down on home plate the day the colored World Series opened. Other famous Negroes of the time who were frequent visitors to Aunt Jemima's box were the comedy duo "Teeth 'n Eyes," who were always seeing g-g-g-ghosts in horror movies, and would amuse the crowd at the ball park with their famous blood-curdling howl when a d-d-d-dangerous hitter came to the p-p-p-plate; and Li'l Ruby, the twittering maid of the airwaves, who had won America's heart with her ridiculous crying jags, and who arrived at the ball park riding sidesaddle on her great Dane, a strapping eighteen-year-old lad imported from Copenhagen, said to be something more than a means of transportation for the actress; "Now ain't that a surprise!" the fans would exclaim, when they saw the diamonds roped around her wrists and her ankles, "I thought she was a little bitty thing!" Yet another Boll Weevil fan was the man rumored to be Aunt Jemima's lover, the distinguished tragedian whose portrayal of the loyal old slave who saves his master's drowning child and subsequently dies of pneumonia in the Civil War epic *Look Away, Look Away* had earned him an Academy Award for the best supporting actor, Mr. Mel E. F. Lewis. And then over the years there were the numerous boxing champions who were like sons to Aunt Jemima: those who come immediately to mind are Kid Licorice, Kid Bituminous, Kid Smoke, Kid Crow, Kid Hershey, Kid Midnight, Kid Ink and his twin Kid Quink, Kid Tophat, Kid Coffee, Kid Mud, and of course, *the* champ, Kid Gloves, whose twenty-year reign as middleweight champion of the world ended in 1948 when he disowned fame, fortune, and

country to become a worker in an aluminum factory in the
Soviet Union. A moody and solitary man, he had always dis-
dained the glitter of Aunt Jemima's box and instead preferred
to sit on the bleacher benches in deep center, surrounded by
barefoot children who clung to his powerful arms and to whom
between innings he sang the songs of the Third International.
In 1948, in a speech from the center of the prizefight ring in
Madison Square Garden, he infuriated Americans of all hues
by denouncing the country that had made him a hero, and the
following day he left by steamer for Murmansk.

Only weeks after his departure, news leaked from behind
the Iron Curtain (how, no one knew, given that the curtain was
iron) that the great Gloves had been exiled to Siberia for mur-
dering with one blow—ironically enough, said the gloating
tabloids, a left—a Commie foreman, who, in his impatience
with the new comrade unable to speak the mother tongue, had
called him by the one English word he had picked up from the
American G.I.s in the war. According to "highly authoritative"
reports released some years later by the U.S. State Department, in the Siberian labor camp poor Kid Gloves had been
cruelly teased and tormented by prisoners and guards alike,
until finally, in that far-off land of blizzards and collectives, the
broken-hearted boxer with the ravished utopian dream perished of homesickness, in his final days languishing for the
American prizefight ring as did his forebears in Georgia for the
jungle villages of the Ivory Coast.

Now, in order to scout the colored players he planned to
poach from Aunt Jemima's league, Frank Mazuma purchased
from a pawnshop a frayed clerical collar and a second-hand
black suit, painted himself with burnt cork, and, wearing beneath his derby a woolly gray wig, went out one Sunday in
1942 to see the Boll Weevils take on the Independence Field
Hands in a doubleheader in his own Reaper stadium. Needless
to say, Mazuma had no intention of "buying" these black boys
like so many slaves—he would just dangle the big leagues
before the best of them, and leave it to them to decide whether
they wished to continue to play for peanuts for the colored
version of the big leagues, or to run off to play for peanuts
for the real thing. So as to be privy to the inside dope on the
star colored players, Mazuma took a seat in a box directly

behind Aunt Jemima. Clever operator that she was, she instantly penetrated his disguise, but said nothing, choosing rather to pass that scandalous information directly to General Oakhart the next day. Let *him* handle the thief—it wasn't for Aunt Jemima to admonish a white man with Mazuma's kind of money . . . "Well," she said, welcoming the clergyman with her biggest, shiningest smile, "howdydo, Reverend! Ain't we honored though!"

Mazuma bowed and presented her with a card from his tattered billfold. It read:

PARDON ME

I AM A NEGRO DEAF MUTE MINISTER

I SELL THIS CARD FOR A LIVING—MAY GOD

BLESS YOU

. . . But we stray from the story of the Mundys on the road. Suffice it to say that foolish and trivial as the events of that day may appear from the perspective of today, it nonetheless would appear that the death knell for the white man's game—and if for the white man's game, for a white man's country; and if for a white country, for a white world—that death knell's first faint tinkle was heard at the moment that Frank Mazuma, in that preposterous disguise, handed his outlandish business card to the famed "mammy" off the flapjack box at a doubleheader between the Boll Weevils and the Field Hands, with Teeth 'n Eyes, Li'l Ruby, and Washington Deesey looking on . . . Impossible, you may say. More than impossible—*outrageous,* to suggest that a greedy scoundrel like Mazuma in circumstances so ludicrous as these, initiated what was eventually to become the greatest advancement for the colored people to take place in America since the Emancipation Proclamation. But of course you must remember, fans, the turning points in our history are not always so grand as they are cracked up to be in the murals on your post office wall.

We return to that knock on the door of the visitors' clubhouse, where the dazed and troubled Mundys are still gathered, following the 14–3 "Ladies Day" loss to Kakoola, and all that had followed upon it. "Mundys? Ruppert Mundys?" A woman giggled. "Are—are you decent, boys?"

All but Frenchy were unclothed and dripping still from the shower, but Big John replied, "Oh sure, we're decent all right. And what about you, honey? Or is your name 'funny'?"

"That voice! It's Big John!"

"Big John!"

"Big John!"

"My, my," said Big John, his eyes darkening with desire, "there's three of 'em . . . Hey, who all are you girls, whatcha after, or can I take a guess?"

Now the three spoke in unison: "We're the Mundy Mommys!"

"The who?" asked John, laughing.

"The Mundy Mothers!"

"The Mundy Moms!"

"And," asked Big John, "just how old would such a Momma happen to be? Twenty-one or twenty-two?"

They giggled with delight.

"Fifty-four years young, John!"

"Sixty-eight years young, John!"

"Seventy-one years young, John!"

Baal pushed the door open a crack—"If she's fifty-four," he whispered to his mates, "Wayne here is a infant. Thanks, ladies," he called, "but we don't need none."

The other players had by now scrambled into their street clothes, and converging upon the door, peered out from behind the first-baseman at the three elderly ladies, wrinkled little walnuts in identical hats, shoes, and spectacles.

"Howdy," said Jolly Cholly, stepping into the hallway. "Now what can we do for you ladies?"

"It's Jolly Cholly!" the women cried. "Oh, look! It's Hothead! It's Chico! It's Deacon! It's Roland!" And then the three were talking all at once—"Oh you poor Mundys! You poor boys! How you must miss your sisters and your wives! Who sews your buttons? Who darns your socks? Who turns your collars and sees after your heels and your soles? Who takes *care* of you, always away from your home?"

"Oh," said Jolly Cholly, with a kindly smile, "we manage

okay, more or less. It ain't so bad missin' a few buttons now
and then. There's a war on, you know.''

"But who feeds Frenchy his toast and his fries? Who
looks after Bud to see he brushes his teeth after games? And
Chico, with the sorest arm in the league—and nobody to cut
his meat!''

"Oh,'' said Cholly, "don't you worry about Chico, he just
sort of picks it up by the bone you know, with the other hand,
and—and, look here, this is nice of you and all, but ain't you
ladies from Kakoola anyway? How come you ain't sewin' buttons on for the Reapers over there, and bein' Moms to them?''

"They don't *need* Moms!'' they cried, triumphantly.

"Well, we don't neither, ladies,'' said Jolly Cholly.
"We're a big league club, you know, so of course thanks for
the offer, very kind of you and all.''

And yet within the hour the Mundys were marching
through the darkening streets of Kakoola behind their self-
appointed "Moms,'' each of the players obediently calling out
the kind of home-baked pie he would like as the grand finale to
his home-cooked meal. So what if it didn't accord with their
"dignity''—so what if Roland Agni turned up his prima
donna nose and refused to join in? Let Agni go back to brood
in that lonely hotel! They might be a homeless ball team, but
that didn't mean they had to do without their just desserts!
Hell, if they were doomed the way Mister Fairsmith said they
were, they would be doing without *everything* soon enough.

"Wayne?''

"Apple!''

"Bud?''

"Cherry!''

"Chico?''

"Banana!''

"Mike?''

"Rhubarb, peach, chocolate cream—''

"Big John?''

"Hair!'' and, laughing, he ducked down a dark alleyway,
dragging Nickname with him.

"Hey, Jawn—what about *my* pie?''

"You miss your momma, do you, Nickname?''

"Well, no.''

"Is that why you was cryin' when she started in talkin' about sewin' on buttons?"

"I wasn't cryin', I got some shit in my eye, that's all."

"Come on, boy, you was bawlin' like a babe! She started in talkin' about darnin' socks, and you wuz about knee-deep in tears."

"Well," admitted the second-baseman, "I *am* homesick, a *little.*"

"Haw! Haw! Sick for home are you? Miss your mom, do you?"

"Oh Jawn, don't kid with me—I—I—I—miss *everythin'* a little," he said, with a sob.

"Well, *niño,* then that's what we are going to get you—everythin'! Just like it used to be for you, boy, back in the good old days!"

And so they set out across Kakoola, Big John telling his protégé, "In a town like this, Nickname, there ain't nothin' money can't buy. And if they ain't sellin' it here, they are sellin' it in Asylum—and if they ain't sellin' it in Asylum, there is always good old Terra Inc. down at the end of the line. Hell, a ballplayer could spend a lifetime roamin' this league, and never lack for entertainment—if, *primo,* you know what I mean by entertainment, and *secondo,* what I mean by a ballplayer! Haw! Haw!" he roared, reaching for Nickname's little handful. "Come on, *muchacho,* I'll get you mothered all right —I'll get you a momma who really plies the trade!"

Oh, did Nickname's heart start in pounding then! A whorehouse, he thought, his very first! What Ohio youngster's heart *wouldn't* be pounding!

But when they finally stopped running they were on a street that looked just like the streets where all the nice families lived in the movies he used to see on Saturdays back home. "Hey, John," he whispered, "this is the wrong place. Ain't it? Look at them houses. Look at them white fences and them green lawns."

"Yeah—and look up there at them street signs. This is it, Nickname. You heard of Broadway and 42nd Street. You heard of Hollywood and Vine. Well, this is the world-famous corner of Tigris and Euphrates. This is the world-renowned 'Cradle of Civilization.'"

"What's that?"

"Haw! Haw! Why, first time I ever heard of it, I guess I was only a lad your age too. Down Nicaragey way, from an ol' sailor off the Great Lakes. He was a shortstop for my paw, till he got the d.t.s and we traded him to a Guatemala farmer for a mule. He says, 'I been everywhere, I been to Shanghai, Rangoon, Bangkok, and the rest, I been to Bali and back—but what they got right up there in Kakoola, Wisconsin, U.S.A., ain't like nothin' in the whole wide wicked world for fixin' what ails you.'" Dragging Nickname with him, he started up the walk to 6 Euphrates Drive, which like numbers 2 through 20, was a white house with green shutters and a water sprinkler turning on the well-kept lawn.

John righted a tricycle overturned on the steps and rang the chimes.

"Hey," whispered Nickname, "some *kid* lives here."

"Kee-rect. And his name is you."

A little peephole opened in the door. "Whattayawant?"

"Say 'I'm home, Mom,'" whispered John.

"But I don't *live* here, Jawn!"

"That don't matter. *Say* it. It's like 'Joe sent me,' that's all."

"Awww—" But into the peephole, Nickname said, "Okay —I'm home."

"'*Mom*'" said Johnny Baal.

"Okay! 'Mom,'" whispered Nickname, and the door swung open just as doors do when the magic words are spoken in fairy tales—and there was a woman looking nothing at all like what Nickname had had in mind. She wore no rouge, smoked no cigarettes, leered no leers. Oh, she was pretty enough, he supposed, and young too—but what the hell was she doing in a blue apron with yellow flowers on it? And holding an infant in her arms!

Instead of winking, or wiggling her hips, she smiled sweetly and said, "Why, my little . . ."

"Nickname," whispered Big John.

"Nicholas?"

"Nick*name*."

"My little Nickname's home!"

"Right on the nose, cutie," said Big John.

"Oh, Nickname," she said, leaning forward to kiss his cheek, "let me just put sister to bed. Oh, you must be so hungry and tired from playing all day with your friends! How you must need your little bath!"

Nickname made a face. "I just had a shower," he said to John. "Down the stadium."

"Well, now you're goin' to get a nice, warm soapy bath."

"Awww, Jawn!"

"Come, darling," said the woman and she turned and started up to the second floor, crooning to the tot in her arms as she mounted the stairs.

"Is she the one we do it to?" whispered Nickname.

"Nope," said Big John, leading the boy over the threshold. "She's the one what does it to you."

"Does *what?* And why's she got to have her baby here, in a place like this?"

"And what's wrong with this place, *niño?* This here is as cozy as you can get."

Sure enough, he could not complain about the accommodations. They were standing in a living room that had two big easy chairs pulled up to the fireplace, a sofa covered in chintz and plump with pillows, and hanging on every wall paintings of bowls of flowers. There was also a playpen in the center of the large round hooked rug. Stepping easily over the bars, Big John sat down among the stuffed animals. "Take your choice," he said, holding an animal in either hand, "the panda or the quack-quack? Well, what are you waitin' for, Nickname? Hop in, *muchacho.*"

"Come on, Jawn. I ain't fourteen months—I'm fourteen *years.* I'm a big leaguer!"

"Hey—a rattle! Ketch!"

"But I'm second-baseman for the Ruppert Mundys!"

"And here's a little fire engine, all painted red! Ding-a-ling! Make way, here comes the fire department!"

"Aww, Jawn, you're makin' fun of me, I think."

"Hey, here she comes—now get in here, you!"

Reluctantly Nickname obeyed. He'd rather be in there with John than out on the rug with the woman with the apron and the apron strings.

"Ah, there's my darling little boy!" she chirped. "There's my . . ."

"Nickname," announced Nickname. "Nickname Damur, second-baseman, lady, for the Ruppert Mundys. In case you ain't heard."

"And all ready for his bath too, my little second-baseman!" Lovingly, she extended her two bare arms over the side of the playpen. "Come now, darling. Mommy's going to clean you and oil you, and then she's going to put you in your nice jammies and feed you and read to you and put you to beddy-bye—isn't that going to be fun?"

Nickname cocked his right arm. "Watch it, lady, I wouldn't come no closer with that kind a' talk!"

"*Bastante,* you little bastard," said John, "all she wants to do is take *care* of you. All she wants to do is give you all the comforts of *home.* Ain't this what all you big leaguers is pissin' and moanin' about? Ain't this what all that clubhouse croakin' is about? Now cut the shit, Nickname, this here is costin' me fifteen smackers! You know what I could get for that kind of dough in this town? Three different redhot nigger gals all at the same time!"

"Let's go get 'em then, John—let's get 'em, and split 'em!"

"You kiddin' me, *niño?* I'm talkin' about jungle pussy, boy, what's got fire in her belly! Now you just travel up them stairs, sonny—and do as your momma says. Go on, go on—here's your little quack-quack. Now git!"

So the second-baseman climbed out of the playpen and balefully followed his "mom" up to a bathroom whose wall-paper was a gay design of clowns and trumpets. There he was undressed and bathed, toweled down, powdered, diapered, and encased in a pair of pale-blue Doctor Dentons, with booties to cover his feet. Though he had long dreamed of being naked with a woman, all he felt while she kneeled on the floor beside the tub and cleaned the insides of his ears, was a desire to knock her down and run. And it didn't help any having Big John in the doorway making wisecracks, and reaching out with his toe to lift her dress and admire her behind.

"Now," said the "mom," "for your little hot dog."

"Hey, that there looks like fun!" roared John, as she soaped between Nickname's legs.

"Only it *ain't*," moaned the humiliated big leaguer.

After his bath came dinner of pea soup and applesauce, spoon-fed him by his "mom"—"Awwww, John!" "Eat it, Nickname—it's costin' fifteen smackers!"—and then he was released from his high chair and led up by the hand to his room, where she read to him the story of Little Red Riding Hood ("What a big pair you got too, Momma!" kibitzed Big John from the doorway) and finally she kissed him good night. "Go to sleep now, baby. It's way past your bedtime," she whispered, tucking the blanket in around his shoulders.

"Hey, Johnny!" cried Nickname from his enormous crib, "it's still light out! It ain't even eight! Enough joke is enough!"

Oh, that amused John greatly too. "Hey," he said to the "mom," "better sing him a lullaby, too."

She looked at her watch. "That'll be à la carte."

"Oh yeah? Since when?"

"It's either a lullaby or a story, Mac—not both."

"At fifteen smackers?"

"I don't make the rules around here, bud. I'm only a working girl. For fifteen dollars you get a Caucasian mother, patient and loving, but without the extras."

"Yeah? And since when is singin' a lullaby to a baby 'a extra'?"

"Look, there's a war on, in case you haven't heard. What with servicemen coming through on their way to the front, we're at it round the clock. Overtime, doubletime—you name it, we're workin' it. I can give you 'Rock-a-Bye-Baby' for ninety-eight cents, but that's the cheapest we got."

"Ninety-eight cents for 'Rock-a-Bye-Baby'? You know what I can get for ninety-eight cents down by the lake?"

"That's your business, Mac, I'm only tellin' you what we got here at the C."

"Where's Estelle?" said Big John.

"Down the office, I suppose."

"You wait here, Nickname! We're goin' to find out about this here war-profiteerin'!"

And Big John was down the stairs and gone. Despite the

vehemence with which he had spoken to her, the woman seemed quite unperturbed; she extracted a pack of cigarettes from her apron, and offered one to Nickname.

"Smoke?" she said.

"Nope. I just chaw."

"Mind if I do?"

"Nope."

"Okay," she said, "take five, pal," and stepping to the window, lit a cigarette; she expelled the smoke with a long weary sigh.

"Look," said Nickname, "I don't need no lullaby, you know."

"Sure, I know," she said, laughing softly. "That's what they all tell me. The next morning they come down all spiffed up and shaved and Aqua Velvaed, and they say, 'You know, I didn't need the light on all night. I didn't need that glass of water, really. I didn't need to wet the bed, I didn't need to fill my diaper three times over'—but it's me who has to change 'em, see, irregardless of what they *really* needed. It's me who has to be up and down the stairs all night long, holding their hand when they wake up from a bad dream. It's me who has to be the nurse when they get a little tummy ache at 2 A.M. and cry like they're going to die. I don't know—maybe it's the war, but I've never seen such colic in my life. See, I used to work the day shift around here. Put 'em in the stroller, wheel 'em around to the park, give 'em a nap, a bottle, play patty-cake, and that was it, more or less. Oh, sure, they act up in the sandbox and comes four o'clock they start whining out of the blue, but believe me, it's nothing like this all-night-long business. Turn the light on. Turn the light off. Hold my hand. Sit over here. Don't go away. I got a pain in my nose. I got a pain in my finger. And on it goes, and I'm telling you, you begin to say to yourself, 'Honey, there's just got to be a better way to earn a living than this.' Sure, the tips are good and I don't have to bother with Internal Revenue, and I get to meet some pretty important people—but, let's face it, I can work the swing shift in a war plant and not do so bad either. I got kids of my own I'd like to see sometime too. You know something? I got a grandchild. You wouldn't know it to look at me, would you? Here, look here—" from the wallet she carried in her apron pocket, she extracted a small photograph. "Here, ain't he somethin'?"

The picture she handed Nickname was of a little tot dressed exactly as he was, and sitting up in a crib, though one not so large as his own.

"He's real cute," said Nickname, handing the photo back through the bars.

"Sure, he is," she said softly, looking at the photo, "but do I get a chance to enjoy him? It seems like half the naval training station was here just on Sunday alone."

"If you're a grandmother," asked Nickname, "how come —if you don't mind my askin'—how come you look so young?"

"I *used* to think it was because I was lucky. Now I'm starting to wonder. Look, look at these legs." She lifted her dress a ways. "Look at these thighs. I used to think they were some kind of blessing. Here, put your hand out here. Feel this." She placed her buttocks against the bars of the crib. "Feel how nice and firm that is. And look at my face—not a wrinkle anywhere. Not a gray hair on my head. And that isn't from the beauty parlor either. That's natural. I just do not age. Know what Estelle calls me? 'The Eternal Mom.' 'How can you quit, Mary?' she says to me, 'How can you go off and work in a factory, looking the way you do, and with your touch. With your patience. Why, I just won't have it.' Where's my loyalty, she asks me. Oh, I like that. Where's my loyalty to the wonderful people who come here to spit pea soup in my face? And what about the boys going off to war—how can I be so unpatriotic? So I stay, Nickname. Don't ask me why. Cleaning the mess out of the diaper of just about everybody and anybody who has fifteen bucks in his pocket and is out looking for a good time. Oh, there are nights when I've got applesauce running out of my ears, nights when they practically drown me in the tub—and I haven't even talked about the throwin' up. Oh, there's just nothing that's out-and-out disgusting, that they don't do it. Sometimes I say to myself, 'Face it, honey, you are just a mother at heart. Because if you weren't you would have been out of this life long ago.'"

When the trouble began down in the street, Nickname's "mother" motioned him over to the window to take a look. "Well," she said, in her unruffled way, "looks like your buddy is going to get it now."

Nickname crawled over the side of the crib and padded to her side. On the front walk, within the glow of the carriage lamp that had been turned up on the lawn, Big John was talking heatedly to two men in white uniforms who appeared to have stepped from a laundry truck parked at the curb; across the side of the truck it said,

C. OF C. DIAPER SERVICE
KAKOOLA

"Who are those guys?" Nickname asked.

"Oh," said Mary, with her soft laugh, "don't be fooled by the name. Those two don't happen to take any crap."

The three men entered the house. "Hey, Nickname!" Big John called up the stairs. "Come on! Put your jock on, *niño!* We're gettin' out of this clipjoint!"

"Whattaya say now, fella, this ain't a barroom," cautioned one of the diapermen. "It's a comfortable middle-class home in a nice neighborhood where people know how to behave themselves. If they know what's good for 'em, anyway."

"It's a racket, is what it is!" John said to the diaperman. "Fifteen bucks and he don't even got a piece of hamburger meat! You probably cut the pablum with water!"

"You're *supposed* to cut pablum with water, wiseguy. Now just quiet down, how about it? Maybe there are people tryin' to sleep around here, you know?"

Nickname by now had made his way to the head of the stairs. "Hi, Jawn . . . What's up?"

"Let's git, *niño.*"

"How come?" asked Nickname, nervously.

"How come? On accounta what they get around here for '*Alouette,*' that's how come!"

"What's an al-oo-etta?"

"It is a French song, that's all it is, keed—and it'll cost you two dollars and fifty cents! Know what they get for 'Happy Birthday'? Four dollars weekdays and five on Sundays! For 'Happy Birthday to You'!"

"Well," said Nickname, watching the two diapermen closing in on his protector, "it ain't my birthday anyhow—I already had it for this year."

"It ain't the birthday, damn it—it's the principle! You

know what you can get for four bucks down by the lake? I hate
to tell you. You know what you can get for two-fifty? You don't
get no French song—you get Frenched itself! Come on, tweak
your mom on the tittie, and let's get out of here!"

Nickname shrugged. "I guess we're goin' now," he said to
Mary.

"Suits me. I been up since four. That'll be fifteen."

Nickname looked down the stairway to Big John. "Jawn?
It'll be fifteen."

"Yeah, well, you tell her it'll be five, what with it bein'
not even nine in the night."

"Sorry, Mac," said Mary. "Fifteen."

Big John said, "Five, slit," and reaching into his pocket
for some change, added, "but here's two bits for yourself, for
givin' us a glimpse of your can. Haw! Haw!"

One of the diapermen was beneath Big John, pinned to the
floor of the playpen—an alphabet block stuffed in his mouth—
and the other was preparing to bring the fire truck down on
the first baseman's head, when the sirens came screaming into the street. "The cops!" cried the diaperman who
could still speak, and he ran for the kitchen door—and there
was a Kakoola policeman pointing a pistol.

"Pimp bastard," said the officer, and fired into the air.

Immediately, from the windows of the little white houses,
men began to leap out onto the lawns, men in diapers and
Doctor Dentons, some still holding bottles and clutching blankets in their hands. Nickname and Big John, charging out
through the front door, found themselves on the front lawn
beside a man in combat boots and a crew cut, clinging to a teddy
bear; apparently he had been in another bedroom of the same
house. "The Japs or the cops," he screamed, "which is it?"

"Haw! Haw!"

Now a squad car turned up off the street and came right at
them there on the lawn, siren howling and searchlight a blind-
ing white. The man with the teddy bear (a sergeant in the U.S.
Marines according to the story in the morning paper about the
raid on "the pink-'n-blue district") broke for the backyard.
Zing, and he fell over into a forsythia bush, his teddy bear
still in his arms.

They came out with their hands in the air after that; some

were in tears and tried to hide their faces with their upraised arms. "Cry babies," mumbled a cop, and he beat them around the ankles with his nightstick as they stepped up into the police van one by one.

Meanwhile, they had begun to empty the houses of the "mothers." Storybooks in hand, they filed out, women more or less resembling Mary, wearing aprons and cotton dresses, and all, it would seem, very much in possession of themselves. They were lined up in the crossbeams of the squad cars and frisked by a policewoman; standing together in the street, they looked as though they might have been called together to give the neighborhood endorsement for 20 Mule Team Borax, rather than to be charged with a crime of vice.

When the policewoman reached into Mary's apron pocket and withdrew a handful of diaper pins, she exploded—"You and your diapers and your diaper pins and your diaper service! Filth! You live in filth! You're a disgrace to your sex!"

"Lay off," said the cop who was covering the "mothers" with a submachine gun.

"Shit and puke and piss! Just get a whiff of them!"

"Lay off, Sarge," said the armed policeman.

But she couldn't. "You perverts make a person sick, you stink so bad!" And she spat in Mary's face, to show her contempt.

The "mothers" stood in the middle of Euphrates Drive listening with expressionless faces to the insults of the policewoman. A few like Mary had to laugh to themselves, however, for nothing the policewoman said could begin to approach the contempt that they felt for their own lives.

Nor did the "mothers" show any emotion when the diapermen, many of them badly beaten and covered with blood, were driven past them with nightsticks, and pushed on their faces into the police van. Only when the body of the dead customer with the teddy bear was carried to the ambulance— diapered down below, and above now too, where they had covered the fatal wound in his head—only then did one of them speak. It was the woman who had fed him that night. "He was just a boy," she said—to which a policeman replied, "Yeah, and so is Hitler."

"I wouldn't doubt it," the "mother" answered, and for her

cheekiness was removed from the line and taken by two policemen into the back of a squad car. "What do you want to hear,
officers," she asked as they led her away, "the Three Bears
or—"

"Shut her up!" shouted the policewoman, and they did.

The van for the "mothers" was over an hour in arriving;
it grew cold out in the street, and though the abuse from the
policewoman grew more and more vile, the "mothers" never
once complained.

Now because of the proximity of "the hog factory" to the
ball park, playing against the Butchers in the Pork Capital of
the World had never been considered a particularly savory experience by Patriot League players, and it was a long-standing
joke among them that they would rather be back home cleaning
out cesspools for a living than have to call Aceldama their
home on a sultry August day. Of course, one full season at
Butcher Field and a newcomer was generally as accustomed to
the aromas wafting in from the abattoir as to the odors of the
hot dogs cooking on the grill back of third. Only the visiting
teams kept up their complaining year in and year out, and not
so much because of the smell, as the sounds. Visiting rookies
would invariably give a start at the noise that came from a
pig having his throat slit just the other side of the left-field
wall, and when a thousand of the terrified beasts started in
screaming at the same time, it was not unheard of for a youngster in pursuit of a fly ball to fall cowering to his knees.

In '43, the Mundys had to come through Aceldama to play
not just eleven, but twenty-two games, and from the record
they made there that year, it would not appear that playing
twice as many times in Butcher Field as each of the other six
clubs did much to accustom them to the nearby slaughterhouse
and processing plant. "Lose to this mess of misfits," the
Butcher manager, Round Ron Spam, had warned his team
when the Mundys—fresh from their disasters in Kakoola—
came to town to open their first four-game series of the year,
"and it is worse than a loss. It is a disgrace. And it will cost
you fifty bucks apiece. And I don't want just victory either—
I want carnage." Subsequently the Bloodthirsty Butchers, as

they came to be called that year, went on to defeat the Mundys
twenty-two consecutive times, yet another of the records compiled against (or by) the roaming Ruppert team. The headlines
of the Aceldama *Terminator* told the story succinctly enough:

MUNDYS MAULED
MUNDYS MALLETTED
MUNDYS MUZZLED
MUNDYS MURDERED
MUNDYS MOCKED
MUNDYS MINED
MUNDYS MOWED DOWN
MUNDYS MESMERIZED
MUNDYS MORGUED
MUNDYS MANGLED
MUNDYS MASHED
MUNDYS MUTILATED
MUNDYS MANHANDLED
MUNDYS MAUSOLEUMED
MUNDYS MACK-TRUCKED
MUNDYS MELTED
MUNDYS MAROONED
MUNDYS MUMMIFIED
MUNDYS MORTIFIED
MUNDYS MASSACRED
MUNDYS MANACLED

—and, after the final game of the season between the two
clubs, in which "the meat end," so-called, of the Aceldama
batting order hit five consecutive home runs in the bottom of
the eighth—

MUNDYS MERCY-KILLED

From Aceldama, which was the third stop on the western
swing after Asylum and Kakoola, the Mundys traveled overnight to the oldest Pony Express station in the Wild West and
the furthest western outpost in any of the major leagues, Terra
Incognita, Wyoming, there to play against the least hospitable
crowd they had to put up with anywhere. No wonder Luke
Gofannon had collapsed and called it quits in the middle of his
first season as a Rustler. After twenty years as the hero of

Rupe-it rootas—loving, tender, loyal, impassioned Rupe-it rootas!—how could he take those Terra Inc. fans in their bandannas and their undershirts, staring silently down at him in that open oven of a ball park? To be sure, in Luke's case, their silence had been punctuated with derisive insults and chilling coyote calls from the distant bleachers, but what nearly drove you nuts out there wasn't the noises, no matter how brutish, but that otherworldly quiet, that emptiness, and that *staring:* the miners, the farmers, the ranchers, the cow-hands, the drifters, even the Indians packed into their little roped-off corner of the left-field stands, silent and staring. Or maybe the word is *glaring.* As though there was nothing more horrible to behold than these Mundys, a bunch of ballplayers who came from, of all places, *nowhere.*

Then there was this matter of the late, great Gofannon— fans out there hadn't forgotten yet the fast one that had been put over on them back in '32. Oh, you could see it plain as day in the set of the jaw of those Indians: a time would come when they would take their vengeance on these white men who had sold them a lemon for a hundred thousand dollars. As though Hothead, or Bud, or the Deacon had made a single nickel off that deal! As though these poor homeless bastards had any-thing to do with what had happened to the people of Terra Incognita ten long years ago! No, it was not pleasant being a Ruppert Mundy in the far western reaches of America. If the white ball emerging out of the acre of white undershirts in deep center wasn't enough to terrify a batsman who was a stranger to these parts, there were those cold, contemptuous, vengeful eyes looking him over from the seats down both foul lines. How they drew a bead on you with those eyes! Why, you had only to scoop up a handful of dust before stepping into the box, for those eyes to tell you, in no uncertain terms, "That there dirt ain't yours—it's ours. Put it back where you got it, pardner." And if you were a Ruppert Mundy and the year was 1943, you put it back all right, and pronto.

And then the long, long train ride back to the East, "the eastern swing" as it was called by the four western clubs, and by the Mundys too, though always self-consciously, for they were hardly a western club in anybody's eyes, including their own. But then strictly speaking they weren't an eastern club anymore either, even if on those eastward journeys, when they turned their watches ahead, the rapid sweep of the minute hand around the dial encouraged them to imagine the present over and done with, and the future, the return to Ruppert, upon them.

Independence, Virginia, where tourists surge through cobbled streets, and taxi drivers wear buckled shoes and powdered wigs, and in the restaurants the prices are listed in shillings and pence; where busloads of schoolkids line up next to the pillory in the town square to have their photo taken being punished, and a town crier appears in the streets at nine every night to shut the place down in accordance with the famous "Blue Laws" after which the baseball team is named. Talk about a place where they make a grown man feel welcome, and you are not talking about Independence, Virginia . . .

And then the worst of it, the coastal journey north from Independence to Tri-City, passing through Port Ruppert on the way . . .

Port Ruppert? Looked more like the Maginot Line. Soldiers everywhere. Two of them, fine-looking young fellows in gleaming boots and wearing pistols, hopped aboard the engine as it slowed in the railroad yard, awaiting clearance to enter the station. Guards in steel helmets and bearing arms stood some fifty feet apart all the way along the tracks, while still other soldiers, in shirt sleeves and blowing on whistles, directed empty flatcars into the roundhouse and back out onto the broad network of tracks. Where were the hobos who used to squat on their haunches cooking a potato at the track's edge, the bums who used to smile their toothless smiles up at the Mundys when they returned from the road? Where were the old signalmen who used to raise their lanterns in salute, and, win or loss, call out, "Welcome home, boys! You done okay!" Where, where were their hundred thousand loyal fans?

"Haven't you heard?" the Mundys chided themselves, "there's a war on."

With a gush from the train (and a sigh from the Mundys), they glided the last hundred yards into the station. "Rupe-it! Station Rupe-it!" the conductor called, and though many disembarked, nobody who played for the team of that name left his seat.

Rupe-it. Oh, how could something so silly as the way they pronounced those two syllables give you the gooseflesh? Two little syllables, Rupe and It, how could they give you the chills?

Hey, listen! They were announcing the arrival of their train in *four* different languages. Listen! English, French, Russian—and *Chinese!* In Rupe-it! And catch them faces? And all them uniforms! Why, you did not think there could *be* so many shades of khaki! Or kinds of hats! Or belts! Or salutes! Or shades of skin, for that matter! Why, there was a bunch of soldier boys wearing *earrings,* for Christ sake! Where the hell are they from—and how come they're on our side, anyway? Damn, who they gonna scare, dressin' up like that! Hey, am I seein' things or is that there big coon talkin' to that other coon in French? Hey, Ass-Start, is them niggers parlayvooin' French? Wee-wee? Hey, Frenchy's cousins is in town, haw haw! Hey—ain't those things Chinks? Yeah? And I thought they was supposed to walk in them little steps! I'll be darned—I never seen so many of 'em at the same time before. Kinda like a dream, ain't it? Hey—lookee there at them beards on *them* boys! Now where you figger those fellers hail from? Eskimos? In this heat? They would be leakin' at the seams, they would be dead. Zanzeebar? Never heard of 'em. And now what do you think them tiny little guys is? Some kind of wop looks like to me, only smaller. And now dang if that ain't some other kind of Chink altogether—over there! Unless it's their Navy! Christ, the Chinee Navy! I didn't even know they had one. And in Rupe-it!

Now the two soldiers who had leaped aboard in the yard came through each car checking the papers of all the service personnel. Because of the crowding the Mundys were huddled together now, three to a seat, in the last car of the train. "You fellas all flat-footed?" the soldier quipped, looking around at the bald pates of the pitching staff. He smiled. "Or are you enemy spies?"

"We are ballplayers, Corporal," said Jolly Cholly. "We are the Ruppert Mundys."

"I'll be darned," the young corporal retorted.

"We are on our way to play four games against the Tycoons up in Tri-City."

"I don't believe it," said the corporal. "The Mundys!"

"Right you are," said Jolly Cholly.

"And you know what I took you for?" said the corporal.

"What's that?"

"All squished up there, looking out the windows with them looks on your faces? I took you for a bunch of war-torn immigrants, just off the boat. I took you for somebody we just saved."

"Nope," said Jolly Cholly, "we ain't off no boat. We're from here. Matter of fact," he added, peering out the window, "probably the only folks in sight that is."

"I'll be darned," said the corporal. "Do you know, when I was just a little boy—"

But no sooner had he begun to reminisce, than the train was moving. "Uh-oh. See ya!" the corporal called, and in a flash he was gone. And so was Rupe-it.

Ballplayers' ballplayers—that was the phrase most commonly used to describe the Tycoon teams that in the first four decades of the twentieth century won eighteen pennants, eight World Series, and never once finished out of the first division. "Play," though, is hardly the word to describe what they were about down on the field. Leaving the heroics to others, without ferocity or even exertion, they concentrated on doing only what was required of them to win, neither more nor less: no whooping, no hollering, no guesswork, no gambling, no elation, no despair, nothing extreme or eccentric. Rather, efficiency, intelligence, proportion—four runs for the pitcher who needed the security, two for the pitcher who liked the pressure, one in the ninth for him who rose only to the challenge. You rarely heard of the Tycoons breaking out, as teams will on occasion, with fifteen or twenty hits, or winning by ten or eleven runs; just as rarely did you hear of them committing three errors in a game, or leaving a dozen men stranded on base, or falling, either individually or as a team, into a slump that a day's rest couldn't cure. Though they may not always have been the most gifted or spectacular players in the league considered one at a time, together they performed like nine men hatched from the same perfect egg.

Of course the fans who hated them—and they were legion, particularly out in the West—labeled them "robots," "zombies," and even "snobs" because of their emotionless, machine-like manner. Out-of-town fans would jeer at them, insult and abuse them, do everything they could think of to try to rattle them—and watched with awe and envy the quietly flawless, tactful, economical, virtually invisible way in which the Tycoons displayed their superiority year in and year out.

Afterwards it was not always clear how exactly they had done it. "Where was we when it happened?" was a line made famous by a Rustler who did not even know his team had been soundly beaten until he looked up at the end of the ninth and read the sad news off the scoreboard. "They ain't human," the other players complained, "they ain't all there," but out of their uniforms and in street clothes, the Tycoons turned out to be fellows more or less resembling themselves, if a little better dressed and smoother in conversation. "But they ain't that *good!*" the fans would cry, after the Tycoons had come through to sweep a four-game series—and yet there never did appear to be anybody that was better. "They *steal* them games! They take 'em while nobody's lookin'!" "It's that park of theirs, that's what kills us—that sunfield and all them shadows!" "The way they does it, they can win all they want, and I still ain't got no use for 'em! I wouldn't be a Tycoon fan if you paid me!" But the even-tempered Tycoons couldn't have cared less.

By '43, the Tycoons had lost just about every last member of the '41 and '42 pennant-winning teams to the Army, but to take their place for the duration, the Tri-City owner, Mrs. Angela Trust, had been able to coax out of retirement the world championship Tycoon team that in the '31 World Series against Connie Mack's A's had beaten Lefty Grove, Waite Hoyt, and Rube Walberg on three successive afternoons. To see those wonderful old-timers back in Tycoon uniforms, wearing the numerals each had made famous during the great baseball era that preceded the Depression, did much to assure baseball fans that the great days they dimly remembered really had been, and would be again, once the enemies of democracy were destroyed; the effect upon the visiting Mundys,

however, was not so salutary. After having traveled on that
train through a Port Ruppert station aswarm with foreigners
of every color and stripe, after having been taken for strangers in the city whose name they bore, it was really more than
the Mundys could bear, to hear the loudspeaker announce the
names of the players against whom they were supposed to
compete that afternoon. "Pinch me, I'm dreamin' again,"
said Kid Heket. "Why not raise up the dead," cried Hothead,
"so we can play a series against the Hall of Fame!" "It must
be a joke," the pitchers agreed. Only it wasn't. Funny perhaps
to others—as so much was that year—but, alas, no joke for
the Ruppert team. "For Tri-City, batting first, No. 12, Johnny
Leshy, third base. Batting second, No. 11, Lou Polevik, left
field. Batting third, No. 1, Tommy Heimdall, right field. Batting fourth, No. 14, Iron Mike Mazda, first base. Batting fifth,
No. 6, Vic Bragi, center field. Batting sixth, No. 2, Babe
Rustem, shortstop. Batting seventh, No. 19, Tony Izanagi,
second base. Batting eighth and catching for Tri-City, No. 4,
Al Rongo . . ."

By the time the announcer had gotten to the Tycoons'
starting pitcher, the Mundys would have passed from bewilderment through disbelief to giddiness—all on the long hard
road to resignation. "Oh yeah, and who's the pitcher? Who is
pitching the series against us—the Four Horsemen, I suppose."

They supposed right. They were to face the four Tycoon
starters who had performed in rotation with such regularity
and such success for over a decade, that eventually the sportswriter Smitty humorously suggested in "An Open Letter to
the United States Congress" that they ought to call the days
of the week after Sal Tuisto, Smoky Woden, Phil Thor, and
Herman Frigg. By '42, Tuisto owned Tri-City's most popular
seafood house, Woden was the baseball coach at the nearby Ivy
League college, Thor was a bowling alley impresario, and
Frigg a Ford dealer; nonetheless, despite all those years that
had elapsed since the four had been big leaguers, against the
Mundys in the first series played between the two clubs in
Tycoon Park that year, each threw the second no-hitter of
his career—four consecutive hitless games, a record of course

for four pitchers on the same team . . . But then that was only the beginning of the records broken in that series, which itself broke the record for breaking records.*

One sunny Saturday morning early in August, the Ruppert Mundys boarded a bus belonging to the mental institution and journeyed from their hotel in downtown Asylum out into the green Ohio countryside to the world-famous hospital for the insane, there to play yet another "away" game—a three-inning exhibition match against a team composed entirely of patients. The August visit to the hospital by a P. League team in town for a series against the Keepers was an annual event of great moment at the institution, and one that was believed to be of considerable therapeutic value to the inmates, particularly the sports-minded among them. Not only was it their chance to make contact, if only for an hour or so, with the real world they had left behind, but it was believed that even so brief a visit by famous big league ballplayers went a long way to assuage the awful sense such people have that they are odious and contemptible to the rest of humankind. Of course the P. League players (who like all ballplayers despised any exhibition games during the course of the regular season) happened to find playing against the Lunatics, as they called them, a most odious business indeed; but as the General simply would not hear of abandoning a practice that brought public attention to the humane and compassionate side of a league that many still associated with violence and scandal, the tradition was maintained year after year, much to the delight of the insane, and the disgust of the ballplayers themselves.

*Some all-time records made by the '43 Mundys:
Most games lost in a season—120
Most times defeated in no-hitters in a season—6
Most times defeated in consecutive no-hitters in a season—4
Most triple plays hit into in one game—2
Most triple plays hit into in a season—5
Most errors committed by a team—302
Worst earned-run average for pitching staff—8.06
Most walks by a pitching staff—872
Most wild pitches by staff in an inning—8
Most wild pitches by staff in a game—14

The chief psychiatrist at the hospital was a Dr. Traum, a heavyset gentleman with a dark chin beard, and a pronounced European accent. Until his arrival in America in the thirties, he had never even heard of baseball, but in that Asylum was the site of a major league ball park, as well as a psychiatric hospital, it was not long before the doctor became something of a student of the game. After all, one whose professional life involved ruminating upon the extremes of human behavior, had certainly to sit up and take notice when a local fan decided to make his home atop a flagpole until the Keepers snapped a losing streak, or when an Asylum man beat his wife to death with a hammer for calling the Keepers "bums" just like himself. If the doctor did not, strictly speaking, become an ardent Keeper fan, he did make it his business to read thoroughly in the literature of the national pastime, with the result that over the years more than one P. League manager had to compliment the bearded Berliner on his use of the hit-and-run, and the uncanny ability he displayed at stealing signals during their annual exhibition game.

Despite the managerial skill that Dr. Traum had developed over the years through his studies, his team proved no match for the Mundys that morning. By August of 1943, the Mundys weren't about to sit back and take it on the chin from a German-born baseball manager and a team of madmen; they had been defeated and disgraced and disgraced and defeated up and down the league since the season had begun back in April, and it was as though on the morning they got out to the insane asylum grounds, all the wrath that had been seething in them for months now burst forth, and nothing, but nothing, could have prevented them from grinding the Lunatics into dust once the possibility for victory presented itself. Suddenly, those '43 flops started looking and sounding like the scrappy, hustling, undefeatable Ruppert teams of Luke Gofannon's day—and this despite the fact that it took nearly an hour to complete a single inning, what with numerous delays and interruptions caused by the Lunatics' style of play. Hardly a moment passed that something did not occur to offend the professional dignity of a big leaguer, and yet, through it all, the Mundys on both offense and defense managed to seize hold of every Lunatic mistake and convert it to

their advantage. Admittedly, the big right-hander who started
for the institution team was fast and savvy enough to hold the
Mundy power in check, but playing just the sort of heads-up,
razzle-dazzle baseball that used to characterize the Mundy
teams of yore, they were able in their first at bat to put together a scratch hit by Astarte, a bunt by Nickname, a base
on balls to Big John, and two Lunatic errors, to score three
runs—their biggest inning of the year, and the first Mundy
runs to cross the plate in sixty consecutive innings, which was
not a record only because they had gone sixty-seven innings
without scoring earlier in the season.

When Roland Agni, of all people, took a called third strike
to end their half of the inning, the Mundys rushed off the
bench like a team that smelled World Series loot. "We was
due!" yelped Nickname, taking the peg from Hothead and
sweeping his glove over the bag—"Nobody gonna stop us now,
babe! We was due! We was *over*due!" Then he winged the
ball over to where Deacon Demeter stood on the mound, grinning. "Three big ones for you, Deke!" Old Deacon, the fifty-
year-old iron-man starter of the Mundy staff, already a
twenty-game loser with two months of the season still to go,
shot a string of tobacco juice over his left shoulder to ward off
evil spirits, stroked the rabbit's foot that hung on a chain
around his neck, closed his eyes to mumble something ending
with "Amen," and then stepped up on the rubber to face the
first patient. Deacon was a preacher back home, as gentle and
kindly a man as you would ever want to bring your problems
to, but up on the hill he was all competitor, and had been for
thirty years now. "When the game begins," he used to say
back in his heyday, "charity ends." And so it was that when he
saw the first Lunatic batter digging in as though he owned the
batter's box, the Deke decided to take Hothead's advice and
stick the first pitch in his ear, just to show the little nut who
was boss. The Deacon had taken enough insults that year for
a fifty-year-old man of the cloth!

Not only did the Deke's pitch cause the batter to go flying
back from the plate to save his skin, but next thing everyone
knew the lead-off man was running for the big brick building
with the iron bars on its windows. Two of his teammates
caught him down the right-field line and with the help of the

Lunatic bullpen staff managed to drag him back to home plate.
But once there they couldn't get him to take hold of the bat;
every time they put it into his hands, he let it fall through to
the ground. By the time the game was resumed, with a 1 and 0
count on a new lead-off hitter, one not quite so cocky as the
fellow who'd stepped up to bat some ten minutes earlier, there
was no doubt in anyone's mind that the Deke was in charge.
As it turned out, twice in the inning Mike Rama had to go
sailing up into the wall to haul in a long line drive, but as the
wall was padded, Mike came away unscathed, and the Deacon
was back on the bench with his three-run lead intact.

"We're on our way!" cried Nickname. "We are on our
God damn way!"

Hothead too was dancing with excitement; cupping his
hands to his mouth, he shouted across to the opposition, "Just
watch you bastards go to pieces now!"

And so they did. The Deke's pitching and Mike's fielding
seemed to have shaken the confidence of the big Lunatic right-
hander whose fastball had reined in the Mundys in the first. To
the chagrin of his teammates, he simply would not begin to
pitch in the second until the umpire stopped staring at him.

"Oh, come on," said the Lunatic catcher, "he's not staring
at *you*. Throw the ball."

"I tell you, he's right behind you and he is too staring.
Look you, I see you there behind that mask. What is it you
want from me? What is it you think you're looking at, anyway?"

The male nurse, in white half-sleeve shirt and white trousers, who was acting as the plate umpire, called out to the
mound, "Play ball now. Enough of that."

"Not until you come out from there."

"Oh, pitch, for Christ sake," said the catcher.

"Not until that person stops staring."

Here Dr. Traum came off the Lunatic bench and started
for the field, while down in the Lunatic bullpen a left-hander
got up and began to throw. Out on the mound, with his hands
clasped behind his back and rocking gently to and fro on his
spikes, the doctor conferred with the pitcher. Formal European that he was, he wore, along with his regulation baseball
shoes, a dark three-piece business suit, a stiff collar, and a tie.

"What do you think the ol' doc's tellin' that boy?" Bud Parusha asked Jolly Cholly.

"Oh, the usual," the old-timer said. "He's just calmin' him down. He's just askin' if he got any good duck shootin' last season."

It was five full minutes before the conference between the doctor and the pitcher came to an end with the doctor asking the pitcher to hand over the ball. When the pitcher vehemently refused, it was necessary for the doctor to snatch the ball out of his hand; but when he motioned down to the bullpen for the left-hander, the pitcher suddenly reached out and snatched the ball back. Here the doctor turned back to the bullpen and this time motioned for the left-hander *and* a right-hander. Out of the bullpen came two men dressed like the plate umpire in white half-sleeve shirts and white trousers. While they took the long walk to the mound, the doctor made several unsuccessful attempts to talk the pitcher into relinquishing the ball. Finally the two men arrived on the mound and before the pitcher knew what had happened, they had unfurled a straitjacket and wrapped it around him.

"Guess he wanted to stay in," said Jolly Cholly, as the pitcher kicked out at the doctor with his feet.

The hundred Lunatic fans who had gathered to watch the game from the benches back of the foul screen behind home plate, and who looked in their street clothes as sane as any baseball crowd, rose to applaud the pitcher as he left the field, but when he opened his mouth to acknowledge the ovation, the two men assisting him in his departure slipped a gag over his mouth.

Next the shortstop began to act up. In the first inning it was he who had gotten the Lunatics out of trouble with a diving stab of a Bud Parusha liner and a quick underhand toss that had doubled Wayne Heket off third. But now in the top of the second, though he continued to gobble up everything hit to the left of the diamond, as soon as he got his hands on the ball he proceeded to stuff it into his back pocket. Then, assuming a posture of utter nonchalance, he would start whistling between his teeth and scratching himself, as though waiting for the action to *begin*. In that it was already very much underway, the rest of the Lunatic infield would begin screaming at

him to take the ball out of his pocket and make the throw to
first. "What?" he responded, with an innocent smile. "The
ball!" they cried. "Yes, what about it?" "Throw it!" "But I
don't have it." "You *do!*" they would scream, converging
upon him from all points of the infield, "You do too!" "Hey,
leave me alone," the shortstop cried, as they grabbed and
pulled at his trousers. "Hey, cut that out—get your hands *out*
of there!" And when at last the ball was extracted from where
he himself had secreted it, no one could have been more surprised. "Hey, the *ball.* Now who put that there? Well, what's
everybody looking at *me* for? Look, this must be some guy's
idea of a joke . . . Well, Christ, *I* didn't do it."

Once the Mundys caught on, they were quick to capitalize
on this unexpected weakness in the Lunatic defense, pushing
two more runs across in the second on two consecutive ground
balls to short—both beaten out for hits while the shortstop
grappled with the other infielders—a sacrifice by Mike Rama,
and a fly to short center that was caught by the fielder who
then just stood there holding it in his glove, while Hothead,
who was the runner on second, tagged up and hobbled to third,
and then, wooden leg and all, broke for home, where he scored
with a head-first slide, the only kind he could negotiate. As it
turned out, the slide wasn't even necessary, for the center-
fielder was standing in the precise spot where he had made
the catch—and the ball was still in his glove.

With the bases cleared, Dr. Traum asked for time and
walked out to center. He put a hand on the shoulder of the
mute and motionless fielder and talked to him in a quiet voice.
He talked to him steadily for fifteen minutes, their faces only
inches apart. Then he stepped aside, and the center-fielder took
the ball from the pocket of his glove and threw a perfect strike
to the catcher, on his knees at the plate some two hundred feet
away.

"Wow," said Bud Parusha, with ungrudging admiration,
"now, that fella has a arm on him."

"Hothead," said Cholly, mildly chiding the catcher, "he
woulda had you by a country mile, you know, if only he'd a
throwed it."

But Hot, riding high, hollered out, "Woulda don't count,
Charles—it's dudda what counts, and I dud it!"

Meanwhile Kid Heket, who before this morning had not been awake for two consecutive innings in over a month, continued to stand with one foot up on the bench, his elbow on his knee and his chin cupped contemplatively in his palm. He had been studying the opposition like this since the game had gotten underway, "You know somethin'," he said, gesturing toward the field, "those fellas ain't thinkin'. No sir, they just ain't usin' their heads."

"We got 'em on the run, Wayne!" cried Nickname. "They don't know *what* hit 'em! Damn, ain't nobody gonna stop us from here on out!"

Deacon was hit hard in the last of the second, but fortunately for the Mundys, in the first two instances the batsman refused to relinquish the bat and move off home plate, and so each was thrown out on what would have been a base hit, right-fielder Parusha to first-baseman Baal; and the last hitter, who drove a tremendous line drive up the alley in left center, ran directly from home to third and was tagged out sitting on the bag with what he took to be a triple, and what would have been one too, had he only run around the bases and gotten to third in the prescribed way.

The quarrel between the Lunatic catcher and the relief pitcher began over what to throw Big John Baal, the lead-off hitter in the top of the third.

"Uh-uh," said the Lunatic pitcher, shaking off the first signal given by his catcher, while in the box, Big John took special pleasure in swishing the bat around menacingly.

"Nope," said the pitcher to the second signal.

His response to the third was an emphatic, "N-O!"

And to the fourth, he said, stamping one foot, "Definitely *not!*"

When he shook off a fifth signal as well, with a caustic, "Are you kidding? Throw him that and it's bye-bye ballgame," the catcher yanked off his mask and cried:

"And I suppose that's what I want, according to you! To lose! To go down in defeat! Oh, sure," the catcher whined, "what I'm doing, you see, is deliberately telling you to throw him the wrong pitch so I can have the wonderful pleasure of being on the losing team again. Oh brother!" His sarcasm spent, he donned his mask, knelt down behind the plate, and tried yet once more.

This time the pitcher had to cross his arms over his chest and look to the heavens for solace. "God give me strength," he sighed.

"In other words," the catcher screamed, "I'm wrong *again*. But then in your eyes I'm *always* wrong. Well, isn't that true? Admit it! Whatever signal I give is *bound* to be wrong. Why? Because *I'm* giving it! I'm daring to give *you* a signal! I'm daring to tell *you* how to pitch! I could kneel here signaling for the rest of my days, and you'd just stand there shaking them off and asking God to give you strength, *because I'm so wrong and so stupid and so hopeless and would rather lose than win!*"

When the relief pitcher, a rather self-possessed fellow from the look of it, though perhaps a touch perverse in his own way, refused to argue, the Lunatic catcher once again assumed his squat behind the plate, and proceeded to offer a seventh signal, an eighth, a ninth, a tenth, each and every one of which the pitcher rejected with a mild, if unmistakably disdainful, remark.

On the sixteenth signal, the pitcher just had to laugh. "Well, that one really takes the cake, doesn't it? That really took brains. Come over here a minute," he said to his infielders. "All right," he called back down to the catcher, "go ahead, show them your new brainstorm." To the four players up on the mound with him, the pitcher whispered, "Catch this," and pointed to the signal that the catcher, in his mortification, was continuing to flash from between his legs.

"Hey," said the Lunatic third-baseman, "that ain't even a finger, is it?"

"No," said the pitcher, "as a matter of fact, it isn't."

"I mean, it ain't got no nail on it, does it?"

"Indeed it has not."

"Why, I'll be darned," said the shortstop, "it's, it's his thingamajig."

"Precisely," said the pitcher.

"But what the hell is that supposed to mean?" asked the first-baseman.

The pitcher had to smile again. "What do you think? Hey, Doc," he called to the Lunatic bench, "I'm afraid my battery-mate has misunderstood what's meant by an exhibition game. He's flashing me the signal to meet him later in the shower, if you know what I mean."

The catcher was in tears now. "He made me do it," he said, covering himself with his big glove, and in his shame, dropping all the way to his knees, "everything else I showed him wasn't *good* enough for him—no, he teases me, he taunts me—"

By now the two "coaches" (as they were euphemistically called), who had removed the starting pitcher from the game, descended upon the catcher. With the aid of a fielder's glove, one of them gingerly lifted the catcher's member and placed it back inside his uniform before the opposing players could see what the signal had been, while the other relieved him of his catching equipment. "He provoked me," the catcher said, "he always provokes me—"

The Lunatic fans were on their feet again, applauding, when their catcher was led away from the plate and up to the big brick building, along the path taken earlier by the starting pitcher. "—He won't let me alone, ever. I don't want to do it. I never wanted to do it. I *wouldn't* do it. But then he starts up teasing me and taunting me—"

The Mundys were able to come up with a final run in the top of the third, once they discovered that the second-string Lunatic catcher, for all that he sounded like the real thing—"Chuck to me, babe, no hitter in here, babe—" was a little leery of fielding a bunt dropped out in front of home plate, fearful apparently of what he would find beneath the ball upon picking it up.

When Deacon started out to the mound to pitch the last of the three innings, there wasn't a Mundy who took the field with him, sleepy old Kid Heket included, who didn't realize that the Deke had a shutout working. If he could set the Lunatics down without a run, he could become the first Mundy pitcher to hurl a scoreless game all year, in or out of league competition. Hoping neither to jinx him or unnerve him, the players went through the infield warm-up deliberately keeping the chatter to a minimum, as though in fact it was just another day they

were going down to defeat. Nonetheless, the Deke was already
streaming perspiration when the first Lunatic stepped into
the box. He rubbed the rabbit's foot, said his prayer, took a
swallow of air big enough to fill a gallon jug, and on four
straight pitches, walked the center-fielder, who earlier in the
game hadn't bothered to return the ball to the infield after
catching a fly ball, and now, at the plate, hadn't moved the bat
off his shoulder. When he was lifted for a pinch-runner (lifted
by the "coaches") the appreciative fans gave him a nice round
of applause. "That's lookin' 'em over!" they shouted, as he
was carried from the field still in the batting posture, "that's
waitin' 'em out! Good eye in there, fella!"

As soon as the pinch-runner took over at first, it became
apparent that Dr. Traum had decided to do what he could to
save face by spoiling the Deacon's shutout. Five runs down in
the last inning and still playing to win, you don't start stealing
bases—but that was precisely what this pinch-runner had in
mind. And with what daring! First, with an astonishing burst
of speed he rushed fifteen feet down the basepath—but then,
practically on all fours, he was scrambling back. "No! No!"
he cried, as he dove for the bag with his outstretched hand, "I
won't! Never mind! Forget it!" But no sooner had he gotten
back up on his feet and dusted himself off, than he was running
again. "Why not!" he cried, "what the hell!" But having
broken fifteen, *twenty*, feet down the basepath, he would come
to an abrupt stop, smite himself on his forehead, and charge
wildly back to first, crying, "Am I crazy? Am I out of my
mind?"

In this way did he travel back and forth along the basepath some half-dozen times, before Deacon finally threw the
first pitch to the plate. Given all there was to distract him, the
pitch was of course a ball, low and in the dirt, but Hothead,
having a great day, blocked it beautifully with his wooden leg.

Cholly, managing the club that morning while Mister
Fairsmith rested back in Asylum—of the aged Mundy manager's spiritual crisis, more anon—Cholly motioned for Chico
to get up and throw a warm-up pitch in the bullpen (one was
enough—one was too many, in fact, as far as Chico was concerned) and meanwhile took a stroll out to the hill.

"Startin' to get to you, are they?" asked Cholly.

"It's that goofball on first that's doin' it."

Cholly looked over to where the runner, with time out, was standing up on first engaged in a heated controversy with himself.

"Hell," said Cholly, in his soft and reassuring way, "these boys have been tryin' to rattle us with that there bush league crap all mornin', Deke. I told you fellers comin' out in the bus, you just got to pay no attention to their monkey-shines, because that is their strategy from A to Z. To make you lose your concentration. Otherwise we would be rollin' over them worse than we is. But Deke, you tell me now, if you have had it, if you want for me to bring the Mexican in—"

"With six runs in my hip pocket? And a shutout goin'?"

"Well, I wasn't myself goin' to mention that last that you said."

"Cholly, you and me been in this here game since back in the days they was rubbin' us down with Vaseline and Tabasco sauce. Ain't that right?"

"I know, I know."

"Well," said the Deke, shooting a stream of tobacco juice over his shoulder, "ain't a bunch of screwballs gonna get my goat. Tell Chico to sit down."

Sure enough, the Deacon, old war-horse that he was, got the next two hitters out on long drives to left. "Oh my God!" cried the base runner, each time the Ghost went climbing up the padded wall to snare the ball. "Imagine if I'd broken for second! Imagine what would have happened then! Oh, that'll teach me to take those crazy leads! But then if you don't get a jump on the pitcher, where are you as a pinch-runner? That's the whole idea of a pinch-runner—to break with the pitch, to break *before* the pitch, to score that shutout-breaking run! That's what I'm in here for, that's my entire purpose. The whole thing is on *my* shoulders—so then what am I doing *not* taking a good long lead? But just then, if I'd broken for second, I'd have been doubled off first! For the last out! But then suppose he hadn't made the catch? Suppose he'd dropped it. Then where would I be? Forced out at second! *Out*—and all because I was too cowardly. But then what's the sense of taking an unnecessary risk? What virtue is there in being foolhardy? None! But then what about playing it too safe?"

On the bench, Jolly Cholly winced when he saw that the batter stepping into the box was the opposing team's shortstop. "Uh-oh," he said, "that's the feller what's cost 'em most of the runs to begin with. I'm afraid he is goin' to be lookin' to right his wrongs—and at the expense of Deacon's shutout. Dang!"

From bearing down so hard, the Deacon's uniform showed vast dark continents of perspiration both front and back. There was no doubt that his strength was all but gone, for he was relying now solely on his "junk," that floating stuff that in times gone by used to cause the hitters nearly to break their backs swinging at the air. Twice now those flutter balls of his had damn near been driven out of the institution and Jolly Cholly had all he could do not to cover his eyes with his hand when he saw the Deke release yet another fat pitch in the direction of home plate.

Apparently it was just to the Lunatic shortstop's liking too. He swung from the heels, and with a whoop of joy, was away from the plate and streaking down the basepath. "Run!" he shouted to the fellow on first.

But the pinch-runner was standing up on the bag, scanning the horizon for the ball.

"Two outs!" cried the Lunatic shortstop. "Run, you idiot!"

"But—where is it?" asked the pinch-runner.

The Mundy infielders were looking skywards themselves, wondering where in hell that ball had been hit to.

"Where *is* it!" screamed the pinch-runner, as the shortstop came charging right up to his face. "I'm not running till I know where the *ball* is!"

"I'm coming into first, you," warned the shortstop.

"But you can't overtake another runner! That's against the law! That's *out!*"

"Then *move!*" screamed the shortstop into the fellow's ear.

"Oh, this *is* crazy. This is exactly what I *didn't* want to do!" But what choice did he have? If he stood his ground, and the shortstop kept coming, that would be the ballgame. It would be all over because he who had been put into the game to run, had simply refused to. Oh, what torment that fellow

knew as he rounded the bases with the shortstop right on his
tail. "I'm running full speed—and I don't even know where the
ball is! I'm running like a chicken with his head cut off! I'm
running like a madman, which is just what I don't want to do!
Or be! I don't know where I'm going, I don't know what I'm
doing, I haven't the foggiest idea of what's happening—and
I'm running!"

When, finally, he crossed the plate, he was in such a state,
that he fell to his hands and knees, and sobbing with relief,
began to kiss the ground. "I'm home! Thank God! I'm safe!
I made it! I scored! Oh thank God, thank God!"

And now the shortstop was rounding third—he took a
quick glance back over his shoulder to see if he could go all the
way, and just kept on coming. "Now where's *he* lookin'?"
asked Cholly. "What in hell does he see that I can't? Or that
Mike don't either?" For out in left, Mike Rama was walking
round and round, searching in the grass as though for a dime
that might have dropped out of his pocket.

The shortstop was only a few feet from scoring the second
run of the inning when Dr. Traum, who all this while had been
walking from the Lunatic bench, interposed himself along the
foul line between the runner and home plate.

"Doc," screamed the runner, "you're in the way!"

"That's enough now," said Dr. Traum, and he motioned
for him to stop in his tracks.

"But I'm only inches from pay dirt! Step aside, Doc—let
me score!"

"You just stay vere you are, please."

"*Why?*"

"You know vy. Stay right vere you are now. And giff me
the ball."

"What ball?" asked the shortstop.

"You know vat ball."

"Well, I surely don't have any ball. I'm the *hitter*. I'm
about *to score*."

"You are not about to score. You are about to giff me the
ball. Come now. Enough foolishness. Giff over the ball."

"But, Doc, I haven't got it. I'm on the offense. It's the
defense that has the ball—that's the whole idea of the game.

No criticism intended, but if you weren't a foreigner, you'd probably understand that better.''

"Haf it your vay," said Dr. Traum, and he waved to the bullpen for his two coaches.

"But, Doc," said the shortstop, backpedaling now up the third-base line, "*they're* the ones in the field. *They're* the ones with the gloves—why don't you ask them for the ball? Why me? I'm an innocent base runner, who happens to be rounding third on his way home." But here he saw the coaches coming after him and he turned and broke across the diamond for the big brick building on the hill.

It was only a matter of minutes before one of the coaches returned with the ball and carried it out to where the Mundy infield was now gathered on the mound.

The Deacon turned it over in his hand and said, "Yep, that's it, all right. Ain't it, Hot?''

The Mundy catcher nodded. "How in hell did *he* get it?''

"A hopeless kleptomaniac, that's how," answered the coach. "He'd steal the bases if they weren't tied down. Here," he said, handing the Deacon a white hand towel bearing the Mundy laundrymark, and the pencil that Jolly Cholly wore behind his ear when he was acting as their manager. "Found this on him too. Looks like he got it when he stumbled into your bench for that pop-up in the first.''

The victory celebration began the moment they boarded the asylum bus and lasted nearly all the way back to the city, with Nickname hollering out his window to every passerby, "We beat 'em! We shut 'em out!" and Big John swigging bourbon from his liniment bottle, and then passing it to his happy teammates.

"I'll tell you what did it," cried Nickname, by far the most exuberant of the victors, "it was Deacon throwin' at that first guy's head! Yessir! Now that's my kind of baseball!" said the fourteen-year-old, smacking his thigh. "First man up, give it to 'em right in the noggin'.''

"Right!" said Hothead. "Show 'em you ain't takin' no more of their shit no more! Never again!''

"Well," said Deacon, "that is a matter of psychology, Hot, that was somethin' I had to think over real good beforehand. I mean, you try that on the wrong feller and next thing they is all of them layin' it down and then spikin' the dickens out of you when you cover the bag."

"That's so," said Jolly Cholly. "When me and the Deke come up, that was practically a rule in the rule book—feller throws the beanball, the word goes out, 'Drag the ball and spike the pitcher.' Tell you the truth, I was worried we was goin' to see some of that sort of stuff today. They was a desperate bunch. Could tell that right off by their tactics."

"Well," said the Deke, "that was a chance I had to take. But I'll tell you, I couldn't a done it without you fellers behind me. How about Bud out there, throwin' them two runners out at first base? The right-fielder to the first-baseman, *two times in a row*. Buddy," said the Deacon, "that was an exhibition such as I have not seen in all my years in organized ball."

Big Bud flushed, as was his way, and tried to make it sound easy. "Well, a' course, once I seen those guys wasn't runnin', I figured I didn't have no choice. I *had* to play it to first."

Here Mike Rama said, "Only that wasn't what *they* was figurin', Buddy-boy. You got a one-arm outfielder out there, you figure, what the hell, guess I can get on down the base line any old time I feel like it. Guess I can stop off and get me a beer and a sangwich on the way! But old Bud here, guess he showed 'em!"

"You know," said Cholly, philosophically, "I never seen it to fail, the hitters get cocky like them fellers were, and the next thing you know, they're makin' one dumb mistake after another."

"Yep," said Kid Heket, who was still turning the events of the morning over in his head, "no doubt about it, them fellers just was not usin' their heads."

"Well, maybe they wasn't—but *we* was! What about Hot?" said Nickname. "What about a guy with a wooden leg taggin' up from second and scorin' on a fly to center! How's that for heads-up ball?"

"Well," said Wayne, "I am still puzzlin' that one out myself. What got into that boy in center, that he just sort of stood there after the catch, alookin' the way he did? What in hell did he want to wait fifteen minutes for anyway, before throwin' it? That's a awful long time, don't you think?''

They all looked to Cholly to answer this one. ''Well, Wayne,'' he said, ''I believe it is that dang cockiness again. Base runner on second's got a wooden leg, kee-rect? So what does Hot here do—he *goes*. And that swellhead out in center, well, he is so darned stunned by it all, that finally by the time he figures out what hit him, we has got ourselves a gift of a run. Now, if I was managin' that club, I'd bench that there prima donna and slap a fine on him to boot.''

''But then how do you figure that shortstop, Cholly?'' asked the Kid. ''Now if that ain't the strangest ballplayin' you ever seen, what is? Stickin' the ball in his back pocket like that. And then when he is at bat, with a man on and his team down by six, and it is their last licks 'n all, catchin' a junk pitch like that inside his shirt. Now I cannot figure that out nohow.''

''Dang cockiness again!'' cried Nickname, looking to Cholly. ''He figures, hell, it's only them Mundys out there, I can do any dang thing I please—well, I guess we taught him a thing or two! Right, Cholly?''

''Well, nope, I don't think so, Nickname. I think what we have got there in that shortstop is one of the most tragic cases I have seen in my whole life long of all-field-no-hit.''

''Kleptomaniac's what the coach there called him,'' said the Deacon.

''Same thing,'' said Cholly. ''Why, we had a fella down in Class D when I was just startin' out, fella name a' Mayet. Nothin' got by that boy. Why, Mayet at short wasn't much different than a big pot of glue out there. Fact that's what they called him for short: Glue. Only trouble is, he threw like a girl, and when it come to hittin', well, my pussycat probably do better, if I had one. Well, the same exact thing here, only worse.''

''Okay,'' said Kid Heket, ''I see that, sorta. Only how come he run over to field a pop-up and stoled the pencil right off your ear, Cholly? How come he took our towel away, right in the middle of the gosh darn game?''

"Heck, that ain't so hard to figure out. We been havin' such rotten luck this year, you probably forgot just who we all are, anyway. What boy *wouldn't* want a towel from a big league ball club to hang up and frame on the wall? Why, he wanted that thing so bad that when the game was over, I went up to the doc there and I said, 'Doc, no hard feelin's. You did the best you could and six to zip ain't nothin' to be ashamed of against big leaguers.' And then I *give* him the towel to pass on to that there kleptomaniac boy when he seen him again. So as he didn't feel too bad, bein' the last out. And know what else I told him? I give him some advice. I said, 'Doc, if I had a shortstop like that, I'd bat him ninth and play him at first where he don't *have* to make the throw.''

"What'd he say?"

"Oh, he laughed at me. He said, 'Ha ha, Jolly Cholly, you haf a good sense of humor. Who efer heard of a first-baseman batting ninth?' So I said, 'Doc, who ever heard of a fifty-year-old preacher hurlin' a shutout with only three days' rest—but he done it, maybe with the help of interference on the last play, but still he done it.''"

"Them's the breaks of the game anyway!" cried Nickname. "About time the breaks started goin' our way. Did you tell him that, Cholly?"

"I told him that, Nickname. I told him more. I said, 'Doc, there is two kinds of baseball played in this country, and maybe somebody ought to tell you, bein' a foreigner and all—there is by the book, the way you do it, the way the Tycoons do it—and I grant, those fellers win their share of pennants doin' it that way. But then there is by hook and crook, by raw guts and all the heart you got, and that is just the way the Mundys done here today.''"

Here the team began whooping and shouting and singing with joy, though Jolly Cholly had momentarily to turn away, to struggle against the tears that were forming in his eyes. In a husky voice he went on—"And then I told him the name for that. I told him the name for wanderin' your ass off all season long, and takin' all the jokes and all the misery they can heap on your head day after day, and then comin' on out for a exhibition game like this one, where another team would just go through the motions and not give two hoots in hell how

they played—and instead, instead givin' it everything you got.
I told the doc the name for that, fellers. It's called courage.''

Only Roland Agni, who had gone down twice, looking,
against Lunatic pitching, appeared to be unmoved by Cholly's
tribute to the team. Nickname, in fact, touched Jolly Cholly's
arm at the conclusion of his speech, and whispered, ''Somebody
better say somethin' to Rollie. He ain't takin' strikin' out
too good, it don't look.''

So Cholly the peacemaker made his way past the boisterous players and down the aisle to where Roland still sat huddled in a rear corner of the bus by himself.

''What's eatin' ya, boy?''

''Nothin','' mumbled Roland.

''Why don'tcha come up front an'—''

''Leave me alone, Tuminikar!''

''Aw, Rollie, come on now,'' said the sympathetic coach,
''even the best of them get caught lookin' once in a while.''

''Caught *lookin'?*'' cried Agni.

''Hey, Rollie,'' Hothead shouted, ''it's okay, slugger—
we won anyway!'' And grinning, he waved Big John's liniment bottle in the air to prove it.

''Sure, Rollie,'' Nickname yelled. ''With the Deke on the
mound, we did not need but one run anyway! So what's the difference? Everybody's gotta whiff sometimes! It's the law a'
averages!''

But Agni was now standing in the aisle, screaming, ''You
think I got caught *lookin'?*''

Wayne Heket, whose day had been a puzzle from beginning to end, who just could not really take any more confusion
on top of going sleepless all these hours, asked, ''Well, wasn't
ya?''

''You bunch of morons! You bunch of idiots! Why, you are
bigger lunatics even than they are! Those fellers are at least
locked up!''

Jolly Cholly, signaling his meaning to the other players
with a wink, said, ''Seems Roland got somethin' in his eye,
boys—seems he couldn't see too good today.''

''You're the ones that can't see!'' Agni screamed. ''*They
were madmen! They were low as low can be!*''

''Oh, I don't know, Rollie,'' said Mike Rama, who'd had

his share of scurrying around to do that morning, "they wasn't *that* bad."

"They was *worse!* And you all acted like you was takin' on the Cardinals in the seventh game of the Series!"

"How else you supposed to play, youngster?" asked the Deacon, who was beginning to get a little hot under the collar.

"And you! You're the worst of all! Hangin' in there, like a regular hero! Havin' conferences on the mound about how to pitch to a bunch of hopeless maniacs!"

"Look, son," said Jolly Cholly, "just on account you got caught lookin'—"

"*But who got caught lookin'?* How could you get caught lookin' against pitchers *that had absolutely nothin' on the ball!*"

"You mean," said Jolly Cholly, incredulous, "you took a *dive?* You mean you throwed it, Roland? *Why?*"

"*Why?* Oh, please, let me off! Let me off this bus!" he screamed, charging down the aisle toward the door. "I can't take bein' one of you no more!"

As they were all, with the exception of the Deacon, somewhat pie-eyed, it required virtually the entire Mundy team to subdue the boy wonder. Fortunately the driver of the bus, who was an employee of the asylum, carried a straitjacket and a gag under the seat with him at all times, and knew how to use it. "It's from bein' around them nuts all mornin'," he told the Mundys. "Sometimes I ain't always myself either, when I get home at night."

"Oh," said the Mundys, shaking their heads at one another, and though at first it was a relief having a professional explanation for Roland's bizarre behavior, they found that with Roland riding along in the rear seat all bound and gagged, they really could not seem to revive the jubilant mood that had followed upon their first shutout win of the year. In fact, by the time they reached Keeper Park for their regularly scheduled afternoon game, one or two of them were even starting to feel more disheartened about that victory than they had about any of those beatings they had been taking all season long.

4

EVERY INCH A MAN

≫ 4 ≪

A chapter containing as much as has ever been written anywhere on the subject of midgets in baseball. In which all who take pride in the nation's charity will be heartened by an account of the affection bestowed by the American public upon such unusual creatures. Being the full story of the midget pinch-hitter Bob Yamm, his tiny wife, and their nemesis O.K. Ockatur. How the Yamms captured the country's heart. What the newspapers did in behalf of midgets. The radio interview between Judy Yamm and Martita McGaff. A description of O.K. Ockatur, who believed the world owed him something because he was small and misshapen. What happened when the midgets collided in the Kakoola dugout. The complete text of Bob Yamm's "Farewell Address." Exception taken to the Yamms by Angela Trust. In which the Mundys arrive in Kakoola to defeat the demoralized Reapers. A Chinese home run by Bud Parusha travels all the way to. the White House; a telegram (purportedly) from Eleanor Roosevelt; wherein a trade is arranged, the one-armed outfielder for the despised dwarf. A conversation between Jolly Cholly Tuminikar and the aging members of the Mundy bench, surprising in its own way. An account of "Welcome Bud Parusha Day," with the difficulties and discouragements that may attend those who would exchange one uniform for another. The disastrous con- clusion to the foregoing adventures.

I N SEPTEMBER of that wartime season, with the Keepers and the Reapers battling for sixth, Kakoola owner Frank Mazuma signed on a midget to help his club as a pinch-hitter in the stretch. The midget, named Yamm, was the real thing; he stood forty inches high, weighed sixty-five pounds, and when he came to the plate and assumed the crouch that Mazuma had taught him, he presented the pitcher with a strike zone not much larger than a matchbox. At the press conference called to introduce the midget to the world, the twenty-two-year-old

Yamm, fresh from the University of Wisconsin, where he'd been the first midget ever in Sigma Chi, praised Mazuma for his courage in defying "the gentleman's agreement" that had previously excluded people of his stature from big league ball. He said he realized that as baseball's first midget he was going to be subjected to a good deal of ridicule; however, he had every hope that in time even those who had started out as his enemies would come to judge him by the only thing that really mattered in this game, his value to the Kakoola Reapers. In the final analysis, Yamm asked rhetorically, what difference was there between a midget such as himself and an ordinary player, provided he contributed to the success of his team?

"The difference? About two and a half feet," said Frank Mazuma, taking the mike from the midget. "And let me tell you something else about little Mr. Yamm here, gentlemen. Every time he comes to bat, I am going to be perched up on top of the grandstand with a high-powered rifle aimed at home plate. And if this little son of a buck so much as raises the bat off his shoulder, I'll plug him! Hear that, Pee Wee?"

Chuckling, the reporters rushed off to the phones (supplied by Mazuma) to get the story to their papers in time for the evening edition.

Sure enough, the first time the midget was announced over the public address system—"Your attention, ladies and gentlemen, pinch-hitting for the Reapers, No. ¼, Bob Yamm"—a man wearing a black eyepatch, an Army camouflage uniform, a steel helmet, and carrying a rifle, was seen to climb out through a trapdoor atop the stadium at Reaper Field and take up a firing position on the roof. Needless to say, he did not find it necessary to pull the trigger; in Yamm's first ten pinch-hitting assignments, not only did he draw ten walks, but he was not even thrown a strike. Even the sinking stuff sailed by the bill of his cap, and of course when the opposing pitchers began to press, invariably they threw the ball into the dirt, bouncing it past the midget, as though he were the batsman in cricket.

In the interest of league harmony, the other P. League owners had been willing to indulge the maverick Mazuma for a game or two, expecting that either the fans would quickly tire of the ridiculous gimmick, or that General Oakhart would make Mazuma see the light; but as it turned out, Kakoolians couldn't have been more delighted to see Yamm drawing balls in the batter's box (and Mazuma taking aim at him from the stadium roof), and General Oakhart was as powerless as ever against Mazuma's contempt for the time-honored ways. When the General telephoned to remind Mazuma of the dignity of the game and the integrity of the league (and vice versa), Mazuma responded by calling a second press conference for the articulate Bob Yamm.

"I have it on very good authority," said Yamm, impeccably dressed in a neat pin-striped business suit and a boy's clip-on necktie, "that the powers-that-be have threatened to pass a law at the next annual winter meeting of the owners of the Patriot Baseball League of America that will bar forever from any team in the league anyone under forty-eight inches in height. This, may I add, even as our country is engaged in a brutal and costly war in behalf of freedom and justice for all. To be sure, such a law, if passed, would only be the outright codification of that very same 'gentleman's agreement' that has operated since the inception of the eight-team Patriot League in 1898 to prevent people of my stature and proportions from competing as professional baseball players.

"It is my understanding that these people now intend to launch a systematic campaign of slander against me, suggesting that I, Bob Yamm, am not entitled to the rights and privileges such as our Constitution guarantees to every American, but rather that I am—and I quote—'a gimmick,' 'a joke,' 'a farce'—and what is more, that my presence on a major league diamond constitutes a 'disgrace' to the game that calls itself our national pastime. Gentlemen of the press, I am sure I speak not only for myself, but for all midgets everywhere, when I say that I will not for a single moment permit these self-styled protectors of the game to deny me my rights as an American and a human being, and that I will oppose this conspiracy against myself and my fellow midgets with every fiber of my being."

Frank Mazuma, whose motto was "Always leave 'em laughin'," immediately quipped, "Every fiber of his being— that's sixty-five pounds worth, fellas!"—and so the reporters departed once again in high spirits; but that Yamm had made a strong claim upon their feelings was more than obvious in

the evening's papers. "A midget to be proud of," one writer
called him. "A credit to his size," wrote another. "A little
guy with a lot on his mind." "Only forty inches high, but every
inch a man." One columnist, in as solemn (and complex) a
sentence as he had ever written, asked, "Why are our brave
boys fighting and dying in far-off lands, if not so that the Bob
Yamms of this world can hold high their heads, midgets
though they may be?" And the following week a famous illus-
trator of the era penned a tribute to Yamm on the cover of
Liberty magazine that was subsequently reprinted by the
thousands and came to take its place on the walls of just about
every barber shop in America in those war years—the meticulously realistic drawing entitled "The Midgets' Midget," showing Bob in his baseball togs, his famous fraction on his back,
waving his little bat toward an immense cornucopia decorated
with forty-eight stars; marching out of the cornucopia are an
endless stream of what appear to be leprechauns and elves
from all walks of life: tiny little doctors with stethoscopes,
little nurses, little factory workers in overalls, little tiny professors wearing glasses and carrying little books under their
arms, little policemen and firemen, and so on, each a perfect
miniature of his or her fully grown counterpart.

All at once—to the astonishment even of Frank Mazuma—
the entire nation took not only brave Bob Yamm to its heart,
but all American midgets with him, a group previously unknown to the vast majority of their countrymen. Until Bob
Yamm's entrance into baseball, how many Americans had
even taken a good long look at a midget, let alone heard one
speak? How many Americans had ever been in a midget's
house? How many Americans had ever taken a meal with a
midget, or exchanged ideas with one? What did midgets eat
anyway? And how much? Where did they live? Did midgets
marry, and if so, whom? Other midgets? Where did they go to
find other midgets? What did midgets do for entertainment?
Religion? Clothes? To all of these questions the ordinary, full-
grown man in the street had to confess his ignorance; either
he knew nothing whatsoever about the American midget, or
what was worse, shared the general misconception that they
were people of dubious morality and low intelligence, belonging to no religious order, befriended only by the sleaziest types,

and constitutionally unable to rise in life above the station of bellhop, if that.

Following the publication of that cover drawing of Bob Yamm, photo stories began to appear with almost weekly regularity in Sunday papers around the country, reporting on the valuable work that local midgets were doing, particularly in behalf of the war effort: photos of midgets with blowtorches crawling down into sections of airplane fuselage far too small for an ordinary aircraft worker to enter; photos of midgets in munitions plants, their feet sticking up out of heavy artillery pieces—according to the caption, spot-checking the weapons against sabotage prior to shipment to the front. There was even a contingent of midgets, recruited from all around the country, shown in training for a highly secret intelligence mission; for security reasons their faces were blacked out in the photo, but there they sat, in what appeared to be a kindergarten classroom, taking instruction from a full-grown Army colonel.

On the lighter side, there were photos of midgets having fun, the men dressed in tuxedos, the women in floor-length gowns, celebrating New Year's Eve at a party complete with champagne, streamers, noisemakers, false noses, and paper hats. There was a photo story one week in the nation's largest Sunday supplement showing a pair of married midgets at home eating a spaghetti dinner ("Doris does the cooking usually, but spaghetti 'n meatballs is Bill's own specialty. From the looks of that big smile—and even bigger portion!—it sure seems like *somebody* enjoys his own cooking in the Peterson household") and another of a midget standing in the Victory Garden out back of his house, pointing up at the corn. ("'Just growin' like Topsy!' says Tom Tucker, of his prize-winning vegetable patch. Tom, known throughout his neighborhood for his green thumb, modestly chalks his outstanding harvest up to 'dumb luck.'")

What one photo story after another revealed, and what was at first so difficult for their fellow Americans to believe, was that midgets were exactly like ordinary people, only smaller. Indeed, after Mrs. Bob Yamm had appeared on Martita McGaff's daytime radio show, the network received letters from over fifteen thousand women, congratulating them for their courage in having as a guest the utterly charming wife of the controversial little baseball player. Only a very small handful found the program distasteful, and wrote to complain that hearing a midget on the radio had frightened their young children and given them nightmares.

"I only wish all of you out there in radioland," Martita began, "could be here in the studio to *see* my guest today. She is Mrs. Bob Yamm, her husband is the pinch-hitter who has major league pitchers going round in circles, and she herself is cute as a button. Welcome to the show, Mrs. Yamm—and just what is that darling little outfit you're wearing? I've been admiring it since I laid eyes on you. And the little matching shoes and handbag! I've never *seen* anything so darling!"

"Thank you, Martita. Actually the sunsuit is something I designed and made myself."

"You didn't! Well, watch out, Paris—there's a little lady in Kakoola, Wisconsin, who just may run you out of business! *Have* you ever thought of designing clothes specifically for women midgets, Mrs. Yamm? Am I correct—it *is* 'women midgets'; or *does* one say 'midgetesses'? Our announcer and myself were talking that over just before the show, and Don says he believes he *has* heard the term 'midgetesses' used on occasion . . . No?"

"No," said Mrs. Yamm.

"Tell me then, what *do* women midgets do about clothes? I'm sure all our listeners have wondered. Do most of them design and make their own, or are you out of the ordinary in that respect?"

"Yes, I guess you could say I was out of the ordinary in that respect," replied Mrs. Yamm. "But since I'm rather thin for my height, and most children's clothes just swim on me, I took to making my own—I guess as a matter of necessity."

"It *is* the mother of invention, isn't it?"

"Yes," agreed Mrs. Yamm.

"And may I say," said Martita, "for the benefit of our radio audience, you are *marvelously* thin. I'm sure the ladies listening in, some of whom have *my* problem, would like to know your secret. Do you watch your diet?"

"No, I more or less eat whatever I want."

"And continue to remain so wonderfully petite?"

"Yes," said Mrs. Yamm.

"Oh, that we were all so lucky! I just *look* at a dish of ice cream—well, let's not go into *that* sad story! Now—what is it like suddenly being the wife of a famous man? Do you find people staring at you now whenever you two step out?"

"Well, of course, they always stared, you know, even before."

"Well, I wouldn't doubt that. You *are* a darling couple. How did you meet Bob? Is there a funny story that goes with that? Did Bob get down on his knees to ask for your hand— or just how did he pop the question?"

"He just asked me if I'd marry him."

"Not on bended knee, eh? Not the old-fashioned type."

"No."

"And just what do you think it was that made you attractive to a man like Bob Yamm?"

"Well, my size, primarily. My being another midget."

"And a very *lovely* midget, if I may say for the benefit of the radio audience what Mrs. Yamm is too modest to say herself. Just to give our radio audience an idea of *how* lovely I'm going to run the risk of embarrassing our guest—I hope she won't mind—but coming into the studio today, for the first moment I did not even realize that she was real. I had seen photographs of her, of course, and knew she would be my guest today—and yet in that first moment, seeing her in that darling outfit, with matching purse and shoes, sitting straight up in the corner of my office sofa with her legs out in front of her, one demurely crossed over the other, I actually thought she was a doll! I thought, 'My granddaughter Cindy has been here and she's left her new doll. She'll be sick, wondering where it is, such a lovely and expensive one too, with real hair and so on'—and then the doll's mouth opened and said, 'How do you do, I'm Judy Yamm.' Well, you're blushing, but it's true. I was literally and truly in wonderland for a moment. And I wouldn't doubt that Bob Yamm was, when he first laid eyes upon you."

"Thank you."

"Was it love at first sight for you, too? Did you ever ex-

pect when you first met him that Bob would be a major league
baseball player?''

"No, I didn't."

"What a thrill then for two young people who only a few
months ago thought of themselves as just an ordinary American couple. By the way, are there any little Yamms at home?"

"Pardon? Oh, no—just Bob and myself."

"Uh-oh, I'm being told to cut it short, time for only one
more question—so at the risk of being as ultracontroversial as
your ultracontroversial husband, Bob Yamm, brilliant pinch-
hitter for the Kakoola Reapers, I'm going to ask it. Do you
think a midget can ever get to be President of the United
States? Now you don't have to answer that one."

"I think I won't."

"Well, I'm no political pundit either, but let me say that
I've been talking to a midget who could certainly get to be
First Lady in my book—and that is the utterly delightful and
charming *and* beautiful Judy Yamm, wife of the famous baseball star, and clothes designer in her own right—and I only
hope our granddaughter Cindy isn't waiting outside here, because one look at you, Judy Yamm, and she's going to want
to take you home for her own! This is Martita McGaff—have
a happy, everyone!"

The enthusiasm that Bob Yamm had generated around the
nation took even the audacious Frank Mazuma by surprise,
and though the owner continued to delight the fans by making
unscheduled appearances on the stadium roof when Yamm
came to bat, he let it be known to the press that of course his
high-powered rifle was loaded only with blanks; in public, he
even stopped referring to Bob as "Squirt" and "Runt,"
allowing the fans to enjoy the midget however they liked.
If they wanted to make a hero out of somebody who was
only forty inches high, that was their business—especially as
it was good for business. In fact, when a midget a full three
inches shorter than Yamm turned up at Mazuma's office one
day, claiming to be a right-handed pitcher, Mazuma promptly
pulled a catcher's mitt out of his desk drawer and took him
down beneath the stands for a tryout. The following day, a

new name was added to the Reaper roster: No. ½, O.K. Ockatur.

For a week, Ockatur sat alone in a corner of the Reaper
dugout, pounding his little glove and muttering to himself
what were taken at the time to be analyses of the weaknesses
of the opposing batsmen. Then the Mundys arrived in town
direct from a series in Asylum, and the right-hander climbed
down off the Reaper bench, and with his curious rolling gait—
for he was not so perfectly formed as Yamm, nor so handsome
either—made his way out to the mound, where he pitched a
four-hit shutout. Using a sidearm delivery, he started low as
he could, actually dragging his knuckles in the dust, and then
released the ball on a rising trajectory, so that it was still
climbing through the strike zone when it passed the batter.
"Why, I never seen nothin' like it," said Wayne Heket. "That
little boy out there, or whatever he is, was throwin' *up* at us."
"The mountain climber," some called the Ockatur pitch; "the
skyrocket," "the upsydaisy"—and as for Ockatur's right
arm, inevitably it was dubbed "the ack-ack gun," and with
characteristic wartime enthusiasm little No. ½ was labeled
"Kakoola's Secret Weapon"—until the players around the
league got the knack of laying into that odd, ascending pitch,
and began to send it out of the ball park, "where," said the
writers, who weren't fooled for too long either, "it belonged
to begin with."

What caused the disenchantment, when it came, to be so
profound was the discovery of Ockatur's fierce hatred of all
men taller than himself, including Bob Yamm. At the outset, his refusal to be photographed shaking Yamm's hand
on the steps of the Reaper dugout had startled those who had
drawn around, in a spirit of good cheer, to observe the historic
event. Visibly shaken by the rebuff, Yamm had nonetheless
told the reporters present that *he* understood perfectly why
Mr. Ockatur had turned away in a huff; in fact, he *admired*
him for it! "What O.K. Ockatur has made clear, gentlemen,
and in no uncertain terms, is that he has no intention of walking in Bob Yamm's shadow." And, in the face of increasingly
blatant provocations, Bob continued to conduct himself as he
had earlier with Frank Mazuma, when the Reaper owner would
do whatever he could to get a laugh out of Bob's size: he

ignored him, and went about his job, which was to draw bases on balls as a pinch-hitter. Only with an adversary like Ockatur, it required a far more heroic effort of restraint, for where Mazuma was a clown who invariably could be counted on to compromise himself by his own exceedingly bad taste, Ockatur was a crazed and indefatigable enemy, who despised him and attacked him with all the ingrained bitterness of a man who is not only a midget by normal standards, but an exceedingly short person even by the standards of the average midget. Though it was not a word Bob himself would ever have used either publicly or privately to describe Ockatur, in the end he had silently to agree with Judy, when she broke down crying one night at dinner, and called Ockatur, who was trying her husband to the breaking point, "nothing but a dirty little dwarf."

If Ockatur came to seem to the Yamms and to the press an insult to the good name of midgets everywhere, to Ockatur, Bob Yamm seemed the last man in the world to bear the title of "the midgets' midget." The sight of Yamm wearing a smaller number than his own made him wild with anger (or envy, as most interpreted it): why, if Yamm was Number $\frac{1}{4}$, then *he* should be $\frac{1}{8}$, if not $\frac{1}{16}$! *He* was the shorter of the two, and with his oversized head and bandy legs, was far more representative of the average little person than this perfectly proportioned, well-spoken, college-educated, smartly dressed, "courageous," "dignified," forty-inch fraternity-boy Adonis, with his spic-and-span Kewpie-doll of a wife! Oh how he hated the kind of midget who went around pretending that he was nothing but a smaller edition of everybody else! who wanted no more than "an even break like everybody else"! As if it were possible for a midget's life to be anything but a trial and a nightmare! As if it were possible sitting in a high chair in a restaurant eating your dinner to feel like "everybody else," while as a matter of fact "everybody else" was either looking the other way in disgust, or openly staring in wonder. And that, only if the management would seat you to begin with. Sorry sir, no room—*no room,* to somebody who weighs only fifty-five pounds and could take his dinner in the phone booth! And what *about* phone booths? What about having to ask the policeman on his beat if he will be kind enough to

pick you up so you can dial—is that like "everybody else,"
Bob Yamm? Is it like "everybody else" to go into a public
urinal and stand on tiptoes at the trough, while "everybody
else" is pissing over your shoulder? And what about the movie
show, where either you sit in the front row and look straight
up at figures that loom over you even worse than in life, or
you go all the way to the back, to the last row, and stand
there on your seat—if the usher will permit. Ushers—*those*
compassionate souls! And what about doorknobs, Bob? What
about stairways! Turnstiles! Water coolers! Is there a single
object that a midget confronts in this entire world that does
not say to him loud and clear, "Get out of here, you, you're
the wrong size." An even break like everybody else! Oh, *that's*
whose midget Bob Yamm was, all right—*everybody else's!*
And that's whose midget he wanted to be, too!

Is it any wonder then that on the afternoon they were to be
photographed shaking hands outside the Reaper dugout, Ockatur muttered at Yamm that insult of midget argot ordinarily applied to the so-called normal-sized people? Chin to
chin, looking into Yamm's clear, kind blue eyes, Ockatur
snarled, "I didn't know they piled shit that high!" then turned
and angrily walked—waddled, alas, would be a more accurate
description—down into the Reaper clubhouse, leaving Bob to
interpret Ockatur's appalling behavior in what he hoped
would be the best interest of their mutual cause.

OCKATUR, YAMM IN DUGOUT SLUGFEST; BRAWLING
MIDGETS DRAW SUSPENSION, FINE FROM MAZUMA;
PINCH-HIT STAR ADMITS GUILT, ADDS: "THIS CLUB
NOT BIG ENOUGH FOR BOTH OF US"; TO QUIT GAME,
MAY RUN FOR CONGRESS AFTER HOLLYWOOD FILMS
LIFE

Sept. 14—The much-feared volcano the Reapers have been worry-
ing over privately for two weeks erupted yesterday in the team
dugout, when the first two midgets in baseball, pinch-hitter Bob
Yamm and pitcher O.K. Ockatur, came to blows. Yamm was just
about to leave the Reaper dugout to pinch-hit against Asylum in
the eighth [Asylum won the game 5–4, tumbling the Reapers into
seventh place. See story p. 43] when a remark from Ockatur
sparked the feud that has been developing between the two since

the midget pitcher joined the Reapers in the stretch drive for
sixth.

Following the bloody battle, both players were taken by
ambulance to Kakoola Memorial for treatment of cuts and
bruises.

Would Suspend Pope

Owner Frank Mazuma promptly slapped a one hundred dollar fine and a ten-day suspension on each player for "conduct
unbecoming a Reaper." Mazuma said: "Of course it's going to
hurt the club. If Bob had walked yesterday he would have
forced in the tying run and we might well be in sixth right now,
where we belong. But there is more to this game than winning."

Mazuma replied with some salty language when asked if he
would have meted out such punishment to the players if either
had been "someone your own size." "It strikes me," said an
angry Mazuma, "as somewhat odd that the guy who has single-
handedly lifted the barrier against midgets should now be accused of picking on them because they happen to be small. I don't
care if they were giants. Throw a punch in my dugout, and I
don't care if you are the Pope himself, out you go on your
————."

[In the Vatican, sources close to the Pontiff said the Holy
Father had not yet been informed of Mazuma's remark. Photo
story on local Catholic reaction, pro and con, p. 7.]

Brilliant Midgets

No one knows yet what exactly passed between the two
players as Yamm was moving out of the dugout to pinch-hit
against the Keepers with the bases loaded and one out. According to other players, ever since Ockatur came up and began his
brilliant winning streak—3–0 to date—he has been needling
Yamm, asking him why he doesn't go ahead and swing away. In
the fifteen times he came to bat prior to his suspension, Yamm
had not swung at a pitched ball. To date there have been only
three strikes called against the forty-inch-high pinch-hitter, each
coming in a different game.

His fifteen consecutive bases on balls already exceed the old
major league record by seven.

Second Volcano

The second volcano erupted in Kakoola—and the nation—at
exactly 9:07 P.M. Central Daylight Saving Time, when Bob Yamm

went on station KALE to read to Reaper fans the letter which he
had just sent by special messenger to owner Frank Mazuma. [See
back page for photo story on midget messenger and his reactions.]

Yamm appeared at the studio with a bandaged head and
hand, accompanied by his wife, Judith. Both were dressed in the
style they have made a nationwide fad in only a matter of weeks.
Bob wore his famous gray double-breasted pin-striped suit, and
Mrs. Yamm a monogrammed yellow sunsuit, with matching yellow
purse, shoes, and hair barrette. Mrs. Yamm maintained her composure throughout, but was seen to dab at her face with a yellow
handkerchief when her husband read the final paragraph of his
prepared statement. [See story "Grown Men Weep" for reaction
of studio technicians to Yamm Farewell Speech, p. 9.]

The Farewell Address

The following is the complete text of the Yamm speech, as
broadcast over KALE:

Good evening. I am Bob Yamm. I have in the past hour sent
a letter to Mr. Frank Mazuma, owner of the Kakoola Reapers,
which I shall now read to you in its entirety.

Dear Mr. Mazuma: I want to tell you that I am wholly to
blame for the violent incident that occurred this afternoon at
3:56 P.M., as I was leaving the dugout to pinch-hit against the
Asylum Keepers. In the five hours that have elapsed since, I
have remained silent as to my responsibility, and have thus caused
a great injustice to be visited upon my teammate O.K. Ockatur.

No Excuse

I have no more excuse to make for this unconscionable delay
than for the incident itself. If I told you that I was too "dazed"
at the time to collect my thoughts, I would be reporting only a
fraction of the truth. I fear that it was unjustifiable anger, and a
cowardly fear of the consequences, that served to seal both my
lips and O.K. Ockatur's fate.

In Anguish Since Five-Thirty

I was discharged from the hospital at 5:14 P.M., clinging
still to my self-righteous attitude and fully intending to maintain my silence. I will tell you now that my conscience has not
given me a moment's peace since 5:30 when I returned home, and,
in anguish, heard the news bulletin announcing your decision to
punish O.K. Ockatur and myself equally. That I allowed three
hours and two minutes more to intervene between your press

conference and my decision to come on the air (reached at 8:32 C.D.S.T.), is, I fear, yet another black mark against my integrity.

Keeps Pitchers Honest

Mr. Mazuma, it will not do any longer to intimate—if only by my silence—that even if I am responsible for this ugly affair, I should be excused from blame because of the burdens I have borne since entering the big leagues. I do not wish to minimize the difficulties and hardships that must befall any man who is a pioneer in his field. I mean rather to suggest that the pressures— and the prejudices—that I have had to withstand as the first midget in baseball, have been as nothing beside those under which my teammate and fellow midget, O.K. Ockatur, has had to labor.

That there might one day be a midget pinch-hitting in the big leagues had long ago occurred to baseball men, if only as a "funny" idea, a curiosity to draw fans to the ball park. Moreover, on the basis of the thousands of letters I have received from midgets around the country since joining the Reapers, I think I can safely say that this dream of a midget pinch-hitter, who one day would stand at home plate testing the control of the best pitchers in the game, has been a secret ambition of American midgets from time immemorial. I have even received letters from nonmidgets, from full-grown baseball fans, who write to wish me well, and to say that the presence of a midget in the batter's box may well be what is necessary to prevent big league pitching from deteriorating any further—to keep the pitchers, as they like to put it, "honest." And many of these correspondents are fans who admit to having scoffed at the idea just a short month ago.

Unfortunately, they continue to scoff at the idea of a midget on the mound. Victorious though he has been in three consecutive outings, in many ways the spark plug of the Reaper drive on sixth, O.K. Ockatur continues to remain to many something less than a major league pitcher. Sad to say, in their estimations he is still "a freak."

Outstanding Freaks

Yes, "freak" is the word that some Americans will use to describe a man whose style of pitching is his own and no one else's, a man who is unusual, unorthodox—in a word, an individualist. Well, if to be one's own man, if to pursue excellence and accomplishment with all that is unique to your being is what is meant by "a freak," then I guess O.K. Ockatur is a freak, all right. And so too, I submit, were the Founding Fathers of this country, so too were the great Greek philosophers, so too were the lonely geniuses who invented the wheel, the steam engine, the cotton gin, and the airplane. And so too is every hero in history who has lived and died by his own lights.

But perhaps what makes O.K. Ockatur "a freak" isn't his unyielding individualism, but the determination he has displayed in the face of every conceivable obstruction, his courage in the face of the most heartbreaking adversity. Yes, perhaps it is his bravery that makes him "a freak"—perhaps it is that to which the fans are paying tribute, when they lean over the dugout roof and cry, "Hey it *is* a midget—I thought it was a monkey!" or when they write letters to him, unsigned of course, in which they tell him to go back to the sideshow. Well, that must be some sideshow, including as it does such freaks as George Washington, Abraham Lincoln, Socrates, the Wright Brothers, and Thomas Alva Edison—in short, every man who has ever dared to pit himself against the ingrained habits and customs of his time, who has dared to brave the jeers of the rabble, the envy of the cowardly, the smugness of the complacent, the sarcasm of the know-it-alls, and the unremitting opposition of the vested interests.

Fails All But Dog

Mr. Mazuma, knowing as I did the extent of the abuse and ridicule that have been O.K. Ockatur's daily fare since arriving in the big leagues, knowing too how even the most proud and independent of men may come to be poisoned by such venom, it was surely incumbent upon me to be understanding, if not forgiving, of his stronger moods. Surely it was not too much to ask that I overlook conduct that might vex an ordinary person, and grant remission where another might condemn. But I failed him, at the very moment that he most needed a friendly smile, a kind remark, a brotherly gesture of solidarity. I failed him, and failed as well: my wife; my teammates; you, Mr. Mazuma; the Patriot League; General Oakhart; Judge Landis; organized baseball; midgets throughout the country, many of them in important war work; those everywhere who have supported the midget in his drive for equal opportunities; and, last but not least, our soldiers across the Atlantic and the Pacific, hundreds of whom have written asking for autographed photos of me at the plate. I don't think it is an exaggeration to say that I failed everyone everywhere, regardless of faith, creed, color, or size, who has clung to the vision of a better world, even as this bloody war rages on. And, of course, most unforgivable of all, I have failed myself.

Though it may seem insensitive of me to be momentarily lighthearted, may I add that just about the only one I seem *not* to have failed is my chihuahua pup, Pinch-hit, who has sat in my lap all the while I have been composing this letter, blissfully ignorant of the fact that his master is not the same man today that he was yesterday, and that he will never be again.

Bows Out

Mr. Mazuma, I fear that my usefulness to the Reapers has come to an end. Much as I continue to respect O.K. Ockatur as an athlete and a man, I cannot expect that, following today's atrocious episode, we two will ever be able to resolve our difficulties amicably. And surely the last thing our team needs, in the midst of a battle for sixth, is a smoldering battle simultaneously taking place on the bench, between an occasional pinch-hitter and a starting pitcher who has not yet lost a game in the majors.

Nor do I think it would be in the interests of O.K. Ockatur himself, if I were to remain with the Reapers as his teammate. Mr. Mazuma, if any of what I have said here will cause you to rescind, or even mitigate, the punishment you have leveled upon O.K., perhaps that may repair to some degree the damage that I have done his reputation. But I do not really believe there is any way to meet his justifiable sense of grievance, or fully to restore his manly dignity, short of my departure from the club.

Great Wife

Because of "the gentleman's agreement" that as we all know continues to exist among the other clubs, leaving the Reapers is of course tantamount for me to retirement from big league baseball. I only regret that I, who entered the drama of this great game so auspiciously, find myself exiting in disgrace. To be absolutely frank, for almost a week now, I have felt an increasing strain, and had begun to worry for my self-control. So too did my wife Judy, who I want to say now, has been a tower of strength right from the day I signed my Kakoola contract. Even though she dreaded the changes my new career would bring to our settled and comfortable domestic life, she knew that I would never be able to count myself a man if I refused to accept the challenge to break down the big league barrier against midgets.

However, as each day she saw more and more evidence of my mental and moral faltering, she could not help but become alarmed, and only yesterday, fearful of just such an incident as erupted this afternoon, begged me to remain at home and take a rest.

Unfortunately, I did not heed her wifely wisdom, and told her that I owed it to the club to continue to play, regardless of my own inner turmoil. Had I the humility to have heeded Judy's advice, a good deal of suffering would have been spared us all. But I would be less than honest if I suggested that it was ever within my power to relinquish a single second of the experience of being a big leaguer. Mr. Mazuma, the time has come for Bob Yamm to bow out of the great game of baseball, but I want you to know, sir, that for these three weeks that I have worn the Kakoola uniform, I have been, not merely the happiest midget, but the happiest man on the face of the earth.

Sincerely,
Robert Yamm

All Men Midgets

Yamm concluded his radio address with an appeal for "human solidarity and brotherhood under God, Our Maker." "I say 'Our' Maker," he continued, "though as we all know there are those in this country who would still have us believe that He who made the full-grown did not make the midget also. Well, let me assure these skeptics, that ever since my own Hour of Crisis began in the Reaper dugout at 3:56 P.M. Central Daylight Saving Time, I have heard His Voice, and it is not runty or pint-sized; let me assure the skeptics that He Who exhorts, chastens, and comforts me is not less a God, nor is He any other God, than He Who made and judges the fully grown. On high, there is but one God Who made us all, and to Him, *all* men are midgets."

Overwhelming Reaction

Reactions to Yamm's forty-two-minute address began coming in from around the nation almost immediately—sports authorities cannot remember another athlete who off the playing field has so captivated the country. Reaper owner Mazuma called Yamm's speech "certainly one of the top ten farewell addresses I've ever heard and just possibly the greatest in history." Mazuma declined to comment further at this time, except to say, "Whether it will be Bob's swan song remains to be seen. The fans are yet to be heard from." [See story on fan mail, "Christmas in September at Kakoola P.O.," p. 26.]

Meanwhile a movement has gotten underway overnight to send Bob Yamm to Congress in the next elections. Republican and Democratic spokesmen declined to comment until Yamm makes known his party affiliation, but interest was more than apparent in the headquarters of both parties here. The sentiment seems to be that perhaps the time is ripe to send a midget to Washington.

"The tragedy of it," said one highly placed political observer, who preferred to remain unidentified, "is that the midgets themselves have always lived scattered about, singly and in pairs around the country, and frankly haven't shown much political savvy. I'm sure they've had other things to worry about, but banded together there's no doubt they would have had one of their own kind in the House long ago. Whether full-grown citizens will elect a midget to represent them in Congress remains to be seen. Up until tonight I would have had to say no. With Yamm's speech, it's a new ballgame. He just could go all the way."

From Hollywood comes word that three major film companies are already bidding for the movie rights to the Bob Yamm story. Talk in the film capital has it that Bob and Judy Yamm will agree to play themselves for one million dollars, with Bob writing the screenplay, to be called "All Men Are Midgets." Part of the proceeds from the projected film are already earmarked to charitable organizations that aid needy and aged midgets.

Angela Trust Outspoken

Strong criticism of Bob Yamm's speech came from Mrs. Angela Whittling Trust, owner of the Tri-City Tycoons, currently in first place in the Patriot League. Mrs. Trust is the outspoken widow of Spenser Trust, who forged Tri-City dynasties in baseball and banking. Of those owners opposed to midgets in the majors, Mrs. Trust has been the most unyielding and vociferous. Newsmen were called to her underground apartment in Tycoon Park at 11:00 P.M., where Mrs. Trust, 72, read the following statement from her wheelchair. Her hip was broken July 4, when she failed in her attempt to field a foul ball lined at her box.

Nix on Siamese

"I never heard such rubbish in my life," Mrs. Trust's statement began. "Just who does he think he is? This Mr. Bob Yamm has delusions of grandeur that would be offensive in a Tri-City

Tycoon, but are utterly bizarre in a player who has pinch-hit a dozen times for a team battling to stay out of seventh, and is a midget besides, with no more business in the major leagues than a sword-swallower or Siamese twins. Yes, you can tell Frank Mazuma that Angela Trust is against Siamese twins too, in case he was planning to bring a pair of them up as a switch-hitter. I know, I am a terrible old New England biddy with a closed mind and the rest of that poppycock, but if Mr. Mazuma's Reapers come to Tri-City, Mass., with a shortstop and a second-baseman who are joined back to back, he will find the door to the visitors' clubhouse locked. I will forfeit the game, I would forfeit the pennant, rather than subject my team to any more of his shenanigans.

Calls Yamm Swiss

"Unfortunately," the Angela Trust statement continued, "what we are witnessing in this country is what I would describe as an outburst of war hysteria. Suddenly anything goes. People are desperate for diversion. Reading the battlefront news I cannot say that I blame them. American women are in tears and cannot sleep. Families are separated, husbands and fathers and sons are gone. The strongest ten million men in America are not with us. We are trying to accustom ourselves to their absence. What could be harder? No wonder the nation appears to be losing its sense of proportion. Who would have believed just one month ago that two ill-tempered midgets dressed up in children's uniforms, with absurd fractions on their backs, would fall to brawling in a major league baseball dugout—and then, *and then*, that one of them would go on the radio for a special broadcast, to bow out of baseball as though he were the King of England abdicating the throne. Yes, a country at war hungers for distractions of a strange sort, but I ask you, my fellow Americans: *how much of this strangeness are we built for?* We must maintain standards! We must return to our senses! We must not account a man 'great' who is nothing more than a presumptuous self-seeking midget with an elephantine sense of his own importance, cashing in during a time of national catastrophe. Truly, I have never in my life heard such cornstarch as he uttered tonight. Why, from the sound of it, you would think Mr. Yamm's conscience was as delicately made as a five hundred dollar Swiss watch. You would think that nobody had a conscience in the world before he appeared at the microphone, with his perfect little wheels whirring away underneath that pretentious little pin-striped suit!

Sorry for Midgets

"Of course I'm delighted he's out of baseball," Mrs. Trust continued. "Good riddance. And his wife with him. Frankly, no baseball wife has ever given me a bigger pain in the neck than this one with her matching shoes and handbags. 'Tower of strength'? Little fashion plate is all she is. Little clotheshorse. A Shetland pony in a child's sunsuit. In this business, the towers of strength are the men on the field. That's why they are there. That's what people pay good money to see. It just will not do to start calling things what they are not. We do not need any more applesauce than there already is in the world. A midget is a midget. I am sorry for them that that has to be the case. I would not wish to be one myself. It must be ghastly. If it were up to me, there wouldn't be any midgets in the world at all. But for some reason that is beyond my understanding, there are, and there is no sense pretending otherwise. As I said, luckily I happen not to be one, but if I were, I assure you I would know my place and have pride enough to make the best of it. And without whining, or what is even worse, going to the opposite extreme and pretending I was some special kind of saint because of it. *That* is what a tower of strength would do, in my judgment.

Won't See Hubby Belittled

"Finally, I will not sit silently by while this sanctimonious, self-inflated, self-admiring, holier-than-thou, stuck-on-himself windbag of a midget announces to the entire country that in his opinion *and* God's, all men are midgets. I have never heard anything so idiotic and insulting in my life. All men are *not* midgets. My husband, Mr. Spenser Trust, who built Trust Savings and Loan, Trust Guaranty Trust, Trust Mutual of Tri-City, as well as the Tri-City Tycoons and Tycoon Park, all before he died at the age of sixty-three, was not a midget in any sense of the word. Nor was my father a midget. He began life as a lumberjack at the age of twelve and by the time he was thirty-five was the greatest timber baron in North America. If the rest of the women in America want to sit idly by while someone calls their men a bunch of midgets, that is their affair. Maybe they know something I don't. But nobody belittles my father or my husband and gets away with it."

The day after Bob Yamm's dramatic broadcast stunned Kakoola and the nation, the Mundys arrived in town. So rat-

tled were the Reapers by the unlikely events of the preceding
afternoon and evening, that the Mundys piled up more runs
in nine innings than they ordinarily scored in a week, edging
Kakoola 6–5 in the ninth. Roland Agni hit two home runs,
bringing his season total to thirty-three (most by a Mundy in
a single season since Gofannon), and with-one on and two out
in the last inning, Bud Parusha set a record of his own, lofting
the first and only home run he or any other one-armed man
would ever hit in the majors. Of course there was a stiff late
afternoon breeze blowing in off the lake and out the left-field
line, and the Kakoola left-fielder also helped to turn into a
four-bagger what should have been an easy out by tipping the
high pop-up off his mitt and into the stands—and then too the
pitch Parusha swung at was described later by the disgusted
Kakoola catcher, Ducky Rig, as "a Lady Godiva ball," meaning it had absolutely nothing on it at all; yet none of this did
anything to diminish the joy in Bud's heart. Obviously under
the sway of Bob Yamm's radio address of the previous night,
Bud told reporters that *he* was the happiest man on the face of
the earth, and then beaming with pride, showed them the telegram that had arrived in the visitors' clubhouse from Washington, D.C., signed "Eleanor Roosevelt," and inviting him
to be co-chairman along with her husband of the upcoming
drive for the March of Dimes.

The Kakoola fans, no less distracted than their players,
seemed for the moment not even to care about the loss that
pushed their team yet another full game behind the Keepers.
It was not to watch the seventh place Reapers take on the
eighth place Mundys that a record-breaking forty-two thousand had assembled in Reaper Field on a weekday afternoon—
rather, they had come, some from as far as two hundred miles
upstate, to see justice done.

For nine full innings of play, whenever the Reapers came
to bat, the fans began their voodoo-like chant. No wonder Jolly
Cholly, throwing his usual wastebasket full of trash, was able
to set the Reapers down looking inning after inning. The Mundys themselves were accustomed by now to all sorts of noise
assaulting their eardrums when they stepped up to the plate,
but the Reapers, for all that they were the property of show-
man Frank Mazuma, and might have been expected to be some-

what more inured to the outlandish, seemed actually to fall into a state of hypnosis when the fans started in calling for the return of their hero. Ptah passed balls (two), Tuminikar wild pitches (two), Mundy fielding errors (five) were as nothing to the transfixed Reaper offense when forty thousand voices set the ball park to rumbling like the heart of a volcano: "YAMM! YAMM! YAMM! YAMM! YAMM! YAMM! YAMM!" Starving savages invoking their potato god for an abundant crop could not have offered up a more impassioned and sustained cry of yearning.

And by nightfall, the deity had delivered. "The fans have spoken," announced Mazuma, his one piratical eye agleam. "As of six o'clock this evening, Bob Yamm, the Midgets' Midget and now the People's Choice, has been reinstated as a Kakoola Reaper. And, in a straight player deal, O.K. Ockatur has been traded to the Ruppert Mundys for slugging outfielder Bud Parusha."

Those sportswriters who hated him of course derided Mazuma for compounding one cruel, corrupt publicity stunt with another. Clearly Mazuma had acquired Parusha—and in the process unloaded the washed-up dwarf—because of the telegram that had converted the Mundy right-fielder from a baseball curiosity into a symbol of courage on a par with the paralyzed President. And even *more* clearly, the telegram purportedly from Mrs. Roosevelt had been composed in his own front office by Mazuma and dispatched by some low-down pal of his in the nation's capital . . . or so whispered his enemies, who claimed that it was only to spare the feelings of poor Bud Parusha that the First Lady, justifiably outraged, had nonetheless decided to allow the telegram to stand as her own —exactly as Mazuma had predicted to his cronies the tender-hearted Eleanor would behave! Admittedly, the name Parusha had once been to the Patriot League what Waner was to the National and DiMaggio to the American, but that was before Angelo and Tony, the Joe and Dom, the Big and Little Poison of the Tycoon outfield, went off to the wars; surely a woman as well informed as Mrs. Roosevelt understood that if Bud Parusha's presence in the big time symbolized anything, it was only the awful depths to which the depleted leagues had

fallen. Still, she held her tongue. Oh, that God damn Mazuma!
He would even go so far as to shit on Eleanor Roosevelt and
the March of Dimes in order to make himself a buck!

To fill the right-field slot left vacant by the departure of Bud
Parusha, Mister Fairsmith had now to look to his bench, and
like schoolchildren who had not done their homework, Mokos,
Omara, Skirnir, Terminus, Hunaman, Khovaki, Kronos, and
Garuda looked the other way. Said Mister Fairsmith's emis-
sary, Jolly Cholly T., "All right, who wants to play right
field?" and the eight, whom he had called together in the
visitors' clubhouse, continued studying the scarred floorboards.
    "Look," said Cholly, "you boys are forty and fifty years
old. When will you ever get a chance like this again? Don't
you want to have somethin' to tell your grandchildren about?"
he asked, figuring this last might have some appeal, in that
all of the Mundy utility players were proud, doting grand-
fathers, who passed much of their time on the bench exchang-
ing snapshots of their offsprings' offspring, while their less
fortunate teammates were out on the field being beaten to a
pulp. "Come on, Mule," said Cholly to Mokos, a great glove
man with the Greenbacks prior to their scandalous demise,
"think how proud little Mickey would be to see your name in
the box score every day. Think how he could say to his school-
chums, 'That's my Grampa out there!' Now how many kids
can do that?"
    "Cholly," said Mokos, sighing, "God knows I'd like to
help you. But frankly it's too much standin' on your feet out
there to suit me."
    "Suppose I say you can sit down, Mule. Suppose I say
you can sit down on the grass and rest up whenever there's an
intentional pass or a new pitcher comes in to warm up. Now
you know with us that can be as much as two, three times an
innin' late in the game, and that's exactly when you'd be
needin' it most."
    The old, tired Mule shook his head. "Sorry, Cholly, I'll sit
here on the bench for you, and watch these games every afternoon, even though the truth be known, I got me a thousand and

one things back home I could do better with my time—but to
be perfectly frank with you, I'll be darned if I'm going to
stand to watch a ballgame, especially when one of the teams
is a last-place club fifty games out of first. I gotta be honest
with you, Cholly. You and me know each other too many years
to start pullin' our punches at a time like this.''

Cholly turned next to Clever Carl Khovaki.

''Can't hear you, Cholly.''

''I said,'' shouted the Mundy coach, ''how would you like
to play right field on a regular basis?''

''Write to who about the bases? I can't but sign my name
with a X, you know that.''

''No, *play right field on a regular basis.*''

''Me?'' bellowed Carl, and broke into a big smile. ''You
must be kiddin'. Can't hear.''

''You don't have to hear!'' shouted Cholly. ''Just field
and hit!''

''Can't hear, though. Can't hear the crowd. Can't hear the
ball bein' struck. Can't hear Agni if he calls for me to catch
it.'' Then, with that wonderful ability to laugh at himself that
had made him the beloved dunderhead of the fans in years gone
by, Clever Carl said, ''Can't even hear myself think. That's
how come I give it up.''

It was true: even in his heyday with Aceldama, though he
could regularly drive a high hard one into the seats, Carl
would be as apt to run back to first as on to third, if someone
hit a single while he was on second. In the thick of things he
seemed to have no more idea as to how the game was played
than a Saudi Arabian. Then he went deaf and lost what little
contact he had with those who could holler and scream at him
what to do next—and then he became a Mundy. ''Get a feller
can hear, Cholly, that's my advice. That is,'' said Carl, ''if
we got one on the club. Otherwise my advice is buy one, and
the hell with the price. Should be one of us ain't hard of hearin'
anyway, just in case of some kind of emergency.''

''Now, look,'' said Cholly, ''somebody has got to play right
field on this club, and it ain't me. I am already pitcher, coach,
mother, and father around here, and that's enough.''

''Well,'' snapped Wally Omara, ''it ain't me, either! Let's
get that clear. Not with my blood pressure—no, sir! If we

had even a shot at seventh, well, that would be a arguin' point, Cholly. But we ain't got a shot at shit as far as I can see, and in the light of that, I really am flabbergasted that you have had the raw nerve, Charles, to even suggest to a feller with my blood pressure—''

"And you?" asked Cholly, turning to Applejack Terminus, who was sitting off by himself, as though nursing some private misery.

"Cholly," said Applejack, looking sadly down at the belly bulging over his belt, "Cholly, if I could still go back for 'em the way I did when I come up, I'd be out there for you every afternoon for the rest of the month. But," said the Apple, closing his eyes against the tears, "them days is gone, Cholly."

"Suppose I say you don't have to go back, Apple. Suppose I say you can play up against the wall, so you only have to come in."

"Cholly," said Terminus, "ain't *nobody* can't catch 'em comin' *in*. Why, that's a insult!"

"But I ain't even sayin' *catch* 'em, Apple. Let 'em drop in for singles and take 'em on the hop. And we'll call that playin' right field. What do you say, fella?"

"Cholly," he moaned, again struggling not to weep, "in my prime, Cholly, when I was playin' center for the Blues, there was times I covered *second* on account of how close in I would play. And you know, 'cause you seen it. You seen where the smart fans used to sit back in them days when I was with the Blues—right out there in the bleachers! And not just paupers either, but millionaires with their chauffeurs. And why? 'Cause they knew. You want to watch a ace outfielder like Apple ply his trade, why, that's the only place *to* sit— right back of him! Yessir! And then watch him go when that ball is hit! Just *watch* him! But then a' course," said Apple, suddenly bitter, "then a' course they put that rabbit in the ball, didn't they? That's what moved us back a' course—*and ruined the whole gosh darn game!* Hell, I remember the first time this feller struck a triple over my head with that new ball a' theirs. Can't even recall his name no more—I don't think he lasted in the big time but fifteen minutes. Anyhow, he struck this darn triple. It was openin' day of 1920. Know what I did? I was so dang mad, I didn't even bother to throw that ball in from center, nosir; I ran all the way to the infield, holdin' that new ball a' theirs in my hand, see, and I run all the way up to that hoofenpoofer, who was a smilin' away to beat the band on third there, as though he had done somethin' special, you understand, and I said, 'Listen, you sorry excuse of a whangdoodle, last year you couldn't a hit the ball above your waist if we give it to you to hold in your hand!' 'Oh no?' says that grinnin' gaboon, 'then how come I done it just now, Apple?' 'How *come?*' says I. '*Here's* how come!' And I ripped off his cap and stuck that ball right up to his ear: 'Juss listen, you wampus cat, juss hold that right up to yer ear you tree squeak of a gazook, and you can *hear* that rabbit's heart a-beatin' away in there!'" And on and on went the fat man, fifteen minutes more on the subject that invariably threw him into a tirade—the introduction twenty-odd years earlier of the lively ball. "Nope," he concluded, spitting on the clubhouse floor to register his vote, "the day I have to rest my fanny on the fence, that is the day I bow out of this game for good. Either you play the outfield shallow, Cholly, like it was meant to be played back before the era of the stitched golf ball, *or you don't play it at all!*"

In the end it was the undernourished six-footer, skinny Specs Skirnir, the Mundy with a year of college education and the least confident of them all, who took the job.

"I just don't want to break my glasses, Cholly."

"You won't, Specs."

"I'm not used to them yet, and I'm afraid I'm going to break them."

"Specs, you've had 'em since '34."

"I know, Cholly, but I just can't get used to them."

"Well, it may just be a matter of playin' with 'em regular. That may do it for you, boy."

"But what happens when they get steamed up?"

"Just take 'em off and clean 'em with your hankie."

"What if it's in the middle of a play, Cholly?"

"Do it before the play."

"But they don't get steamed up *before*. They get steamed up *during*."

"Well, then," said Cholly, patiently, "do the best you can, and clean 'em after."

"But *after's* too late! What if because they're steamed up I can't see—and get hit with the ball! Suppose I'm at bat and get hit in the mouth! Suppose a grounder jumps up and breaks my nose! And all because my glasses got steamed up!"

"Ah, come on, Specs, none of that's goin' to happen. It hasn't yet."

"That's because since I got them in 1934 I've been *benched!* And even with *that* they get steamed! Look, look how I chipped my tooth on the water fountain in Independence. My glasses got steamed up on account of the heat, and I went in too close for a drink, and I chipped my tooth on the spout. Look, Cholly, look at my shins, they're all black and blue— tripped over Big Jawn's foot just going down to the clubhouse in Terra Inc. to take a leak. Imagine—just taking a leak is dangerous in these damn things! Cholly, I shouldn't even really be in the *dugout* during the game, let alone on the *field!* Nine innings just on the bench and at the end of the game I'm a wreck! If I don't go in and get a rubdown and a hot shower, I ache in every muscle for a week! Cholly, this is crazy—this is insane! I don't get what's going on around here at all. I've been to school, Cholly, and I can tell you this much—you don't trade away a perfectly decent one-armed outfielder to put in his place a guy who wears *glasses*. What kind of baseball strategy is that? And look what we got in return, Charles—a dwarf! It wasn't bad enough to have Chico with that awful squeak of his, now we got to have a twisted little dwarf coming in out of the bullpen for the grand finale every afternoon! Cholly, I don't like it! Nine years now, Cholly, one way or another, I've managed to stay alive wearing these God damn things—and now suddenly this crazy little dwarf shows up to help us finish last, and I'm supposed to take my life in my hands playing in glasses for a big league team. *Cholly, I'm only forty-three years old!*"

"Specs," said Cholly, laying a fatherly hand upon the sopping uniform of the terrified utility player on the brink of becoming a regular again, "I have just spent a mornin' here goin' over this club's reserve strength, and if it'll be any comfort to you, I don't believe this here *is* a big league team any more, in the original way that they meant that word."

"Well, maybe *we* ain't a big league team, but we're play-

ing *against* big league teams—and, Cholly, that's what's scariest of all!''

After a moment's reflection, Cholly said, ''I suppose that
is what's scariest, come to think of it. Still and all, we gotta
do it,'' and he entered Specs Skirnir on the line-up card for
that day's game. ''You're battin' seventh, son. And don't
forget your hankie.''

Query: Who back in Port Ruppert had arranged the trade
anyway? As far as the players knew, the paneled, carpeted
stadium offices of the Mundy management had been turned
over to the Army, along with the beautifully manicured field,
and the patriotic Mundy brothers had rented for the duration
a nondescript cubbyhole in a rundown office building at the
very edge of Port Ruppert's colored section. According to one
of the rumors with which the players around the league liked
to tease and taunt the Mundys, the office was tended only by
an old woolly-haired janitor who came in to raise and lower
the blackout shade each day, and to forward whatever mail had
accumulated on to the exotic cities of Latin America, where
the Mundy brothers were said to be recuperating from the
hard winter of negotiation that had landed their ball club on
the road.

''Hey,'' said Big John, laughing as usual, ''maybe the
nigger done it. Maybe Mazuma called when he was sweepin'
up, and the nigger said, 'Okay wiff me, boss,' and hung up.
What do you say to that, Venus de Milo? Some nigger janitor
back in Rupe-it swapped you even up for a fella the size of a
mosquito!''

''Hey, would that be legal?'' asked Nickname. ''If a nigger
done it? I mean, ain't they got their own leagues?''

''That depends whether the Mundy brothers give 'im the
authority,'' said old Wayne Heket. ''Why, down home I know
a feller signed everythin' over to his dog, then just lay down
and died.''

''Could be Nickname's right, though,'' said Hot. ''I'm
gonna look that up. It just could be that if a nigger has done it,
that Bud here ain't got no choice but to go over to their
leagues—and for life!''

''Now wouldn't that be somethin'! If on top of havin' just

one arm for hittin' and throwin' and wipin' his bee-hind, poor
Buddy wound up by mistake playin' outfield for a bunch of
niggers!''

"Hell, I'druther go on home and shovel hoss manure than
have to play ball with jigaboos every day!''

"At least you'd have your self-respect!''

"Poor Buddy! Eatin' all that shit they eat too, instead a'
real food!''

"And how's he ever goin' to know what they're sayin'
when they're talkin' to him? I hear tell over in them leagues,
that instead of havin' signals they just holler out 'Bunt!',
figurin' the other team don't know enough English to guess
what's comin' next. Them spades is always scratchin' themselves so much, half the time what you figure for a hit-'n-run
sign ain't nothin' but the manager goin' after his coot-
ies.''

"Poor Buddy!''

"Poor Bud!''

While this exchange took place in the Mundy locker room,
Bud continued to separate out of his locker what belonged to
the Mundys and what belonged to him. Earlier in the day he
had wondered just how unhappy he would be when the time
to leave his old teammates rolled around. He was a sentimental
sucker from way back, and he knew it. But as it turned out,
he found he was just too damn happy about going to be sad.
Why, if anything it was the other players who looked to be on
the brink of tears, as they watched him pack his cardboard
suitcase with his few things, and render unto Ruppert what
was the team's.

"Poor Buddy,'' they said, "I don't envy him if he winds
up with a bunch of blooches to have to sit down next to in the
dugout on a hundred degree day. Pee-*you!*''

Oh, but did they envy him! With the exception perhaps of
John Baal, who considered a home a joke, there was hardly a
Mundy who wouldn't have given his right arm to have been
Big Bud Parusha, the new Kakoola Reaper.

"Well, fellas,'' said Bud, "that's it, I guess.'' He waited
a moment to see if he might stop being so damn happy and
start in being just a little sad, if only for auld lang syne. But
it was not for him to be miserable that day—not quite yet.
"Well, I won't forget you fellers, don't worry,'' said Bud,

and suitcase in hand, he left the Mundy clubhouse, never to wear that uniform again.

O.K. Ockatur arrived shortly thereafter to take his place; no observations about niggers from the Mundys, either, not a word in fact about anything in this whole wide world, while the misshapen midget stripped out of his little street clothes and climbed into the scarlet and gray.

Frank Mazuma, having already designated the opener of the Mundy-Reaper series "Welcome Bud Parusha Day," held one of his press conferences before the game, this one to introduce Buddy to the Kakoola newspapermen, and even more important, "to squelch at the outset a most detestable rumor that," said Mazuma, "reflects not simply upon that doormat known as Frank Mazuma's integrity, or upon the integrity of this fine young man bearing the honored baseball name of Parusha, but what is of far greater moment, upon the integrity of the wife of the President of the United States, and, by extension, of the Commander-in-Chief himself, the leader of the world's greatest democracy in its do-or-die battle against the forces of evil."

Bud, standing sheepishly beside the Reaper owner, wore a Reaper home uniform of creamy white flannel, bearing on its back the orange numeral 1½. The fraction, of course, had come off O.K. Ockatur's uniform; as Mazuma explained to the reporters, it was not intended to suggest that Bud was missing anything ("the empty right sleeve of his uniform, gentlemen, tells that story eloquently enough") but rather that he was endowed with about fifty per cent more courage than the ordinary mortal.

"Why not go all the way then, Frank," asked one reporter, "and give him 1–5–0 for a number?"

"Well, the fact is, Len, I talked that over with Bud here, but he said he thought it might seem to the other ballplayers that he was trying to lord it over them, if he had three numbers to their two. So we settled on the half. In fact, I said to him, 'Bud, do you think you can restore this fraction to a place of dignity in the baseball world?' and Buddy here said in reply, 'I sure can try, Mr. Mazuma.'"

Then a reporter asked, "How the hell does he tie his shoelaces, Frank?"

"Good question, Red, but if you don't mind, we're going to save those exhibitions for the pregame ceremonies. Right now I want, for everyone's sake, to turn to that rumor that has swept the league ever since I purchased- Buddy from the Mundys late yesterday afternoon. I needn't tell you gentlemen that over the years I have grown somewhat accustomed to having my motives maligned by the self-styled protectors of this game—the people I call (and I'm not mincing initials here either) the s.o.b.s of O.B. But I really must confess that I was not prepared for their latest smear campaign. I simply did not believe that they could sink to such depths as to claim that this fine young ballplayer whom you see before you, who only yesterday struck the first four-bagger ever hit in the majors by a one-armed player, is not in fact one-armed at all, but that beneath his uniform he has a perfectly good second arm tied down to his left side."

"They *didn't!*" someone cried (someone perhaps in Mazuma's employ?).

"Gentlemen of the press, I have asked you here to help me scotch this despicable lie of theirs before this boy goes out on the field today to have bestowed upon him the honors he earned yesterday with one mighty swing of his bat, and I remind you, against my own ball club. I am going to ask my little daughter, Doubloon, to come out here to assist Bud in removing his new Reaper shirt. She's been clamoring all summer for a job out at the ball park, and I thought maybe this would be as good a time as any. Honey? Doubloon?"

Here a voluptuous young woman in brief white shorts and a clinging orange blouse (and the word "Over" stitched across her back, just above the number "21") rushed in a clatter of high heels up to the microphone, kissed her daddy on the mouth, and then, to the applause and catcalls of the assembled reporters, began to fumble with the buttons of Bud's uniform shirt.

"By the way," ad-libbed Mazuma, " 'Doubloon' doesn't mean what some of you fellas think it does. Strange to say, it has nothing to do with things that come in pairs."

The newspapermen had to chuckle at the famous Mazuma

humor which he could direct even at the members of his own family.

"I'm all thumbs," giggled Doubloon, as she loosened Bud's belt so as to extract his shirttails from his trousers. "Oh what a stupid thing to say to *you!*" she cried, fluttering her eyelids at the new Kakoola Reaper.

"Nor," said Mazuma, lighting up a cigar, "is 'Doubloon' a mispronunciation of the capital of Ireland, for all that this kid could get anybody's Irish up, if you know what I mean by 'Irish.'"

By now Bud's shirt had been removed and Doubloon was drawing his orange sweatshirt out of his shorts.

"Actually," said Mazuma, continuing with the witty patter, "'Doubloon' is just another way of saying 'Do-re-mi.' Tell the boys the names of your brothers and sisters, sweetheart."

Turning momentarily from her task, she wiped the perspiration from her upper lip with a raised shoulder ("Oh baby!" cried one of the reporters, oddly moved by the gesture) and in her whispery voice, said, "Jack, Buck, Gelt, and Dinero."

Then, with a little jump into the air, Doubloon yanked the sweatshirt over Bud's head and the athlete was nude to the waist.

"Ucch," cried Doubloon, unable to suppress a shiver of revulsion.

"Well," said Mazuma, gravely now, "there it is, gentlemen. The truth for all to behold. Not a trace of a left arm. Not a *suggestion* of a left arm."

Here, at a nod from Mazuma, the photographers surged forward and the room was incandescent with flashbulbs.

"How about from the back, Bud!"

"Smile, Bud, cheer up! This is your day, boy!"

"Make a muscle, Bud, with the one you got!"

"Cheese, Bud, cheese! *Thatta* boy!"

When the photographers receded—with a promise from Mazuma that there was more to come—one of the reporters said, "Frank, you may not like this, but how do we know that this isn't some kind of trick make-up job such as they do in the movies? How do we know that Bud's missing arm isn't in fact hidden away under a phony layer of skin made out of wax or some such substance?"

"Doubloon," said Mazuma, "would you do Daddy a favor? To assure the reporters that there's no arm hidden away inside a false covering of skin, would you just pass your hand up and down Bud's side?"

"Do *what?*"

"Just press lightly up and down his left side, so they see that it is really and truly him. Well, come on now, honey."

"Oh, *Daddy.*"

"Now, Dubby, you're the one who wanted a summer job, you know that. You're the one who wanted to wear the number 'Over 21,' remember? You're a big girl now and sometimes big people have to do things they don't necessarily like to do. Touch his side, sweetheart."

"Oh, Daddy, I *can't.* It's so *uccchy.*"

"Look, young lady, either you touch him as I tell you to, or I am going to put you over my knee! You may be over twenty-one, you know, but you're still not too old for your daddy to give you a good old-fashioned spanking, press conference or no press conference!"

Here the photographers came surging forward again, cameras in the air.

"What a clown," mumbled a reporter known to be no great admirer of Mazuma's.

"Clown my ass, Smitty!" snapped the Reaper owner. "Do you think I want you boys leaving here half-believing that you've been had? *Do* you? Do you think I want the people of this country to suspect that the wife of the President of the United States, the First Lady of the Land, has asked somebody to be honorary co-chairman of the March of Dimes who has been disguised by me, Frank Mazuma, for reasons of publicity or profit, to look like some kind of freak, when in fact he isn't? Do you think I want our brave allies to harbor the slightest suspicion that this is a country run by con-men and crooks? Do you boys know what Tokyo Rose could do with a little tidbit like this? Do *you,* Doubloon, my innocent daughter? Do you realize the kind of venom that Jap bitch could pour into the ears of—?"

"Oh, *please,*" cried Doubloon, "I can't *bear* you, Daddy, when you sound like a minister!"

"And what's wrong with sounding like a minister, may I

ask? Since when is religion a dirty word in this country, may
I ask?"

"Oh, all right, I'll *touch* him—just stop *lecturing* me!"

"Okay then, okay," said Mazuma, subsiding, and nodded
to the photographers to get ready.

Doubloon meanwhile readied herself. First, she squeezed
her eyes shut very tightly like a little girl preparing to swallow
a spoonful of cod-liver oil. Then she rose up on tiptoes so that
her narrow white heels came popping up out of her orange
shoes ("Oh baby!" cried that same reporter, now moved
apparently by the sight of her heels); and then, with great
reluctance and much wiggling of the can, she extended the
finger of one hand very, very slowly in the direction of Bud
Parusha's body, which all the while he had been standing
shirtless before the crowd, had been turning a deep shade
of crimson.

Because of the lightning storm of flashbulbs that accompanied the contact of Doubloon's fingertip with Buddy's flesh,
the effect of her gesture upon the former Mundy was not immediately apparent. But when at last everyone's vision was
restored, there for all to see was a bulge of substantial proportions in Buddy's new flannel trousers.

"My, my," laughed the reporters.

Mazuma, never at a loss for words, quipped, "Well,
gentlemen, I'll tell you one thing my new right-fielder ain't
missin'," and with that, brought the house down.

What a clown indeed. Is it any wonder that when Mazuma
beckoned, the reporters came in droves? And is it any wonder
that those like General Oakhart, who had struggled all their
lives to prevent the great American game from becoming
just another cheap form of popular entertainment, wished
that Frank Mazuma, and all his kind, might be lined up against
the outfield wall and shot?

The jubilant mood in which the press conference ended continued on through the pregame ceremonies of "Welcome Bud
Parusha Day"—baseball stunts and feats of skill performed
by the visiting Mundys. "Their tribute," announced Frank
Mazuma, to the forty-odd thousand who had of course turned

out not to welcome Bud Parusha but to witness the return of Bob Yamm, "their tribute to their former teammate, a great ballplayer and an even greater human being, brother of the great Tycoon Parushas, now serving so gallantly with the United States Marines, Angelo and Tony—" here the fans rose and accorded Angelo and Tony a standing ovation that lasted two full minutes—"Bud Parusha!"

Scattered applause as Bud ran from the Reaper dugout waving his mitt at the stands. From the steps of the visitors' dugout, the Mundys looked on in awe at Buddy all in home team white. How like a bride he seemed to them in their own tattered road uniforms of gray! Jolly Cholly, the kindest coach who ever lived, flashed the V for Victory sign—"Good luck, kid!" he called, and Parusha was all at once washed over with an emotion so strong, so engulfing, that he even felt it in his missing limb. *Take me back,* cried the heart of the bride-to-be, *take me back before it's too late. Maybe you're where I belong!* But what American in his right mind ever wanted to be back with an eighth place team when he could be up with one in seventh? So, instead of bolting for the Mundy dugout, Bud continued on to home plate, to his deliverers, Mazuma and Doubloon.

And now the first of the Mundys who had agreed to perform that afternoon was introduced to the fans. On the sly, Mazuma had approached each of the disgruntled Ruppert players, but in the end only two of the regulars and one of the relief pitchers was so desperate, or so gullible, as to be taken in when the owner promised to make Reapers out of them too if they proved to be "crowd pleasers" in the manner of Buddy P.

"Ladies and gentlemen," Mazuma announced into the mike that had been set up at home plate, "it is a pleasure and an honor to introduce to you the youngest player in the history of the major leagues, Mundy second-sacker, fourteen-year-old Nickname Damur!"

Nickname came charging full-speed from the visiting team's dugout and made a perfect (and he hoped, crowd-pleasing) hook slide around Doubloon's leg and into the plate.

"Cut it *out*," snapped Doubloon.

"Reputed to be the fastest base runner in the game today

—by those, that is, who've had the rare opportunity of *seeing* him on base—only kidding, Nickname!" quipped Mazuma, clapping the boy on the back, while the mob howled—"Nickname Damur is today going to match his speed around the bases with none other than the second cousin by marriage to the great Seabiscuit, my own Doubloon's polo pony—Graham Cracker!"

Here a snorting little chestnut filly danced up out of the Reaper dugout. "Grahams!" called Doubloon, and she ran to where the batboy, who had led the horse up past the water cooler and on to the playing field, was holding the pony by the reins. "Oh Grammies!" cried Doubloon and buried her lips in the pony's mane. Then, in high-heeled shoes, shorts, and blouse, she was hoisted up onto her mount by the batboy; her riding crop was tossed up to her and she was off—galloping all the way to the center-field wall and back.

"Graham Cracker will be carrying one hundred and seven pounds. Or," said Mazuma, "to put it so that you folks who don't follow the ponies understand, 38–22–36."

Now Nickname and Graham Cracker lined up with their noses even at home plate and pointed in the direction of first base. "As you fans know," said Mazuma, "thanks to General Douglas D. Oakhart there are still no pari-mutuel windows allowed in Patriot League parks. But speaking for myself and fun-loving men everywhere, I don't see what's to stop you from placing a friendly little wager with your neighbor . . ."

While the hubbub of betting excitement swept through the stadium, Doubloon took the opportunity to lean down across Graham Cracker's neck, and as though talking into the horse's ear, whispered to the Mundy second-baseman, "Wouldn't crowd us on the turn, Nickname—not if you want to come out of this thing in one piece."

And they were off!

"It's Graham Cracker in the lead as they break from the plate," announced Mazuma, dropping into a deep gravelly voice and firing his words like bullets— "It's Graham by half a length down the first-base line! At the bag, Graham turns wide—and it's Nickname making his dash on the inside as they head for second! And now they're neck and neck, Nickname's right there! So is Graham! They're around second heading for third, and it's Nickname now by a length, a length and a half with a third of the way to come—and now Graham Cracker is making her move as they pass the shortstop position! Graham Cracker is not beaten yet! She's coming with a rush! If she don't get blocked, she'll give that Mundy an awful drive! Now they're around third, they're heading for home, *and here comes Graham Cracker*—'' and now forty thousand screaming, hollering fans were on their feet, and even as Doubloon's whip curled across his mouth, even as the blood sprang from his nose, Nickname could imagine victory— himself a Kakoola Reaper, second-baseman for an authentic big league team, a club with a park of its own, fans of its own, and an owner of whose presence you could never for a moment be in doubt—ah, but there was the blur of Graham Cracker pulling past him, and once again that whip as it flailed backwards to crack open the skin of his brow, and no, he would *not* be defeated, no, he would *not* be a Mundy for the rest of his born days—"Don't!" hollered Jolly Cholly, as Nickname began to go into his slide—but he did, he did: at the risk of being crushed to powder beneath Graham Cracker's four plunging legs, the ambitious fourteen-year-old, who wanted only to improve his lot in life (as who doesn't?), who wanted only to better himself (as who wouldn't?), went in under the horse's hoofs.

"Crazy little prick!" cried Doubloon, and swerving to avoid a collision at the plate, allowed Nickname to score. She herself went hurtling headlong out of the saddle and flew some thirty feet through the air, then bounced into the Mundy dugout, where Big John, taking her on the short hop, was able to squeeze just about whatever he wanted before the stretcher arrived to hurry the broken body of the unconscious young woman to the emergency operating room of Kakoola Memorial. Then, with forty thousand flabbergasted fans looking on —yes, even the Kakoola fans were staggered, even their expectations of a lively afternoon of thrills were exceeded by this calamitous turn of events—Mazuma borrowed a pistol from a stadium guard and put a bullet through Graham Cracker's skull.

"Gee," gulped Nickname, as the pony, who had lain twitching in agony only inches from home plate, died with a whish of fumes from her exhaust, "I was *only* tryin' to win."

In his grief, Mazuma had to smile. "Well, if Doubloon kicks the bucket, Damur, you'll see what you won. When the fans get through with you, Nickname, you'll envy the unenviable Gamesh. My educated guess, kid, is that even if Doubloon survives, you yourself are washed up. To coin an appropriately paradoxical phrase, 'You're out of the running, flash-in-the-pan.'"

"At fourteen?" cried the bloodied Mundy.

"Kee-rect," said Mazuma. "I believe you have just Mundied yourself for life."

"But how *could* I? I *won!*"

"Tell it to them, Nickname," said Mazuma, lifting his gaze to the mob howling now for Nickname's unsportsmanlike hide. "Like the feller says," quipped Mazuma, covering his ears, "where you're concerned, it's all over but the shouting."

Minutes passed before Mazuma could even hope to make himself heard; then he stepped to the microphone, raised one hand, and into the red roaring mouth of the crowd, tossed this tender filet: "Official time, fourteen and four-fifths seconds. The winner—Damur!"

"Murderer! Killer! Monster! Fiend!"—yes, those were the nicknames they were now suggesting for the youth perennially in search of the right monicker for himself.

After the groundskeepers had dragged Graham Cracker's carcass across the field and out through the Mundy bullpen, and had raked away the last of her poignant hoof prints, Mazuma announced to the crowd that he intended to continue with "Welcome Bud Parusha Day" ceremonies as planned. And when, in a breaking voice, he said, "I can't help but think that Doubloon would want it that way," the fans once again came to their feet to deliver a standing ovation.

To the surprise and delight of everyone, the next person to be introduced was a stout, gray-haired woman in a longish print dress and sturdy shoes who was helped up out of the Reaper dugout and escorted to the microphone by a small army of Boy Scouts. "Ladies and gentlemen," said Mazuma, pecking her once on the cheek, "this little lady happens to be— my mom! And with her, Troop 40 of Mazuma Avenue School!"

The Boy Scouts came instantly to attention and saluted—

some saluted Mother Mazuma, others Frank Mazuma, still
others the American flag in center field, and a few simply
saluted each other. Mrs. Mazuma waved shyly at the crowd
with her handbag. "Today," she said into the mike, but so
softly the fans had to lean forward in their seats to hear . . .
Today, came the even gentler echo . . . "I consider myself—"
I consider myself . . . "the happiest mother—" *the happiest
mother* . . . "on the face of the earth—" *of the earth* . . .
Yet another standing ovation.

"Now, fans," said Mazuma, "as you all know, there is a
custom in baseball, old as the great game itself, for the team
at bat to attempt to rile up the team on the field by that benign
form of badinage known as bench-jockeying. And as you also
know if you've been out to the park this year to see our erst-
while visitors at play, there is probably no player in the entire
league who the bench-jockeys can rile up quicker and easier
than the man I am about to introduce. All you have to shout
from the bench is 'Hothead, bet you a bottle of suds you
couldn't throw out my own mother!' and then watch that
Mundy fume. Folks, let's give a big welcome to Bud Parusha's
former teammate and fellow defective, Ruppert Mundy catcher,
Hothead Ptah!"

Wearing but one shin guard—"Only got but one shin!"
Hot would snarl at the wiseguys—and his chest protector, and
carrying his mask and his glove, Hot came racing out of the
Mundy dugout at what for him was top speed. Oh, was he
eager!

"Well," said Mazuma when the laughter died down, "here
she is, Hot—my mom!"

"Howdy!"

"Good day, Mr. Ptah."

"Well, Hot," said Mazuma, "think you can throw her
out at second, two out of three? Personally, I have to say I
got my doubts, knowin' Mom here and her speed."

The crowd went wild as Hothead proceeded instantly to
lose his temper. "You'll eat those words, Mazuma!"

"And—and," said Mazuma, having to wait now for his
own laughter to subside ("His daughter's in the hospital,
surgery is being performed on her spinal column at this very
moment, and he can still laugh! What a guy!" said the Reaper

sportscaster to the hundreds of thousands tuned to KALE),
"to assist Hothead in his attempt to cut down my mother
stealing two times out of three, here is the proud owner of the
sorest arm in baseball, Mundy relief ace—"

Yes, to the delight of the multitude, Chico Mecoatl began
the long sad walk in from the Mundy bullpen. "Eeeep!" they
cried, "eeeep!" imitating that little yelp he made when he
pitched. Oh, how the crowd loved it—while the Mundys themselves were dumbstruck. Chico, even *Chico,* with an E.R.A. of
14.06, could no longer bear the indignity of wearing the Ruppert R!

"And," continued Mazuma, "covering second, to take the
throw from Hothead—" "No!" the fans roared. "—Mundy
second-sacker—" "No! No!" "—Nickname—"

"MURDERER! KILLER! THUG!" they shrieked, as
Nickname, tipping his cap, ran gamely out to his position.

When Big John rose from the Mundy bench to go out to
cover first, he quickly assured his startled teammates that *he*
was only doing it for the kicks involved. "Don't worry, boys.
I ain't no turncoat. Only trade I'd consider is to the Gypsys—
wouldn't mind dancin' with a bear before I die! Haw! Haw!"

Mrs. Mazuma, meanwhile, had retired to the Reaper dugout, to leave her purse for safekeeping with the Boy Scouts
of Troop 40, and to change into her spikes.

To spare himself some suffering, Chico rolled his warm-up
pitch on the ground to Hot, who then pegged the ball down to
Nickname at second. Ducky Rig, the Reaper catcher, came out
to pretend to be the batter, and to yet another standing ovation
—seven in all during the pregame ceremony, "let me check—
yes sir, that's it all right, a major league record," said the
sportscaster, "for standing ovations in a pregame ceremony
in regular season competition"—Mazuma's mom walked to
first in her baseball shoes, being careful to avoid stepping
down on the freshly laid foul line.

"How do you do, Mr. Baal," she said, and Big John gave
the fans their money's worth by sweeping off his cap and
bowing in the manner of Sir Walter Raleigh.

Then the Mexican right-hander went into his stretch; he
looked cursorily back over his left shoulder to first—and sure

enough, the old lady in the print dress came climbing down off the bag, and taking one inch, and then another, and then another, wound up taking herself a very healthy lead indeed. Engaging Chico's eyes, she began to move her arms in a slow swinging motion, looking for all the world as though she would be breaking for second as soon as he went into his delivery.

Well, let her. Chico hadn't thrown to first to hold a *regular* base runner to the bag so far this year, and he wasn't starting up at this late date with an old lady. Not with *his* arm, he wasn't. So, into his snake-like wind-up he went, and with that yelp of his—"Eeeeep!"—looped the ball into the dirt. Hot blocked it neatly with his wooden leg, and Mrs. Mazuma held at first.

On the second pitch she went! The pitch, when it finally arrived, was high, but Hot, playing inspired ball, leaped to grab it and still in the air, fired down to Nickname.

Dress and all, Mrs. Mazuma slid, and her son, who was serving now as umpire at second, called, "Y'r out!"

The look she gave him when she rose to brush the dirt off herself could hardly be described as maternal. "He missed the tag, Frank."

"I call 'em the way I see 'em, Mom," said Mazuma into the hand mike he was carrying.

"He never touched me, Frank," said Mrs. Mazuma, kicking angrily at the bag.

"Look, no favors around here just because you happened once upon a time to have nursed the umpire! If I said 'Y'r out!', y'r out!"

Shaking her head in dismay, she trotted back to first, but not before turning to toss a few words Nickname's way.

Nickname now walked the ball to the mound, waving for Hot and Big John to join him and Chico for a conference. "Look," he said, "you ain't gonna believe this—but know what Mrs. Mazuma just told me? She flashes me this look, see, and she says, 'Don't block that bag, sonny, or next time I'll cut your ears off!'"

"Well, whattayaknow! Just as I suspicioned! That card Mazuma done it to us again—the she is really a he! Haw!"

"Look," snarled Hot, "I don't care if it's a *it!* You block that bag good, Nickname! And Chico, don't you give her no jump like that, you hear? Fire to first when she takes that lead!"

"Oh, Caldo, no, please Caldo, I don't be happy fire to first —too much hurt, Caldo—"

"And what about bein' a friggin' Mundy, don't that hurt? Hold that slit to first, you yelpin' little spic, or the whole lot of us is doomed to Rupe-it forever!"

"Haw! Doomded we is anywhichway," said Big John, and strode back to first base as though doom was so much lemonade to him. "How they hangin', honey?" he asked Mrs. Mazuma, placing a wad of tobacco juice between her spikes.

"Here, here," retorted Mrs. Mazuma, "we don't need any of that, young man," and stepped down off the bag with her lead.

Chico's sorry throw to first, preceded as it was by a squeak, enabled Mrs. Mazuma to get back to the bag in plenty of time.

"Ain't you afraid you'll tear your nice dress, sweetie, if you have to hit the dirt again?" asked Big John.

"I can look after myself perfectly well, thank you," and she broke for second! Again Hot's peg was perfect, but with a slide reminiscent of the Georgia Peach himself, Mrs. Mazuma swept in on her back to the right of the bag—and the tag—while reaching behind to tick the base with the fingers of her left hand.

"Safe!" called Mazuma, extending his arms, palms down. "She is *safe!*"

With the crowd on its feet again, Mrs. Mazuma rose to clap the dust out of her dress and to adjust her rubberized hose. And all the while, in a voice that was no less menacing for being muted, she issued a warning to the Mundy second-baseman, who though he could not believe his ears, listened as politely as he would to any lady her age dressed in that kind of dress: "Now back in the kitchen, sonny," she told him, brushing herself clean, "I have got me a special grinding stone for honing my carving knives—and you know what I do with it? I sit around with the other nice ladies in the after-noon over a cup of coffee and some petit fours, and I sharpen up my spikes. Now this is the last time I'm telling you: that basepath, in case you ain't heard, belongs to the runner. You get in the runner's way one more time, and she is going to take you, buster, clothes and all. I'm stealing this next one for a kid in the hospital, Nickname, little girl name a' Doubloon— so just you give me room, boy, if you want to have a face left."

"But," replied Nickname, "she *whipped* me—with her *whip!* Look, this blood is *mine!*" But Mrs. Mazuma was trotting back to first, accompanied by a joyous roar from the crowd.

As the two stood together on the bag, Big John came up to within an inch of her jaw, and inquired, "Just couldn't be, under that wig and make-up and all, that you are the outlawed and unfamous Gil Gamesh pickin' up a few pesos—could it, Mrs. M.? That couldn't be you under there, playin' the slit again, could it, Gilly boy?"

"Now you just watch your tongue, Mr. Baal. One more crack—"

"You call it how you want—haw! haw!"

"—and I will report you to General Oakhart for even mentioning that name on a big league diamond, and what's more, to an American Mom." And like a big, calm, cunning cat, she started inching away from that bag.

Behind the plate, Hothead was already screaming, "Hold her to the—!" But it was too late now; the old lady had gotten the jump and was already midway to second while Hot was still waiting for Chico's slow ball to arrive at the plate. According to some of the ironists in the league, you really had to feel sorry for that pitch—slow is slow, but that poor thing was retarded. Hot, too frantic to think, did the unthinkable: while the ball was still on its way to the plate, he rushed forward to meet it, thus putting himself directly in the path of the bat, should the man at the plate decide to take a cut at either the ball or the catcher.

"Swing!" the fans cried to Duck Rig. "Knock the cover off his skull!"

Ducky was really of a kindly nature (and the fans of course were only kidding), but still and all, it was his job up there to keep the whole thing honest, and so he swung—a kind of golf stroke, was all, at Hothead's wooden leg, driving it cleanly off the stump and down the third-base line—"Foul!"

according to the sportscaster up in the radio box. One of the
Boy Scouts ran instantly out to retrieve it, even as Hot, balancing on just one leg, burned one down to second and then
went toppling after it on to his face. God, did ever a man want
to be traded as much as Hothead Ptah?

"A perfect peg!" the sportscaster cried—only Mrs. Mazuma was sliding in with her right leg so high in the air, you
could for a moment see the sunlight glinting off her spikes.
Then shoe, leg, and the flying folds of her long dress disappeared into the crumbling figure of Nickname, who went down
as if in slow motion, closing over Mrs. Mazuma's lower ex-
tremities like the jaws of a crocodile.

Silence in the ball park, the silence of the spheres, while
the dust cleared and Mazuma looked to ascertain whether the
runner had managed to separate the second-baseman from his
head, which had pretty much seemed her intention. But no,
though she had sliced his uniform open diagonally from the
shoulder to the waist, Nickname himself was intact; the second-
baseman had, however, been separated from the ball, which lay
fifteen feet beyond him at the edge of the grass.

"Safe!" exclaimed Mazuma, and as they said next day in
the papers, you could have renamed Reaper Field Pandemonium Park.

Halfway to the mound, the Mundy catcher lay pounding
the dirt with his fists, and howling, as though those tears he
wept were scalding his face.

Suddenly a Boy Scout appeared at the side of the fallen
catcher, holding the wooden limb in his two outstretched hands.
"Here, sir, your leg."

"Aww, stick it up your ass," wept Hothead. "*You* go
through life a jelly-apple!"

"You mean," cried the Boy Scout, a look of pure delight
breaking across his freckled face, "I can keep it? And the
baseball shoe, too? Wow! Hothead Ptah's leg!" he called,
running back with his prize to the troop in the Reaper dugout.
"He said I can *have* it!"

And now Nickname was kneeling beside him, and Big
John too. "How could you do it?" Hot cried, grabbing the
second-baseman by the shirt, "How could you be afraid of a
sixty-year-old lady's spikes?"

"Aw, lay off, Hot," said Big John. "It warn't no old lady.
If you ask me, it was a ringer named Gamesh."

But Nickname, wiping the warpaint of his own blood and
tears across his cheek with the back of his mitt, blubbered,
"But it *was* a old lady, Jawn, that's the worst of it. *That's*
how come I dropped the ball! It weren't them spikes that
scared me, Hot. Look, I took 'em full in the letters."

"Then *what?*" screamed Hot. "Was you bein' *polite* to
her that you lost the ball?"

"No! No! It's, it's when she raised up her leg—that's
how come I lost it! I damn near went unconscious."

"*Why?*" demanded Hothead.

"Aw jeez, Hot, I ain't never smelled nothin' like that at
second base before. Or in a cathouse even. It stunk like somethin' that's been left out somewhere and turned green. I ain't
lyin' to you, Hot—I thought maybe it was a shrimp boat
dockin' at the bag. Only worse! Then my whole life flashed
before my eyes, and I thought, by Jesus, I'm gonna *die* from
whatever it is!"

"That keen, huh?" said Big John.

"Keen? I'druther be drownin' in a swamp!"

"Well," said Big John, consoling the catcher as he and
Nickname each took the dumbstruck Hothead by an arm and
helped him back to the Mundy dugout, "old or young, they all
of them knows how to get the use out of that thing, don't they?
Cheer up now, ol' Hothead, you ain't the first feller to get done
in by the black hole of Calcutta—or the last either."

And Chico? No sooner had Hot's leg been driven foul than
he ran from the field to the visitors' clubhouse, climbed inside
his locker and pulled the door shut behind him. A devout and
simple man (albeit an ingrate), he had taken what happened
as a judgment upon himself. Through the airholes of the locker
he whispered a plea, "I like Mundy! I be Mundy! I stay
Mundy!" and though Jolly Cholly shortly appeared to open
the locker and remove the trembling reliever from his makeshift confessional, thereafter Chico's sleep was plagued with
visions of limbs being batted back at him out of the box, of
eyeballs dropping like bunts, and whole heads, severed at the
neck, that he took with a shriek on one hop . . . oh, in torment
he would roll from his hotel bed to the floor, and there on his

face, in yet another strange town, beg to be forgiven for his
disloyalty to the team that owned him, and his hatred of the
uniform he wore. He prayed to the Holy Mother to keep him
a Mundy forever—hoping against hope of course, that because
he was so unworthy, his prayers would go unanswered.

In the name of mercy (and narrative brevity, fans), let us pass
over Bud Parusha's protracted demonstration of how he tied
his shoelaces, and over the eight and two-thirds innings of
baseball that ensued, to arrive at the final bloodletting of
"Welcome Bud Parusha Day," wherein the refugees from
Ruppert, bereft of the player whose name at least had endowed
their line-up with some small claim to big league legitimacy,
went from being simply the most inept and ludicrous team in
the history of Organized Baseball, to the most universally despised. In that nobody on the Kakoola club had any idea of how
to remove the ball from between their new right-fielder's jaws
when in his anxiety it would become lodged there (as it did in
one out of every two chances he had during his first day as a
Reaper), what should have been an easy 8–0 victory for the
home team, went to the last of the ninth with the score tied
8–8, thanks to Bud Parusha's big mouth.

The bottom of the ninth then, score tied, two men down,
and the bases full of Reapers—could it have happened any
more dramatically in a storybook? With a weary, wild fifty-
year-old on the hill for the Mundys, and the winning run
on third, the longed-for words were uttered:

"Your attention, please. Pinch-hitting for Kakoola, Number ¼—"

His name was lost in the roar.

But for a small (a very small) Band-Aid across the bridge
of his nose, Bob Yamm bore no marks of the fierce combat of
the previous afternoon. Nor was there any indication in his
bearing that the decision made by an entire nation "in the
long dark night of its soul" (to hear Frank M. describe it)
"to bring Bob back to baseball and baseball back to Bob" had
affected by so much as one iota, by so much as one micron, by
so much as one *millimicron,* his exquisite sense of propriety.
He emerged from the Reaper dugout swinging his two little

bats and proceeded on to home plate with the grave, determined manner of a man with a job to do, no more, no less. The
tumultuous ovation being accorded him he acknowledged only
by pulling on the bill of his cap. And when he looked for the
briefest second to the stands, it was not to the roaring multitude, but to a seat in Frank Mazuma's box back of first, where
Judy Yamm, perched on two Kakoola telephone directories,
chewed upon her manicured and polished nails. To her alone
Bob smiled.

On the mound, Deacon Demeter, who had already walked
fourteen full-grown men in the course of the long, harrowing
afternoon, leaned way down off the rubber and searched for
that narrow slot in space through which the ball must now
pass to be considered a strike. He looked and he looked and
he looked—the Deacon was a patient man—and then instead
of rearing back to pitch, he walked off the field and out of the
game, all on his own. "Believe me, Cholly," he told the Mundy
coach in the dugout, "if it was possible, I'd a tried. But, hell,
you couldn't even a got a nickel in there to make a phone call."

"Ladies and gentlemen, your attention please: coming in
to pitch for the Mundys, Number 1/16—"

The rest is Patriot League history, or was, when P.
League history was still extant around here. Pitching to someone approximately his own size, Number 1/16—who was of
course O.K. Ockatur, wearing on his Mundy shirt the number
of his dreams and of his own devising—cut loose with two
overhand curveballs, quite normal little pitches such as a
pretty good fifth-grader might throw; each broke in across the
waist of the immobile Yamm and over the outside corner for
strikes one and two. Now, Yamm was as unfamiliar with an 0
and 2 situation as a man from Mars, or Budapest; likewise he
was utterly without ability as a hitter, which was why Mazuma
had warned him at the outset that he wasn't to lift the bat off
his shoulder if he wanted to live to tell the tale. But Bob did
not intend to go down looking at called strike three. It wasn't
a matter of sparing *his* pride, either; what concerned him was
the pride of respectable, honest, hardworking midgets everywhere, the average American midget whose dignity he em-
bodied and trust he bore. He stood for too much to too many
little people, to stand there helpless and impotent before

Ockatur's third strike. It came down to this: he was loved and Ockatur was loathed. One had only to listen to that crowd to know that.

Of course with two quick strikes on the hitter, Ockatur decided to waste his next pitch—as who wouldn't, freak or Hall of Famer? Yamm, however, imagining that the high hard one sailing toward his hands was going to break down and away like the two preceding curveballs, went lunging after it with his bat. He swung with all his might, and he missed, even as the ball kept right on coming at his face.

The first bulletins from the hospital were hopeful. Millions of Americans went to bed at midnight September 15, 1943, believing that the crisis had passed. Then, at 4:17 A.M. Central Daylight Saving Time, Frank Mazuma emerged from Kakoola Memorial and wearily mounted the hood of a police car. He was unshaven and his face was streaked with tears. To the gathering of newsmen, to the hundreds of fans and well-wishers who had continued to stand vigil outside the hospital even as a fine morning drizzle had begun to fall, Mazuma announced that the ball that had struck Bob Yamm between the eyes had blinded him for life. When he came to deliver the rest of his report, he broke down completely and had to be helped from the police car by his sons Jack and Gelt, and hurried away. It was only a matter of minutes, however, before a hospital orderly who wanted his picture in the paper collared the sportswriter Smitty and revealed that the curvaceous Doubloon would never wiggle her sweet ass again, as she was paralyzed from her twenty-two-inch waist clear to the ground.

And after those two stories went crackling out over the wire services, not even Bud Parusha, miserable and solitary misfit that he was to be with a team of commonplace duffers like the Reapers, ever longed to return to the Mundys again.

5

THE TEMPTATION OF ROLAND AGNI

❧ 5 ❧

*A word on the Mundy winning streak and an observation on
the law of averages. The secret meeting between Roland Agni
and Angela Whittling Trust, in which Roland delivers a mono-
logue on his batting prowess that approaches the condition of
poetry. The history goes backward to recount the adventures
of Mrs. Trust: a description of her love affairs with Ty Cobb,
Babe Ruth, Jolly Cholly Tuminikar, Luke Gofannon, and Gil
Gamesh. Her great address to Agni on her transformation
from a selfish woman into a responsible human being. A dire
warning to Agni, in which the reader will be no less astonished
than the rookie to learn of the international conspiracy against
the Patriot League. Concluding with an account of the history
of the Greenbacks under Jewish management, including
scenes of Jewish family life which will appear
quite ordinary to most of our readers,
albeit they are enacted in
a ball park.*

N EAR THE END of September, just as the '43 season was
coming to a close, a phenomenon so unlikely occurred in the
Patriot League that for a couple of weeks the nation ceased
speculating upon when and where the Allied invasion of the
European fortress would be launched and turned its attention
to the so-called "miracle" of the sports world. The pennant
races themselves had people yawning: in a hapless American
League, the Yanks were running away with the flag on an
un-Yankeeish team batting average of .256, and in the National,
the Cardinals, who still had Musial to hit and Mort Cooper to
pitch, were eighteen games ahead of the second place Reds and
twenty-three in front of Durocher's Dodgers. The only race
that might have been worth watching was over in the P.
League, where for months the Tycoons had remained only
percentage points ahead of the Butchers; by September, however, both clubs were playing such uninspired ball that it
seemed each had secretly come around to thinking that winning the flag in that league in that year might not be such an

honor after all. No, the "miracle" in the Patriot League
wasn't taking place at the top of the standings, but at the
bottom. The Ruppert Mundys were winning.

The streak began on September 18, with a fourteen-run
explosion against Independence, and it did not end until the
final day of the season, and it took Tri-City to do it: Tycoons
31, Mundys 0, the worst defeat suffered by the Mundys all
season, and unquestionably the worst game ever to be played
by any team in the history of the major leagues.

Nonetheless, that the Mundys should give up thirty-one
runs on twenty-seven hits and twelve errors—nineteen runs in
a single inning—on the final day of that grim year was not
beyond human comprehension; what was, were those eleven
consecutive victories by scores of 14–6, 8–0, 7–4, 5–0, 3–1, 6–4,
11–2, 4–1, 5–3, 8–1, and 9–3. How in the world had a team like
that managed to score eighty runs in little more than a week,
when they had barely scored two hundred in the five months
before?

"They wuz due maybe," said the fans.

"Law of averages," wrote the sportswriters.

But neither explanation made any sense; nobody who is
down and out the way the Mundys were is *ever* due—that is
not the *meaning* of "down and out"—and as for the "law of
averages," it doesn't exist, certainly not in the sense that he
who has lost over a considerable length of time must, on the
strength of all that accumulated defeat, inevitably begin to
win. There is no mechanism in life, anymore than at the gaming
tables, that triggers any such equalizing or compensatory
"law" into operation. A gambler at the wheel who bets the
color black because the red has turned up on ten successive
turns may tell himself that he is wisely heeding the law of
averages, but that is only a comforting pseudoscientific name
that he has attached to a wholly unscientific superstition. The
roulette wheel has no memory, unless, that is, it has been fixed.

How the Miracle Came to Pass

It all began when Roland Agni, an Ace bandage wound
round his face and over his blond curls, broke into Tycoon
Park one night, bound and gagged the night watchman, and

then, having relieved the old man of his key-ring, made his
way to the underground bunker of Angela Whittling Trust,
owner of Tri-City's team of aging immortals. The only weapon
Agni carried was his bat.

Silently he pushed open the heavy steel door and slipped
into the vestibule of her apartment. From floor to ceiling the
walls were lined with glass showcases containing cups and
trophies two and three feet high, topped like wedding cakes
with figurines in baseball togs, and lit from above by spot-
lights: the Patriot League Cup, the Honey Boy Evans Trophy,
the World Series Cup, the Douglas D. Oakhart Triple Crown
Award . . . Roland could identify each by its size and shape
even before stealing down the corridor to gaze upon the hallowed objects. Further on gleamed a row of goldfish bowls,
each containing a single baseball bearing the Patriot League
insignia and hung with a small silver medallion identifying
the relic within:

Phil Thor's
61⅓ Scoreless Innings
in a Row
1933

Vic Bragi's
535th Lifetime Home Run
1935

Smoky Woden's
Perfect Sixteen-Inning Game
1934

Double Play Number
216 of the 1935 Season
"Rustem-to-Izanagi-to-Mazda"

Like any American who had been a kid growing up in the
era of the faultless Tycoon clubs of the early thirties, Agni
was overcome when he discovered himself only inches from
these record-breaking baseballs out of the Patriot League past.
To be sure, the Tycoon stars of the Depression years whose
names Agni read with such reverence were the same old-timers
against whom he and the Mundys had been playing baseball
all season long. Yet, to see *the* very ball with which Smoky

Woden had registered the last out against the Butchers in
that perfect sixteen-inning game back in '34 was a thrill
bearing no resemblance to playing against old Smoky himself.
That was no thrill at all, but downright humiliating. Yes, the
more legendary the star, the more anguished was Roland to
take the field with his eight clownish teammates, and thus
come to be associated with them in the mind of someone he had
idolized ever since he was a nine-year-old boy, dreaming of
the Patriot League as of Paradise.

Now to the naked eye the ball with which Smoky had
finished up his sixteen perfect innings back in '34 looked to be
an exact replica of the one Vic Bragi had driven into the
stands for his five hundred and thirty-fifth P. League home
run in '35—be that as it may, there was no confusing the
depth and quality of the awe that each inspired in someone
with Agni's exquisitely refined feel for the game, one who could
sense within his own motionless body that synchronization of
strength, timing, and concentration that each achievement
must have called forth. For all that he was an outfielder—and
what an outfielder!—Roland had only to read "Double Play
Number 216" for his muscular frame to vibrate with the
rhythms that carry a ball from short to second to first, from
second to short to first, from first to second and back to first
for two! "Ah oh ee," he moaned, "ee oh ah . . . ah ah ah . . .
whoo-up whoo-up pow . . ." Two hundred and sixteen times
and never the same way twice! Every double play as different
from the next as one snowflake from another—and each just
as perfect! Oh this game, thought Roland, shuddering with
ecstasy, how I love and adore this game!

Tommy Heimdall's
65th Double
1932

Tuck Selket's
23rd Pinch-Hit
1933

"All right, Agni," said Angela Trust, who had rolled her
wheelchair to within point-blank range of her ecstatic and
spellbound intruder, "drop the bat."

At the sight of the black revolver, Agni instinctively fell
back from the display of famous balls, as though from a wild
pitch.

"Drop it, Roland," repeated Mrs. Trust. "Pretend you've
just drawn ball four, and drop it at your feet—or I'll send you
to the showers for life."

The Louisville Slugger slipped from his hands to the
carpet. "How," he muttered through the Ace bandage, while
raising his hands over his head, "how do you even know for
sure it's me?"

The elderly woman, a beauty still beneath the wrinkles,
and imposing even in a wheelchair, kept the revolver trained
on his groin. "Who else has been sending me candy and flowers
for a week?" she said coldly.

"You didn't answer my letters!" cried Agni. "I didn't
know what to do. *I had to see you.*"

"So you decided on this," she said, contemptuously.
"Take that absurd thing off your face."

He did as he was told, returning the bandage to his right
knee, which he had twisted the previous week stealing home
against the Blues. "Boy," he said, adjusting his trousers,
"that was really startin' to ache, too. I just didn't want the
night watchman to recognize me, that was all."

"And is he dead? Did you crack his head for a home run,
you fool?"

"No! Of course not! I just tied him up and gagged him . . .
with . . . well . . . with a couple of my jocks. But I didn't
do him no harm, I swear! Look, I wouldn't have done nothin'
like this—but I had to! If I call, you don't even come to the
phone. When I write you, you ignore me even worse. My telegrams—do you even *get* them?"

"Daily."

"Then why don't you answer! I am the league's leading
batter and the outstanding candidate for rookie of the year—
or I would be, if I was a Tycoon! Oh, Mrs. Trust, how can you
be like this to someone who is hittin' .370!"

"The answer is no."

"But that don't make *sense! Nothin'* makes sense no
more! *I don't understand!*"

"You're a center-fielder, Agni; nobody expects you to

understand. There is more at stake than you can ever comprehend.''

"But the pennant's what's at stake right now! Bragi can hardly swing from his rheumatism killin' him so—and Tommy Heimdall's so darn tired he don't even come out for battin' practice! And Lou Polevik is pooped even worse! Them guys are goin' on sheer nerve! On what they was, not what they are!''

Sharply, she replied, ''They are fine, courageous men. There will never be another outfield like them. In their prime, they made Meusel, Combs, and Ruth look nothing more than competent.''

"But you'll lose the pennant—and to them two-bit Butchers! I could put you over the top, I swear!''

"And is that what you came here to tell me? Is that why you tied a night watchman in athletic supporters and stole in here with your mighty bat? Did you actually think I would negotiate a trade just because you threatened to fungo my brains against the wall? Or did you plan to rape me, Roland, to assault a seventy-two-year-old woman with a Louisville Slugger if she did not give in to your wishes? My God! Not even Cobb was that crazy!''

"But, holy gee, neither am I! I wouldn't *dream* of anything like that! Gosh, Mrs. Trust, what a thing to say to—to me! About you! And my bat!''

"Why then *bring* the bat, Roland?" she snapped.

"Why else?" he said, shrugging—and smiling. "To show you my form.''

"And you expect me to believe that? Don't you think I've had the wonderful privilege of seeing your perfect form already?''

Of course he could tell from her tone that Angela Trust was being sarcastic, but that didn't make what she had said any less true: his form *was* perfect, and he knew it. Blushing, he said, ''Not close up, though.''

God, it's so, she thought. He wasn't going to bludgeon her into buying him—he was only going to try to seduce her with his form. Oh, he was a .370 hitter, all right—a peacock, a princeling, a prima donna, just like all the other .370 hitters she had known. They think they have only to step to the plate for the whole of humankind to fall to its knees in adoration. As though there is nothing in this world so beautiful to behold as the stride and the swing and the follow-through of a man who can hit .370 in the big leagues. *And is there?*

"Pick it up," she said, without, however, lowering the pistol, "and come into my parlor. But one false move, Roland, and you're out."

"I swear, Mrs. Trust, I only want to show you my swing. In slow motion."

At each end of Mrs. Trust's parlor was a life-sized oil painting, one of her husband, wearing a dark suit and a no-nonsense expression, and seated before a vault at Trust Guaranty Trust; the other was of her father, also in a business suit, but posed with an ax over his shoulder; behind him stretched a sea of stumps. Projecting from the two side walls, some fifteen feet above the floor and at an angle of forty-five degrees, were several dozen baseball bats; at first glance, they looked like two rows of closely packed flagpoles. Slowly walking the length of this old lady's parlor, from the portrait of the great banker who had been her husband, to the portrait of the great lumber baron who had been her father, one could gaze up on either hand at the bat of each and every Tri-City Tycoon who had ever hit .300 or more in a single season. They formed an unbroken shelter beneath which Angela Whittling Trust conducted her affairs.

Agni pointed with his own bat to the one directly over his head.

"Wow. Who's *that* belong to?"

"A forty-two ouncer," she replied. "Who else? Mike Mazda."

"Look at the length of that thing!"

"Thirty-eight inches."

Agni whistled. "That's a lot a' bat, ain't it?"

"He was a lot of man."

"Mine here is thirty-four inches, thirty-two ounces, ya' know. That's how come the writers say I 'snap the whip.' That's how come I got that drivin' force, see. It ain't because my wrists is weak that I like the narrow handle, it's because they're so damn strong. And that's the truth. My forearms and my wrists are like steel, Mrs. Trust. Want to feel them

and see for yourself? Want to see me take my cut now? In
slow motion? I can swing real slow for ya', and ya' can follow
it to see just how damn level it is. Hey, want to try an experi-
ment with a coin? When I'm standin' in there, waitin' for the
pitch, ya' know, I hold the big end of the bat so straight and so
still, ya' can balance a dime on the end of it. And that's the
truth. Most fellas, when they start that sweep forward, they
got some kind of damn hitch or dip in there, so tiny sometimes
you can't even see it without a microscope—but just try to
balance a coin on that big end there when they start their
swing, and you see what happens. They see that ball acomin'
at them, and they will drop their hands, maybe only that much,
but that is all it takes to throw your timin' to hell. And your
power too. Nope, there is only one way to be a great hitter
like me, and it ain't movin' the bat in two directions, I'll tell
ya'. Same with the stride. Me, I just raise up my front foot
and set it back down just about where I raised it up from. You
don't *need* no more stride than that. I see fellas take a big
stride, I got to turn away—that's true, Mrs. Trust, it actually
makes me nauseous to look at, and I don't care if it's Ott himself. They might just as easy put a knife to themselves and
slice off two inches of good shoulder muscle, because that's
what they are givin' away in leverage. I just don't understand
why they want to look like tightrope walkers up there, when
all you got to do with that foot is just *raise* it up and *set* it
down. A' course, you got to have eyes too, but then I don't have
to tell you about my eyes. They say my eyes are so sharp that
I can read the General's signature off a fastball comin' up to
the plate. Well, if that's what the pitchers wanna tell each
other, that's okay with me. But between you and me, Mrs.
Trust, I ain't some eagle that can read handwritin' comin' at
me at sixty miles a hour—all I *can* tell is if the thing is goin'
to break or not, because of the way them stitches are spinnin'.
If you want, I could stand behind home plate with you durin'
battin' practice, and you tell the pitcher to mix 'em up however he likes and ninety per cent of the time I promise I will
holler out the curveballs even before they break. Maybe I *could*
read General Oakhart's signature on a change-up, but frankly
I ain't never bothered to try. It ain't goin' to help me get a

base hit, is it—so why bother? Want to see me swing again?"

By now the pistol lay in her lap like a kitten.

"Want to see me take my cut now?" Agni repeated, when the old woman remained frozen, seemingly uncomprehending in her chair. "Mrs. Trust?"

He's Luke Gofannon, she was thinking, *it's Luke Gofannon all over again.*

There had been five men in her life who mattered, and none had been her husband; her affair with him had begun only after he was in the ground. Of the five—two Mundys, a Greenback, a Yankee, and a Tiger—she had loved only one with all her heart, the Loner, Luke Gofannon. Not that he was a fiercely passionate man in the way of a Cobb or a Gamesh; no, it was the great haters who made the great lovers, or such had been Angela's experience with America's stars. To yield to the man who had stolen more bases than anyone in history— by terrifying as many with his menacing gaze as with his surgical spikes—was like nothing she had ever known before as a woman; it was more like being a catcher, blocking home plate against a bloodthirsty base runner, than being a per- fumed beauty with breasts as smooth as silk and a finishing school education; she felt like a base being stolen—no, like a bank being robbed. Throughout he glared down at her like a gunman, snarling in his moment of ecstasy, "Take that, you society slit!" But then, where another would collapse with a shudder, shrivel up, and sleep, the great Ty would (as it were) just continue on around the bag and try for two; and then for three! And then he would break for the plate, and to Angela's weary astonishment, make it, standing! a four-bagger, where another player would have been content with a solid base hit! The clandestine affair that had begun in his hotel room in 1911 —on the day he won the batting crown with an average of .420 —came to a violent end at the conclusion of the 1915 season, when he decided to perform upon her an unnatural act he described as "poling one out of the ball park foul." Actually she did not so much resist as take longer to think it over than he had patience for, or pride. Having stolen his record-breaking ninety-six bases that year, he was not accustomed to waiting around for what he wanted.

According to the next day's newspapers, Mrs. Trust suffered her broken nose in the bath of a Detroit hotel room; true enough, only she had not got it by "slipping in the tub," as the papers reported.

The Yankee was Ruth. How could she resist?

"George? This is Angela Whittling Trust. We happen to be in the same hotel."

"Come on up."

"With Spenser or without?"

"Surprise me." He laughed. It was October of 1927; he had already hit sixty home runs in the course of the regular season, and that afternoon, in the third World Series game against the Pirates, he'd hit another in the eighth with two on.

Surprise me, the Bambino had said, but the surprise was on her when he answered her knock, for the notorious bad boy was unclothed and smoking a cigar. Still slender, still silken, Angela was nonetheless a white-haired woman of fifty-five in the fall of '27, and in her silver-fox cape the last woman in the world one would think to greet in anything but the manner prescribed by society. Which was of course why the Babe had chosen to appear nude at the door—and why Mrs. Trust had entered without any sign that she was discomfited in the slightest. Of course he was a clown, a glutton, an egomaniac, a spoiled brat, and a baby through and through . . . but what was any of that beside those tremendous home runs?

"I been expectin' ya', Whittlin' Trust."

"Have you now." She removed her cape and draped it over a trophy that the Babe had placed to ice in a champagne bucket. What wit. What breeding. She took a good look at him—what legs. But who cared, with all those home runs?

"Since when?" Angela asked, removing her gloves in a most provocative way.

"Since 1921, Whittlin' Trust."

"Really? You thought I'd ring you up for fifty-nine home runs, did you?"

He smiled and sucked his cigar. "And one hundred seventy r.b.i.s. And a hundred seventy-seven runs. And a hundred nineteen extra-base hits. Yeah, Whittlin' Trust,'' said the Yankee immortal, chortling, ''as a matter of fact, I thought you might.''

''No,'' she said, as she set down her watch and her rings and began to unbutton her blouse, ''I thought it would be best to wait. I have my reputation to consider. How was I to know you weren't just another flash-in-the-pan, George?''

''Come 'ere, W.T., and I'll show you how.''

A season with Ruth—and then in '29, the first of her pitchers, the first of her Mundys, the speedballer, Prince Charles Tuminikar. Yes, they called him a prince when he came up, and they called swinging and missing at that fastball of his ''chasin' Charlies.'' That was all he bothered to throw back then, but it was enough: 23–4 his rookie year, and by July 4 of the following season, 9–0. Then one afternoon, locked in a 0–0 tie going into the fourteenth, he killed a man. Everyone agreed it was a chest-high pitch, but it must have been coming a hundred miles an hour at least, and a dumb rookie named O'del, the last pinch-hitter off the Terra Inc. bench, stepped into the damn thing—exactly as Bob Yamm was to do against Ockatur thirteen years later—and he was pronounced dead by the umpire even before the trainer could make it out to the plate with an ice pack. Everyone agreed O'del was to blame, except Tuminikar. He left the mound and went immediately to the police station to turn himself in.

Of course no one was about to bring charges against a man for throwing a chest-high pitch in a baseball game, though maybe if they had, he could have served four or five years for manslaughter, and come on out of jail to be his old self on the mound. As it was, he never threw a fastball of any consequence again, or won more games in a season than he lost. Or was worth much of anything to Angela Whittling Trust.

And so it was, in her sixtieth year, that she came to Luke Gofannon, the silent Mundy center-fielder who had broken Ruth's record in 1928, as great a switch-hitter as the game had ever known, a man who made both hitting and fielding look like acts of meditation, so effortless and tranquil did he appear even in the midst of running with the speed of a locomotive, or striking at the ball with the force of a pile driver.

''You're poetry in motion,'' said Angela, and Luke, having reflected upon this observation of hers for an hour (they were in bed), remarked at last:

"Could be. I ain't much for readin'."

"I've never seen anything like you, Luke. The equanimity, the composure, the serenity . . ."

To this he answered, in due time, "Well, I ain't never been much for excitement. I just take things as they come."

His exquisitely proportioned, powerful physique in repose—the repose itself, that pensive, solitary air that had earned him his nickname—filled Angela with a wild tenderness that she had not known as mistress to the ferocious Tiger, the buffoonish Yankee, and the ill-fated fireballer they now called Jolly Cholly T.; he awakened an emotion in her at once so wistful and so full of yearning, that she wondered if perhaps she should not have been a mother after all, as Spenser had wanted her to be, a good mother and a good wife. But before another season began, she would be sixty. Her face, her breasts, her hips, her thighs, for all that she had given them everything money could buy (yes, these had been her children), soon would be the face, breasts, and thighs of a thirty-five-year-old woman. And then what would she do with her time?

"I love you, Luke," she told the Loner.

Another hour passed.

"Luke? Did you hear me, darling?"

"I heard."

"Don't you want to know *why* I love you?"

"I know why, I guess."

"Why?"

"My bein' a pome."

"But you *are* a poem, my sweet!"

"That's what I said."

"Luke—tell me. What do you love most in the world? Because I'm going to make you love me just as much. More! What do you love most in the entire world?"

"In the entire world?"

"Yes!"

It was dawn before he came up with the answer.

"Triples."

"Triples?"

"Yep."

"I don't understand, darling. What about home runs?"

"Nope. Triples. Hittin' triples. Don't get me wrong, Angela, I ain't bad-mouthin' the home run and them what hits 'em, me included. But smack a home run and that's it, it's all over."

"And a triple?" she asked. "Luke, you must tell me. I have to know. What is it about the triple that makes you love it so much? Tell me, Luke, tell me!" There were tears in her eyes, the tears of jealous rage.

"You sure you up to it?" asked Luke, as astonished as it was in his nature to be. "Looks like you might be gettin' a little cold."

"You love the triple more than Horace Whittling's daughter, more than Spenser Trust's wife—*tell me why!*"

"Well," he said in his slow way, "smackin' it, first off. Off the wall, up the alley, down the line, however it goes, it goes with that there crack. Then runnin' like blazes. 'Round first and into second, and the coach down there cryin' out to ya', 'Keep comin'.' So ya' make the turn at second, and ya' head for third—and now ya' know that throw is comin', ya' know it is right on your tail. So ya' slide. Two hunerd and seventy feet of runnin' behind ya', and with all that there momentum, ya' hit it—whack, into the bag. Over he goes. Legs. Arms. Dust. Hell, ya' might be in a tornado, Angela. Then ya' hear the ump—'Safe!' And y're in there . . . Only that ain't all."

"What then? Tell me everything, Luke! What then?"

"Well, the best part, in a way. Standin' up. Dustin' off y'r breeches and standin' up there on that bag. See, Angela, a home run, it's great and all, they're screamin' and all, but then you come around those bases and you disappear down into the dugout and that's it. But not with a triple . . . Ya' get it, at all?"

"Yes, yes, I get it."

"Yep," he said, running the whole wonderful adventure through in his mind, his eyes closed, and his arms crossed behind him on the pillow beneath his head, "big crowd . . . sock a triple . . . nothin' like it."

"We'll see about that, Mr. Loner," whispered Angela Trust.

Poor little rich girl! How she tried! Did an inning go by during the two seasons of their affair, that she did not know his batting average to the fourth digit? You're batting this much, you're fielding that much, nobody goes back for them like you, my darling. Nobody swings like you, nobody runs like you, nobody is so beautiful just fielding an easy fly ball!

Was ever a man so admired and adored? Was ever a man so worshipped? Did ever an aging woman struggle so to capture and keep her lover's heart?

But each time she asked, no matter how circuitously (and prayerfully) she went about it, the disappointment was the same.

"Lukey," she whispered in his ear, as he lay with his fingers interlaced beneath his head, "which do you love more now, my darling, a stolen base, or me?"

"You."

"Oh, darling," and she kissed him feverishly. "Which do you love more, a shoestring catch, or me?"

"Oh, you."

"Oh, my all-star Adonis! Which do you love more, dearest Luke, a fastball letter-high and a little tight, or me?"

"Well . . ."

"Well what?"

"Well, if I'm battin' left-handed, and we're at home—"

"Luke!"

"But then a' course, if I'm battin' rightie, you, Angel."

"Oh, my precious, Luke, what about—what about a home run?"

"You or a home run, you mean?"

"Yes!"

"Well, now I really got to think . . . Why . . . why . . . why, I'll be damned. I got to be honest. Geez. I guess— you. Well, isn't that somethin'."

He who had topped Ruth's record, loved her more than all his home runs put together! "My darling," and in her joy, the fading beauty offered to Gofannon what she had withheld even from Cobb.

"And Luke," she asked, when the act had left the two of them weak and dazed with pleasure, "Luke," she asked, when she had him just where she wanted him, "what about . . .

your triples? Whom do you love more now, your triples, or your Angela Whittling Trust?"

While he thought that one through, she prayed. *It has to be me. I am flesh. I am blood. I need. I want. I age. Someday I will even die. Oh Luke, a triple isn't even a person—it's a thing!*

But the thing it was. "I can't tell a lie, Angela," said the Loner. "There just ain't nothin' like it."

Never had a man, in word or deed, caused her such anguish and such grief. This illiterate ballplayer had only to say "Nothin' like it" about those God damn triples for a lifetime's desire to come back at her as frantic despair. Oh, Luke, if you had only known me in my prime, back when Ty was hitting .420! God, I was irresistible! Back before the lively ball, oh you should have seen and held me then! But look at me now, she thought bitterly, examining herself later that night in her mirrored dressing room—just *look* at me! Ghastly! The body of a thirty-five-year-old woman! She turned slowly about, till she could see herself reflected from behind. "Face it, Angela," she told her reflection, "thirty-six." And she began to sob.

"Luke! Luke! Luke! Luke! Luke!"

It was only the name of a Patriot League center-fielder that she howled, but it came so piercingly from her throat, and with such pitiable yearning, that it might have stood for all that a woman, no matter how rich, beautiful, powerful, and proud she may be, can never hope to possess.

And then he was traded, and then he was dead.

And so that spring she took up with a Greenback rookie, a beautiful Babylonian boy named Gil Gamesh.

"Till I was eight or nine, I knew we was the only Babylonian family in Tri-City, but I figured there was more of us out in California or Florida, or some place like that, where it was warm all the time. Don't ask me how a kid gets that kind of idea, he just gets it. Bein' lonely, I suppose. Then one day I got the shock of my life when my old man sat me down and he told me we wasn't just the only ones in Tri-City, or even in Massachusetts, but in the whole damn U.S.A. Oh, my old man, he was a proud old son of a bitch, Angela—you would a' liked that old fire-eater. He wouldn't change his ways for nobody or

nothin'. 'What do you mean you're a Babylonian?' they'd ask
him when he filled out some kind of form or somethin'—'what
the hell is God damn Babylonian supposed to be? If you're
some kind of wop or Polack or somethin', say it, so we know
where we stand!' Oh, that got him goin' all right, callin' him
those things. 'I Babylonian! Free country! Any damn thing—
that *my* damn thing!' That's just what he'd tell 'em, whether
it meant gettin' the job or losin' it. And so that's what I wrote
down in school too, under what I was: Babylonian. And that's
how come they started throwin' them rocks at me. Livin' down
by the docks in those days, there wasn't any kind of person
you didn't see. We even had some Indians livin' there, Red
Indians, workin' as longshoremen, smokin' God damn peace
pipes on their lunch hour. Christ, we had Arabs, we had
everythin'. And they'd all take turns chasin' me home from
school. First for a few blocks the Irish kids threw rocks at me.
Then the German kids threw rocks at me. Then the Eye-talian,
then the colored, then them Mohawk kids, whoopin' at me like
it was some honest to Christ war dance; then down by the
chop suey joint, the Chink's kid; then the Swedes—hell, even
the Jew kids threw rocks at me, while they was runnin' away
from the kids throwin' rocks at them. I'm tellin' you, it was
somethin', Angela. Belgian kids, Dutch kids, Spanish kids,
even some God damn kid from Switzerland—I never seen one
before, and I never ever heard of one since, but there he is,
on my tail, shoutin' at the top of his lungs, 'Get outta here,
ya' lousy little Babylonian bastard! Go back to where you
belong, ya' dirty bab!' Me, I didn't even know what a bab was.
Maybe those kids didn't either. Maybe it was somethin' they
picked up at home or somethin'. I know my old man never
heard it before. But, Christ, did it get him mad. 'They you call
bab? Or *bad?* Sure not *bad?*' 'I'm sure, Poppa,' I told him.
'Bab,' he'd say, 'bab . . .' and then he'd just start goin' wild,
tremblin' and screamin' so loud my old lady went into hidin'.
'Nobody my boy bab call if here I am! Nobody! Country *free!*
God damn *thing!* Bab they want—we them bab show all right
good!' Only I didn't show them nothin', 'ceptin' my tail. When
those rocks started comin' my way, I just up and run for my
life. And that just made my old man even madder. 'Free!
Free! Underneath me?' That's how he used to say 'under-

stand.' Or maybe that's how all Babylonians say it, when they speak English. I wouldn't know, since we was the only ones I ever met. Don't worry, it got him into a lot of fights in bars and stuff, sayin' 'underneath' for 'understand' like that. 'Don't again to let you them call bab on my boy—underneath? *Ever!*' 'But they're throwin' rocks big as my head—at my head!' I told him. 'Then back throw rock on them!' he told me. 'Throw them big rock, throw you more big!' 'But there are a hundred of them throwin', Poppa, and only one a' me.' 'So,' he says, grabbin' me by the throat to make his point, 'throw you more *hard*. And *strong! Underneath?'*

"So that's how I come to pitchin', Angela. I got myself a big pile a' rocks, and I lined up these beer and whiskey bottles that I'd fish outta the bay, and I'd stand about fifty feet away, and then I'd start throwin'. You mick bastard! You wop bastard! You kike bastard! You nigger bastard! You Hun son of a bitch! That's how I developed my pick-off play. I'd shout real angry, 'Run, nigger!' but then I'd spin around and throw at the bottle that was the wop. In the beginnin', a' course, out on the street, bein' so small and inexperienced and all, and with the pressure on and so forth, I was so damn confused, and didn't know what half the words meant anyway, I'd be callin' the wops kikes and the niggers micks, and damned if I ever figured out what in hell to call that kid from Switzerland to insult him—'Hey,' I'd say, 'you God damn kid from God damn Switzerland,' but by the time I got all that out, he was gone. Well, anyway, by and by I got most of the names straightened around, and even where I didn't, they stopped laughin', on account of how good I got with them rocks. And about then I picked up this here fierce way I got too, just by imitatin' my dad, mostly. Oh, those little boys didn't much care to chase me home from school anymore after that. And you should a' heard my old man crowin' then. 'Now you them show what bab do! Now they underneath! And good!' And I was so damn proud and happy, and relieved a' course, and a' course I was only ten, so I just didn't think to ask him right off what else a bab could do. And then he up and died around then— they beat the shit out of him in a bar, a bunch of guys from Tierra del Fuego, who had it in for Babylonians, my mother said—and, well, that was it. I didn't have no father no more

to teach me, so I never did know how to be the kind of Babylonian he wanted me to be, except by throwin' things and
sneerin' a lot. And that's more or less what I been doin' ever
since.''

A callow, untutored boy, a wharf rat, enraged son of a
crazed father—no poem he, but still the greatest left-handed
rookie in history, and nothing to sneer at at sixty-one . . .
But then he threw that pitch at Mike Masterson's larynx, and
Gil was an ex-lover too. To be sure, in the months after his
disappearance, she had waited for some message from the
exile, a plea for her to intervene in his behalf. But none came,
perhaps because he knew that she was not the kind of woman
whose intervention anyone would ever take seriously. ''Speak
a word to the Commissioner about that maniac,'' her husband
had cautioned her, ''and I will expose you to the world, Angela,
for the tramp that you are. Every loudmouth Ty and Babe and
Gil who comes along!''

Even in her grief she found the strength to taunt him.
''Would you prefer I slept with bullpen catchers?''

''Look at you, the carriage of Caesar's wife, and the
morals of a high school harlot who pulls down her pants for
the football team.''

''I have my diversions, Spenser, and you have yours.''

''Diversions? I happen to be the patron and the patriarch
of a great American metropolis. I have made Tri-City into the
Florence of America. I am a financier, a sportsman, and a
patron of the arts. I endow museums. I build libraries. My
baseball team is an inspiration to the youth and the men of the
U.S.A. I could have been the Governor of this state, Angela.
Some say I could have been the President of the country, if
only I did not have as my wife a woman whose name is scribbled on locker room walls.''

''You diminish my accomplishments, Spenser, though, I
must say, you certainly do justice to your own.''

''Babe Ruth,'' he said contemptuously.

''Yes, Babe Ruth.''

''What do you do after you make love to Babe Ruth? Dis-
cuss international affairs? Or Benvenuto Cellini?''

''We eat hot dogs and drink pop.''

''I wouldn't doubt it.''

"Don't," said Angela Whittling Trust.

"A woman," he said bitterly, "with your aristocratic profile."

"A woman does not live by her profile alone, my dear."

"Oh? And in what ways is a baseball player able to gratify you that a billionaire is not?" He was a fit and handsome man, with no more doubt of his prowess in sex than in banking. "I'd be interested to learn wherein Babe Ruth is more of a man than Spenser Trust."

"But he isn't more of a man, darling. He's more of a boy. That's the whole point."

"And that is irresistible to you, is it?"

"To me," said his wife, "and about a hundred million other American citizens as well."

"You gum-chewing, star-struck adolescent! Hear me now, Angela: if at the age of sixty-one you should now take it into your selfish, spoiled head to sirenize a Tri-City Tycoon—"

"I assured you long ago that I would not cuckold you with any of your players. I realize by what a slender thread your authority, as it were, hangs."

"Because I am not running a stud farm for aged nympho-maniacs!"

"I understand what you are running. It is something more on the order of a money-making machine."

"Call it what you will. They are the most accomplished team in Organized Baseball, and they are not to be tampered with by a bored and reckless bitch who is utterly without regard for the rules of civilized life. A fastball pitcher's floozie! Whore to whomever hits the longest home run! That's all you are, Angela—a stadium slut!"

"Or slit, as the players so neatly put it. No, it wouldn't do for the Governor of the state to be married to a slit instead of a lady, would it, Spenser? And whoever heard of the President being married to a wayward woman? It isn't done that way in America, is it, my patron and patriarch?"

"To think, you have kept me from the White House just for the sake of debauching yourself with baseball stars."

"To think," replied his wife, "you would keep me from debauching myself with baseball stars, just for the sake of getting into the White House."

That winter, while Angela waited in dread for the news that Gil Gamesh was dead (if not beaten to a pulp like his father before him, stomped to death by Tierra del Fuegans whom he had insulted in some poolroom somewhere, then dead by his own wrathful hand), her own husband was fatally injured in a train wreck. His broken body was removed from the private car that had been speeding him to Chicago for a meeting with Judge Landis, and Angela was summoned to the hospital to bid him farewell. When she arrived she found his bed surrounded by his lawyers, whom he had called together to be sure that the dynasty was in order before he took his leave of it; all fifteen attorneys were in tears when they left the room. Then the Tri-City Tycoons were called in. The regulars, like eight sons, stood on one side of the bed, the pitching staff lined up on the other, and the remaining players gathered together at his feet, which he himself could no longer feel; they had come in uniform to say goodbye. Hospital regulations had made it necessary for them to remove their spikes in the corridor, but once inside his room, they had donned them again and crossed the floor to the dying owner's bedside with that clackety-clack-clack that had always been music to his ears.

Angela stood alone by the window, hers the only dry eyes in the room. Dry, and burning with hatred, for Spenser had just announced that he had passed the ownership of the club on to his wife.

The players moved up to say farewell, in the order in which they batted. He grasped their powerful hands with the little strength that remained in his own, and when he spoke his last words to each of them, they had virtually to put their ears to his lips to understand what he was saying. He was fading quickly now.

"Lay off the low ones, Tom, you're golfin' 'em."

"I will, Mr. Trust, I will—s'long, Mr. Trust . . ."

"Mike, your ass is in the dugout on those curveballs. Stand strong in there, big fella."

"Yes, sir. Always, sir . . . See ya', sir . . ."

"If I had a son, Tuck, I'd have wanted him to be able to pinch-hit like you."

"Oh, jeez, Mr. Trust, I won't forget that, ever . . ."

"Victor—Victor, what can I say, lad? If it's 3 and 0, and he lays it in there, suit yourself."

"I will, Boss, I will. Oh thank you, Mr. Trust."

"Just make sure it's in there. No bad pitches."

"No, never, sir, never . . ."

Finally there was just his wife and himself.

She had never despised him more. "And me, Spenser?" she asked, shaking with rage at the thought of all he had burdened her with. "Just what am *I* supposed to do with your wonderful team?"

He beckoned for her to come around to the side of his pillow. In one of his bandaged hands, it turned out, he was clutching a baseball. With a final effort of his patriarchal will, he tossed it to her. "Learn to be a responsible human being, Angela," and with that, the Lorenzo de' Medici of Massachusetts closed his eyes and passed into oblivion.

. . . Now, to the Roland Agni who would woo her with his swing and his follow-through, Angela Trust said, "For your information, Agni, I had you scouted when you were eleven years old. What do you think of that?" Nothing wistful in her voice, nothing flirtatious or lascivious, much as he reminded her of the Loner who had been the love of her life; no, remembering what she had been, she remembered who she was— *a responsible human being.*

Yes, a decade earlier Spenser had died, leaving her holding the ball, and the ball had been her salvation.

"You *did?*" Agni said.

"I have a dossier on you going back to the fifth grade. I have photographs of you at bat against your uncle Art on a family picnic in the year 1936, him in his shirtsleeves and mustache, and you in overalls and sneakers."

"You *do?*"

"Young man, the day you graduated from high school, who was the first on line to offer you a contract? That was no 'hunch' on my part, I wasn't just hopping on the bandwagon like the rest of my colleagues. I had arrived at my decision about you when you were still playing in that vacant lot at the corner of Chestnut and Summit."

"You *had?*"

"But you and your dad went with the Mundys instead. Well, so be it. Life must go on. I have reports on my desk right

now of six-year-old boys, little tykes who still won't even go
to sleep with the light off, who nonetheless have the makings
of big leaguers. They're my concern now, not you.''

"*But*—''

"But what? Win the pennant? I'd give my eyeteeth for
that flag. If any Tycoon team ever deserved it, it's these stars
of a decade ago, who have come out of retirement so as to keep
us all above water during these terrible years. Sure they need
help right now. But there are the Mundys to think of, too.''

"But the Mundys are fifty games out of first! They're
finishing the lowest last in history!''

"And without you, they would not finish at all.''

"So what! They don't *deserve* to finish! *And they don't
deserve me!* Mrs. Trust, I am a Tycoon dressed up in a Mundy
baseball suit, and that's the truth! Ya' have to trade for me,
Mrs. Trust—ya' gotta!''

"And win the flag in a seven-team league? You are all
that makes the Mundys major league. I tremble to think of
them without you.''

"I tremble thinkin' of them *with* me! Now we even got
Ockatur! The dwarf who blinded Yamm! And Nickname
Damur, who crippled that beautiful girl! It's like livin' with
criminals—and all I want to do is just play *ball!*'' And here,
seated beneath Mike Mazda's forty-two-ounce bat, the .370
hitter fell to weeping.

"Roland,'' she said, unable to bear the sight of him in
tears, "I'm going to tell you something now that's going to
astound you. Stop crying, Roland, and listen carefully to what
I have to say.''

"You're tradin' for me!'' he shouted triumphantly.

"*Listen* to me, I said. You may not understand this, it may
well be beyond you—God knows, it's beyond older and more
worldly men than yourself—but the fact is this: there is nothing that the enemies of this country would like *better* than for
Angela Whittling Trust to buy Roland Agni from the Ruppert
Mundys.''

"The who?''

"The enemies of America. Those who want to see this
nation destroyed.''

"And if you buy me, they'll like it?''

"If I buy you, they will adore it."

"But—"

"But why? But how? Believe me, I do not talk tommyrot.
I do not have the largest army of baseball scouts in America
in my employ for nothing. It isn't just about exceptional young
athletes that my scouts keep me informed. They live close to
the people. In many cases they are not even suspected of being
Tycoon scouts at all, but appear to their friends and neighbors to be ordinary townsfolk like themselves. As a result, I
know what goes on in this country. Not even the Federal Bu-
reau of Investigation knows what I do, until I tell them."

"But—but why me? I don't get it, Mrs. Trust. Why does
Hitler—"

"Hitler? Who mentioned that madman? Oh no, Roland,
we are dealing with an enemy far more cunning and insidious
than that deluded psychopath out to conquer the world with
bombs and bullets. No, even while this war rages on against the
Germans and the Japs, the other war against us has already
begun, the invisible war, the silent assault upon the very fabric
that holds us together as a nation. You look puzzled. What *does*
hold this nation together, Roland? The stars and the stripes?
Is that what men talk about over a beer, how much they love
Old Glory? On the streetcars, on the trains, on the jitneys,
what does one American say to another, to strike up a conversation, 'O say can you see by the dawn's early light?' No! He
says, 'Hey, how'd the Tycoons do today?' He says, 'Hey, did
Mazda get himself another homer?' Now, Roland, now do you
remember what it is that links in brotherhood millions upon
millions of American men, makes kin of competitors, makes
neighbors of strangers, makes friends of enemies, if only while
the game is going on? *Baseball!* And that is how they propose
to destroy America, young man, that is their evil and ingenious
plan—*to destroy our national game!*"

"But—but *how?* How can they do a thing like that?"

"By making it a joke! By making it a laughingstock! They
are planning to laugh us into the grave!"

"But—*who* is?"

"The Reds," said Mrs. Trust, studying his reaction.

"Aww, but they're finishin' in the money, Mrs. Trust,
back a' the Cards. I don't get it. What's their kick?"

"No, no, not Cincinnati, my boy. If only it were . . . No, it's not Bill McKechnie's boys we're up against this year, but General Joe Stalin's. The *Russian* Reds, Roland. From Stalin-to-Lenin-to-Marx."

"Well, I'm sure glad to hear it don't involve Johnny Vander Meer. That'd be like Shoeless Joe again."

He could not understand—but then could General Oakhart? Could Kenesaw Mountain Landis? "Roland, it may sound outlandish and far-fetched to you, and yet, I assure you, *it is true.* In order to destroy America, the Communists in Russia and their agents around the world are going to attempt to destroy the major leagues. They have selected as their target the weakest link in the majors—our league. And the weakest link within our league—the Mundys. Roland, why do you think the Mundys are homeless? Whose idea do you think that was?"

"Well . . . the Mundy brothers . . . no?"

"The Mundy brothers are only *pawns.* Not even fellow travelers—just stupid pawns, who can be manipulated for a few hundred thousand dollars without their even knowing it. Much as I despise those playboys, the fact remains that the plan to send the Mundys on the road while the U.S. government takes over the stadium in Port Ruppert was not hatched in the Mundy front office. *It began in our own War Department.* Do you understand the implications of what I have just said?"

"Well, I don't know . . . for sure."

"The plan was conceived in our own War Department. In other words, *there are Communists in the War Department of the United States government. There are Communists in the State Department.*"

"Gee, there are?"

"Roland, there are even Communists in the Patriot League itself . . . *right . . . this . . . minute!*"

"There *are?*"

"The owner of the Kakoola Reapers, to name but one."

"Mr. *Mazuma?*"

"Yes, Mr. 'Mazuma,' as you call him, is a Communist spy."

"But—"

"Roland, who else is making such a mockery of baseball?

Who else so mocks and shames the free enterprise system?
Yes, through the person of our friend, Mr. Frank Mazuma,
they are going to turn the people, not only against the national
game, but simultaneously against the profit system itself.
Midgets! Horse races! And he'll have colored on that team
soon enough, just wait and see. I've had him under surveillance
now since the day he came into the league, I know every move
he makes before he makes it. Colored, Roland, colored major
league players! And that is only the beginning. Only wait until
Hitler is defeated. Only wait until the international Communist conspiracy can invade every nook and cranny of our
national life. They will do to every sacred American institution, to everything we hold dear, just what Mazuma has done
to the integrity and honor of our league. They will make a
travesty of it! Our own people will grow ashamed and bewildered as everything they once lived by is reduced to the
level of a joke. And in our ridiculousness, our friends and our
neighbors, those who have looked to us as a model and an inspiration, will come to despise us. And all this the Communists will have accomplished without even dropping a bomb or
firing a bullet. They will have Frank Mazumas everywhere,
they will do to General Motors and to U.S. Steel just what they
have done to us—turn those great corporations into cartoons
out of a Russian newspaper! They've given up on the idea of
taking over the working class, Roland—that didn't work, so
now they are going to take over the *free enterprise system
itself.* How? By installing spies as presidents of great companies, and saboteurs as chairmen of the board! Mark my
word, the day will come when in the guise of an American
capitalist, a friend of Big Business and a member of the Republican Party, a Communist will run for President of the
United States. And if he is elected, he will ring down the curtain on the American tragedy—a tragedy because it will have
been made into a farce! And when that terrible day comes,
Roland, when a President Mazuma is installed in the White
House, they won't need a Red Army marching down Trust
Street to blow up the Industrial and Maritime Exchange; the
poor bewildered American people will do it themselves . . .
But then they won't be Americans by then, no, no, not as you
and I know them. No, when baseball goes, Roland, you can kiss

America goodbye. Try to imagine it, Roland, an American summer Sunday without doubleheaders, an American October without the World Series, March in America without spring training. No, they can call it America, but it'll be something very different by then. Roland, once the Communists have made a joke of the majors, the rest will fall like so many dominoes.

"You don't believe me, do you? Well, neither do the men at the top of the leagues—'Angela, you're blaming the Communists for what you people have brought upon yourselves. You've let the league go to pot, and now you are paying the price with playboys like the Mundys, and clowns like Mazuma, and undesirables like the little Jew.' But, Roland, who *is* the little Jew? Now, I have no final proof as yet, this is still only conjecture, but it all fits together too neatly to be dismissed out of hand. The Jew who bought the Greenbacks in 1933, this seemingly comical little fellow in his dark suit and hat, this foreigner with an accent who plunged what we believed to be his life's earnings into those scandal-ridden Greenbacks, *is a Communist agent too.* Yes, taking his orders from Moscow —*and* his money! But tell this to Frick, or Harridge, or Oakhart, or even Judge Landis. Behind my back, they call me a fanatic, a bitter old woman who has lost her looks and her lovers and now has nothing better to do than cause them trouble. But I have not 'lost' anything—I have only fulfilled the request my husband made of me on his deathbed. 'Become a responsible human being,' he told me. I hated him for saying that, Roland. In my selfish womanish ignorance, I did not even know the meaning of the words. I wanted poetry, passion, romance, adventure. Well, let me tell you, there is more poetry and passion and romance and adventure in being a responsible human being than in all the boudoirs in France! And I do not intend to be irresponsible ever again!"

"In other words," said Agni, tears once more welling up in his eyes now that he saw that she was finished, "in other words, on account of your husband and what he said and so on, and all that other stuff you just said, I am stuck with the Mundys for the rest of my life!"

"Would you prefer to be 'stuck' with Communism, you stupid boy? Would you rather that you and your children and your children's children be 'stuck' with atheistical totalitarian Communism till the end of time?''

"But I ain't *got* no children—or children's children. *I swear!*"

"Roland Agni, if you make a deal to be traded you will have to make it with the enemies of the United States, *as* an enemy of the United States. However, if you care more for your country than for yourself, you will play ball not with the Communists, but with the Ruppert Mundys!"

"But you could win the *pennant*, Mrs. Trust—"

"And enslave mankind in the bargain? You must be mad!"

As usual in Tri-City, while the Tycoons battled to win the flag, across town the team once considered their rivals, if not in league standings then in the hearts of the local fans, made their annual attempt to climb out of the second division and finish in the money. It was a feat that the Greenbacks had not managed yet in the years since Gil Gamesh and the Whore House Gang had been driven from the league, not even when they won more games than they lost. Eager and accomplished as the players might be, invariably they began to falter in August, and by the season's end the team was firmly ensconced in fifth or sixth. At first glance it seemed (to the moralists, that is) that the scandals that had destroyed the fiery Greenback teams of '33 and '34 had left behind "a legacy of shame" which inevitably eroded the confidence of newcomers to the club, just as it had poisoned the spirit of the veterans of those unfortunate years. Comparison had only to be made to what had befallen the Chicago White Sox of the American League, after it was discovered at the tail-end of the 1920 season that the pennant-winning 1919 team, the team of Shoeless Joe Jackson and Eddie Cicotte, had thrown the World Series to Cincinnati: as all the world knows, it was sixteen years before the demoralized White Sox finished in the first division again.

Popular as such explanations proved to be with the punitive masses, those inside the game suggested that what stood between these perfectly competent Greenback teams and a first division finish was really the odd family who were now the

Greenback owners. In actuality, none of the rookies who joined the club after the '34 season ever appeared at the outset to be intimidated by the team's scandalous past; the youngsters were mostly country kids, and when a Greenback scout appeared in the midst of the Depression with a fistful of bills and a big league contract, they grinned for the camera, and right out there in the pasture, beside their overalled dads, signed on the dotted line. How were they to know, those eager innocent kids and their impoverished dirt farmer dads, that when the rookie got up north to Tri-City to meet the owner, he would turn out to be a *Jew*, an oily, overweight, excitable little Jew, whose words came thick and fast from his mouth, in sentences the likes of which none of them had ever heard before. Down on the farm a pig was a pig and a cow was a cow —whoever heard of a Jew with the same name as an island in New York harbor? A real Goldberg—only called Ellis!

"De immigration took one look at de real name," explained the Greenback owner to the farmboy who sat before him, his cardboard suitcase in his lap and tears of disappointment in his eyes, "and dat vas dat. Vee vuz Ellis."

"But . . ." the rookie stammered.

"But vat? Speak up. Dun' be shy."

"Well, sir . . . well, I don't think . . . well, that you is what my daddy and me had in mind."

"I ain't vat my daddy and me had in mind needer, Slugger. But dis is de land of opportunities."

"But—what kind of opportunity," the boy blurted out, "is playin' big league ball for a *Jew!*"

Ellis shrugged; sarcastically he said, "A vunz in a lifetime. Okay? Now, vipe de tears and go put on de uniform. Let's take a look on you, all dressed up."

Reluctantly, the boy changed out of his threadbare church suit and his frayed white shirt into a fresh Greenback home uniform. "Nice," Ellis said, smiling, "*very* nice."

"Ain't the seat kind a' baggy?"

"The seat I can take in."

"And the waist—"

"De vaist I can fix, please. I'm talkin' general appearance. Sarah," he called, "come look at de new second-baseman."

A roundish woman, her hair up in a bun and wearing an apron, came into the office, bucket and mop in hand.

"Vat do you t'ink?" he asked his wife.

She nodded her head, approvingly. "It's him."

"Toin aroun'," said Ellis, "show her from de beck."

The rookie turned.

"It's him," said Mrs. Ellis. "Even the number is him."

"But—but how about down here, M'am," asked the rookie, "in the seat here—?"

"Dun' *vurry* vit de seat," said Ellis. "De important t'ing is de shoulder. If it fits in de shoulder, it fits."

The rookie squirmed inside the suit, miserable as he could be.

"Go ahead, sving. Take a cut—be sure you got room. I don't vant it should pinch in de shoulder."

The rookie pretended to swing. "It don't," he admitted.

"Good! Vundaful! She'll pin de seat and de vaist, and you'll pick up Vensday."

"*Wednesday?* What about tomorrow?"

"Please, she already got t'ree rookies came in yesterday. Vensday! Now, how about a nice pair of spikes?"

Dear Paw [the letters went, more or less] we bin trikt. The owner here is a ju. He lives over the skorbord in rite so he can keep his i on the busnez. To look at him cud make you cry like it did me just from lookin. A reel Nu York ju like you heer about down home. It just aint rite Paw. It aint big leeg like I expeck atal. But worse of all is the sun. Another ju. A 7 yr old boy who is a Gene Yuss. Izik. He duz not even go to skule he is that much of a Gene Yuss. His i cue is 424 same exack as Wee Willie Keeler hit in '97. Only it aint base hits but brains. Paw he trys to manig the team. A seven yr old. It just aint what we had in mind is it Paw. What shud I do now. Yor sun Slugger.

Isaac. *There* (according to those in the know) was *precisely* what had stood between the Greenbacks and the first division all these years. In the end most of the players could swallow being fathered and mothered by the Ellises—but that crazy little genius kid of theirs, this Isaac, with his charts, his tables, his graphs, his calculations, his formulae—with his *ideas!* According to him, every way they had of playing baseball in the majors before he came along was absolutely *wrong*. The sacrifice bunt is *wrong*. The intentional pass is *wrong*. With less than two outs the hit-and-run is preferable to hitting away, *regardless of who is at the plate*. "Oh yeah?" the players would say, "and just how'd you figure that one out, Izzy?" Whereupon the seven-year-old would extract his clip-on fountain pen from his shirt pocket, and set out to show them how on his pad of yellow paper.

"First off, you must understand that the hit-and-run is the antithesis of the sacrifice bunt, a maneuver utterly without value, which by my calculations results in a *loss* of seventy-two runs over the season. I calculate this loss by the following formula," and here he wrote on the paper which he held up for them to see—

$$1Ys = 5.4376\,CRy + .2742 = .4735$$

"On the other hand," said Isaac, "compare the total runs scored by hitting away versus the hit-and-run, which of course is your remaining alternative with a man on base. As you can see from the graph—" Shuffling through his briefcase, he came up with a chart, prepared on the cardboard from a laundered shirt, a maze of intersecting lines, each carefully labeled in block letters, "*CRy* performance," "*Ys* probability," "probable total DG attempts," etc.—"as you can see, wherein the broken line represents hitting away—"

"Uh-huh," said the ballplayers, winking at one another, "oh, sure, clear as day—you're a real smart little tyke, Izzy—" they said, signaling with an index finger to the temple that actually in their estimation the child was a little touched in the head.

"If then," concluded Isaac, "the hit-and-run were employed at four times the ordinary frequency of the sacrifice bunt, we could anticipate another sixty-five to seventy-five runs per year for the Greenbacks. Now you ask, what are the consequences in the standings of these sixty-five to seventy-five runs per year for the Greenbacks? Let us look at Table 11, which I have here, keeping in mind as we do that of course the fundamental equation for winning a baseball game is $1\ Y = (Rw)\ (Pb/Pd)$."

But by now most of his audience would have drifted away, some to the batting cage, others off to sprint and shag flies in the outfield, and so Isaac would pack his briefcase, and with his pad under his arm, wander down to the bullpen to give the day's lesson to the utility catchers and relief pitchers. He removed a cardboard from his briefcase and attempted to pass it among them. It read—

$$d = \frac{{}^c L\ P\ V^2\ t^2\ g\ C^2}{7230\ W}\ \text{feet}$$

"Aww, what the hell is that, Izzy?" they said, handing it right back.

"A formula I've prepared to tell how much a ball will curve. Don't you think that is something you ought to be familiar with?"

"Well, we is already, kid—so go on out of here."

"All right, if that is the case, what does d stand for?"

"Doggie. Now get out. Scat."

"d equals displacement from a straight line."

"Oh sure it does, everybody knows that."

"Or should," said Isaac, "if they pretend to any knowledge whatsoever of the game. How about ${}^cL$?"

Silence. Weary silence.

"${}^cL$ equals the circulation of the air generated by friction when the ball is spinning," said Isaac. "And P equals the density of the air, of course—normal at .002–.378. V equals the speed of the ball, t equals the time for delivery. And g equals the acceleration of gravity—32.2 feet per second per second. C equals—well, you tell me. What *does* C equal?"

"Cat," they said, as though the joke were on him.

"Wrong. C equals the circumference of the ball—9 inches. And W? What about W?"

"W is for Watch Your Little Ass, sonny," whispered a rookie, in disgust.

"No, W equals the ball's weight, which is .3125 pound. 7230 relates other values of pounds, inches, feet, seconds, and so forth, to arrive at an answer in feet."

"Yeah? And so what! What of it!"

"Only that I know whereof I speak, gentlemen. You must believe me. If only you would cease being slaves to the tired, conventional, and wholly speculative strategies of the game as it has been mistakenly played these fifty years, and would apply the conclusions I have reached by the mathematical analysis of the official statistics, you could add three hundred runs to the team's total production, thus lifting the Tri-City Greenbacks from fifth to *first*. *Your* conclusions are based on nothing but traditional misconceptions; *mine* are developed from the two fundamental theorems of the laws of chance, proposed by Pascal in the seventeenth century. Now, if you will agree to be patient, I am willing to try once again—"

"Well, we ain't! Get lost, Quiz Kid! This is a game for men, not boys!"

"If I may, it is 'a game' for neither. It is an applied science and should be approached as such."

"F off, Isaac! F-U-C-K off, if you know what *that* equals!"

As the seasons passed, and Isaac developed into even more of a genius than he had been when he first came to the Greenbacks at the age of seven, relations with his father's team became increasingly bitter; having confirmed his theories over the years by subjecting the entire canon of baseball records to statistical analysis, he found he no longer had the patience to explain ad infinitum to these nincompoops why they were playing the game all wrong. The antagonism he had had to face in his first years in the majors had hardened him considerably, and by the age of ten the charming pedantry and professional thoroughness of the seven-year-old (who had deemed it necessary to convince as much by his eloquence as by the facts and the figures) had given way to a strident and demanding manner that did not serve to endear him to players two and three times his own age. For this tone he now regularly took toward the Greenback regulars, he more than once had been rewarded with a wad of tobacco juice. "I'll worry about *why,* you idiot—*just do as I say!* You wouldn't understand *why* if I told you—which I have anyway, *a thousand times. Just no more sacrifice bunts!* Because what you are sacrificing is sixty-two runs a year! When he says bunt,

I want the hit-and-run! Do you understand that? *Do not bunt under any circumstances.* Hit-and—" And just about then came the tobacco juice, a neat stream, or a dripping wad, expertly placed right down through his open mouth, putting that voice box of his out of commission, at least for a time.

"Isaac," said his father, "I'm payink a high-class baseball manager fifteen t'ousand dollars a year, dat he should tell dem to bunt, dat behind his back, you should tell dem hit-and-run?"

"But I am a mathematical genius!"

"And *he* is a baseball genius!"

"He is a baseball *ignoramus.* They *all* are!"

"And so who should be de manager, Isaac—you? At de ripe age of ten?"

"Age has nothing to do with it! We are talking about conclusions I have reached through the scientific method!"

"*Enough* vit dat method! You ain' gung to manage a major leek team at age ten—*and dat's dat!*"

"But if I did, we would be in first place within a month!"

"And day vud t'row me from de leek so fast you vud'n know vat *hit* you! Isaac, day ain' lookin' already for somet'ink day could tell me goodbye and good riddintz? Huh? Day ain' sorry enough day let a Jew in to begin vit, now I got to give dem new ammunition to t'row me out on my ear? *Listen* to me, Isaac: I didn't buy no baseball team juss for my own healt'—I bought it for *yours!* So you could grow up in peace an American boy! So ven came time to give it to de Jews again, day couldn't come around to my door! Isaac, dis is a business vere you could grow up safe and sound! Jewish geniuses, go look how long is de average life span in a pogrom! But own a big leek team, my son, and you ain' got for to vurry never again!"

"But what good is a big league team if the big league team plays the game *all wrong!*"

"In *your* eyes all wrong. But not to de big leekers! Isaac, please, if de goyim say bunt, let dem bunt!"

"But the hit-and-run—"

"*Svallow* de hit-and-run! *Forget* de hit-and-run! It ain' de vay day do here!"

"But the way they do it here is *wrong!*"

"But here is vere it *comes* from!"

"But I can prove they're wrong SCIENTIFICALLY!"

"You're such a genius, do me a favor, prove day're *right!*"

"But that's not what geniuses *do!*"

"I dun *care* about de oder geniuses! I only care about *you!* Dis is big leek baseball, Isaac—vat vuz here for a t'ousand years already! *Leaf vell enough alone!*" And here he related to Isaac yet again the long, miserable story of anti-Semitism; he told him of murder and pillage and rape, of peasants and Cossacks and crusaders and kings, all of whom had oppressed the Jewish people down through the ages. Only in America, he said, could a Jew rise to such heights! Only in America could a Jew ever hope to become the owner of a major league baseball team!

"That's because they only *have* baseball in America," said Isaac, scowling with disgust.

"Oh yeah? Vat about Japan, viseguy?" snapped Ellis. "Day dun' got baseball dere? You t'ink a Jew could own a baseball team in Japan so easy? Isaac—listen to me, for a Jewish pois'n dis is de greatest country vat ever vas, in de history of de *voild!*"

"Sure it is, 'Dad'," said the contemptuous son, "as long as he plays the game their way."

Thus the seasons passed, the Greenbacks regularly finishing fifth and sixth in the Patriot League, and the genius son no less contemptuous of his father's old-country fearfulness than of the Greenbacks, who were bound by ignorance and superstition and habit to self-defeating taboos. Before Isaac's tirades and tongue-lashings, even the staunchest players eventually came to lose faith in the instructions they received from the bench, and by midseason most of them would wind up playing entirely on their own, heeding neither the conventional tactics of that season's manager, nor the unorthodox strategies of "the little kike" as the little tyke was now called; or, what was even worse, rather than following their own natural instincts, independent of seasoned manager or child prodigy, they would try to *reason* their way out of the dilemma, with the result that time and again, in the midst of straining to think the problem through, they would go down looking at a fat one. Finally, it was not the increase in Greenback strike-outs, but a sense of all the bewilderment that lay back of them, that caused the Greenback fans to become increasingly uneasy in the stands, and to emerge from the stadium at the end of nine innings as exhausted as if they had spent the preceding two hours watching a tightrope walker working without benefit of a net. So exhausting did it become to watch their team's strained performance, that even those Greenback fans whose interest had survived the expulsion of Gamesh and who had made their peace with the idea of a true-blue Yid as owner, eventually preferred to stay at home and wash the car on their day off, rather than going out to Greenback Stadium to see a perfectly competent ball club struggling in vain against eighteen men—the nine on the opposing team and the nine on their own.

6

THE TEMPTATION OF ROLAND AGNI

(continued)

≈ 6 ≈

The arrival of Agni at Greenback Stadium; what befalls him
amongst the Jews he there meets with, containing several dia-
logues between a Jew and a Negro that cause Roland to con-
sider taking his life. Newspaper coverage of his suicide imag-
ined by the rookie sensation. Isaac Ellis . makes another
appearance; a conversation on "the Breakfast of Champions,"
wherein the desperate hero of this great history learns the
difference between the Wheaties that are made in Minneapolis
by General Mills and those that are manufactured in an under-
ground laboratory by a Jewish genius, and something too
about Appearance and Reality. Roland succumbs. Concerning
winning and losing. A short account of the Mundy miracle,
with assorted statistics. The bewilderment of Roland; his fears
and hallucinations. In which the character of Mister Fair-
smith appears, with an explanation as to why he disappeared
from the scene so early in the book. A long digression on base-
ball and barbarism, with a very full description of Mister Fair-
smith's adventures in Africa; his success there with our na-
tional pastime, his disappointment, his bravery, and his narrow
escape from the savages who blaspheme all he holds sacred and
dear. His faith in a Supreme Being is tested by the Mundys.
A disputation between a devout and the manager on whether
Our Lord loves baseball. The Mundy winning streak settles
the issue. A heartwarming scene on a train to Tri-City. The
disastrous conclusion of the foregoing adventure, in which
Nickname's attempt to stretch a double into a triple with the
Mundys thirty-one runs behind the Tycoons in
the ninth constitutes the coup de grâce.
Isaac and Agni have it out.
Mister Fairsmith is laid
to rest.

L̲ATE ONE NIGHT, not very long after his visit to Mrs. Trust,
Roland Agni once again stole out of his hotel room after Jolly
Cholly's bed check and made his way through the unfamiliar
streets of Tri-City, this time toward the harbor instead of the
business district. The Tycoons were at home fattening them-

selves on the visiting Mundys, the Greenbacks were on the
road; nonetheless, a light was shining in a window above the
scoreboard in right field, exactly as it had on each of the two
previous excursions that Agni had secretly made to Greenback
Stadium. As yet, however, he had not found the courage to ring
the bell in the recessed doorway on the street side of the right-
field wall. But was "courage" the word? Wasn't it more like
"treachery"?

If you make a deal, Roland, Mrs. Trust had told him,
*you'll have to make it with the enemies of America, as an
enemy of America . . .*

"Vat *is* dis? Who *is* dis?" came a voice from a window
some twenty-five feet above his head. For he (or the traitor in
him) had rung the bell at last!

"Vat kind of joke is dis! Vat's gung on down dere!"

"I—I thought there was a night game . . . sorry . . ."

"At 2 A.M.?" cried Ellis. "Get outta here, viseguy, de
Greenbacks is on de road!"

"I—I have to see the owner."

"Write de complaint department, dummy!"

But as the Jew's head withdrew, the miserable Mundy
star cried out, "It's—it's Roland Agni, Mr. Ellis!"

"It's *who?*"

"Me! Roland! The leading hitter in the league!"

Agni was led up a steep circular stairway through the
interior of the scoreboard, as terrified as if he were climbing
the spinal column of a prehistoric monster. A single bulb
burned at the very top, no larger than you would imagine a
monster's brain to be, and with about as much intensity. Black
squares of wood were fitted into the thirty or forty apertures
that faced out onto the field, as though the mouths, ears, and
nostrils, as well as all the eyes, had lids to pull shut when the
great beast wasn't out breathing fire. . . . In all, mounting
the dim hollow interior of the scoreboard produced the most
eerie sensation in Roland—or maybe it was just walking behind a Jew. He did not believe he had ever even seen one up
close before, though of course he'd heard the stories.

Mrs. Ellis immediately put up some hot water for tea. "A
.370 hitter," she said, pulling a housecoat over her night-

gown, "and he goes out in the middle of the night without a
jacket!"

"I wasn't thinkin', ma'm. I wanted a little air, ya' see,
and got lost . . ."

She put her hand to his forehead. "This I don't like," she
told her husband, and left the room, returning in a moment
with a thermometer. "Please," she said to Agni, who at first
refused to rise from his chair, "you wouldn't be the first big
leaguer what I seen with his pants down."

So, scaling new heights of humiliation in his desperate
attempt to shed the scarlet-and-gray, Roland did as he was
told.

While Mrs. Ellis sat beside him, waiting for his fever to
register, the Jew owner returned to the ledgers which lay open
beneath the lamp on his desk. "You know vat I clear in a
veek?" he asked the Mundy star. "Last veek, know vat I
cleared in cash, after salaries, after rent and repairs, after new
balls and new resin bags? Take a guess."

"A thousand?" said Agni.

"Who you talkin' to, Mrs. Trust from de Tycoons, or
me? Guess again."

"Shucks, I can't, Mr. Ellis, with this here thing stickin'
in me . . ."

"Sha," whispered Mrs. Ellis, checking the second hand on
her watch.

"Guess again, Roland!" said Ellis.

"A hundred a week?"

"Come again!"

"Ninety? Eighty? Look, how do I know—I got my own
troubles, Mr. Ellis!"

With the enemies, as an enemy . . .

"Tventy-t'ree dollars a veek!" cried Mr. Ellis. "Less den
de ushers! Less den de groundkipper! Less den de hooligan
vat sells de beer! *And I'm de owner!*"

Mrs. Ellis extracted the thermometer. "Well," she said,
"I'll tell you the name of one .370 hitter who ain't running
around Tri-City no more tonight! The league's leading hitter
and he's out looking for pneumonia!"

"It's . . . it's bein' a Mundy, Mrs. Ellis . . ." whispered
Agni.

"It's *what?*"

"Nothin'," he said, but instead of getting up and getting the hell out, he allowed himself (or the traitor in him) to be bundled into a pair of Mr. Ellis's pajamas and buried beneath three blankets on the sofa.

It wasn't making a deal with the enemy, was it, to stay overnight?

In the morning his temperature was normal, but Mrs. Ellis would not hear of his returning to his hotel without breakfast. "Please, you're not playing against the Tycoons on an empty stomach." And he had to agree that that made no sense.

"Tell me somet'ink," grumbled Ellis from across the breakfast table, "vy do vee haf all dese pitchers? Can somebody give me vun good reason?"

"Abe," said his wife, from the stove, "enough with the pitchers."

"God forbid dey should lift a finger around here between assignments! To get dem to pinch-*run* even, you got to get down on your knees and beg! Years ago, a pitcher who vas a pitcher would t'row bot' ends of a doubleheader! Ven I fois' came to dis country, belief me, you didn't *haf* eight pitchers sittin' dere on dere behinds for every vun vat vas on de mound! You had two, t'ree iron men, and dat vas it! Today, *nine pitchers!* No vunder I'm goink to de poor house! And *you*—" he cried, as into the room came his worst enemy of all, "Mr. Argument! Mr. Ideas! Mr. Sabotage-his-own-fad'er!"

"You sabotage yourself," mumbled Isaac, and stuffed a sugar bun into his mouth.

"Isaac," said Mrs. Ellis, "see who's heré? Roland Agni! The league's leading hitter!"

"Bat him first," said Isaac, "instead of eighth, and he'd be leading the league in runs scored, too."

"I *would?*" said Agni. "I thought fourth."

"First!" shouted Isaac. "Players should bat in the descending order of run-productiveness! $Dy = rp \times 1275$. But try to explain that to the morons who manage this game!"

"Mr. Know-it-all!"

"They don't see eye-to-eye," explained the kindly Mrs. Ellis.

"Neither does me and my dad," Agni said.

"Vell, listen to him den!" snapped Ellis. "Maybe you'll loin somet'ink!"

"I did," whined Agni, "that's how come everythin' that's wrong with me is wrong. On account of my father! Oh, Mr. Ellis," cried Agni, "I—I—I—"

As an enemy, with the enemies, Roland.

"I—I want—I want—"

"What is it?" cried Mrs. Ellis, clutching her heart at the sight of the young hero suddenly in tears.

"I—I want to be a Greenback! To play for you! Oh, buy me, Mr. Ellis—and I'll play for nothin'! But I just can't be a Mundy no more!"

Stunned, Ellis said, "For nuttink?"

"Yes! Yes! I play for my allowance of two-fifty a week as it is! Oh, buy me, please! I'll bring in fans by the tens of thousands! I'll be the greatest Greenback since Gil Gamesh!"

"A star like you—you vud play for a Jewish pois'n?"

"Mr. Ellis, I don't care if you was the worst Jew in the world—*I'll do anything! I'll eat scraps! I'll sleep on the club-house floor!*"

"Not in my stadium," said Mrs. Ellis.

"Sarah," said Ellis, "get me de Mundy front office. Ve're makink a deal!"

Isaac Ellis stood by, sneering, while his mother called long distance to Port Ruppert. "Hello?" she said. "This is the Ruppert Mundys? . . . You *sure?*" Shrugging she handed the phone to her husband.

"Vat?" he asked her.

"To me," she said, "sounds like the *shvartze.*"

"Abe Ellis talkink here."

"What you want, Abe Ellis dere?"

"To speak vit one of de Mundy boys, if you dun' mind."

"Day ain' here. Day in South America. What you want?"

"Who is dis talking to me like dis?" demanded Ellis.

"Dis here George. Now what you want befo' I hang up?"

"I vant to talk to de Mundy brut'ers about a trade, if dat's all right vit' you!"

"Who all you wanna trade?"

"Listen, who is dis, may I ask, de colored janitor or somebody?"

"Das right. Dis here is George Washington, de colored janitor. Who all you wanna trade? Don' tell me no dwarf now, 'cause I jus' bought me a li'l dwarf."

"*You* bought?"

"Das right."

"And since ven you got de right to buy and sell in de Patriot Leek?"

"Since when do *you*, Jew?" and the Ruppert front office hung up.

"A *shvartze* janitor," said Ellis, "runnink a big leek team!"

"A what?" asked Agni.

"A colored pois'n!" cried Ellis. "George Vashington no less! He sveeps de floor—and he makes de trades!"

"Then that's him," said Agni, "who traded Buddy to Kakoola—just like the fellers said!"

"I dun' belief it! Sarah," said Ellis, "call again—and call *right!*"

"This the Mundys?" she asked, after dialing long distance and waiting to be connected. "Yes?" She handed the phone to her husband. "It's him."

"Hello?" said Ellis, "Ruppert Mundys?"

"Das right."

"Look—I vant to buy from you a center-fielder."

"Well, ain' dat somethin'. De Jew, he wanna buy de bess playuh we done got! And how much you wanna pay, Jew?"

"Vatch de vay you talk to me, sonny boy!"

"How much you wanna pay, Jew? Dis here de league leadin' batter we's talkin' about. Dis here a nineteen-year-ol' boy, strong as de ox, quick as de rabbit, smart as de owl, and hungry as de wolf!"

"How much *you* vant?"

"Oh, jus about as much as you ready to part wid, Jew—and den some!"

"Vell, frankly I vas t'inkink more alonk de line of a svop—svoppink players."

"Oh, I betch you wuz," chuckled George. "Only we don' *need* no mo' players."

"De Mundys dun' need *players?*"

"We juss fine in de player department. We wan' yo' *money.*"

"Listen, vat is dis! Vat's goink on! Who gave you de right—I demand to know!"

"Same one gave *you*," and the phone went dead.

"Can't be!" cried the Greenback owner. "Dis is somebody tryink to drive me crazy! It couldn't be a real *shvartze*—no, it can't be true!"

Sneering, Isaac said, "Why not, Dad? It's the land of opportunity, *Dad*."

"For everybody," thought Agni, bursting into tears again, "but me! And *I'm* the All-American star! It ain't fair! It don't make sense no more! I'm the greatest rookie of all time! I'm another Cobb! I'm another Ruth! I'm everybody great rolled up into one—and a Jew and a nigger is bargainin' for my hide!"

This time Ellis himself did the phoning. "You sure," he asked the operator, "dis is de big leek team? You sure dis ain't a practical joke?"

"This is not A Practical Joke, sir," the operator informed him. "If you want A Practical Joke you will have to get that number from information. I have the Ruppert Mundy Baseball Organization of the Patriot League on the wire. Go ahead, please."

"Hello—Mundys? *Ruppert* Mundys?"

"De same."

"Dis is de *shvartze* again?"

"De same."

"How much for Roland Agni?"

"A cool qwata of a million."

"*Dollars?*"

"De *same*, Jew."

Agni descended through the dim interior of the right-field scoreboard; halfway down he walked out along a gangway to lift one of the boards and peer through the aperture at the playing field that might have been his home, if only he wasn't so great and didn't cost so much to buy . . . Far below, the pasture beckoned. He saw the headlines.

AGNI LEAPS FROM SCOREBOARD

Rookie Slugger Suicide; Jews, Niggers, Commies, Cripples, Dwarfs, and Other Freaks Held Responsible; Landis Orders

Disreputable Elements Barred from Game Forever; "Clean-up
long overdue," says Mrs. Trust; "Could have been greatest of all
time," Managers agree; Mundy Brothers Jailed; Mazuma Gets
Death Penalty; Agni's Father Weeps at Funeral: "I was only
trying to teach him humility"—Stoned by Grief-Stricken Fans;
"This day shall live in infamy," says F.D.R.; Nation-wide
Mourning Ordered; Pathetically Broken Beautiful Body To Be
Cremated in Ceremony at Hall of Fame; Ashes To Be Scattered
from Air Force Bomber on Fans at Opening Game of World
Series; Number To Be Retired; Shoes To Be Bronzed; Bat and
Glove To Be Taken on Round-the-World Tour of G.I.s by Bob
Hope; Name To Live Forever; "Lesson to Mankind," says Pope;
Fred Waring's "Ballad of Roland Agni" Number One on Hit
Parade; Big Four To Meet

It almost seemed worth it . . .

Except, thought Agni, that's not what would happen at
all—not with my luck! No, even if he leaped to his death in a
perfect swan dive, he would get no more than a few grudging
lines on page seventy-two, he was sure . . .

MUNDY DEAD IN FALL, AS IF ANYONE CARES

Tri-City, Sept. 16—One of the Ruppert Mundys, the joke team
of organized baseball, in a typical stupid Mundy stunt, fell out
of the scoreboard at Greenback Stadium and died. God only
knows what he was doing there. His name was Nagi or something
like that and he was said to be their best player. The Mundys' best
player. Terrific.

"No luck, Agni?"

"What!"

"It's me."

"Who? It's so dark!"

"Down here. Isaac Ellis. The ungrateful son."

"Oh . . ."

"Down here. Keep coming, Roland, keep coming."

"What—what is all this?"

"My laboratory."

"Where am I?"

"Under the stadium. You missed the door to the street."

"What—what are you doing?"

"Oh, this? Splitting the atom."

"What—what's that mean?"

"Just something to pass the time, Roland, until I get to manage the Greenbacks the way they ought to be managed."

"But you're only seventeen."

"And a Jew and a genius, I know."

"Boy, you must be lonely to sit down here like this, doin' that. Well, I better be going, you know. How do I get out a' here?"

"Not so fast. Sit down. I wanted to talk to you, Roland."

"But I got to be at Tycoon Park—I gotta game to play."

"Don't be frightened, Roland. I only want to talk, that's all. You're a great baseball player, Roland. They don't make them like you anymore."

"I know they don't. They never did, like me. I've got practically everything you could want."

"Roland, I'd like to manage you some day. Your body, my brains—there'd be nothing like it in the history of the game."

"But I'm a Mundy, in case you ain't heard."

"I could buy you from the Mundys, don't worry about that."

"Oh yeah! And where *you* goin' to get two hundred and fifty thousand dollars from?"

"A seventeen-year-old Jewish genius can always lay his hands on a few bucks, Rollie."

"Oh sure."

"My friend, I could make that quarter of a million just between now and the end of the season by betting on the Mundys to win all their remaining games."

"You could, huh? And how they gonna do that? A miracle from God?"

"See this that I am holding in my hand? You can read by the light of my Bunsen burner."

"It's just a box of Wheaties."

"Wheaties, the Breakfast of Champions."

"Well, that's pure baloney, that champion stuff. We get 'em free, by the case. And look at all the good they done us."

"You get your Wheaties from the General Mills Company in Minneapolis, Minnesota. That is why they don't do what they're advertised to do. These Wheaties are manufactured by a seventeen-year-old Jewish genius.''

"But—it's the same box, ain't it?''

"The same box. The same flavor. The same in every visible way. Only one invisible difference.''

"What?''

"They do the job. If the Ruppert Mundys were to eat these Wheaties made by me in Tri-City, if only a few little flakes were to be sprinkled on top of those Wheaties they already eat made by the Wheaties company in Minneapolis, your team would be unbeatable.''

"Oh yeah? And what makes them so special again?''

"Let's call it extra energy.''

"That's what they all say. Vitamin X, Y, and Z. It's all words.''

"Roland, if only you will slip these Wheaties into their breakfast in the morning, there will be no holding down the Mundys on the field.''

"I suppose they're going to wake up old Wayne Heket while they're at it, too.''

"They'll do more than just wake him up, I can assure you of that.''

"Oh sure, sure.''

"Stupid *goy*, I am splitting the atom! I am fifty years ahead of my time in nuclear physics alone! The Wheaties I could do with a frontal lobotomy! I am telling you the scientific facts—the Mundys will eat my Wheaties, and they will win all of their remaining games! And by betting on them I will win a quarter of a million dollars—and buy yóu for my father's team—and become the Greenback manager, at long last! And either my old man says yes, or he winds up on the street, begging with a cup!''

"But—but, if I feed the boys these Wheaties—is that what you want me to do?''

"Exactly! Every morning, just a little sprinkle!''

"And we win—?''

"Yes! You win!''

"But—that'd be like throwin' a game.''

"Like *what?*''

"Like throwin' it. I mean, we'd be winnin' when we're

supposed to be losin'—and that's wrong. That's illegal!''

"Throwing a game, Roland, is *losing* when you're supposed to be *winning*. Winning instead of losing is what you're
supposed to do!''

"But not by eatin' Wheaties!''

"*Precisely* by eating Wheaties! That's the whole *idea* of
Wheaties!''

"But that's *real* Wheaties! And they don't make you do
it anyway!''

"Then how can they be 'real' Wheaties, if they don't do
what they're supposed to do?''

"That's what *makes* them 'real'!''

"No, that's what makes them *unreal*. *Their* Wheaties say
they're supposed to make you win—and they don't! *My*
Wheaties say they're supposed to make you win—and they
do! How can that be wrong, Roland, or illegal? That is keeping your promises! That is being true to your word! I am
going to make the most hopeless baseball team in history into
a team of red-blooded American boys! And you call that
'throwing a game'? I am talking about *winning*, Roland, *winning*—what made this country what it is today! Who in his
right mind can be against *that?*''

Who, indeed. Winning! Oh, you really can't say enough good
things about it. There is nothing quite like it. Win hands down,
win going away, win by a landslide, win by accident, win by a
nose, win without deserving to win—you just can't beat it,
however you slice it. Winning is the tops. Winning is the name
of the game. Winning is what it's all about. Winning is the
be-all and the end-all, and don't let anybody tell you otherwise. All the world loves a winner. Show me a good loser, said
Leo Durocher, and I'll show you a loser. Name one thing that
losing has to recommend it. You can't. Losing is tedious. Los-
ing is exhausting. Losing is uninteresting. Losing is depress-
ing. Losing is boring. Losing is debilitating. Losing is compromising. Losing is shameful. Losing is humiliating. Losing
is infuriating. Losing is disappointing. Losing is incomprehensible. Losing makes for headaches, muscle tension, skin
eruptions, ulcers, indigestion, and for mental disorders of every

kind. Losing is bad for confidence, pride, business, peace of
mind, family harmony, love, sexual potency, concentration, and
much much more. Losing is bad for people of all ages, races, and
religions; it is as bad for infants as for the elderly, for women
as for men. Losing makes people cry, howl, scream, hide, lie,
smolder, envy, hate, and quit. Losing is probably the single
biggest cause of suicide in the world, and of murder. Losing
makes the benign malicious, the generous stingy, the brave
fearful, the healthy ill, and the kindly bitter. Losing is universally despised, as well it should be. The sooner we get rid of
losing, the happier everyone will be.

But winning. To win! It was everything Roland remembered.

14–6 against Independence, nine runs scored in the first inning.
Seven Mundy home runs! Eight Mundy stolen bases! WAYNE
HEKET STEALS HOME!

8–0, knocking the Blues out of the pennant race. THE
MUNDYS KNOCK THE BLUES OUT OF THE PENNANT
RACE! Deacon Demeter goes all the way, scattering three
hits. Four Mundy double plays. WAYNE HEKET STEALS
TWO BASES! FIFTY YEARS OLD AND HE STEALS
TWO BASES! Home runs: Rama (2), Skirnir, Agni, and
Damur. NICKNAME DAMUR, FOURTEEN YEARS OLD
AND NINETY-TWO POUNDS, HITS A HOME RUN INTO
THE UPPER DECK!

Asylum. Four home games against the Mundys for the
Keepers. This should land them in fifth for sure. This is their
chance to overtake the Greenbacks for sure. MUNDYS
SWEEP FOUR IN A ROW. Demeter, Tuminikar, Volos,
Buchis hurl COMPLETE GAMES! TUMINIKAR UN-
LEASHES FASTBALL OF YORE! HEKET STEALS
FIVE BASES! PTAH HITS SAFELY IN SIXTH CON-
SECUTIVE GAME! Home runs in Asylum: Rama (4), Skir-
nir (3), Baal (6), Agni (2).

Kakoola. Mundys take three in a row. Ho-hum. Ockatur
two-hits old mates. Rama-Baal home run barrage continues.
Heket scores from first on long Damur single! Steals everything except the catcher's underwear. Skirnir's great catch

breaks back of Reaper rally! Reliever Chico Mecoatl fans last seven Reaper batters! Tuminikar whiffs sixteen with blazing fastball. Mazuma delighted as incredulous capacity crowds witness massacre of locals. "Know that R that used to stand for 'Ridiculous'?" says Mazuma. "Stands for 'Renegades' now. One more season without a home, and they'll be the greatest team in the history of the game. And the most dreaded!"

Then Terra Inc. 8–1, 9–3. Simple as that. The Mundys, boom, boom, boom; the Rustlers, swish, swish, swish. Eleven in a row.

Assorted statistics for the miracle: Heket, 14 stolen bases; Rama, 12 home runs; Baal, 10 home runs, 4 triples, 2 doubles; Ptah, hit safely 11 consecutive games; Damur, batting average for 11 games, .585 (in contrast to .087 for previous 142); complete games pitched, Tuminikar 3, Ockatur 2, Demeter 2, Volos 1, Buchis 1. Wild pitches, none. Passed balls, none. Errors, 3, all on Skirnir, trying to make acrobatic never-say-die shoestring catches.

Oh it was wonderful, it was glorious, it was heavenly— except at night, when he could not sleep because of those nightmares in which he stood before the conscience of the game, the Commissioner himself, and received his just deserts. "But I didn't eat any myself, Your Honor—I swear I didn't! Not a one!" "You fed the others, Roland." "They fed *themselves*. They lifted the spoons to their own mouths and chewed and swallowed all on their own, I swear!" "But who brought those boxes of illegal Wheaties to the table, Roland? Who sprinkled them in with the others?" "But it was that smart little Jew that put me up to it, Commissioner! He forced me to, by playin' on my hopes!" "Roland, I have no more love for a smart little Jew than the next fellow. Baseball has always been a Christian game, and so it shall remain, if I have anything to do with it. But if Jews don't belong here, neither do ballplayers who fall for their schemes to make an easy buck." "But *I* didn't want to make a buck. The little *Jew* did. I only wanted to play baseball with a real big league team!" "Well, that's unfortunate, because as it now stands, you are never going to play baseball with any team again. You are banished for life, Roland Agni. You are a traitor and a crook." "No! No!"

And leaping from his bed he would run down into the hotel lobby to telephone Tri-City.

"Look, Isaac, what if somebody dies!"

"Nobody's going to die, Roland."

"But maybe this stuff can kill somebody who isn't supposed to have any."

"Roland, you just keep feeding them the Breakfast of Champions, and don't worry about a thing."

"But—but you should see Old Wayne. He starts packin' it away—well, I get worried! Suppose he ups and croaks. That'd be murder!"

"You want to be a Mundy forever, do you?"

"Well, no. But I don't want to get the chair, either! Or get banished! I mean, you watch those guys out there, the way they're playin', and you think, if they keep this up, they're going to *die!*"

"Die? Why?"

"Well, they're too good, that's why! I just think sometimes in the middle of an innin', when we're battin' around and scorin' and goin' crazy on the bases, that all of a sudden, I'm goin' to look in the dugout *and they'll all be dead!*"

"Nobody's died yet from winning, Roland, not that I've ever heard of."

"But maybe if they lost *one,* sort of to give their systems a rest . . ."

"Just what the bookies are waiting for. Why I'm still getting six and seven to one, Agni, is because Las Vegas expects the collapse to come every day, and it doesn't. And it won't, so long as you do your job. Understand me?"

"Well, just so long as nobody gets harmed . . . or paralyzed . . . or somethin' like that. I keep thinkin', one mornin' they're all goin' to be eatin' breakfast, and then they're all just goin' to get paralyzed from head to toe. That could happen too, you know."

"No, it couldn't."

"Why not!"

"Because I'm a scientific genius, Roland, that's why not."

But, thought Roland, if you're such a scientific genius, you smart little Jew, why don't you use them Jewish Wheaties on the Greenbacks to make them win? Why don't you use

them on your own father's team? Because they give people
something awful, that's why! Because one day, right out on
the field, the whole damn team is going to turn purple in the
face and fall down dead! I know it!

But of course all that happened to the Ruppert Mundys
from eating "the Jewish Wheaties" was that they kept on
winning games—and started in giving Roland friendly tips on
how to hit the ball, for as it happened, during the course of the
winning streak his was the lowest batting average on the club.
"You're pressin', kid," said Nickname, at the pregame batting
practice, "just meet the ball." "Believe you're droppin' your
head there, Rollie," advised Skirnir, "keep the old bean up."
"You're uppercuttin' the low ones, Agni—give in the knees
more." And who said that? The dwarf, Ockatur, who barely
came to Agni's knees!

And what of Ulysses S. Fairsmith? Do you fans even remember
the name? If not, then you are in about the same fix by this
time as the players themselves.

Where has the Mundy manager been all season long? Why
isn't he in his famous wooden rocker in the corner of the
Mundy dugout, moving the defense around with the gold tip
of his bamboo cane? What happened to *him?*

Sadly, this: managing the Mundys on the road was worse
than anything the grand old man of baseball could ever have
imagined. Of course, ever since the death of Glorious Mundy
in 1931, he had known his share of disappointment and frustra-
tion, beginning with the Mundy brothers selling out from
under him the pennant-winning clubs of the twenties and replacing all those greats with the lowest-priced players they
could find; certainly when they sold Luke the Loner to the
Rustlers, no one would have thought any the less of the venerable manager had he bid Ruppert goodbye. But out of loyalty
to the city of Port Ruppert and all the friends he had made
there, out of loyalty to the memory of the incomparable Glorious M., Mister Fairsmith accepted without complaint what
any other manager of his record would have interpreted as a
cynical disregard for his professional dignity. Even his enemies, who ridiculed him behind his back for his ministerial

ways, had to admire so impressive a display of character.
"There is more to human life than what you read in the won-
and-lost column, my good friends," said Mister Fairsmith,
and he was a manager, mind you, who had known the taste of
victory and who had cherished it.

But what happened to the Mundys in '43 was more even
than a man of his forbearance and compassion could bear to
witness—or be a party to. Calamity, catastrophe, cataclysm—
of course he had expected no less; he had *prayed* for no less,
praying too that the Lord would give him the strength, the
will, and the wisdom to inspire his homeless flock to prevail
over every conceivable form of suffering that he expected
would be visited upon them. But what shook Mister Fairsmith's faith, what brought him at the age of eighty to the
very edge of an abyss even more terrifying than the one he had
glimpsed twenty years earlier in Africa, was that rather than
being the most profoundly religious experience of a Christian
life, shepherding the Ruppert Mundys from one P. League
town to the next had turned into a farce and a travesty. Where
there was to have been meaningful torment and uplifting anguish and ennobling despair, there was ridiculousness—and
worse. These were the most unprofessional, undignified, *immoral* athletes he had ever seen gathered together on a playing
field in his life—if you could even call them "athletes"! This
wasn't suffering deserving of his compassion—this was just
downright disgusting behavior! Why, not even those African
savages, with their filed teeth and carved flesh, not even those
black devils with their hateful abominations, had sickened and
revolted him as did the '43 Ruppert Mundys!

. . . And those savages had sickened him, all right. The
barbaric ceremony that they had forced him to witness some
twenty years earlier had been the most hideous culmination
imaginable to a round-the-world trip that, till then, the American newspapers had hailed as a brilliant success, particularly
those wonderful weeks proselytizing for the national pastime
in Japan. With the assistance of an erudite young theology
student, a nephew of his who was as adept with a fungo bat as
with the language of this remote jungle tribe, Mister Fairsmith had penetrated a thousand miles into the primitive interior of Africa, the last thirty miles by foot through the

jungle, with native carriers bearing upon their backs the bags
of bats, gloves, and bases he had borne from America. The villagers, numbering no more than a hundred and fifty men,
women, and children, lived in a circle of grass huts not so much
larger than a regulation infield. Beyond the village in all directions was half a mile of high grass—beyond that, the jungle.

Using a machete-like tool with a hooked blade that they
swung two-handed—using a nice level stroke and practically
no stride at all—the men of the village cleared a hundred square
yards of grass for their white visitors, solemn and silent
as gravediggers while they worked. Here Mister Fairsmith
conducted his classes and organized the first game of baseball
ever played on the continent of Africa between all-native
teams. With equipment donated at their playgrounds by the
schoolkids of Ruppert, and which was to be left behind with
the villagers once they had mastered the skills of the game,
Mister Fairsmith demonstrated the fundamentals of hitting,
bunting, catching, pitching, fielding, baserunning, sliding, and
umpiring. The moment he saw the men clearing the field, he
realized that he had stumbled upon a tribe of great long-ball
hitters. Stumbled? Or had the Lord a hand in this? They were
something to watch in the batter's box; not even their fastest
pitcher could intimidate a hitter once he had dug in with his
bare feet at the plate, and when they swung it was as though
the bat was a blade with which they intended to cut the ball in
two. No, Mister Fairsmith did not have to remind these savages, as he did his own rookies throughout spring training, to
follow through on the swing. The follow-through was in their
blood. They were naturals.

The trouble erupted over sliding. Though the men were
clothed only in genital pouches tied around the waist with
rawhide, they did not for a moment flinch from "hitting the
dirt." To the contrary, they slid with abandon whether a slide
was in order or not, with the result that by the time a runner
had come round to score he was covered with dust from head
to foot. No matter how sternly Mister Fairsmith would address them on this matter, they would not even remain on their
feet going into *first*.

It was not a decision that it pleased him to make, but at
the end of the first week, he called the native men together and

through the person of his young nephew announced that henceforth any runner sliding into first base would automatically be called out. He regretted having to resort to a measure of this kind, but he simply did not know how else to curb this stupid passion of theirs.

The spears appeared from out of nowhere. One moment the tribesmen were standing around, listening in their silent, solemn way to what they must have imagined was to be an impromptu class on the finer points of the game—a review, perhaps, of the previous day's lesson in the squeeze play—and the next they were pressing in upon him with their long weapons of warfare. And to protect himself, Mister Fairsmith, in khaki short pants, half-sleeved shirt, and pith helmet, had nothing but a thirty-four-ounce Hillerich and Bradsby.

Then came the wailing of the women, as horrifying a sound as Mister Fairsmith had ever heard—and he had spent his life in baseball parks, he had known crowds to cry for blood before. But not even in Aceldama, Ohio, or Brooklyn, New York, had he ever heard anything to match this. All at once the shaven-headed women were rushing from the circle of huts, some with painted babies still at their scarred breasts, and making a noise as though they were gargling with fire. Oh they were ecstatic, these savage women—tonight they would be dining out on the flesh of Christian gentlemen!

Incredible! Horrendous! Or—or was it not a miracle? Yes! They were going to eat him *because he had decided to add to baseball a rule of his own devising, a rule that did not really exist.* In their own savage African way, they were responding as would the fans at any major league park in America, if the umpire had arbitrarily suspended or altered the code that governs their national pastime. What they had come to understand in one short week was that this was no game for children he had come six thousand miles to teach them, this was no summertime diversion for adults—it was a sacred institution. And who was he, who was *anyone,* to forbid sliding into first when not even the Official Playing Rules Committee of the three leagues forbade it?

The natives were right and he was wrong, and being the man he was, Sam Fairsmith told them so.

At once the women ceased their yowling and the men fell

back with their spears. And his young nephew, who had barely
had voice enough to translate his uncle's words, removed the
catcher's mask and began to undo the chest protector behind
which he'd taken refuge when the tribesmen had charged
Mister Fairsmith; however, like a catcher who may or may not
get a turn at bat in the inning, he continued to wear the shin
guards.

Now the leader of the village, a giant of a man for whom
Mister Fairsmith had high hopes as a fastballing right-handed
pitcher on the style of Walter Johnson, separated himself
from his fellows and stepped forward to address Mister Fairsmith in the language of his tribe. He spoke—as they all did on
the rare occasions they were moved to speak—with much glow-
ering and eye-rolling.

Mister Fairsmith's nephew translated. "Walter Johnson
says that it pleases his people that Mister Baseball has chosen
not to burden them with a regulation against sliding that would
be punishable by an out."

"Tell Walter Johnson," replied "Mister Baseball," "that
I shall try never again to be so mindless and foolish as to place
such a burden upon them."

The gigantic native glowered upon hearing the good news,
and spoke again.

"Walter Johnson says that he is grateful. He says, however, that now that the issue of sliding has been raised, he
wishes to make it known that he and his braves believe they
have been deprived of still another opportunity to enjoy the
pleasure and thrill of the slide. He says that players wish to
know if there is any rule that forbids them from sliding into
first following a base on balls."

Mister Fairsmith said, "You mean, after receiving a *walk,*
they want to slide into first?"

"It would appear from his tone," said Fairsmith's
nephew, reaching for the catcher's mask again, "to be on the
order of a smoldering grievance, Uncle Sam."

"Now, that *is* ridiculous. The primary object of the slide
is to reach the base without being tagged out by the fielder. As
they surely must understand by now, if a batter in his turn at
bat receives four pitches outside of the strike zone he is
awarded first base. Consequently there is no need to avoid

being tagged or thrown out; all that is required of the batsman
is that he proceed to first base, where, merely by touching the
bag it becomes 'his'.''

"You want me to tell him all that?''

"Why, of course I do. And over and over, until he gets it
into his head. Now, why are you putting that chest protector
on again? Good Lord, son, don't show *fear,* of all things.''

"But—I'm frightened.''

"Of a tribe of heathen black men?''

"Of their *spears,* Uncle. Look!''

Sure enough, the men of the village who had fallen back
when Mister Fairsmith had rescinded the prohibition on sliding into first, were advancing again with spears upraised,
ready to lunge, it would appear, if he should fail to grant this
new request. Nonetheless, the Mundy manager said, "You will
repeat my words to Walter Johnson. You will tell him that
sliding into first after a walk is just plain foolishness and I
won't have it. I wouldn't allow American players to do it, and
I surely am not going to extend to a village of black Africans
a prerogative that I would deny my own countrymen and kin.''

When Walter Johnson had heard Mister Fairsmith's
message, he responded in a voice so thunderous that it caused
the scrawny village dogs to go yelping off into the high grass.
And then the women started instantly to yowl and screech in
their bone-chilling fashion.

"What now?'' asked the exasperated American.

"He says, 'On what authority will Mister Baseball not
allow us to slide into first following a walk?' He demands to
know the number of *that* rule in the Official Baseball Rules as
recorded, amended, and adopted by the Professional Baseball
Playing Rules Committee.''

Chagrined as he was by this renewed outburst of wailing
from the women, and distracted as he was by the spears pressing toward his throat, Mister Fairsmith was once again deeply
gratified by all that Walter Johnson had remembered from his
very first lecture on the Rules. Not only did he have a hopping
fastball and fine control, not only was he an excellent hitting
pitcher, but he appeared to have, in that head decorated with
triangular scars on either cheekbone, a brain. "Well, of
course,'' said Mister Fairsmith, "my authority in this in-

stance does not derive from a written regulation, and consequently I cannot give him the number of a rule. You must explain to him that what we are dealing with here is a matter of *unwritten* law, or custom, but one so universally respected as to have the force and effect of every last rule in the rulebook.''

No sooner were these words translated, than the women, like a flock of squawking crows, rushed off to the far end of the village circle, and then swept back again, pushing through the dust a black kettle, five times the size of a beer keg. Meanwhile the children, who had disbanded in search of wood, were already carrying it to a spot at the outskirts of the village, where the older girls of the tribe had begun to assemble the branches for a fire.

When his nephew pulled the catcher's mask over his face, Mister Fairsmith instantly snatched it away and threw it to the ground. ''Now, you must stop this nonsense immediately. I want to know what exactly is going on with these people. Why in God's name are they behaving like this *now?* What did he just say to me?''

''He—he said they were a proud race.''

''Pride he calls it? The men with spears? The women screaming like banshees? And from the looks of it, preparations underway for an outright act of cannibalism? That isn't pride in my book, and you may tell him as much!''

''But, Uncle, he says that though they will follow to the letter the *rules* of the white man's game, they refuse to be enslaved by arbitrary strictures designed to rob them of their inalienable cultural rights. By denying the men the right to slide into first after having been awarded a base on balls, you have grievously insulted their masculinity.''

''To the contrary,'' said Mister Fairsmith, while only fifty feet away the women set to scrubbing the interior of the immense kettle with sand and river water, ''sliding into first after a walk is as sure a way as I know of for a ballplayer to compromise himself *and* his professional stature in the eyes of the spectator.''

''Apparently,'' said the youngster, after translating Mister Fairsmith's remarks to Walter Johnson, ''that isn't the way they see it.''

''Oh, isn't it? In other words, a tribe of black men who

had not even seen a ball or a bat prior to last week, is going
to tell Ulysses S. Fairsmith, manager of the Ruppert Mundys,
what constitutes professionalism in baseball?''

"I think that is the meaning of the spears, Uncle, yes."

"Well, suppose you just make it perfectly clear to Mr.
Walter Johnson here that if there is anything in the world I
hate worse than a cheat, it's a bully. I am afraid these people
are really starting to rub me the wrong way, and I am a man
who is known and respected throughout the world of sport for
his patience."

"But, Uncle—what if they eat us! What if because you
won't let them slide into first after a walk, they put us into
that pot and boil us alive!"

"My dear young fellow, if despite all we have tried to
teach them in this last week they want to continue to be loathed
and despised by civilized men the world over, in the final analysis, that is their business. They're the ones who are going to
have to live with themselves, once the 'fun' is over. I, however,
have a responsibility to my countrymen and to the game which
is their national pastime. Surely, it must be clear to you now
that where sliding is concerned, if you give these people a finger,
they will take a hand. Allow them to slide into second, third,
and home and they want to slide into first for no good reason.
Allow them to do so on a batted ball and they want to do it
after a *walk*. And where will it stop, I ask you? No, either I
draw the line right here, at the cost of my life if need be, or
else, simply to save my skin, I yield to force, I yield to just the
kind of violence I detest with all my heart and soul, and give
baseball over, lock, stock, and barrel, to these savages to pervert and destroy."

"Listen!" cried the young seminarian. "A drum!"

Yes, somewhere in this village, the hands of a warrior
had begun to thump out a rhythm whose ominous meaning
was all too clear . . .

"No," said Mister Fairsmith, "I will not be the man who
allowed baseball to become a primitive rite for savages. I
would rather die a martyr to the national pastime, if such is
the will of the Lord."

"But—" cried his young companion, "what about *me?*"

"You?" said Mister Fairsmith. "I believed when I took

you with me, that your ambition in life was to be a Christian
missionary.''

"It was! It is! But why should I die for *baseball?*''

Mister Fairsmith raised his face to the African sun:
"Father, forgive him, he knows not what he says.''

By midnight two fires burned. The one back of home plate had
been ignited by an ancient bony creature of indeterminate sex,
who seemed weighted to the ground only by virtue of the mask
and the chest protector that he (or she) wore. The fire midway
between the pitcher's mound and second base appeared to be
the special property of the women of the tribe, who throughout
the evening had chanted a monotonous incantation in rhythm
with the village drum, meanwhile feeding the flames with oil so
that they reared high into the air, casting a red gleam over the
entire infield. The outfield was lit by the moon and the stars.
From beyond the black wall of foliage, there came a shrill,
insistent piping, as though all the beasts of the jungle were
being directed to seats in the treetops by the African night
birds.

The two white men were bound by their wrists and ankles
to stakes driven into the coaching boxes, Mister Fairsmith at
third, young Billy Fairsmith at first. They had been hanging
there since noon.

When the kettle was rolled by six naked warriors across
the infield and hoisted up over the fire back of the pitcher's
mound, the villagers who had gathered two and three deep
along the infield foul lines began to wail with excitement. They
too were unclothed now, and all their protuberances seemed
swollen to the bursting point in the flickering shadows; many
bore white phosphorescent markings on their heels and shoulder blades, and when they leaped in place, their movements
dazzled and confused the eye. As what didn't?

Two tiny boys—matchsticks with bellies—now appeared
upon the diamond, dragging Mister Fairsmith's ball bag.
Hobbling behind, making signs in the air, came the creature in
the mask and the chest protector. When the little boys had
finally pulled the heavy bag up on the rubber, this creature—
wise man? wise woman?—directed them to empty the bag of

its contents. Meanwhile, the water crested and slid over the
edge of the kettle and into the fire, the sizzle greatly exciting
the villagers, causing them to wail as though in torment—
though in fact they appeared from their sporadic leaping
about to be in some savage version of seventh heaven.

And now Walter Johnson strode out to the mound. He
dismissed the tiny boys with a wave of the hand, and immediately took to examining the several dozen baseballs they had
emptied on to the ground. It was a while before he found the
one that most suited him. After rubbing it three times in his
immense hands—"*Omoo! Omoo! Omoo!*" the women chanted
—he passed it, with a deep bow and a friendly bark, to the
Wise One in the mask and chest protector. The Wise One, ball
in hand, hobbled toward the fire. Raising the ball once toward
the villagers lined up along the first-base foul line—"*Omoo!*"
—then to the villagers lined up along third—"*Omoo!*"—the
Wise One went into a windup more elaborate than any Mister
Fairsmith had seen in his entire career, and let fly the ball in
the direction of the kettle.

When the wailing had subsided, the boy children of the
tribe ran out to the mound, where they squatted on their
haunches around Walter Johnson. He addressed them in so
fearsome a manner that several instantly wet the ground beneath them. Then each was handed a baseball, and just as the
Wise One had earlier, threw it into the kettle. "*Omoo! Omoo!
Omoo!*" With the mound empty of baseballs, the women
moved in again, chanting in rhythm to the drum, and swaying
now, as they watched the balls jump and spin like fabulous
curves and knucklers in the roiling waters. From time to time
a woman approached the fire, and dipping a net on a long pole
into the kettle, extracted a ball. Walter Johnson tested the
stitches with a thumb, and then directed her to return the
steaming ball to the pot. In the end he took the pole himself
and dipped deep into the kettle, collecting all the balls in the
net. Then, swinging the pole three times over his head—
"*Omoo! Omoo! Omoo!*"—he sent the boiled baseballs sailing
into the air.

As though unchained, the tiny boys broke across the
diamond, two or three of them invariably leaping upon the
same ball, biting simultaneously into the cover, teeth to teeth,

nose to nose—and kicking all the while at one another's shins in wild windmill fashion. When, finally, one or another of the boys had the ball to himself and firmly in his own grasp, he dropped to his knees to devour the covering with the ferocity of one who had been denied food for twenty-four hours; perhaps that was the case. Having eaten clear down to the yarn, the child then raced to the sidelines to deposit the carcass with one of the village elders—presumably his own grandfather—and sped off in search of another ball. Along the sidelines, the parents and relatives of the children shrieked directions at them, pointing and shouting to draw their attention to balls that remained unclaimed at the far edges of the diamond. For all their ardor, however, they were obviously amused by the ceremony, and the most ancient members of the community had to be held up on their feet, so wracked were they with laughter. To be sure, here and there spectators were covering their eyes with their fingertips—a gesture apparently signifying shame. These, it would seem, were relatives of the few youngsters who kneeled retching in the basepaths or rolled around the mound, in the full glow of the fire, clutching their stomachs and whimpering with pain.

Finally there was not a ball that had been donated by the generous little boys of Port Ruppert whose cover had not been wholly devoured. On their haunches again, the panting, sweating little children waited while Walter Johnson and the Wise One moved along the foul lines, counting the skinned baseballs that had been dropped at the feet of the village elders.

The winner of the competition was a burly little fellow, no more than seven, who had eaten the covers off five regulation baseballs. Hoisted up on to Walter Johnson's marvelous shoulders, he was carried ceremoniously around the basepaths, while the villagers chanted, *"Typee! Typee! Typee!"*

The next competition turned out to be not so amusing, or so successful, and left the villagers oddly dispirited, as though they might be wondering, "What's the matter with the kids these days?"

It was a hitting contest. The object fired down off the hill by Walter Johnson was not a baseball, however—there was no longer a single baseball intact on the entire continent of Africa —but a black, shriveled head, slightly larger in circumference than the nine and a quarter inch ball considered "official" in the big leagues. Invariably Johnson got two quick strikes past a youngster before he had even gotten the bat off his bare little shoulder; then he would throw him a head wide or low of the plate, and strike him out swinging. Now, from the way the spectators hissed and spat at the children from the sidelines, it would seem that to bring the meat-end of a bat into contact with what had once been the face of a tribal enemy, or traitor, appeared to them to be as easy as pie; the fact that the youngsters could not even rouse themselves to swing until they were already down by two strikes, bespoke a timidity that particularly enraged the menfolk. Yet, for all that the fathers barked angry instructions at the tiny little hitters, leaping high into the air and showing their filed teeth to communicate their disappointment, their offspring remained frozen in fear at the plate, even though Walter Johnson was clearly throwing nothing but half-speed pitches, and curves that turned so slowly you could virtually see the glum expression on the face as it broke down the middle.

Only the burly little seven-year-old who had skinned and eaten the most hides managed to get so much as a *piece* of a head, ticking an ear or an eyelid so lightly however, that after examination by the Wise One, the head was deemed undamaged enough to be thrown back into play. Nonetheless, he managed to stay alive in the batter's box longer than any of his little friends, and was thus declared the winner once again.

Now the tribesman whom Mister Fairsmith had come to call Babe Ruth—as much for his barrel-chested, bandy-legged physique as his power at the plate—was called out of the crowd of spectators to satisfy the expectations that the fledglings of the village had so miserably disappointed. And did he! *There* was the old sound of wood against bone! The moment the bat met the skull, you just knew that that old head was *gone*. What a night for the Babe! Fourteen heads thrown, fourteen heads smashed to smithereens.

No sooner was the exhibition over, than the village children, and even some of the men, surged forward to capture a sliver of cranial bone as a souvenir of the occasion.

And now came the ceremony of the virgins and the baseball bats. The tribe, stirred to a frenzy by Babe Ruth's performance at the plate, went silent as worshippers when the first demure native girl, with brass hoops dangling from her ears, and her shaved head covered by a Mundy baseball cap, was led slowly in from the bullpen and across the dark outfield by the Wise One. The women tending the fire reached out to touch the lithe naked body when she moved past the flames, and on the sidelines the spectators whispered excitedly to see the tears of joy in her large brown eyes. Under the direction of Walter Johnson—as gentle now with the maiden as he had been severe with the young boys—the girl arranged herself upon home plate, as she did so darting a shy glance toward the "hitter" in the on-deck circle. Then Walter Johnson gently pulled the oversized Mundy cap down over her eyes and the women of the tribe began to sing.

A jug of boiling water dipped from the kettle was used to wash down the plate after the initiate had taken her turn in the box. With a broom of twigs the Wise One brushed away every last grain of dust, and then examined the bat to be used next, giving particular attention to the handle, to be sure that it had been cleansed of the resin that Mister Fairsmith had encouraged the players to use in order to improve their grip in this tropical climate. From the meticulous hygienic ritual that preceded each deflowering—and too from the tender way in which Walter Johnson covered their eyes to prevent them from growing skittish, in the manner of fillies—it would appear that the girls of this tribe were a pampered lot indeed. Each bat was used but once and then discarded, yet another indication of the singular care and concern lavished upon the pubescent female in this remote corner of the world.

Then came the feast.

Gloves had been boiling in the kettle all the while the girls had been up at the plate. By now they were cooked to a turn, and when they were removed from the water and scattered about the field the villagers fell upon them with ferocity —in the end they did not even leave uneaten the tough lacing that edged the first-basemen's mitts. The eyelets through which the lacing was drawn they spit on the ground like so many pits, but everything else they devoured, thirty-six gloves in all: four right-handed catchers' mitts, four first-basemen's mitts (two left-handed, two right-handed), and eighteen right-handed fielders' gloves eaten by the men; ten left-handed fielders' mitts divided among the women and the children. The chest protectors were boiled for dessert, and while the adults sucked and chewed on the canvas, the children gobbled down the filling. Some of the tots were carried off to sleep still clutching tufts of hairy wadding in their little pink palms.

Long after the village was asleep, when only embers burned where the huge fires had illuminated the infield, Mister Fairsmith, hanging still from his post in the third-base coaching box, was stirred to consciousness by the noise of creatures scurrying back and forth across the diamond. In the dim light he gradually was able to bring his eyes to focus upon the crones of the village, bone-thin women, bent and twisted in the spine, who were scrambling and darting about like a school of crabs over the ocean floor. Combing the playing field, they had collected all the bats that had been discarded earlier on, and now with no regard for the sanctity of the ritual, for hygiene or for decorum, they proceeded to ape the ceremony of the virgins and the bats. Two and three together would roll in the dust around home plate, cackling and moaning, whether in mockery of the young virgins or in imitation, it was impossible for Mister Fairsmith to tell.

Then, with a blast of heat right up from Hades, the African dawn—and fast as they could, the old women departed, using the serviceable Louisville Sluggers for crutches and canes.

Across the field Billy still hung from his pole in the first-base coaching box. He too had escaped the kettle. But that was all he had escaped.

"Old . . . old-timers' day . . ." he called to his uncle, looking with a lopsided smile after the departing hags.

To which Mister Fairsmith cried out twice, a cry that was no more than a breath: "The horror! The horror!"

In the morning, with the sun really cooking, one of the village boys came skipping out to the field, apparently without any idea at all that the season in the Congo had come to an end. Or maybe he was hoping that even if his friends and their fathers had returned to the round of life such as had existed in the village before Mister Fairsmith and his bearers had emerged from the jungle, the Mundy manager might at least play a game of "pepper" with him. It was the boy Mister Fairsmith had christened Wee Willie, after Wee Willie Keeler, whose famous dictum, "Hit 'em where they ain't," had taken a strong hold upon the youngster's imagination. He was exceedingly bright for a dusky little fellow, and in the week's time had even come to learn a few words of English, along with learning how to switch his feet and punch the ball through to the opposite field.

For several minutes he stood before the stake to which Mister Fairsmith was fastened, waiting to receive his instructions. Then he spoke. "Mistah Baseball?" He reached up and tugged at the Patriot League buckle on the manager's belt. "Mistah Baseball?"

Nothing. So he ran clockwise around the diamond, sliding into second on his bare behind, then into first, before approaching the white man hanging from the stake in the first-base coaching box. Looking up into the lopsided smile, he gave him the bad news. "Mistah Baseball—he dead."

The canoe in which the two Americans were discovered was decorated on either side with what must have been the tribe's symbol for Death, a stick figure holding in one of his outstretched arms an oval shield looking something like an oversized catcher's mitt. The bodies had been wrapped from head to foot in the yarn off the two dozen balls whose hides had been eaten by the boys of the tribe. They were discovered (just barely this side of the afterlife) in a stream twenty miles from Stanleyville, from whence they were borne by friendly natives through the jungle to a hospital in the city. And there they lay for weeks and weeks, first Mister Fairsmith, then young Billy, about to land, like a called third strike, in the Great Mitt of Death.

When they could walk again, it was the older man who led the younger through the gardens. Every time they came upon a doctor or a nun, Billy would launch into a description of the marvelous night game that he and his uncle had witnessed in the interior. He told them of the nine girls who had come up to the plate to "pinch-hit," he told them of "the Old-Timers' Game," that had taken place just before dawn, but in that by and large the staff was composed of Belgians, they listened politely, without any understanding that the young American had lost his mind.

Thereafter, for so long as the Mundys made their home in Port Ruppert, Mister Fairsmith arranged for Billy and a nurse from the institution to be chauffeured out to the ball park on Opening Day, and for the two to be seated in a box directly beside his honor the mayor. That was the least he could do, for, loosely speaking, he was responsible for the boy's mind having become forever unhinged. Not, mind you, that Mister Fairsmith would have conducted himself any differently if he'd had to live through that nightmare again. True, a bright young man whose ambition had been to become a missionary in the service of Christ had lost his bearings in the world. But suppose, on the other hand, Ulysses S. Fairsmith had consented to allow African baseball players to slide into first after a walk . . . suppose he had been the one responsible for an entire continent of black men turning the great American game of baseball into so much wallowing in the mud . . . No, he could never have borne that upon his conscience.

To return now to the trial facing the venerable manager in his eightieth year, the hopeless '43 Ruppert Mundys—how could they disgust and horrify him even more than those African savages? Precisely because they were *not* African savages, but Americans! (by and large), big leaguers! (supposedly). For heathen barbarians to defile the national pastime was one thing, but American men wearing the uniform of the major league team to which Ulysses S. Fairsmith had devoted his entire life? That was beyond compassion and beneath contempt.

So far-reaching was his disgust that when they arrived (on separate trains) in a P. League town, Mister Fairsmith would not even stay at the hotel where he might have the misfortune of running into one of his players in the lobby or the dining room. Instead he went off as a guest to the home of the local evangelist, as much for the sake of religious succor as for the relief it afforded him to be out of sight of those degenerates impersonating his beloved Mundys.

"First African savages. Then the Emperor of Japan. And now, now my own Mundys. Billy," he asked the evangelist, "how can God exist and sanction such as this?"

"The Lord has his reasons, Samuel."

"But have you ever been to watch this team on the field of play?"

"No. But I read the box scores. I know what you are suffering."

"Billy, the box scores are as nothing beside the games themselves."

"We can only pray, Samuel. Let us pray."

And so instead of traveling out to the ball park, where nothing he could say or do would change these impostors into Mundys, Mister Fairsmith would remain on his knees throughout the afternoon, praying that the Lord might accomplish the transformation that was beyond his own managerial powers.

Each evening, after dinner, Jolly Cholly traveled out from the hotel to tell Mister Fairsmith the results of that day's game. The minister's wife always prepared a plate of cookies to bring to the Mundy coach while he sat in a chair beside Mister Fairsmith's bed and, scorecard in hand, described the horrors of the afternoon, play by play.

Down in the living room, the minister asked his wife, "How is he taking it?"

"He just lies there, looking into space."

"I'll go to him, when Jolly Cholly leaves."

"I think you had better."

At the door, the minister would say to the Mundy coach, "And who will be the starting pitcher tomorrow, Mr. Tuminikar?"

And as often as not, Jolly Cholly shrugged and answered, "Whoever feels like it, I guess. We sort of have given up on any kind of rotation, Reverend. Whoever wants the exercise, he just grabs his mitt and goes on out there."

Carrying his Bible and wearing his collar, the minister would enter Mister Fairsmith's room.

"In victory," cried the Mundy manager, "I was magnanimous. In defeat I was a gentleman. In Africa, I would have martyred myself rather than permit those savages to sully the national game. Why, why is this happening!"

"Tell *me* why, Samuel. Say what is in your heart. Why has the Lord chosen you for such suffering and pain?"

"Because," said Mister Fairsmith, bitterly, "because the Lord hates baseball."

"But Our Lord is just and merciful."

"No, He hates baseball, Billy. Either that, or He does not exist."

"Our Lord exists, Samuel. Moreover, He loves baseball with a love that is infinite and all-encompassing."

"Then why is there such a team as the '43 Mundys? Why a Hothead Ptah! Why a Nickname Damur! And now a dwarf who blinded a midget! A dwarf in a Ruppert uniform! *Why?*"

"Samuel, you must not lose faith. He will answer our prayers, albeit in His own time."

"But they are already in last place *by fifty games!*"

"Many that are first by fifty games shall be last, Samuel, and the last by fifty, first. Let us pray."

So he prayed: in Tri-City with the Reverend Billy Toll-house, in Aceldama with the Reverend Billy Biscuit, in Independence with the Reverend Billy Popover, in Terra Incognita with the Reverend Billy Scone, in Asylum with the Reverend Billy Zwieback, in Kakoola with the Reverend Billy Bun. Yes, the most famous radio preachers of the era sought to save the great manager from apostasy; but, alas, by the middle of September, with the Mundys having won but twenty-three of one hundred and forty-two games, those who patiently tried to explain to him that perhaps he would have to wait until next year for his prayers to be answered, feared that if the Lord did not intervene in behalf of the Mundys before the season's end, Ulysses S. Fairsmith's faith would be extinguished for-ever.

And then it happened. Mundys 14, Blues 6. Mundys 8, Blues 0. Mundys 7, Keepers 4. Mundys 5, Keepers 0.

Hallelujah! Hallelujah! Hallelujah!

"So there is a God on high, and He does love baseball."

"It would appear so, Billy."

"And He has tested His servant, Ulysses S. Fairsmith, and He has not found him wanting."

"Then *that* was His reason."

"It would appear so, Samuel, it would appear so."

Hallelujah! Hallelujah!

Perhaps they were a last place team with the worst record ever compiled in the history of the three leagues, but on the train ride back across the country following the 9–3 home-run extravaganza against Terra Incognita—their eleventh in a row—they were as joyous and confident as any Ruppert team Mister Fairsmith could recall, including the great pennant winners of the twenties.

The train was bound for Tri-City, where they were to play their final game of the year, a contest rained out earlier in the season against the Tycoons. And what a victory that was going to be! Oh sure, the bookmakers had them down as four-to-one underdogs (how on earth could they do it again? how could the Mundys knock the Tycoons out of first on the last day of the season?) but there wasn't a Ruppert Mundy who heard those odds, who didn't have to laugh. "Well, you want to be a rich man, George," they told the grinning porter, "you lay down two bits and see if you ain't got yourself a dollar in your pocket by tomorrow night."

Soldiers on board the eastbound train continually drifted back to the dining car during the evening meal to get a peek at the miracle team of the Patriot League. "Our pleasure, our pleasure," the Mundys said, when the G.I.s asked for autographs. The soldiers said, "You don't know what it means to a feller headed to he-don't-know-where, just to be ridin' the same train with a team what's done what you guys have. Wait'll I write home!"

"Good luck, soldier! Good luck, G.I. Joe!" the Mundys called after them. "You make it hot for old Hitler now!"

"We will! We will!"

"Good luck, lads! You're brave boys!"

"And good luck to you—in Tri-City!"

"Oh, tell that to them Tycoons! Them's the ones need luck!"

They were up till midnight in the diner, playing spit-in-the-ocean and smoking Havana cigars. The waiters, who ordi-

narily would have shooed them off to their berths hours ago—
after having flung their food at them, cold and greasy—were
more than happy to stay and do their bidding, just for the
privilege of hearing the rampaging Rupperts recount inspirational anecdotes from their amazing eleven-game streak. After
all, if the Mundys could rise from ignominy to glory virtually
overnight, who in this world could consider himself doomed?

"Yes, *suh,* Mistah Hothead! Yes, *suh,* Mistah Nickname!
Mistah O.K.—you want sump'n, suh?"

"A new pack of Bicycles, George!"

"Yes, *suh!*"

At midnight, leaning on Jolly Cholly's arm, Mister Fairsmith entered the dining car. Nickname doused his cigar in his
beer, and Ockatur, who had the lion's share of the winnings
piled on the tray of the high chair in which he was seated,
slipped the money surreptitiously into his pocket.

Following the two victories in Independence and the four
in Asylum, Mister Fairsmith had rejoined the team in the
dugout, remaining with them throughout their last five tri-
umphs in Kakoola and Terra Inc. His cane across his lap, a
beatific gleam in his blue eyes, he slowly rocked to and fro on
his chair, as one Mundy runner after another crossed home
plate. He was a far more decrepit figure than they remembered
from Opening Day—the wear and tear of all that prayer. Indeed, if anything had the power to subdue these spirited
Mundys, who now virtually quivered with energy from breakfast to bedtime, it was that look in Mister Fairsmith's eye of
exceeding wisdom and benevolence.

With Jolly Cholly's assistance, Mister Fairsmith was
helped into a chair drawn into the aisle at the head of the car.
"I have a telegram to read to you before I retire for the night,"
he said, studying the face of each of the redeemed. "It has
just this minute arrived, and was brought back to me by the
engineer. 'Dear Sam. No matter what the outcome of tomorrow's game, I want you to know how proud I am of you and
the Ruppert Mundys. As a result of what you have accomplished against the most insuperable odds, the R that once
stood for Ruppert must henceforth be considered to stand for
nothing less than this great Republic. The Mundys are a homeless team no more—they belong to an entire nation. Sam, I

will consider it a great privilege if I may board the train in
Port Ruppert tomorrow morning and accompany you and your
team to their final game in Tri-City.' Signed, 'General Douglas
D. Oakhart, President of the Patriot League.' ''

With this, Mister Fairsmith signaled for Jolly Cholly to
help him to his feet. ''Good night, Mundys. Good night, my
Ruppert Mundys,'' and his creased and craggy face beamed
with love.

Rupe-it!

There was a band to greet them—at 6 A.M.! And all along
the tracks into the station, Rupe-it rootas, waving hand-let-
tered signs wildly in the air.

MUNDYS WE MISS YOU!

GONE BUT NOT FORGOTTEN!

MUNDYS COME HOME ALL IS FORGIVEN!

The players pressed their noses to the windows and waved
at the crowd that had turned out at dawn just to watch their
train pass through on the way to Massachusetts.

When the train stopped to receive passengers, mobs of
schoolchildren surged to the side of the sleeping car to gape at
the heroes whose names had all at once become legendary
throughout the land. The players winked and laughed and
blew kisses, and then, when they were moving again, lay back
in their berths, not a few with tears on their faces. Winning!
Winning! Oh, you just can't say enough good things about
winning!

Festooned with ribbons, General Oakhart stood at the entrance
to the dining car to receive them; Mister Fairsmith, supported
by Jolly Cholly, introduced the victorious players one by one.
When the last Mundy was seated before his orange juice, the
President of the league addressed them:

''Before I drink a toast to this brave and courageous ball
club''—he amused the players, who were easy to amuse these

days, by tapping a fingernail on his juice glass—"I have a telegram to read to you date-marked yesterday noon. 'Dear General. No one could be more delighted than I am by the remarkable Mundy winning streak. As you know, at the outset of the season, I shared your fears that the burden they had chosen to bear might ultimately do serious damage to their morale. And indeed, there were moments during the season when being a permanent road club seemed to be weighing too heavily upon the shoulders of the Ruppert team. But just when it appeared that our worst fears were about to be realized, they have astounded and heartened the entire country with the most incredible display of Big League ball many a fan has seen this season, or *any* season. It is a great moment, not only for the Mundys and Mister Fairsmith, not only for you and the Patriot League, not only for baseball, but for the nation. I am deeply honored by your invitation to join you in your box at Tycoon Park to watch this final contest of the Patriot League season, and wish to inform you that despite pressing business here in the Commissioner's office, I will leave Chicago in time to be in Tri-City to address the Mundys in their clubhouse before the game begins.' And, gentlemen, the telegram is signed by the Commissioner of Baseball, Judge Kenesaw Mountain Landis."

And there he was, craggier even than Mister Fairsmith, the czar of baseball, waiting to greet them as they entered the visitors' clubhouse at noon. If till then the Mundys had any doubt that they had passed from being the most despised to the most beloved baseball team in America, it surely disappeared when the Commissioner, of his own accord, kneeled to exchange a few pleasantries with O.K. Ockatur. Then, while the flashbulbs popped, the fearless judge—so aptly named for an American mountain—read the following telegram to the team:

"'My dear Judge Landis. It has been a bracing experience for me, as for my fellow Americans, to watch the Ruppert Mundys turn a season of seeming catastrophe into a gallant triumph. I firmly believe that the farmers and the factory workers, the children in our schools and the women who keep the home fires burning, and above all, our brave fighting men around the globe, cannot but draw inspiration from the "Never

Say Die'' spirit of these illustrious men. Though I cannot join you today at Tri-City to watch this undiscourageable nine in their final battle of the season, I assure you I will, from the War Room, be in continual telephone contact with the stadium in order to remain abreast of the inning-by-inning developments. Accepting your most kind and thoughtful invitation in my behalf will be my wife, a baseball fan in her own right, and one who has seen in the resurgence of the team everyone had counted out, a stirring example for all underdogs everywhere. With every best wish, very sincerely yours, Franklin D. Roosevelt.' ''

So, along with Mrs. Trust and General Oakhart and Judge Kenesaw Mountain Landis, the wife of the President of the United States sat that afternoon in a box behind the Tri-City dugout, there to pay tribute to the Ruppert team in behalf of America's Chief Executive. The game, in fact, was delayed thirty minutes while Mrs. Roosevelt went down into the visitors' dugout to shake the hands of the players and ask them what states they were from. Then she rejoined the other dignitaries in the box, and the Tycoons, weary from their season-long battle against the surging Butchers, and visibly unnerved by all the attention being heaped upon their adversaries, took the field. Though the day was breezy, and he had taken no more than a dozen warm-up pitches, Smoky Woden's uniform was already gray with perspiration when Frenchy Astarte stepped up to the plate and the umpire cried, ''Play ball!''

No need to chronicle here the records compiled in a game about which tens of thousands of words were written during that fall and winter: the record number of times Hothead Ptah tripped on his mask going back for foul pop-ups, the record number of times that Mike Rama knocked himself unconscious against the left-field wall, the record number of times Specs Skirnir ''lost'' ground balls in the sun—every stupid and humiliating mishap of that afternoon was recounted by the sports columnists of the nation no less frequently than the third strike that Mickey Owen dropped in the '41 World Series, or the error that earned Bonehead Merkle his nickname in 1908, and lost the Giants the pennant.

With two out in the ninth and his team down by thirty-one runs, Nickname Damur got the fifth Mundy hit of the day—

Agni had the other four—a clean shot up the alley in left center, and then was out when he tried to stretch the double into a three-bagger. The Tycoon fans, by reputation as sober and scholarly a crowd as you could find anywhere, were so busy laughing at the sheer idiocy of Nickname's base-running, that it was a while before they even realized that their team had just won the '43 flag. In the dugout, streaming tears, Nickname stood before Mister Fairsmith and tried to think of some sort of explanation for what he had just done.

"I don't know, sir," he said, shrugging. "I guess you could say I gambled."

"Thirty-one runs behind in the ninth . . . and you say . . . you say you *gambled?* My God," moaned Mister Fairsmith, "my God, why hast thou forsaken me?" and rolling off his rocker, died on the floor of the visitors' dugout.

"What happened, you son of a bitch?"

"I couldn't—I couldn't do it."

"Why, Roland, *why* couldn't you?"

"Don't you know who all was eatin' breakfast with us? General Oakhart! You know who all was in the box? Judge Landis, the Commissioner! And Mrs. Eleanor Roosevelt! And you know who sent us a telegram? *The President of the United States!*"

"And what do they have to do with anything?"

"They just happen to be the most important people in the world, that's all!"

"Idiot! They are the most important people in the world just like the Wheaties they make in Minneapolis are the Breakfast of Champions!"

"But they kept sending these *telegrams*. Everybody kept sayin', 'I just got this telegram,' and it would get all hushed and everythin', and then when they start in readin' it, it would sound just like the Gettysburg Address or somethin'! It would give me the gooseflesh!"

"And that's why you couldn't do it—because of the gooseflesh?"

"But we had enough money anyway, Isaac! You said we had the quarter million to buy me already!"

"Oh, we had it all right."

"What—what do you mean, Isaac! You said on the phone we had *more*—two hundred and seventy-five thousand dollars —you told me that just last night!"

"And just last night we did."

"But if you lost twenty-five today, you still have enough— well, *don't you?* They didn't go raise the price on me, on account of my goin' four for four—*did they?*"

"You know what the odds were today, Roland? 4–1. Two hundred and seventy-five thousand dollars would get you a million and change, if the Mundys did it again."

"Yeah—*so?*"

"So I thought, since the Mundys *are* going to win, why buy just Roland Agni? Why not a whole franchise while I'm at it?"

"*So?*"

"So I bet the wad, Rollie."

"You *did?*"

"See, I didn't figure on the league's leading hitter getting gooseflesh from all those telegrams. I didn't figure on being betrayed by a weakling and a coward!"

"You bet it *all?*"

"All."

"Then—*there's nothin' left!*"

"Correct. I go back to splitting atoms, you go back to being a Ruppert Mundy for the rest of your life."

"But *I can't!*"

"Oh yes you can, you All-American asshole. Gooseflesh from telegrams!"

"But it was just my *respect* comin' out!"

"*Respect?* For *who,* for *what?*"

"For the President of the United States! For—for the whole country!"

"But *I'm* the one you should respect, Roland. The one you should have gooseflesh over is *me!* Ah, go on back to the Mundys, Agni. That's where you belong anyway."

"I *don't!*"

"You do, my cowardly, simple-minded, patriotic pal. Because that's all you really are when it comes down to it—a Ruppert Mundy."

"And you—you're a lousy loudmouth little kike! You're
a dirty greedy money-mad mocky! You're a Shylock! You're
a sheeny! *You killed Christ!* I'd rather be a *nigger* than be
one of you!"

"Well, good, Roland. Because before this is over, you
may get your chance."

And so the '43 season came to an end.

Mister Fairsmith's body was borne by train directly from
Tri-City to Cooperstown, New York. The journey of less than
three hundred miles lasted through a day and a night, for in
every village and hamlet along the way the train would draw
to a halt to allow those who had gathered together at the station to say goodbye to the great Mundy manager. The local
high school team, with heads bowed and eyes closed, was invariably to be found at the siding with their coach, as were
numerous children in baseball togs, some so small they had to
be held in their mothers' arms.

In the village of Cooperstown, the flag-draped coffin was
removed from the train by members of the Mundy team and
placed upon a horse-drawn caisson. To the slow, mournful
pace set by the corps of drummers from the service academies,
and escorted by an honor guard drawn from every team in the
three leagues, each wearing his gray "away" uniform, the
Mundys walked behind the coffin down the main street of Cooperstown. At the National Baseball Hall of Fame, the coffin
was unlashed and the pallbearers—Astarte, Damur, Baal,
Ptah, Rama, Heket, Skirnir, and Agni—carried it through the
gate and up the steps of the Museum and into the gallery of
the Hall of Fame, a room nearly as long as the distance from
home to first, and flanked by black marble columns hewn from
the earth of Mister Fairsmith's native Vermont.

There, beneath the bronze plaques upon which are sculp-
ted the faces of baseball's immortals, brief eulogies were
delivered by General Oakhart and Judge Landis. Each noted
that Ulysses S. Fairsmith and the pillars came from the same
state, and drew the appropriate conclusions. Judge Landis
described him as "baseball's ambassador to mankind," and
said that throughout the world, people of all races and nations

would mourn the passing of the man known to many of them simply as "Mister Baseball." Slowly, he read the "roll call" of the seven continents to which Mister Fairsmith had traveled as the ambassador of the national pastime. "Yes," he said, in conclusion, "even Antarctica. That was the kind of human being that this man was." Then the doors to the street were opened and throughout the afternoon the fans filed past the open coffin, made of hickory wood by Hillerich and Bradsby.

They buried him on a hillside that looks down upon the spot where (legend has it) Abner Doubleday invented the game in 1839. And if it *is* only legend? Does this make the shrine any less holy?

"Oh God," said the Reverend Billy Bun, "Thy servant, having played his nine innings upon this earth . . ."

When the last prayer had been uttered by the last of the Billies, each of the Mundy regulars stepped up to the grave, and with a bat handed him by the minister, fungoed a high fly ball in the direction of the setting sun. Then a solitary bugle played "Take Me Out to the Ballgame," and the mourners turned and made their way back down into the town that is to baseball fans the Lourdes, the Canterbury, the Kyoto of America.

7

THE RETURN OF
GIL GAMESH; OR,
MISSION FROM MOSCOW

➳ 7 ➳

An extraordinary letter of reference. A project of Mrs. Trust's, and her trip with General Oakhart to visit a penitent sinner. Gil Gamesh relates his history; his wanderings; student days at SHIT, and other adventures in Soviet Russia. The Soviet spy system revealed to the General. The author puts in a brief recorded appearance. In which the history leaps ahead seven months with an excerpt from General Oakhart's testimony before a Congressional Committee. The press conference wherein Gamesh is reinstated; he relates a history appropriate to the occasion. America opens its heart—with a notable exception. A series of lectures on Hatred and Loathing. Roland returns to a vengeful team; his chagrin; the surprising discovery he makes in the locker room; his death. In which General Oakhart names names and Gil Gamesh pays tribute to a great American. The Patriot League cleans house and the Mundy Thirteen appear before the House Un-American Activities Committee. In which the author puts in an appearance before the Congressional Committee and expresses his opinion in no uncertain terms. Wherein the history draws to a conclusion, with a few last-minute disasters.

McWILEY'S GROCERY STORE
141 Kakoola Blvd., Kakoola, Wisconsin
Wm. McWiley, Prop.

March 1, 1944

To Whom It May Concern:

This is to affirm that Gil Gamesh was formerly employed under a variety of aliases by the Kakoola Citizens Action Committee for Americanism and the Kakoola Council to Keep America Free in doing investigative and research work.

During the period of his employment, Mr. Gamesh's services were entirely satisfactory and I have no hesitation in recommending him for any type work in which a thorough knowledge of Communism and Communist methods is necessary. He made an

321

excellent witness in executive session of the statewide Citizens Action Committee for Americanism held here in Kakoola at McWiley's Grocery Store for November 23–24, 1943, and his services were much in demand by the investigative units of both the Committee and the Council throughout the Middle West.

His knowledge of Communism and Communist methods can be utilized in the fields of dissemination of information concerning Communism, as well as the field of investigation.

Yours very truly,
Wm. McWiley
President, Kakoola CACA
Legal Director, Kakoola KAF

"Mrs. Trust," said the General, returning the letter to the old lady of the league, "the Ruppert Mundys have just this afternoon lost their first exhibition game of the '44 season by a score of 12–4 to Asbury Park High. I have just this moment learned by phone that they would not even have scored their four runs if the high school coach hadn't put in his junior varsity for a couple of innings' experience against a big league club, once he had the game sewed up. I have Roland Agni, the league's leading hitter, out there in Michigan sulking in his bedroom, refusing to join the Mundys in New Jersey for spring training, or ever again, from what he tells his poor father—I have a league, in other words, that is just about coming apart at the seams, Mrs. Trust, and you arrive here with a letter for me to read from some greengrocer in Kakoola."

"This greengrocer happens also to be the President of the Kakoola Citizens Action Committee for Americanism and the Legal Director of the Kakoola Council to Keep America Free."

"Organizations unknown to me, I'm afraid."

"And I suppose the name Gil Gamesh is unknown to you as well?"

Wearily he said, "It rings a bell, Madam."

"You banished him from baseball."

"And would again, for all that it appears to have cost us."

"*And* him."

"That a criminal should be stigmatized for his crime seems to me one of the few reassuring facts of this life; that the victim should be stigmatized, therein lies the tragedy. My dear lady, I long ago lost interest in the fate of Gil Gamesh. I assumed, as I think you did, that the man was dead. Nor did I grieve at the thought that he might have come to a violent end. At the risk of being indecorous, let me say that I understood how your feelings might have been otherwise. I would not have expected them to be my own. Nonetheless, ever since you assumed the ownership of the Tycoons, I have had every reason to believe that you joined in the opinion of baseball's leaders that I had acted in the best interests of the game and the league, and the cause of decency and justice, when I expelled Gamesh in '33. I can't believe that with all that threatens the integrity and existence of our league at this moment, you would want now to divert my attention in any way from the serious work at hand."

"To the contrary," said Angela Trust, hammering the floor with her cane, "I want you to see how much more serious it is than you may wish to know!"

"Madam, we have had our conversations on the subject of Communism. Surely you know I am no friend of the Reds."

"Nor is Will Harridge! Nor is Ford Frick! Nor is that eminent jurist Kenesaw Mountain Landis! And yet all the while you four stalwarts are not befriending the Reds, the Reds continue making inroads into the Patriot League! General, you talk to me of *stigmas,* but there is no stigma—there is only subversion! There is only conspiracy and sabotage!"

"Mrs. Trust, that is just so much foolishness."

"And is *this?*" she cried, rattling the letter in the air. "Would it still seem foolish if what I have been telling you for years were told to you now by a man who has consorted with the Communists for a decade? Would it be foolishness if you heard my own warnings from the mouth of a man who studied for four years in Moscow at the International Lenin School of Subversion, Hatred, Infiltration, and Terror? Who now takes his orders directly from *the highest placed Communist agent in America?*"

"You mean this *grocer,* this McWiley?"

"*I mean Gil Gamesh.*"

"Gamesh? A Communist *spy?*"

"As far as the Communists are concerned, yes. But I

know otherwise. And now, General, so too do you: Gil Gamesh, who loathed America, loves it once again. He has defected back to us.''

"How can you say these things *seriously?* Who *told* you all this?''

Beneath the thousand wrinkles, she was suddenly as radiant as she had ever been. "Gil," she answered.

Mrs. Trust's limousine carried them to the no-man's land between Greenback Stadium and the waterfront, amidst the looming warehouses and grimy factories of what had been Tri-City's "Docktown," a workers' quarter once as lively with petty intrigue, as squalid, as "colorful" as anything bordering the docks of Marseilles or Singapore. Here and there a dirt path still opened up through the weeds back of a trucking platform, and beside a heap of charred rubbish or the rusted-out bones of a dismantled car, stood one of those lean-to shacks that used to house Docktown families of five, six, and seven—a brawling immigrant couple, their ragged children, the toothless Old World parents. By 1944, of course, a few two-by-fours nailed together in Tri-City at the tail-end of the previous century hardly resembled any sort of human habitation, and, in fact, seemed to be home only to the barnswallows that swooped toward the General's glittering Army insignia as he followed angrily along the rutted path behind the grande dame, who set a feverish pace, cane and all.

The General looked at him in disbelief. No yellow linen suit; no perforated two-tone shoes; no brilliantine making patent leather of the hair; no *hair;* no swagger either; no scowl; no crooked smile; no *smile*—no expression at all, other than a terrifying blankness fixed upon bones as prominent as the handles of a valise. The man appeared to have been stripped of hide, meat, and muscle, boiled down to bone, then wired together again like the extinct displayed in the biology lab—and finally covered over in a shroud of wax a size too small for his carcass. The clothes too looked like retreads, just such outfits as are issued to those corpses selected to rise from the dead to go and walk among the living in Automats and public library reading rooms: fraying gray cotton jacket, thread-worn tweed trousers thickly cuffed, narrow black knit tie, and dark shoes with a wedge of heel thin as a wafer and the leather worn membranous over the corns. The uniform, not of the dandy, but the "loner."

"General Oakhart," said the ghost, gravely.

"I am he. But who may I ask are you?"

"Just who Angela says I am."

"I don't believe it. You don't look like the Gil Gamesh I knew. You don't *sound* like that Gil Gamesh, either."

"Nor do I feel like that Gil Gamesh any longer. Nonetheless, that is the Gil Gamesh I am doomed to remain forever. I can never hope to unburden myself of his foolishness, his treachery, or his despair. My hair is gone. My arm is gone. My looks are gone. So what. I am what I have been. Can I now become what I would be? It seems once again, General, that my future is in your hands."

"What future? Who are you, man? Do you live in this dump?"

"This dump and worse dumps. This dump and palaces. I've driven dynamite over the Rockies in a broken-down Ford. I've fought gun duels in the Everglades with the F.B.I. Prison in Poland. Sturgeon with Stalin. Cocktails with Molotov."

"Mrs. Trust, only listen to this impostor—just *look* at him! This is not Gil Gamesh!"

"If you like, General," said the ghost, "I will recount to you in detail the substance of my meetings with you and Mike the Mouth in the summer of '33. 'Gil,' he said, 'somebody in this world has got to run the game. Otherwise, you see, it wouldn't be baseball, it would be chaos. We would be right back where we were in the Ice Ages . . .' "

"If you are Gamesh, where did you learn to speak like a radio announcer, instead of a roughneck off the streets?"

"Where else?" said Gamesh. "Night school."

"And how do you come to *look* like this?"

"Rage, hatred, suffering—you name it."

"And you live here, is that the idea? Is this your hideout, or some such nonsense?"

"It is my *yafka*, yes."

"Meaning what! Speak English!"

"I hide here, General, from time to time. It also happens

to be the house where I was born. A fitting place to be reborn.
General, there is no need for you to doubt my identity. I am
Gil Gamesh, an agent of the Communist Party, just returned
from six years in Moscow, four of them at the International
Lenin School from which I received the equivalent of a Ph.D.
in espionage and sabotage. My mission is to complete the de-
struction of the Patriot League of Professional Baseball
Clubs."

"Madness!" cried General Oakhart to Mrs. Trust. "Sheer
madness, all of it!"

"I agree, General," replied Gamesh. "I have indeed been
a mad, enraged creature. All my life I found my strength in
rancorous resentment, but only after my banishment from
baseball did I plunge headlong into a barbarous world of violence and vengeance, and dedicate myself wholly to destroying
what had destroyed me. Only listen to my story, General, and
perhaps it will explain even to your satisfaction how I come
to look as I do . . ."

After he had been banished, he said, he had made his way
west, robbing and raping as he went, teaming up along the
way with other vengeful men. In those years they were not
hard to come by. There was no Germany or Japan to hate then
—only one's own, one's native land. Whom did he meet in
those Depression years who had not been abused, humiliated,
cheated, thwarted, and wrecked (to hear the victim tell it) by
America? Was there a man in a bar between Port Ruppert and
Seattle without a score to settle, without reparations due him,
without hatred boiling in his heart? While busting miners'
heads for a copper company in Nevada, he met a man named
"Bill Smith"—a Commie in scab's clothing. It was the Communists who sent him to night school to learn the three Rs;
Russian they taught him on their own. They gave him books
to read. They gave him fraudulent birth certificates. They
gave him dynamite. They gave him guns. They told him America was on its last legs—brave revolutionary leaders like Gil
Gamesh would deal the deathblow to their homeland. They
told him a new day was dawning for mankind, and he pretended to be happy to hear the news. But what did he care
about mankind? That was just another highfalutin' name for
the sons of bitches who screwed you out of what was yours.

Mankind? That was for "Bill Smith" and "Bob White" and "Jim Adams," and the hundreds of others with names out of grade school primers, Yids most of them, who kept him awake at night with fervent speeches about "the new day that was dawning." Only it wasn't dawn that interested Gil Gamesh, it was night.

"In 1938 I was called to Moscow, the highest honor that can be accorded a struggling young Communist agent. I was enrolled in the International Lenin School for Subversion, Hatred, Infiltration, and Terror, known popularly as SHIT."

"You expect me to believe that that is the name of a school in Moscow, Mr. Gamesh?" asked the skeptical General.

"General, they are nothing if not contemptuous of human decency and dignity. Irreverence and blasphemy are their business, and they know how to practice it, too. Let me go on, please. As a student at SHIT I attended classes fourteen hours a day, seven days a week. To school in the dark, home in the dark, and once a week in winter, out of bed again to perfect the 4 A.M. arrest on somebody down the hall. Summers off in the country, in slave labor camps, administering beatings and conducting interrogations while the regular torturers are on vacation—occasionally driving a prisoner insane or torment- ing an intractable suspect into a confession, but by and large the usual student stuff, cleaning up after suicides, seeing that the bread is stale and there's nothing nourishing in the soup, and so on. And the talk, General. The unending lectures. The study groups. And then the murders, of course. Three room- mates murdered in their beds during my senior year. My freshman year at SHIT there were eighty-seven of us, hand- picked from around the globe. We graduated a class of twenty- four. Sixteen strangled, nineteen poisoned, five run over, eleven shot, three knifed, one electrocuted by a high-voltage toilet seat, and thirteen 'suicides'—out of windows, off roof- tops, and down the stairwell. I pushed two of them myself to pass 'Defenestration.' General Stalin spoke at our graduation. I was class valedictorian. When Stalin shook my hand, he said, 'The final conflict will be between the Communists and the ex-Communists.' The idea startled me. I had thought the final conflict would be between the Communists and the Wall Street Dogs. Only in the next year did I understand Uncle

Joe's curious remark, or warning, to the SHIT valedictorian of '42. The higher I rose in espionage circles the more disillusioned I became. Oh, I could stomach the brutality easily enough—it didn't take more than two minutes, if that, to get over missing a murdered friend, and of course a murdered enemy was so much gravy. Then to be graduated directly from SHIT to one of the highest planning positions in Sabotage in the Kremlin restored me to just the sort of power and prestige that I had known so briefly and that I had imagined I had lost forever. No, for that monster of vengeance, Gil Gamesh, Communism was like a dream come true, it was an evil man's paradise, except for one small thing. No baseball.

"Yes, after all those years away, I began missing the hell out of baseball. It wasn't so bad during the winter, but when spring finally came I found myself turning to the back pages of *Pravda* looking for the scores. I'd walk by a vacant lot, hear some kids screaming, and expect to see a gang of boys shagging flies—instead they would be playing 'Purge,' running around arresting each other and dragging the girls into the bushes for mock trials. World Series time was the worst. I understood then what it meant to have betrayed my country. You see, it was the first time in my life that I realized that it *was* my country, that a country, that *anything,* could really be mine. God knows, I wasn't a Russian. Nor was I ever a Babylonian, really, in anything other than name. Least of all was I a member of mankind. No, it wasn't for humanity, or the working class, that my heart ever bled, but only for *me,* Number 19. Or so I thought, until I looked out of my window on Red Square one night last October and saw that while I had been eighteen hours at my desk, planning the destruction of the Patriot League, three feet of snow had fallen on Moscow. And I thought: what the hell am I doing in snow-covered Russia, when in Mother America it is crisp, bright fall? The Cardinals, the Tycoons, and the Yanks are playing in the World Series, even as I sit here! *Who's pitching? What's the score?* And then I did a stupid, reckless thing—I fear still that one day it will cost me my life. At 3 A.M. I walked down the corridor into the shortwave radio room of Soviet Military Intelligence, where I knew there was a man on duty monitoring the opening game, and I sat there until dawn, listening to Spud Chandler pitch a three-hitter against the Tycoons. When Keller grand-slammed Woden I let out a cheer. That's right, Angela, still the Greenback in my heart—still the crosstown rival, even in Moscow! Fortunately the radioman was asleep. Though was he? Who knows? I left before Etten hit his in the eighth, but Keller's was enough. I knew then that I wasn't any longer just Gil Gamesh looking out for himself, I wasn't just Number 19 in this world and no more—I knew then that down beneath the dreams of glory and vengeance, beneath the contempt, the isolation, the loneliness and the hatred, I happened to be an American.

"Of course it was pretty late in the day to be making such a discovery. I was due to return to America in only one week, my mission to personally initiate and oversee our next, and, hopefully, our final assault upon your league, General. As I have said, planning the infiltration and the destruction of the Patriot League has been my primary task ever since my gradu-ation from SHIT. It was with a program such as this in mind that the Party had latched on to me back in '34, though of course it was not until I had proved myself as an underground agent in twenty-two states that I was called to my training in Moscow. In that time the Politburo handed down a different directive on baseball each season. Not only was the program uncoordinated and haphazard, but it became a dangerous bat-tleground for party factions. That is what invariably happens when there is no firm theoretical grasp of the issues. Nine comrades who opposed the destruction of baseball were tried and sentenced to death in 1940 for Incurable Right-Wing De-viationism, and the following year, directly after the All-Star game, nine who *favored* the destruction of baseball were tried and sentenced for the same crime. The fact of the matter is that nobody in all of Russia had the slightest understanding of the political and cultural significance of baseball and its relationship to the capitalist mystique, until I arrived on the scene. It is no secret that my senior honors paper entitled 'The Exploitation of Regional Pride by the Profit-Mongers of Pro-fessional Sport' provided the theoretical foundation for the revised plan of attack that eventually resulted in the expulsion of the Mundys from Port Ruppert. Stalin himself, you should know, tended to side at the outset with the faction, now jailed,

who were for the expulsion of the Tycoons from Tri-City. Or
so he led us to believe. I realize now that he was only testing
my strength and my staying power. I am sure he understood
from the beginning that any attempt to dislodge the Tycoons
would inevitably result in failure, and even worse, exposure
of the entire conspiracy against the league. Furthermore,
ironic as General Stalin can be at the expense of Mrs. Trust,
he is a shrewd judge of character, and a careful student of the
reports filed by Colonel Chichikov. He knows just how tough
and wily a foe International Communism is up against in the
person of Angela Whittling Trust."

"Colonel Chichikov?" said General Oakhart. "And just
who is this Colonel Chichikov, if I may ask?"

"Colonel Chichikov of the General Staff. You know him
under the alias Frank Mazuma."

"Oh this *is* preposterous! You're telling me now that
Frank Mazuma, the owner of the Kakoola Reapers, is a member of the General Staff of the Red Army?"

"Was at one time, yes. Since 1928, Colonel Chichikov has
been one of Russia's most valuable agents in America."

"But in 1928 the man was a well-known bootlegger!"

"Among other things, General, among other things. It is
Colonel Chichikov who through his American experiences has
provided Stalin with the witticisms he has been dining out on
for years. Chichikov's definition of capitalism, for example, is
one of Stalin's favorites: 'From each according to his stupid-
ity, to each according to his greed.' "

"Please, Mrs. Trust, how much more of this hallucinatory,
psychopathic rot must I stand here and listen to!"

"As much as it takes," said Mrs. Trust, "to make you
face the facts! To make you see that the greatest conspiracy in
the nation's history is taking place right under your nose! Of
course Colonel Chichikov is operating within our midst. Who
with eyes in his skull and a brain in his head could have
watched the antics of our Mr. Mazuma just this last season
and concluded otherwise? *I* have been calling that man a Communist for years, General—now here is Gil Gamesh, fresh
from six years in Moscow, four of them a student at SHIT, to
tell you that in actuality Mazuma is none other than Colonel
Chichikov of the General Staff, and you *still* refuse to believe!

What will it take, General, to rouse you from this mindless sloth to do your duty as an American, as a soldier, and as President of the Patriot League? General Oakhart, fail to heed this warning, sir, and you will go down in history with Benedict Arnold, your name like his will be a synonym for treason and betrayal for as long as decent patriots draw breath! For the sake of God, for the sake of America, attend to what this man is telling you. He has been there—he knows!''

"True," said Gamesh, nodding sadly. "I have seen the future, General, and it stinks."

"Gil, tell him who else is an officer in the Russian armed forces. Tell him the name of the man you met in Moscow in 1941.''

"O.K. Ockatur," said Gamesh.

"You mean—the dwarf who pitches for the Mundys?" cried Oakhart.

"The dwarf who pitches for the Mundys," said Gamesh. "Formerly Captain Smerdyakov, a tank officer in the Leningrad Military Unit of the Red Army.''

"You met him, you're telling me, in *Moscow?*"

"He came to address the school."

The words "Benedict Arnold" had undermined the General's confidence more even than he knew. It simply could not *be* that he who had devoted his entire life to defending the Rules and Regulations could go down in history as neglectful of his responsibilities to be vigilant, honorable, and upright! "Gamesh," cried the aging warrior, "are you sure of this? Are you telling me the truth? Are you absolutely sure it wasn't some *other* dwarf?"

"After four years in the Communist underground, and four more at SHIT, you learn to be able to distinguish between dwarfs, General, easily enough. It was Ockatur. The fact of it is, I am here to spy on him as well as to become the manager of the Mundys.''

"Become *what?*"

"That is my mission. I was assigned here the very night news was flashed to the Kremlin of the death of Ulysses S. Fairsmith. 'You will return to America, Comrade Gamesh. You will become the manager of the Mundys. The last there will ever be.' Those were Stalin's words. I said to him, 'Comrade Stalin, that is more easily said than done.' To which he replied, 'Where there is an iron will, Comrade, there is a way.' On my departure, there were those in my own faction who said that Stalin is grooming me to be his heir—on the other hand, there are those among my adversaries who maintain that whether I fail or succeed, my usefulness to the Party will have been exhausted and I will be earmarked for liquidation, precisely as Ockatur is now.''

"Liquidation? Ockatur? *Why?*''

"No complicated political motive there, General. Simple, in fact. Stalin is a heartless man who despises dwarfs. Of course, he is curiously drawn to them as well—undoubtedly for pathological reasons. As soon as a new dwarf appears in the Party, he is inevitably elevated with great rapidity to a position of trust in the Kremlin. And then even more quickly annihilated, so that not a trace of him remains. General, if the life of the ordinary citizen in the Soviet Union is fraught with danger and uncertainty, the life of a dwarf there is even worse. That is why you see so very few dwarfs these days in Russia. In the time of the czars, nearly every village and hamlet had at least one misshápen little gnome-like person, if not a dwarf, then a hunchback, if not a hunchback, at leaśt a hydrocephalic or something along that line. Today there's hardly a trace of them. You can ride from one end of Russia to the other on the Trans-Siberian Railroad and look in vain for somebody, other than a child, under four feet tall. Either they have risen to the top in the Kremlin, only to be swallowed up in the void, or else, if they have any wits at all, they are in the forests, in hiding, living off nuts and berries, and there they will remain so long as this madman is the ruler over Russia. This madman, General, who would rule the world. And will—unless we stop him, here and now.''

"But—but—'' There were a thousand questions, a million, a hundred million. And for a Douglas D. Oakhart who would not be a Benedict Arnold, the gravest of all: *what if this is so?*

"But this letter?'' said Gamesh.

"Well, yes! Among other things, this letter—from the grocer named McWiley. In Kakoola!''

"Colonel Raskolnikov of the Russian Secret Police.''

"You mean—*he* is a spy too?"

"He is *the* spy, General. Raskolnikov is the number one underground espionage agent in the United States. As President of CACA and Legal Director of 'Keep America Free,' he's able to keep abreast of just who in the Middle West has information about the Communist conspiracy to destroy the American way of life. At the same time, his own humble position as a grocer, and his deliberately crackpot behavior, tend to give the whole anti-Communist crusade a bad name. But that's the least of his cunning. Every deadly plan begins with him. In the Soviet Union they say there has never been a hatchet man to match him. At SHIT, of course, his name is legend."

"Mrs. Trust," said the confused and demoralized General, "you—you know this? When you showed me this letter, you knew that William McWiley was in actuality—"

"Of course."

"In other words, you deliberately deceived me!"

"As the Communists learned to their satisfaction a long time ago, to deceive the President of the Patriot League is not such a difficult task."

"True enough," said Gamesh. "Comrade Stalin himself said to me triumphantly at dinner one night, 'Roosevelt in Washington, Oakhart in Massachusetts—as the great Russian proverb has it, When the farmer and his wife hold the jug too long to their lips, the wolf steals through the snow to sink his teeth in the throat of the cackling chicken.' "

The following phone conversation was monitored and recorded on the evening of March 16, 1944, by agents of the F.B.I. and subsequently introduced into the hearings of a subcommittee of the House Un-American Activities Committee, presided over by Congressman Martin Dies of Texas, and held in Room 1105, United States Court House, Port Ruppert, New Jersey, October 8, 1944.

SMITTY: Why doesn't he go to the F.B.I.?

OAKHART: He claims the F.B.I. is infiltrated from top to bottom with Communists and Communist sympathizers. He says he wouldn't get out of there alive.

SMITTY: Why not Landis then?

OAKHART: He doesn't trust him. Smitty, neither do I. Landis would use the scandal to make us look bad and himself like a hero. He'd use this thing to shut the league down once and for all. Exactly, Gamesh says, what the Communists would want him to do in the first place.

SMITTY: Then why doesn't he go to the top?

OAKHART: According to him, the Soviet agents in the War Department who arranged the leasing of Mundy Park are Roosevelt appointees. They'd bury it, he says—and him too.

SMITTY: And the papers? What about talking to me? I know the son of a bitch.

OAKHART: Because that would be premature. Right now he could finger only Mazuma and Ockatur—but there are others, just as highly placed, whose identities are a mystery even to him. Then there are the party members and fellow travelers among the players—

SMITTY: And where does he find evidence for that, General?

OAKHART: That's what he's *out* to find. As manager of the Mundys he'll appear to Stalin to be carrying out his mission, but in actuality he'll be in the best possible position to work in our behalf to uncover and expose the entire conspiracy. Up close, inside, managing the team that's been their number one target, he'll be right at the center, able to employ all the skills he's learned from them, against them. At SHIT he was first in his class, Smitty—so he tells us, anyway.

SMITTY: Also at bullshit, my old friend.

OAKHART: You don't buy it.

SMITTY: Do *you?* The guy is crazy. Some lunatic off the street hired by that dried-up old slit. Whatever it is, it ain't on the level.

OAKHART: You think it's not even Gamesh?

SMITTY: Suppose that it is. Why would you believe *him,* of all people? If ever there was a grievance-monger with a score to settle, it's that maniacal bastard. "Sturgeon with Stalin. Cocktails with Molotov." It's all too ridiculous.

OAKHART: Ridiculous, yes—*but what if it's also true?* What if baseball *is* destroyed from within?

SMITTY: When that happens, my dear General, it'll be a sad day indeed, but it won't be the atheistical materialistic Communists who will have done it.

OAKHART: Who then?

SMITTY: Who? The atheistical materialistic capitalists, that's who! A' course that's just one man's opinion, General—fella name a' Smith.

The following is excerpted from General Oakhart's testimony before the subcommittee of the House Un-American Activities Committee on October 8, 1944, in Port Ruppert.

THE CHAIRMAN: General, would you tell the Committee why, having solicited the advice and opinion of your friend Mr. Word Smith, the well-known sportswriter, you decided the following morning to disregard it and to recommend the appointment of Gamesh as manager of the Mundys?

GENERAL OAKHART: Well, Mr. Dies, it was because of that startling phrase that Mr. Smith used, "atheistical materialistic capitalists."

MR. THOMAS: In other words, General, until he used that phrase, it just had not entered your head at any time during the previous years that this man might have Communist leanings or might even be an outright agent of a foreign power dedicated to overthrowing our government by violent means.

GENERAL OAKHART: Frankly, sir, I have to say no, it did not. I am afraid I had been completely taken in by him until that evening. Perhaps I might not even have been alert to the implications of the phrase "atheistical materialistic capitalists" if I had not spent those hours earlier in the day with Mrs. Trust and Mr. Gamesh. You must realize—indeed, I know you do—that I have not been alone in believing the Russians and General Stalin to be, in President Roosevelt's words, "our brave allies in the fight against Fascism."

MR. THOMAS: Along that line, General—would it be your opinion, as a former military man, that the war against the

Germans and the Japanese has been used by the Communists to mask their subversive activities here in the United States?

GENERAL OAKHART: Absolutely. There is no better example of that particular kind of Communist treachery than the cynical way in which patriotic feelings were manipulated by the Communist agents in the War Department in order to secure the lease to Mundy Park and drive the Ruppert Mundys from their home. I'd like to take this opportunity, if I may, Mr. Thomas, to inform the Committee that I was one of those who from the very outset opposed leasing Mundy Park to the War Department. At that time, of course, I had no idea that Communists had so thoroughly infiltrated the executive branch of the United States government, and that it was they who were plotting the destruction of my league. On the other hand, that destruction was imminent if the Mundys should be dispossessed from Mundy Park—well, that seemed to me a foregone conclusion.

THE CHAIRMAN: General, following your March 16 phone conversation with Mr. Smith, in which he used the phrase "atheistical materialistic capitalists," did you have any specific recollections of other catchphrases or slogans he had used in the past, either in conversation or in his writings, that had a subversive or propagandistic flavor?

GENERAL OAKHART: Well, of course, his speech and his writings were peppered with phrases that caught you up short by their sardonic or barbed quality, but generally speaking, I shared the view of most everyone, that this show of irreverence was more or less in the nature of a joke, much like all that alliteration he's so famous for.

MR. MUNDT: A joke at the expense of his country.

GENERAL OAKHART: It seemed benign enough, Mr. Mundt, at the time. As everybody knew, he had been a pinochle-playing crony to several American presidents.

MR. THOMAS: Did you know, General, that he has also been a ghostwriter for the present incumbent of the White House?

GENERAL OAKHART: No, sir. I have only learned that through these hearings. But let me tell you, Mr. Thomas, that when he used that phrase, "atheistical materialistic capitalists," I could not have been any more shocked had I known that the man who spoke such a phrase happened also to be a speech-writer for the President of the United States.

MR. THOMAS: Well, I'm glad to hear that. Because it would have shocked *me* profoundly to learn that the hero of the Argonne Forest and the President of a major American baseball league could permit such a traitorous, slanderous, propagandistic remark to leave no impression on him whatsoever.

GENERAL OAKHART: Well, you needn't be shocked, sir, because it didn't. It is not for me, Mr. Thomas, to describe the action I took within the next twenty-four hours as "daring" or "courageous" or "far-sighted," but given the tone of your last remark, I feel I must remind the Committee that Angela Trust and myself, alone in the entire world of baseball, have been fighting tooth and nail against the hammer and sickle—and to this day, *to this day,* have earned little more than the scorn of our colleagues and the disbelief of the nation. Admittedly, it was not until that fateful night in March that I came to recognize the enemy for who and what he was, but since that time, as I am sure you know, I have been in the forefront of the battle against the Red menace, and no less than the members of this Committee, have done everything within my power to fight to preserve the Constitution of the United States and the great game of baseball against Communist subversion and treachery.

(*Loud applause. The Chairman raps his gavel.*)

THE CHAIRMAN: I appreciate that the spectators may from time to time wish to express their admiration for a witness, but I must ask you to restrain your enthusiasm in the hearing room. I'm sure that General Oakhart, who just prior to this morning's hearings announced his intention to run for the presidency of the United States in the coming election, would just as soon you express yourselves through the ballot box anyway.

(*Laughter.*)

GENERAL OAKHART: And, Mr. Dies, I am equally sure that if in August either of our great political parties had nominated for the presidency a candidate who had seen at first hand how the Communists work, a man who knew from hard and tragic experience what an unscrupulous, ruthless, and murderous gang they are, if the American people had been given the opportunity by either the Democrat or the Republican parties to vote for a man who was equipped to fight and to defeat the Communist enemy in our midst, then they might not be roused to display such enthusiasm for my words. But the fact of the matter is, sir, that the people will be silent no longer. Their eyes have been opened—they know the struggle that America will face in the postwar years with those who now pose as her friends. And so do I. And if Mr. Franklin D. Roosevelt and the Democrat Party do not know—and Mr. Roosevelt does not!—and if Mr. Thomas E. Dewey and the Republican Party do not know—and Mr. Dewey does not!—then the American people will look elsewhere for leadership. They will look to one who is not afraid to speak the unspeakable and to do the undoable, to one who is not afraid to call an enemy an enemy, at whatever cost and peril to himself! To one whose party is his country and whose platform is the law of the land!

(*Loud applause.*)

It was a warm and hospitable welcome that Gil Gamesh received when General Oakhart announced to the members of the press assembled in his Tri-City office on St. Patrick's Day 1944 that the former Greenback pitching ace standing beside him, whom he himself had banished a decade earlier, was now to be reinstated in the league, as manager of the Ruppert Mundys. With one notable exception, the writers broke into spontaneous applause as the ghostly Gamesh (bewigged, as he would be henceforth, in a raven-black hairpiece, and wearing his old Number 19) stepped to the microphone, removed his spectacles (the General's idea—adds seriousness) to wipe at an eye with the back of his big left paw, and then proceeded to express his gratitude, first to General Oakhart, for granting him amnesty and a chance to begin life anew; then to Mrs. Trust, for going to bat for him with the General; and then to the American people, who by giving him a second chance, attested to nothing less than their faith in mankind itself . . . Then he told them what he had seen and what he had learned

in his ten years of exile. It was not the story he had told to the
General and Mrs. Trust, but one devised for public consump-
tion by the three of them. It had mostly to do with "our greatest natural resource, the kids of America, this country's future
and its hope." In his guilt and his shame, said Gamesh, he had
wandered the length and breadth of the land under a number
of aliases—Bill Smith, Bob White, Jim Adams—working for
weeks and months at a time as dishwasher, handyman, grocery
clerk, and farmhand; he had lived beneath forty-watt bulbs in
rooming houses in each of the forty-eight states, lonely as a
man could be, without a friend in the world, except, except for
"the kids." At the end of the work day, having downed his
bowl of chili at the counter of the local greasy spoon, he would
step out into the street and listen. For what? For the sound of
the ball striking the bat, or landing with a whack in the pocket
of a catcher's mitt. On many a night he had walked a mile just
to watch a bunch of kids batting a taped-up ball around. Was
he even alive in those years, other than during those twilight
hours on the sandlots of America? Did his heart stir otherwise?
No, no—the remaining twenty-three hours of the day and night
he was a corpse embalmed in shame. "Hey, mister," they'd
call over to him as he stood on the sidelines smoking his two-
cent after-dinner cigar, "wanna ump?" "Hey, mister, fungo
some out to us, hey?" "Hey, mister, ain't that right? Ain't Gil
Gamesh the greatest that ever lived?" "Walter Johnson!"
"Gil Gamesh!" "Rube Waddell!" "Gil Gamesh!" "Grover
Alexander!" "No, Gamesh! Gamesh! Gamesh!" Dangerous as
it was for this man who wished to be forgotten by America
to come anywhere near a pitcher's mound, it was simply
beyond him sometimes not to give a youngster in need a
little advice. "Here, boy, do it this way," and taking the ball
from the little pitcher's hand, he'd show him how to set the
curveball spinning. Oh, there were idyllic summer nights in
small Middle Western towns when he just couldn't resist,
when he would rear back with that taped-up lopsided ball and
hurl a perfect strike into the mitt of the twelve-year-old catcher
—in the process (Gil added, with a tender laugh) knocking him
onto his twelve-year-old fanny. Oh, the mouths of those
youngsters sure hung open then! "Hey, who are you anyway,
mister?" "Nobody," Gil answers, "Bob White, Bill Smith,

Jim Adams . . ." "Hey, know who he looks a little like, guys?
Hey, guys, know who he *is?*" But by then Gil would be sham-
bling off to the sidelines, headed for his rooming house, there
to pack up and move on out to some place new, a strange town
where he could live another day, another week, another month,
as an anonymous drifter . . . Then, said Gil, the war came.
He went around after Pearl Harbor trying to enlist, but always they would ask to see his birth certificate and always
he would refuse to show it; oh, he had one all right, only it
did not say Bob or Bill or Jim—it said, for all the world
to see, this here is Gil Gamesh, the man who hated his fellow
man. Then one day down in Winesburg, Ohio, unable to bear
any longer his life as a lonely grotesque, he turned that self-
incriminating document over to the recruiting sergeant.
"Yep, he's me," he finally admitted—and the fellow turned
red, white, and blue and immediately ran back to show the
thing to his commanding officer. For over an hour Gil sat in
that office, praying that his exile had ended—instead, the
sergeant came back with a captain and a major at his side and
handed Gil a little card stamped U, meaning that as far as
the U.S. government was concerned he was and forever would
be an "Undesirable." The major warned him that if he did not
present the card to his draft board whenever they might call
him up for induction, he would be liable for arrest and im-
prisonment. Then the officers withdrew, and while the Undesirable stood there wondering where he might steal a belt
to hang himself with, the sergeant, in a whisper, asked if he
might have his autograph.

Months of wandering followed, months too desperate to
describe—Black Hawk, Nebraska; Zenith, Minnesota; up
in Michigan; Jefferson, Mississippi; Lycurgus, New York;
Walden, Massachusetts . . . One night he found himself in
Tri-City—it had taken a decade to wend his way back to the
scene of the crime. There he waited outside Tycoon Park for
a glimpse of the great lady of baseball, Angela Whittling
Trust. It was she whom he begged to intercede in his behalf.
"For I knew then," said Gil, "that if I could not regain my
esteem and my honor in the world whose rules I had broken
and whose traditions I had spat upon, I would be condemned
to wander forever, a stranger and an outcast, in this, my own,

my native land. Of course I knew my pitching days were over, but what with the war raging and so many major leaguers gone, I thought perhaps I might be taken on as a bullpen catcher, as someone to throw batting practice, as a batboy perhaps . . . Gentlemen, I did not dream, I did not dare to dream—'' et cetera and so forth, until he came around again to the kids of America, who were his inspiration, strength, salvation, and hope. To them he owed his redemption—to them he now committed heart and soul.

ONE MAN'S OPINION

by Smitty

Talking to Myself

''And not a word about Mike the Mouth. Has anyone happened to notice?''

Look, that was a decade ago. Isn't it a sign of human goodness and mercy to be able to forget about what happened to the other guy ten years back? Besides, Mike the Mouth is dead by now anyway. Or else out there still in the boondocks, demanding some nutcake's version of Justice. Be reasonable, Smitty. So Gamesh robbed him of his voice—the old geezer happened to rob Gil of something too, remember? A *perfect* perfect game. Look, Smitty, don't you believe in people changing for the better? Don't you believe in human progress? Why don't you see the good in people sometimes, instead of always seeing the bad?

''I'm not talking about good men or bad men,'' said Smitty, signaling for another round for the two of them. ''I'm talking about madmen.''

Oh sure, everybody in this world is cracked, except you know who.

''Not everybody,'' said Smitty. ''Just the crackpots who run it. Crackpots, crooks, cretins, creeps, and criminals.''

You left out cranks—how come? Cranks who write columns and cry crocodile tears. Maybe you scribblers worry too much.

''If we don't, who will?''

What the h. do you think you are, anyway? The unacknowledged legislator of mankind?

''Well, that was one man's opinion.''

Whose, Smith? Yours?

"No. Fella name a' Percy Shelley."

Never heard of him.

"Well, he said it."

Well, don't believe everything you hear.

"I don't. But what about what I don't hear?"

What's that?

"A word, a single word," said Smitty, "about Mike the Mouth," and called sharply this time to the waiter for drinks for himself and his friend.

Said Frank Mazuma: "Gamesh? Great gimmick. Why don't I think of things like that? Who'd they get to coach at first, Babyface Nelson?"

FIRST DAY BACK IN THE BIG TIME

Gentlemen, the name is Gil Gamesh. I am the manager who is replacing the gentle Jolly Cholly Tuminikar, who himself replaced the saintly Ulysses S. Fairsmith. My lecture for today is the first in our spring training series on the subject of Hatred and Loathing. Today's talk is entitled "Ha Ha."

Let me begin by telling you that I think you gentlemen are vermin, cowards, weaklings, milksops, toadies, fools, and jellyfish. You are the scum of baseball and the slaves of your league. And why? Because you finished last by fifty games? Hardly. *You are scum because you do not hate your oppressors. You are slaves and fools and jellyfish because you do not loathe your enemies.*

And *why* don't you? They certainly loathe *you*. They mock you, they ridicule you, they taunt you; your suffering moves them not to tears, but to laughter. You are a joke, gentlemen, in case you haven't heard. They laugh at you. To your face, behind your back, they laugh and they laugh and they laugh.

And what do you do about it? You take it. You try not to hear. You pretend it isn't happening. You shrug your shoulders and tell yourself, "It's fate." You say, "What difference does it make, no skin off my nose," and other such philosophical remarks. No wonder they laugh. A team not of baseball players, but philosophers! Stoics and fatalists instead of hitters and fielders! Of *course* they laugh. Gentlemen, *I* laugh!

Ha ha ha ha ha ha ha ha ha ha! Hear me, Mundys? I am laughing, *at you.* Along with the rest of America! At your resignation! At your fatalism! At your jellyfish philosophy of life! Ha ha ha ha ha ha ha ha ha ha ha! Ha ha ha ha ha ha ha ha ha! Ha ha ha ha ha ha ha ha!

Second Day Back

Welcome, Mundys, to another in our spring lecture series on Hatred and Loathing. Before I begin I have to tell you that you surely did outdo yourselves yesterday on the playing field in being laughable. What a wonderful comedy show that was! A regular *Hellzapoppin'!* I near wet my pants watching you standing out there on the field with your heads hanging like the old tried and true victims you are, while those high school lads (or were they lasses?) scored those eight runs in the first inning. What got you down so, "men"? I figured you were going to go out there and really start hating and loathing your enemies and oppressors, and instead you were the jellyfish and cowards and vermin of old, if not more so. Maybe you are ready for our second lecture then, entitled "How To Hate, and Whom."

Boys, it's easy. Just think of all the things you haven't got that other people have. Shall I name a few just to get you going? The obvious first. Other people have all their limbs. Other people have all their hair. Other people have all their teeth and twenty-twenty vision in both eyes. Other people have admiration, luck, fun, something to look forward to. Other people—and this may come as a surprise—have something to be *proud* of: self-respect, love, riches, peace of mind, friends—why, other people have sirloin for breakfast, champagne for lunch, and dancing girls for dinner. And more!

Now you may ask, "Okay, I ain't got none of that and they got all of that—where's the hatred come in?" Mundys, that you can ask such a question is the measure of just how ruthlessly oppressed you have been. Don't you *understand,* boys? It isn't *fair!* It isn't *just!* It isn't *right!* Why should those who have have and those who have not have not? For what reason do they have everything and you nothing? In the name of what and whom? It makes my blood boil just talking about it! I feel the hatred for those haves coursing through my veins just thinking about all that you boys live without that other people have more of than they know what to do with! Brains! Strength! Self-confidence! Courage! Fortitude! Wit! Charm! Good looks! Perfect health! Wisdom! Why, *even Common Sense!* Oh, I could go on forever naming the things that other people have in excess, but that you Mundys haven't a trace of, singly, or taken all together. Talk about being deprived! My cowards, my jellyfish, my fools, you have absolutely *nothing* to recommend you—and on top of that, *you haven't even got a home! A home,* such as every little birdie has in a tree, such as every little mole has in the ground, such as every major league team in creation has, *excepting you!* Talentless, witless, luckless, and as if all that wasn't unfair and unjust enough, *homeless too!*

And you ask me, "But what's there to hate about, Gil?" *They robbed you of your home! They drove you out like dogs!* and you say, "Hey, where's the hatred come in?"

THIRD DAY BACK

Fellas, we had to cut it short yesterday so you could go out there and get your asses whipped by the naval station team, with the result that I did not get around to telling you whom to hate for having deprived you of just about everything a baseball team could want. Let me make it easy for you. Just so you don't go wrong—being new as you are to this great adventure of loathing—why don't you begin by hating your fellow man *across the board?* That way you won't grow confused. If you see a guy in a Mundy uniform, he's all right, *but everybody who is not in the Ruppert scarlet and gray, you are to hate, loathe, despise, vilify, threaten, curse, slander, betray, mock, deceive, revile, and have nothing further to do with.* Is that clear? All mankind except those in the scarlet and gray. Any questions?

Nickname, did I happen to hear you say *"Why?"* Because they live off your misery, Damur! Because the nightmare that is your life at second base *gives them pleasure!* Your errors are their solace, your strike-outs their consolation. Mundys, don't you get it yet? You bear their blame! You suffer in their

stead! The worse your luck, the better for them—the greater
your misery, the happier they will be! Look, haven't you
heard? Do I have to tell you *everything?* THE RUPPERT
MUNDYS ARE THE OFFICIAL SCAPEGOATS OF THE
U.S.A.!

And who *made* you scapegoats, boys? Was it writ in the
stars, Specs? God's will, Tuminikar? Well, that's what they
tell the peasants, all right, when those poor bastards don't
happen to like their lot anymore. That's what they tell the
slaves, when they happen to look up from their shackles and
ask, "Hey, what the hell is goin' on around here?" Sorry,
sorry, nothing to be done for you downtrodden today. God's
will. He wants it this way, with you on the bottom and us on
the top. Back to work now—we'll tell you if and when there's
to be any change with those chains . . .

Mundys, it isn't *God* that put you on the road! It isn't
fate, and it isn't *nothing,* either. *It is your fellow man!* Who
made you scapegoats, Mundys? The United States government and the brothers M.! The country whose flag you salute,
the owners whose names you bear! That's who joined forces
to rob you of honor and dignity and home! The state and the
owners! Your country and your bosses!

It did not come easy at first, but that's what spring training is
for, Gil told them, getting that old unused venom running
again, getting out there first thing in the morning to start in
working on those old weaknesses of character, like ingrained
habits of courtesy and that old bugaboo, the milk of human
kindness. Get that gee-whiz out of your voice, Damur—this is
no high school dance! Cut out that grinning, Rama, nothing is
funny about hate! *Snarl,* Heket, *snarl* at your oppressor—he
lives off your old age! I want to hear some *hatred* in there
when you shout "Hate!"

Ah, but it was hard. How could you go around insulting
some player on the other team when you knew he was better
than you by far? How expect to frighten somebody with your
bark or your bite who had you pegged for a busher long
ago—somebody who in fact frightened *you.* No, it just wouldn't
work. Besides, it wasn't that the other players *always* teased

and kidded them—sometimes they were downright amiable,
even sympathetic with the Mundys for having to be Mundys.
Why, if they went around hating everybody, they were going
to wind up losing what few friends they still had left in the
league.

"You have no friends! You have only enemies! Their
smiles oppress you as much as their sneers! You don't want
their sympathy—you want their *blood!*"

Oh, but it was so hard. How do you go about hating and
loathing those crowds you've been working so hard to placate
and appease? How can you possibly hate all those people who
you don't even know? Christ, when you come down to it, they're
just people, like you and me.

"No, they are not! They are your tormentors! They im-
prison you by their ridicule! You are in bondage to their contempt! You are shackled by their smirks and their smart-ass
remarks! There is no such *thing* as 'people just like you and
me' if you are Ruppert Mundys! There are the oppressed and
the oppressors! The Mundys and the rest of mankind—or
mancruel, to be precise!"

Oh, but it was hard spreading that hatred around the way
Gil wanted. Hate the Mundy brothers *too?* Hell, they didn't
even know what they looked like. How can you hate somebody
you wouldn't even recognize if he sat down next to you on the
trolley car? And they don't even travel on trolleys—those guys
travel in limousines! These are important people, these are
powerful men!

"And they sold you down the river, boys, kicked you and
your pitiful asses out of the inn, just like Jesus and his Mom!
That's what important people do. That's how they get to *be*
important."

But, but we're their team, they pay the wages—their
father was *the* Glorious Mundy who is back in Port Ruppert
buried in deep center field. Their name is our name. How can
we hate our own name, if you know what we mean?

"Because their name *isn't* Mundy anymore. It's Muny,
good old-fashioned dough! They have maligned the name—
mangled it beyond repair! *You* are the true Mundys, boys, and
not because it was the name of your robber-baron father,
either! No, because it is short for Mundane! Meaning *common,*

meaning *ordinary*—meaning the man in the street who's fed
up to here with the Muny brothers and their ilk dancing the
rhumba down in Rio while the ordinary Joe toils without honor
and without reward! The Mundane, who do the dirty work of
this world, their noses to the ground or the grounder, their
tails to the whip, while the Mundy boys stash it away in Fort
Knox! Their name your name? Their team your team? *Says
who!*"

Oh, but it was hard, hardest of all hating the U.S. of A.
Why, if it wasn't for our country 'tis of thee, there wouldn't
even be baseball to begin with!

"Or homeless baseball teams! Look," cried Gamesh,
"what the hell good is a country to you anyway, if there is no
place in it you can call your own?"

Oh, it was hard, but as it turned out in the end, not *that*
hard. By the time the '44 season had begun, they had trampled
out the vintage where the grapes of wrath are stored. Their
hatred knew no bounds.

SECRET SPRING TRAINING REPORT ON COMMUNIST INFILTRATION OF PATRIOT LEAGUE

Excerpts from Memorandum prepared by Gil Gamesh, Manager
of the Ruppert Mundys and Chief Investigator, Patriot League
Internal Security Affairs Division, for General Douglas D. Oakhart, President of Patriot League, and Mrs. Angela Whittling
Trust, Presidential Adviser for Internal Security Affairs, submitted 4/17/44:

1. *Summary.* It is now clear that (a) Communist infiltration of
   the Patriot League is far more extensive than our most pessimistic preseason estimates; and (b) that the Ruppert Mundys,
   as had been hypothesized, occupy a pivotal position in the
   Communist plans for the subversion of the Patriot League.
   The clarification of (a) has been achieved by (c) continuous
   surveillance of Ruppert Mundy activities throughout spring
   training and (d) an analysis of same. Clarification of (b)
   has been achieved by way of (a) (c) and (a) (d), with equal
   emphasis given to each. Current trends, unless reversed before
   conclusion of '44 season, will lead to a Communist-controlled
   league, with complete dissolution to follow, from all indica-
   tions, during '45 season, so as to coincide with Communist
   takeovers in Europe and Asia at conclusion of international

hostilities. The situation is very disturbing, as will be reflected in the following percentages, based on the evidence supplied by (c) and (d):

	Mundys		P. League as Whole	
	April 1933	April 1944	April 1933	April 1944
Communist agents	0%	8%	0%	6%
Communist Party members	4%	16%	3%	14%
Fellow travelers	8%	24%	6%	16%

2. *Analysis of percentages* (charts attached) . . .
3. *Communists detected*
   a. Communist espionage agents
      (1) O.K. Ockatur (P). As reported earlier, Ockatur is in actuality Captain Smerdyakov, formerly a tank officer in the Leningrad Military Unit of the Red Army, now affiliated with the Main Intelligence Directorate of GRU of the Armed Forces General Staff. Because of the blinding of Bob Yamm his reputation is currently at a low ebb in Moscow, where the latest official explanation of that act is that it was committed solely out of personal animosity, in direct defiance of orders. Ockatur argues that he acted in direct *compliance* with orders and accuses his enemies of attempting to ruin him with a charge of "incurable dwarfism." It would appear from all this that Stalin, in the Russian phrase, has already begun "turning the little fellow on his head in the earth," and that sooner or later he will be liquidated, perhaps by being beaned by a Communist pitcher during his turn at bat. We must be prepared for this eventuality.
      (2) Hothead Ptah (C). Ptah is none other than Major Stavrogin, the infamous "One-Legged Man," probably the most admired *agent provocateur* ever to be graduated from SHIT.
   b. Communist Party members
      (1) Frenchy Astarte (SS). Astarte was an active member of the Communist Party in Canada, Latin America, and the Far East before entering the United States under the guise of an infielder. He is fluent in six lan-

guages, though pretends to understand nothing but French. On instruction from Moscow Astarte dropped the pop fly in the last of the ninth of the last game of the '42 season, the error that cost the Mundys a tie for seventh, and set the stage for thé expulsion from Port Ruppert.

(2) Big John Baal (1B). Trained in the jungles of Central America by local Communist insurrectionists; highly motivated. Cell leader of Mundys, certainly one of the top two or three party members in the league.

(3) Chico Mecoatl (P). Roots in Mexican insurgency movement. Two brothers, three sisters, six cousins, and two stepfathers jailed in Mexico for political activities. Noises he makes while pitching may be code signals.

(4) Deacon Demeter (P). ''The Red Deacon,'' liaison between party members in organized baseball and party members infiltrating organized religion. Top Southern ''white trash'' Communist in U.S.

c. Fellow travelers
   (1) Jolly Cholly Tuminikar (P)
   (2) Nickname Damur (2B)
   (3) Specs Skirnir (RF)
   (4) Carl Khovaki (UT)
   (5) Applejack·Terminus (UT)
   (6) Mule Mokos (UT)

4. *The Isaac Ellis Development*

a. Background and summary; or, ''From Surmise to Certainty.'' It has long been suspected by the Presidential Adviser and the Chief Investigator of the Internal Security Affairs Division of the Patriot League that the owner of the Tri-City Greenbacks, Abraham Ellis, and his wife, Sarah Ellis, were, like so many of their co-religionists, either ''tools'' of the Communists, party members, or fellow travelers. It has now been established with maximal certainty *that the entire Ellis family comprises the key intelligence and secret police unit in all of organized baseball.*

b. J.E.W.; or, ''The Ellis Mission.'' The Ellis mission appears to be threefold: (J) to contribute by their very presence to undermining faith in the Patriot League; (E) to mastermind ad hoc espionage activities within the league; and (W) to spy on their fellow Communists within the league and transmit all data as to the loyalty, dedication, and competence of agents and party functionaries to the appropriate

Kremlin offices. With a foot in both the GRU (Main Intelligence Directorate of the Armed Forces General Staff) and the KBG (Intelligence Service of the Soviet State Security Service, or Secret Police), the Ellises hold the position of *highest-ranking Communist agents in the Patriot League,* outranking Frank Mazuma (Colonel Chichikov) and the Chief Investigator of the Internal Security Affairs Division of the Patriot League. Their identity is probably known only to Colonel Raskolnikov himself.

c. Isaac Ellis; or, "Moscow Makes Her Move." On April 12, 1944, three days before the opening of the Patriot League season, Isaac Ellis, the seventeen-year-old son of Abraham Ellis, requested an interview with Gil Gamesh in a cafeteria in Tri-City, where the Mundys were playing a final exhibition game against the Greenbacks. There Ellis made the following proposal:

(1) That he become a Ruppert Mundy "coach" under manager Gil Gamesh

(2) That he be given complete managerial control over team strategy until the All-Star break

(3) That during this "trial" period he be permitted to institute the following changes—

   (a) Do away with the sacrifice bunt as an offensive maneuver and the intentional pass as a defensive maneuver

   (b) With a runner or runners on base and less than two outs, rely almost exclusively on the hit-and-run

   (c) Bat the hitters in descending order of run productiveness

   (d) Instead of removing pitchers "randomly and haphazardly" in a game for defensive reasons, rotate for offensive reasons; start with "a relief pitcher" who works approximately two innings, follow with "a starting pitcher" who goes approximately five, and finish up with "a second relief pitcher" who pitches the final two

   (To justify this bizarre and outlandish system, Ellis offered a wealth of spurious statistics and pseudoscientific explanations [see charts attached]; he argued that if instituted on opening day, the system would land the Mundys in the first division by the All-Star break and the team

would be in contention for the pennant by the
season's end.)

d. Analysis. It was of course immediately apparent to the
Chief Investigator that (J) Isaac Ellis was a Communist
agent assigned to spy on Gil Gamesh; (E) that if hired by
Gil Gamesh to be a Ruppert Mundy coach he might well be
able to act to inhibit the counterespionage activities of
Gamesh; but (W) that if he were *not* hired, it would be
immediately apparent to Moscow that Gamesh, by refusing
to capitalize on Ellis's brilliantly destructive scheme, had
acted to preserve rather than to undermine the Patriot
League—in short, that he had (as indeed he has) resumed
his loyalty to his native land.

When, at the end of June, the Mundys moved up into undis-
puted possession of fourth place, Roland Agni found himself unable to justify any longer, either to his father or to
Manager Gamesh, his refusal to honor his Ruppert contract.
Never mind that a day didn't pass now without a Mundy player
being thrown out of a ballgame for cursing the ump or taking
a poke at an opposing player; never mind that there were fist
fights with fans and rumors of knives in the Mundy dugout;
never mind the invective spewed forth from the Mundy bench,
the likes of which had never before been heard in big league
ball. The point was this: how could he continue to call them
the worst team in history when there now appeared to be four
teams even worse in the Patriot League alone—and only three
that were better! Just what kind of prima donna was he to
refuse to play ball on a major league team with a better
than .500 average? "What about Walter Johnson, Roland—
twenty years with the Senators and only two pennants—and
did he complain? Did he run home and refuse to leave his
room?" "But it's a fluke, Daddy!" cried Roland from the
bed where he now lay for weeks on end. "I know these fellas—
they can't even *field* .500!" "Yet," said his father, peering into
the darkened room, "here are today's official standings, for
all to see. Tycoons first. Butchers second. Keepers third. And
Mundys fourth, with thirty wins and twenty-nine losses. In
ten weeks, they have won almost as many without you as they
won *with* you during an entire season of play." "But that

wasn't my fault—*I won the batting championship of the entire
league!*" "Yet oddly it didn't help that team one bit. From
the looks of things, it may even be what hindered them. You
and your superior ways may well have been what crushed the
confidence of that entire team. Oh, son, when will you understand that no man is an island unto himself?"

So the fatal, final step was taken: the incomparable Roland
Agni, who had never wanted any more from life than that it
should reward him with the dignity and honor commensurate
with his talent, returned to don the uniform whose scarlet R—
heretofore the initial letter of "Ridiculous" and "Refugee"
—was now said to stand for "Ruthless" and "Revenge."

And it was ghastlier than ever. Winning every other game
through a systematic program of hatred and loathing was
worse even than losing them all through ineptness and stu-
pidity. Enraged, his teammates were even more repulsive to
Roland than they had been cowed and confused; at least then,
in a weak moment, he could feel a little *pity*. But now they could
not even step bareheaded to the top step of the dugout to listen
to the National Anthem without hissing among themselves
like a pack of venomous snakes—despicable bastards!

"Fuckin' Betsy Ross!"

"Fuckin' Francis Scott Key!"

"Fuckin' stripes!"

"Fuckin' stars!"

And that was just the pregame vitriol. By the time nine
innings had elapsed there was nothing around that had not
been traduced and vilified by the Ruppert team, beginning of
course with the opposing ballplayers, their parents, wives,
sweethearts, and children, and proceeding right on down to the
local transportation system and the drinking water. It did not
let up for a moment, neither from the field nor the bench, and
certainly not from the third-base coaching box, where No. $\frac{1}{16}$,
the most vengeful of the vengeful, could turn an opposing
pitcher into a raving madman by saying what was more disgusting even than what Hothead used to whisper to the Southern boys about their moms—referring as it did, in O.K.'s
case, to their little tiny daughters in kindergarten, girls just
about the right size and shape, insinuated O.K., for a fella of

his dimensions. Oh, could that vile little dwarf make those pitchers balk! Why, he could score a man all the way around from first on three well-timed remarks about some little bit of a girl just out of diapers.

And could old Jolly Cholly make them bastards jump! Oh, did they go down when he threw that fast one back of their shoulder blades! "Know who that is out there?" Hothead would whisper to the batter with his face in the dust. "Tumini-kar, that once killed a guy. Fella just about your size too."

"Tag 'em, Kid, right in the gazoo!" Nickname would shout across to third, and Heket—grinning sheepishly—would feint one way, and then, the old man's revenge, slam the ball and the glove right up between the base runner's thighs.

"Yeeeeowwwwww!" cries the base runner.

"Out!" cries the ump, even as the fans swarm on to the field screaming for Heket's scalp, and the most aged of the Mundys swarm up out of the dugout, armed with two bats apiece to protect their decrepit brother.

Inning after inning, day in and day out, Gil Gamesh sends his pitcher back out to the mound with only three words of instruction: "Knock somebody down."

"Who?"

"Anybody. They live off your suffering, *each and every one.*"

"Those dirty bastards!"

"What right have they to be batting last all the time?"

"The filthy pricks!"

"Who are they to mock and ridicule you?"

"They're nobody! They're nothin'!"

"They're *worse* than nothing, boys! They're *not Ruppert Mundys!* They're baseball players *who don't wear scarlet and gray!* They're Keepers, they're Greenbacks, they're fucking *Tycoons!*"

"The filthy slimy shits!"

"Ah, that's the spirit! *That's* my Mundanes! Cut his face, Nickname! Crush his balls, Kid! Defame his wife! Threaten his life! Calumniate his kids! I want blood! I want brawls! I want hate! I want a baseball team that nobody is ever going to laugh at again!"

CHANSON DE ROLAND

"The end justifies the means. All we're trying to do out there is win a ballgame."

"But it ain't a ballgame anymore—not by anybody's standards!"

"What then?"

"It's hatin', threatenin', and cursin'—it's wantin' to kill the other guy, wantin' him dead—*and that ain't a game!*"

"Never heard of Ty Cobb, did you? Mugsy McGraw? Leo the Lip?"

"But they ain't nothin' compared to this! And that's only three. This is a whole team that's gone crazy! And you goadin' and goadin' em, till one day they is goin' to take the ump and rip him into little pieces! It's got to stop, Mr. Gamesh! Why do they have to hate the whole country? Even Cobb didn't do that! And Leo Durocher don't go around cursin' Abraham Lincoln and Valley Forge! *What does that have to do with baseball?*"

"Hatred makes them brave and strong—it's as simple as that."

"But it ain't brave *or* strong—it's just stupid! They are just a bunch of stupid fellers to begin with, and all you are doin' is makin' them stupider!"

"And what was so smart about being in last?"

"I ain't sayin' it was smart—it was just *right*. That's where they belong!"

"And you, where do you belong? Let me tell you, Roland. Away where they put the rest of you guys who go around trading in *phony breakfast foods.*"

"But they weren't *mine*. Who told you *that?*"

"Who do you think?"

"But *he's* the one who made 'em, the little Jew! Did he tell you that, too? *He* made 'em, not me!"

"But you're the one who dropped them in their breakfast bowls, All-American Boy."

"But I *had* to."

"Tell it to the Commissioner, Roland, tell it to General O. Or would you prefer me to?"

"No! No!"

"Then keep your clean-cut ideas to yourself, Roland—underneath me? That's Babylonian, Star, for understand. The Mundys are fourth in the league—and without the benefit of your clean-cut advice."

"But they don't *deserve* to be fourth!"

"What about all that winning, Roland?"

"But they don't deserve to be *winning!*"

"And who does in this world, Roland? Only the gifted and the beautiful and the brave? What about the rest of us, Champ? What about the wretched, for example? What about the weak and the lowly and the desperate and the fearful and the deprived, to name but a few who come to mind? What about losers? What about failures? What about the ordinary fucking outcasts of this world—who happen to comprise *ninety per cent of the human race!* Don't they have dreams, Agni? Don't they have hopes? Just who told you clean-cut bastards you own the world anyway? Who put you clean-cut bastards in charge, that's what I'd like to know! Oh, let me tell you something, All-American Adonis: you fair-haired sons of bitches have had your day. It's all over, Agni. We're not playing according to your clean-cut rules anymore—we're playing according to our own! The Revolution has begun! Henceforth, the Mundys are the master race!"

"Ellis."

"What do *you* want?"

"Ellis, why did you tell the skipper about them Wheaties? *Nobody's supposed to know.*"

"Nobody's supposed to know what, Agni? That Mr. Perfect isn't Mr. Perfect after all?"

"He's goin' to blackmail me!"

"Not if you keep your clean-cut mouth shut, Roland."

"But this ain't baseball anymore at all! This is worse than last year even! Him and his hatin' and you and your charts—you two are destroyin' the game!"

"Let's say we're changing things."

"But it's all wrong! A Jew at first, a dwarf at third—whoever heard of coaches like that! You can't even catch a ball, Isaac! All you know is numbers! To you we're just pieces

of arithmetic! Somethin' you can multiply and divide—and to
him, to him we're wild savages! We're somethin' that you open
the cage and let 'em out to run wild! It's gotta stop, Isaac!''

"Why is that?"

"Because—this ain't the time-honored way!"

"Neither was feeding them 'Jewish Wheaties' the time-
honored way. But you did it."

"But I *had* to!"

"In order to be the hero you are, right, Golden Boy?"

"Oh, why is everybody against me bein' great—when I
am! Why does everybody hate me for somethin' I can't help!
It ain't my fault I was born superior!"

"Well, maybe the same holds true for the inferior,
Roland."

"But I ain't tellin' them *not* to be inferior. That is their
right! Only give me mine! Instead there is this plot to beat me
down!"

"Poor little .370 hitter."

"But if I wasn't always goin' crazy with this here team, I
could hit more! I could be a *.400* hitter—instead they're drivin'
me mad!"

The Shot Heard Round the League

Then, fans, it was over: Roland Agni was dead and the
Mundys were no more.

Fifty-five thousand Kakoolians were already in their seats
when the Ruppert team came out for batting practice on the
Fourth of July 1944. All around the P. League now the sight
of the Mundys emerging from their dugout set the spectators'
mouths to foaming, but nowhere did the resentment reach
such a pitch even before the first pitch as in Kakoola, in part,
of course, because the ingenious Kakoola entrepreneur was
always on hand to get the day's frenzy under way—"Renegades! Roughnecks! Rogues! Rapscallions! Rowdies"—but
also because Gamesh's snarling, scowling nine was still the
bunch that had crippled Doubloon and blinded Bob Yamm,
and sold the Reapers that one-armed lemon named Parusha.

(Afterwards, when that day's tragedy was history, the editorialists around the nation were to lament this "climate of
hatred" that had gripped the city of Kakoola on "the fateful

Fourth" and prepared the way for the bloodshed—though Mayor Efghi was quick to remind the papers that it was not a Kakoolian who had pulled the trigger, but "a deranged, embittered loner . . . whose barbarous and wanton act is as repugnant to Kakoolians as it is to civilized men the world over.")

When the visitors departed the clubhouse that day for the pregame workout, one Mundy stayed behind. Seated before his locker wearing only his support, he was as striking and monumental a sufferer as any sculptor had ever hewn from stone. "What am I to do? Go home again? No, no," he realized, "you *can't* go home again. Who ever heard of anybody great going home—who ever heard of a great man who lived with his mom and his dad!" Oh, he could just see himself, lying there in his bedroom till his hair turned white and his teeth fell out, his high school trophies and that year in the majors all he had to prove that he would have been and *should* have been the greatest center-fielder of all time. He could just imagine those meals at the family dinner table, himself ninety and his father a hundred and twenty-five. "No man is an island unto himself, Roland." "But they were not men!" "All ballplayers are men, Roland. The Ruppert Mundys were ballplayers. Therefore the Ruppert Mundys are men." "But all ballplayers are not men. Some are freaks and bums!" "But freaks and bums are men. The freak and the bum are your brothers, my son." And would it be any better down in the town? "See that one there, with the cane and the beard. That's old Roland Agni. Let him be a warning to you, children." "Why, what'd he do wrong, Mommy?" "He never thought about others, that's what, only about himself and how wonderful he was . . ."

Roland was drawn from the horrible vision of a lifetime of paternal reprimand and unjust obscurity by the strange conversation coming from the clubhouse entryway. What the hell language was that anyway? It wasn't German, it wasn't Japanese—he knew what they sounded like from the war movies. What was that language then—and who was talking it anyway?

When he peered around the row of lockers he saw a stolid little man wearing a big padded blue suit conversing with the manager of the Ruppert Mundys. Gamesh had his eyes riveted to the foreigner's face, a face broader than it was long and heavily padded, like the suit. The stranger was holding a base-ball bat at his side. He handed it to Gamesh, *Gamesh saluted,* and the man in the suit was gone.

That was all he heard and saw, but it left the center-fielder reeling.

Then Gamesh saw *him.*

"You again? What are you sulking about now, Goldilocks? Who excused you from batting practice, Big Star?"

"That—that was Russian!" Agni cried.

"Get out on the field, Glamor Puss, and fast."

"But you were talkin' *Russian* to that man!"

"That man, Agni, happened to be my uncle from Baby-lonia, and what we were talking was pure, unadulterated Baby-lonian. Now get your immortal ass out on the ball field."

"If it was your uncle, why did you salute him?"

"Respect, Roland—ever hear of it? All Babylonians salute their uncles. Don't you know ancient history, don't you know anything except what a star you are?"

"But—but why did he give you a bat?"

"Jesus, what a question! Why shouldn't he? Don't Baby-lonians have kids? Don't Babylonian kids like autographs, too?"

"Well, sure, I guess so . . ."

"You guess so . . ." snorted Gamesh, that master of in-timidation. "Here," he said, handing Agni a pen to finish him off, "ink your famous monicker—be the first on your team. And then get out of here. You've got hitting to do. You've got *hating* to do. And loathing, God damn it! Oh, we'll make a Mundy out of you yet, Mr. All-American Boy!"

Thirty-two was the number chiseled into the wood at the butt end of the bat, but Roland Agni had only to lift it in his right hand to know that it did not weigh a gram over thirty-one ounces. An ounce of bat was missing. *Somewhere it was hollow.*

He reeled again, but not so the Soviet terrorist and sabo-teur could see.

Even from deepest center, Agni followed the skipper's every movement down in the dugout: he watched him use it as a pointer to move his infield around, watched him hammer

with it on the dugout floor to rattle the Kakoola hitters,
watched between pitches when he rested his chin on the flat
end, as though it were a bat and he were a manager like any
other. For six full innings the center-fielder kept one eye on
the game and the other on Gamesh—with that great pair of
eyes, he could do it—and then at the top of the seventh, a
Damur foul zinged back into the Mundy dugout, and when the
players went scrambling, Agni landed like a blockbuster in the
manager's lap.

"Hey! Give that here!" snarled Gamesh. "Hey—!"

But on the very next pitch, Nickname drew a walk; Terminus, pinch-hitting for the pitcher, moved up to the plate;
and Roland, who according to the Isaac Ellis Rotation Plan
(and with the reluctant permission of his father) batted first,
leaped from the dugout to the on-deck circle, swinging round
and round over his head the bat he had wrested from the
Mundy manager with all the strength in his body, the bat that
was missing an ounce.

Now rarely during that season did the Mundy manager
step onto the field if he could help it; he had his reasons—and
they were to prove to be good ones. To remove a pitcher from
the game, he sent the Jewish genius out to the mound, and to
talk to the batters he had the notorious Ockatur waddle on
down from the third-base coaching box. Those two misfits gave
a crowd plenty to holler about, without Gamesh (who was
of course *the* Mundy they had turned out to see and to censure
—though his popularity had plummeted, the charisma held)
running the risk of liquidation.

But now the threatening notes that he had been receiving daily since opening day must have seemed to him as
nothing beside the danger of discovery by the incomparable
center-fielder, whose demoralization and incipient derange-
ment (any inning now, Gamesh reported daily to his superiors)
had fit precisely into his sinister timetable. So he called for
time and came up out of the Mundy dugout as though to talk
strategy with Terminus at home plate. What a Fourth of July
treat for that crowd! At the sight of the cadaverous Mundy
manager, wearing on his back the number he had made infamous a decade earlier, the Reaper fans roared as only they
could. *There he was* at last, the hero who spoke to them of rage,

ruination, and rebirth, a white Jack Johnson, a P. League Jesse James—the martyred intransigent, the enviable transgressor, and something too of the resurrected who had died for their sins and returned.

At home plate, Gamesh took Applejack Terminus aside to tell the fifty-two-year-old to remember to keep his eye on the ball, then headed back to the Mundy dugout by way of the on-deck circle, the crowd raving on all the while. With Gamesh looming over him, Roland remained down on one knee, the fingers of his right hand curled like a python around the handle of the Babylonian's bat.

"Okay, Champ," said the manager, clapping him lightly on the back, "give it here and go back down and get your own."

"Communist! Dirty Communist!"

"Tsk, tsk. What sort of language is that for a clean-cut lad from a big middlewestern state?"

"*True* language!" said the center-fielder, and opening his clenched left fist, showed Gamesh that he had the goods on him at last. "It's all clear now—you traitor!"

"What's clear, Roland? To me you sound confused, boy."

"That you're a spy, a secret Soviet spy! Just like Mrs. Trust warned me about!"

"Now what on earth are you holding in your hand, Rollie?"

"Film! A tiny little roll of secret film!"

"Where'd you buy it, from some dirty old pervert downtown? Tsk, tsk, Roland Agni."

"I got it out of this here bat! You know that! By unscrewin' the bottom of the bat! And out it dropped, right in my hand!"

"Play ball!" the umpire called. "You gave 'em their thrill, Gil—they've seen your frightenin' mug—now let's play the game!"

"Film?" said Gamesh. "Oh, sure. My uncle. He's the super-duper photographer in the family. Babylonians love pictures, you know—worth a thousand words, we say."

"Your uncle's a Communist spy! You're one too! *That's* why you're teachin' them hate!"

"*Play ball!*"

Before the umpire could descend upon them, Gamesh

started back to the dugout—but his parting words were chilling, their meaning as well as their tone: "Use your head, Hero.
I can ruin your life, destroy your reputation forevermore."

After working the count to 2 and 2, Terminus popped up
foul on an Ellis hit-and-run and not all the abuse in the new
Mundy lexicon could cause the Kakoola third-baseman to drop
the fly ball, nor was he intimidated by Applejack's bat as it
came careening toward his ankles. The put-out made, however,
the third-baseman started after Ockatur (later, from his hospital bed, he claimed that the dwarf had spit in his eye as he
crossed the coaching box in pursuit of the pop-up), whereupon
the Mundys sprang from the bench and were kneeing (some
said knifing) the fielder before he could lay hold of the misshapen coach. Scores of police charged on to the field from
beneath the stands—on hand, as of old, when Gamesh came to
town—and when finally spikes were plucked from flesh and fingers from eyeballs, Ockatur, Astarte, and Rama were ejected
from the game, and the Kakoola third-baseman, as well as the
shortstop—the sole Reaper who had dared to come to his defense—were carried unconscious from the diamond. How times
do change! Who would have believed this of the Mundys only
the season before?

The field clear at last of law-enforcement officers (and
their horses), Gamesh came off the Mundy bench once again
and started out to home plate, where Agni waited for the
Reaper utility infielders to take a practice throw before stepping in for his turn at bat.

Making no effort to hide his disgust, the umpire said,
"Now what, Gamesh? You gotta start in too? Ain't they crazy
enough from Mazuma?" he asked, motioning out to the bleachers, where the irrepressible Kakoola owner, in an Uncle Sam
beard and suit to celebrate the day, and with the assistance of
daughter Dinero, was loading an iron ball into a mock cannon
aimed in the direction of the Mundy bullpen.

"So what do you say, Rollie," Gamesh whispered, "you
don't want to go down in recorded history like Shoeless Joe,
do you? You wouldn't want the world to know about those
W-h-e-a-t-i-e-s, would you? Why not give over the fil-um then,
okay? And then go get yourself a nice new bat, and we will forget we ever crossed swords today—what do you say, Roland?

*Otherwise your name will be anathema for centuries to come.
Like Caligula. Like Judas. Like Leopold and Loeb.''*

"What—what's anathema?" asked the young center-fielder, weakening under Gamesh's maniacal, threatening gaze.

"*Mud,* my boy, *mud.* You will be an outcast from decent society worse even than me. You who could be greater than Gofannon, greater than Cobb, greater than the great Joe D.''

"But—but you're out to destroy America!''

"America?" said Gamesh, smiling. "Roland, what's America to you? Or me, or those tens of thousands up in the stands? It's just a word they use to keep your nose to the grindstone and your toes to the line. America is the opiate of the people, Goldilocks—I wouldn't worry my pretty little reflexes about it, if I was a star like you.''

When the bang sounded, all faces turned—grinning—toward the open center-field bleachers, where the bearded, top-hatted Mazuma, and daughter Dinero, clad for a summer day in a strip of red, a cup of white, and a cup of blue, were still wrestling with the cannonball (and one another). The fans whooped and barked with delight. Then came the second report, and with it the realization that it wasn't Mazuma setting off firecrackers, and it wasn't a joke.

Spectators turned up afterwards (publicity hounds, one and all) who claimed to have heard as many as six and seven shots ring out, thus giving rise to the "keystone combo" conspiracy theory of assassination bandied about for months and months in the letters column of the Kakoola papers; however, the investigation conducted by General Oakhart's office in cooperation with the Kakoola Police Department concluded "beyond a shadow of a doubt" that only two bullets had been fired, the one that shattered Gil Gamesh's left shoulder before ricocheting into Roland's throat, and the bullet that penetrated Agni's head directly between his baby-blue eyes, at the very instant, it would seem, that he was either to betray his country so as to save his name, or sacrifice his name so as to save his country.

From the stands it was at first assumed that the bodies lying atop one another across home plate were both dead; but though Gamesh's famed left arm lay stretched in the dust, lifeless as a length of cable, the right edged slowly down

Roland's bloody shirtfront, and while pandemonium reigned in the stadium, Gamesh reached into Roland's pants and fished the microfilm out from where the innocent youngster had (predictably) secreted it.

The assassin was dead within minutes. Kakoola mounted police, low in their saddles, charged the scoreboard, placing as many as twenty bullets into each of the apertures from which the shots appeared to have come. As a result, they got not just the assassin, but also the scorekeeper—a father of four, two of whom, being boys, were assured within the week of admission to West Point when they should come of age. At a memorial service at Kakoola City Hall, a service academy spokesman standing in full-dress uniform beside the two small boys, Mayor Efghi, Frank Mazuma, and a veiled, voluptuous Dinero, would call the appointments "a tribute to the brave father of these two proud young Americans, who had perished," as he put it, "in the line of duty" (perished along with Mike the Mouth Masterson, who was, as the reader will already have surmised, the murderer).

The coroner's inquest revealed that of the two hundred and fifty-six slugs fired by the Kakoola police, one had grazed Mike's ear; however, the long night he had spent with his high-powered rifle in a remote corner of the scoreboard, sucking chicken bones and drinking soda pop and dreaming his dreams of vengeance, followed by the excitement of the assassination itself, apparently had been enough to cause him to keel over, at eighty-one, a victim of heart failure.

THE ENEMY WITHIN

Two days after Agni's death, from the studios of TAWT, Angela Whittling Trust's Tri-City radio station, General Oakhart revealed to the American people the magnitude of the plot to destroy the Patriot League, Organized Baseball, the free enterprise system, democracy, and the republic. Seated to either side of the microphone from which the General read his statement were Gil Gamesh, Angela Trust, and Mr. and Mrs. Roland Agni, Senior, parents of the slain center-fielder, who, it was now revealed, had not been the accidental victim of a vengeful madman, "a loner" acting on his own, but had been murdered deliberately for refusing to play ball with America's enemies.

"My fellow Americans, and ladies and gentlemen of the press," General Oakhart began. "I have here in my hand the names of thirteen members of the Ruppert Mundy baseball team who have been named as dues-paying, card-carrying members of the Communist Party, secret agents of a Communist espionage and sabotage ring, and Communist sympathizers."

He proceeded then to outline the scheme hatched over a decade ago in the inner sanctum of the Kremlin, and that had erupted in violence two days earlier with the tragic murder of the 1943 Patriot League batting champ, and the attempt upon the life of Gil Gamesh. "I am shortly going to ask the Mundy manager to tell you his own remarkable story in his own words. It is a story of defeat and dejection, of error and of betrayal; it is a story of the horror of treason and the circle of loneliness and misery in which the traitor moves. I know that some of you will ask, How can you have any respect for the integrity of a man who now admits to such a heinous past, who admits to us now that he did not tell anything like the whole truth about himself the first time he appeared before the nation only a few brief months ago? My answer is not one of justification but of extenuation. My fellow Americans, is it not better to tell the whole truth in the end than to refuse to tell the truth at all? Is it not better to be one who has been a Communist than one who may still be one? I think one need only contrast the searing frankness and the soul-searching courage of Gil Gamesh with the deviousness and treachery of the Mundy Thirteen—twelve of whom still staunchly refuse to admit to the crime of treason—to conclude that Gil Gamesh is indeed an American who deserves not only our respect, but our undying gratitude for this warning he has given us of the conspiracy we face and the battle that lies ahead."

General Oakhart now read into the microphone the names of the Mundys whom he was suspending that day from the Patriot League for their Communist activities. Full files, he said, were available on each and every one of these cases, and had been turned over that morning to the F.B.I., along with the files on another thirty-six Communists and pro-Communists presently active in the league. In that the Thirty-Six hadn't yet been afforded an opportunity, in closed session with the General, either to refute the charges or to make a full confession, General Oakhart said that he did not consider it "fair play" to make their names known to the public at this time. To date, he reported, not a single one of the Mundy Thirteen that he had interrogated in his office had been able to disprove the allegations to the satisfaction of himself or Mrs. Trust, who had served throughout as his associate in this investigation; and so far only one Mundy—after having laughingly denied his Communist affiliations in the morning—had returned to the General's office in the afternoon and made a clean breast of his lifelong service as an agent of the Soviet Union. He was John Baal, the Mundy first-baseman. Having confessed to his own conspiratorial role, he had then proceeded to confirm the identities of his twelve Communist teammates, who were, in alphabetical order, Jean-Paul Astarte, Oliver Damur, Virgil Demeter, coach Isaac Ellis, Carl Khovaki, Chico Mecoatl, Eugene Mokos, Donald Ockatur, Peter Ptah, George Skirnir, Cletis Terminus, and Charles Tuminikar.

General Oakhart concluded his remarks with the assurance that the Patriot League would be cleansed of its remaining thirty-six Communists and the plot against American baseball destroyed before the week was out.

Now Gamesh, his left arm in a sling beneath his Ruppert warm-up jacket, stepped to the microphone. After being accorded a standing ovation by the assembled reporters (with one notable exception), he delivered himself of the story he had previously told the General in the old family hovel in Docktown. At the request of the reporters, he twice recounted his experience in the radio room of Soviet Military Intelligence, where he had listened one night to the first Yankee-Tycoon World Series game while snow fell upon the Communist capital he never could call home. "I feared that some day I would pay with my life for the longing that had drawn me to that room. And so," said Gamesh, as the reporters (with one notable exception) scribbled furiously, "I nearly did, two days ago. My fellow Americans, that the Communists should have chosen from their ranks former Patriot League umpire

Mike Masterson to be my assassin is an indication of just how
shrewd and cynical is the enemy secretly conspiring against
us. For had I been killed two days back by the bullet that has
instead only shattered my arm, it would have appeared to the
world that I was the victim of an act of vengeance taken
against me and me alone by a crazed and senile old man who
could never find it in his heart to forgive and forget. And it
would have been assumed, as indeed it has been until this moment, that Roland Agni was merely an unintended victim of
the homicidal umpire's bullets. But the truth is far more
tragic and far more terrifying. Mike Masterson, the umpire
who never called one wrong in his heart, was no less a dupe of
the Communists than I was—and in his obedience to his Communist masters, deliberately and in cold blood destroyed the
life of a very great American—a great hitter, a great fielder,
and a great anti-Communist crusader. I am speaking of the
youngster I came to know so well, and admire so deeply, in
the few brief weeks I was privileged to be his manager. I am
speaking of the one Mundy who did not jump to the bait that
I dangled before his teammates to determine just which were
the Red fish swimming in the Ruppert Mundy sea. I am speaking of the young American who the Communists so feared
that in the end they ordered his execution, the youngster who
fought the Reds at every turn, at times blindly and in bewilderment, but always armed with the conviction that there
was only one way to play the game, and that was the way
Americans played it. I am speaking of the player, who, had he
lived in happier times, would have broken all the records in the
book and surely one day would have been enshrined in Cooperstown with the greats of yesteryear, but whose name will live on
nonetheless in the Anti-Communist Hall of Fame soon to be
constructed here in Tri-City by Angela Whittling Trust: I am
speaking of Ruppert center-fielder Roland Agni.''

Here Gamesh turned to the parents of the slain young
man. The elder Mr. Agni, no less impressive a physical speci-
men than his son, rose to his feet and extended a hand to
Roland's mother; together the bereaved father and his petite
and pretty wife stepped to the microphone. Mr. Agni's voice
was husky with emotion when he began, and his wife, who
had been so brave all along, now gave in to tears and wept

quietly at his side while he spoke. Mrs. Trust, in a gesture recorded in the Pulitzer Prize photograph of that year, reached up and with her own withered hand took hold of Mrs. Agni's arm to comfort the younger woman.

Said Mr. Agni: "My wife and I have lost our nineteen-year-old son. Of course we cannot but grieve, of course our hearts are heavy. But I should like to tell you that we have never in our lives been prouder of him than we are today. To others Roland was always a hero because he was a consummate athlete—to us, his parents, he is now a hero because he was a patriot who made the ultimate sacrifice for his country and for mankind. Where is there an American mother and father who could ask for anything more?"

The last word that afternoon was Mrs. Trust's. It was her answer to the Communists, and it was "Applesauce!"

As General Oakhart had promised, within the week thirty-six more Communists and Communist sympathizers were suspended from the Patriot League and their names released to the press: nine Reapers, eight Greenbacks, seven Keepers, six Butchers, four Blues, and two Rustlers. Even more shocking than this list of thirty-six was the exposure of the Communist owners, Frank Mazuma and Abraham Ellis, as well as the Soviet "courier," Ellis's wife Sarah. When both owners immediately issued statements in which they categorically denied the charges—calling them outrageous, nonsensical, and wickedly irresponsible—General Oakhart traveled to Chicago to confer with Judge Landis. The incensed Commissioner had already informed reporters that he for one did not intend to do the job of "rodent extermination" for General Oakhart that the P. League President should have been doing for himself while the Communists were infiltrating his league over the last decade; nonetheless, following their three-hour meeting, Landis made a brief statement to reporters in which he announced that Organized Baseball lent its "moral support" to the General's decision to suspend from league play the Kakoola Reapers and the Tri-City Greenbacks until such time as the accused owners either proved their innocence or divested themselves of their franchises. But in the matter of any legal suits resulting

from the suspension of the two teams, Judge Landis made it
altogether clear that they would be the sole responsibility of
those who had gotten themselves into this mess to begin with.

Thereafter chaos reigned in General Oakhart's league.
The teams decimated by suspensions had to call on local high
school boys to fill out their rosters, if, that is, they could find
high school boys of any ability whose fathers were foolish
enough to compromise their sons' prospects by associating
them with a P. League club. The suspended players meanwhile loudly proclaimed their innocence in bars and poolrooms
all over the country—causing brawls aplenty—or else, following the example of Big John Baal, willingly admitted to whatever it was they were being charged with in the hope that an
admission of guilt and a humble apology ("I'm just a country
boy, I didn't know no better") would lead to reinstatement.
Frank Mazuma did go ahead and bring a damage suit for four
and a half million dollars against the Patriot League President, but the Ellises seemed virtually to acknowledge their guilt
by locking the gates to Greenback Stadium and disappearing
from Tri-City without leaving a trace. Even dedicated P.
League fans indifferent to the dangers of Marxist-Leninism
(and there were many) grew increasingly exasperated by the
shifting schedule, by fourteen- and fifteen-year-old relief pitchers, and by the vociferous American Legion pickets forbidding
them entrance to the bleachers. Consequently, by the end of
the '44 season there wasn't a team in the league, not even the
untainted Tycoons, who could draw more than three hundred
people into the park to watch them play baseball.

The day after Max Lanier picked up the final Cardinal
victory in the '44 World Series, the House Un-American Activities Committee began hearings on Communist infiltration of
the Patriot League in Room 1105 of the federal court house
in Port Ruppert, New Jersey. The Vice President of the United
States, Mr. Henry Wallace, in a speech that very morning before the convention of the East-West Educational and Rehabil-
itation Alliance of the Congress for the Promotion of Hu-
manitarianism in the United Post-War World, described the
investigation as "a despicable affront to our brave Russian
allies," and Mrs. Roosevelt, in her daily newspaper column,
agreed, calling it "an insult to the people and the leaders of

the Soviet Union." F.D.R. was reported to have laughed the whole thing off as so much "electioneering." "By whom, Mr. President?" "Doug Oakhart," the Chief Executive was supposed to have said. "The old war-horse still wants my job."

Each day hundreds of Port Ruppert citizens congregated near the statue of Lincoln at the foot of the Port Ruppert court house steps to watch the subpoenaed witnesses arrive; so did they once line the sidewalk ten and fifteen deep outside the Mundy clubhouse door to catch a glimpse of the great Gofannon as the shy star exited Mundy Park in an open-neck shirt and overalls at the end of a good day's work. Only the crowd back in those days was head over heels in love.

One by one the Mundys whom General Oakhart had suspended arrived with their lawyers to testify before the Committee.

"Traituh!"

"Toincoat!"

"Spy!"

In that entire week only one Port Rupe-it roota was seen weeping, a midget in a messenger's uniform who broke from between a policeman's legs at the sight of Ockatur stepping out of his taxi, and called in a high, breaking voice, "Say it ain't so, O.K.!"

"It ain't, you little asshole!" replied Ockatur, and waddled arrogantly up the steep court house steps one at a time.

Of the thirteen, ten maintained their innocence right down to the end, despite repeated warnings from the chairman that they were testifying under oath and if found guilty of perjury would receive stiff fines and heavy jail sentences; at least half of these ten would undoubtedly have made a confession too, had it not been for Ockatur, who emerged as the strong man of the group, tongue-lashing the fainthearted like Skirnir and appealing to the conscience of the preacher, Demeter, in night-long arguments at their hotel. Of the three who admitted to being Communists, Big John Baal had of course done so prior to being called before the Committee—indeed, he had just gone around the corner from General Oakhart's office and after an hour in a bar "seen the light": "Sure I was a Communist for the Communists," he told the press. "Sure I was trained by the Reds down there in Nicaragey—hell, they wuz all over the place. Sure the Mundys is mostly Commies. I think some of 'em is queers, too. Ha ha ha ha!'' The two who changed their story at the hearings and admitted to affiliations they had previously denied, and of which they were now deeply ashamed, were Nickname Damur (reportedly whipped by his daddy till he told the truth) and Chico Mecoatl, who testified with the aid of an interpreter. At the conclusion of their testimony, in which they fingered not only themselves but the other Communist members of the team, they were lauded by the Committee chairman. "Mr. Damur, Mr. Mecoatl, we appreciate your cooperation with our Committee," said Congressman Dies. "It is only through the assistance of people such as you that we have been able to make the progress that has been made in bringing the attention of the American people to the machinations of this Communist conspiracy for world domination.''

"*Muchas gracias, Señor Dies*," said Chico, but Nickname wept.

The most troublesome of the Mundy Thirteen were the coaches, Isaac Ellis and O.K. Ockatur, both of whom created such commotion at the hearings that they had to be forcibly removed by federal marshals and subsequently were found in contempt of a Congressional committee and each sentenced to a year in jail, Ockatur to the federal penitentiary at Lewisburg, Pennsylvania, and Isaac to a farm for delinquent boys in Rahway, New Jersey, where, within a month of his arrival, he was beaten to death in the shower by his entire dormitory, apparently for suggesting that the great Mundy martyr, Roland Agni, had been involved with him in feeding doped-up breakfast food to his teammates toward the end of the '43 season.

Frenchy Astarte was the only other Mundy to die after giving testimony to the Committee, he by his own hand on the family farm at Gaspé.

The "surprise" witness called by the committee in Port Ruppert was the sports columnist of the Finest Family Newspapers, Word Smith, who refused to answer questions having to do with purported friends of his, "highly placed officials in the executive branch of the government" allegedly involved in the leasing of Mundy Park by the War Department, in accordance, it now turned out, with the Soviet plot to destroy the Patriot League.

"Mr. Chairman," said Smitty, after supplying his name, his address, and his occupation, "this Committee and its investigation is a farce. I refuse to be a party to it. I refuse to answer any more of your questions, particularly questions about my associations, past, present, or in the life to come. I refuse to answer any questions having to do with my political beliefs, my health habits, my sex habits, my eating habits, and my good habits, such as they are. I refuse to apologize or explain or verify any remarks I have ever made to anyone over the telephone, face to face, in my sleep, in my cups, or in my solitude. I refuse to participate in this lunatic comedy in which American baseball players who could not locate Russia on a map of the world—who could not locate *the world* on a map of the world—denounce themselves and their teammates as Communist spies out of fear and intimidation and howling ignorance, or, as is the case with that case named Baal, out of incorrigible human perversity and curdled genes. Truly, sir, I have never seen anything in sixty years of astonishment to compare with these shameful shenanigans. Over the past two seasons it has been my misfortune to follow the Patriot League through one incredible and ludicrous crisis after another. Things have happened on the field of play that I would not have believed if I had not been there to see them with my own eyes. Frankly, I still don't believe them. But for sheer unabashed, unabetted, unabridged, unaccountable, unadorned, unallayed, unamusing, unanticipated, unassailable—"

(Laughter. Scattered applause.)

CHAIRMAN: Now, just a minute—

SMITTY: —uncalled for, unchecked, uncoherent, unconditional—

CHAIRMAN: Counsel, I think you had better advise your client—

SMITTY: —unconnected, unconscionable, unconstrained—

CHAIRMAN: It is you, sir, who is unconstrained. I think you are describing yourself. Now—

SMITTY: —uncontrollable, uncurbed, undecipherable, undefinable—

CHAIRMAN (*pounding gavel*):   Now, you will have to stop or you will leave the witness stand. And you will leave the witness stand because you are in contempt. And if you are just trying to force me to put you in contempt, you won't have to try much harder. You won't have to get to the end of the alphabet to go to jail, you know.

SMITTY: —undesirable, undiluted, undisguised, undreamt-of, unearthly, unequaled, unfaltering, unfathomable, unforgettable—

CHAIRMAN: Officers, take this man away from the stand.

(*Applause and boos as witness is approached by federal marshals.*)

SMITTY: —unreality, Mr. Chairman, for sheer *unununununreality*, I cannot think of anything to compare with what has transpired at these hearings.

CHAIRMAN: Is that all you wanted to tell us?

SMITTY (*being led from the stand by two marshals*):   That ain't exactly nothin'.

CHAIRMAN: But surely as a writer, Mr. Smith, you know the old saying that truth is stranger than fiction.

SMITTY: So are falsehoods, Mr. Chairman. Truth is stranger than fiction, but stranger still are lies.

(*Applause and boos as he is led out of the room.*)

For his defiance Smitty was held in contempt of the Committee and was sentenced to a year in the federal penitentiary at Lewisburg; he was paroled after six months, but never again did his by-line appear in an American newspaper.

November 1944. General Douglas D. Oakhart runs as a write-in candidate for President of the United States. Receives one-tenth of one per cent of the popular vote.

February 1945. HUAC concludes investigation of all Patriot League teams; calls for federal grand jury to investigate baseball.

March 1945. Twenty-three more Communists expelled from Patriot League, bringing total (exclusive of owners) to seventy-two. General Oakhart regretfully suspends league operations until end of war when returning veterans will restore P. League play to "peacetime caliber."

August 1945. Destruction of Fairsmith Stadium in Hiroshima.

October 1945. Publication of *Communism Strikes Out,* by Douglas D. Oakhart (Stand Up and Fight Press, Tri-City, Mass.).

January 1946. First contingent of P. League ex-G.I.s proclaim themselves "free agents." Refuse to honor reserve clause of contracts drawn with "Communist-dominated" teams. Backed by American Legion and Veterans of Foreign Wars. Frank Mazuma promises to carry case to Supreme Court.

March 1946. Gil Gamesh disappears from Tri-City editorial office of Angela Trust weekly national newsletter, *Stand Up and Fight!* Revenge by Communists feared. Mrs. Trust offers hundred thousand dollar reward for information pertaining to Gamesh's whereabouts.

April 1946. Angela Whittling Trust, in surprise preseason move, releases "loyal" Tycoon players from contracts, signaling demise of Patriot League. Says of third major league, "Better dead than Red." Mazuma labels act "mad," promises to fight to restore league "integrity." Publication of *Switch-Hitter, or I Led Two Lives,* by John Baal (Stand Up and Fight Press, Tri-City).

September 1946. War Department dismisses four who engineered lease of Mundy Park from Ruppert franchise. Department of Justice reconvenes grand jury investigating baseball.

March 1947. Wreckers begin demolition of Mundy Park for exclusive harborside luxury apartments. Port Ruppert City Council votes unanimously to change city name by January 1948; contest announced for name appropriate to "new era of expansion and prosperity."

April 1947. Aceldama, Asylum, Independence (Va.), Kakoola, and Terra Incognita follow Port Ruppert example, to be rechristened by '48. Frank Mazuma courtroom heart attack victim; survivors drop legal actions instituted by embittered entrepreneur named by P. League as Soviet spy. "Our family," says Doubloon Mazuma from wheelchair, "has suffered enough from this savage national pastime."

November 1948. General Oakhart runs for President of the United States on Patriot Party ticket; running mate Bob Yamm. Receives surprising two per cent of popular vote; strongest in California. "Crusade under way," says General.

May 1949. Pravda photograph of Moscow May Day celebration reprinted in American papers; hatted figure between Premier Stalin and Minister of State Security Beria identified as Marshal Gilgamesh. Angela Whittling Trust May 2 suicide in underground stadium bunker. May 3, Tri-City councilmen vote to join former P. League towns in search for new name.

June 1952. Tycoon Park, last remaining P. League stadium in U.S., to make way for multi-billion dollar "Maine to Montevideo" highway.

October 1952. Oakhart-Yamm seek McCarthy endorsement; share TV platform when Wisconsin Senator raps Stevenson: "If somebody would only smuggle me aboard the Democratic campaign special with a baseball bat in my hand, I'd teach patriotism to little Ad-lie." Political analysts interpret remark as boost to Patriot Party presidential ticket. Splinter Republicans wave signs, "General E, no! General O, yes!"

November 1952. Oakhart-Yamm receive 2.3 per cent of popular vote, despite charge by Dems. and Reps. that Oakhart dupe of Soviet agent.

March 1953. Pravda photograph of Stalin funeral mourners reprinted in American press; hatted figure between Minister of State Beria and First Secretary Malenkov identified as Marshal Gilgamesh.

December 1953. Lavrenti P. Beria executed in Soviet Union by Stalin's heirs; hatted figure between First Secretary Khrushchev and Minister of Defense Bulganin identified as Marshal Gilgamesh in *Pravda* photo.

March 1954. Marshal Gilgamesh sentenced to death as "double agent" and executed. *Pravda* carries full confession wherein "enemy of people" admits secret connection to American and National Baseball leagues. Leagues in joint statement label Gamesh confession "a preposterous fraud . . . typical act of Communist treachery to which no American in his right mind could possibly give credence." Oakhart calls for full-scale investigation of league presidents Frick and Harridge; McCarthy reported "ready and willing."

August 1956. Private plane en route to Patriot Party Convention in Palm Springs disappears without trace; General Douglas D. Oakhart, Bob and Judy Yamm, and aircraft millionaire pilot assumed dead. Communist sabotage suspected.

EPILOGUE

The drama's done. Why then here does one step forth?—Because one did survive the wreck of the Patriot League. One did survive the madness, the ignorance, the betrayals, the hatred, and the lies! One did survive the Fairsmiths and Oakharts and Trusts and Baals and Mazumas and Gil Gameshes! Survived (somehow!) the writing of this book! O fans, forgive the hubris, but I'm a little in awe of my own fortitude. Rage, we know, can carry a writer a long long way, but O the anguish en route, the loneliness, the exhaustion, the self-doubt. But I will not describe again the scorn and the derision to which I've been subjected (see Prologue); believe me when I say, *they don't let up, they're out there being smug and self-satisfied and stupid every single day!* Charges of lunacy from senile old goats! Literary criticism from philistine physicians! Vile aspersions cast upon my probity, my memory, my dignity, my honor—and by whom? By the fogeys in the TV room watching *The Price Is Right!* O try it, fans, try plying your trade day in and day out with all around you sneering and calling you cracked. Do an old man a favor and see how far you get laying your bricks and selling your salamis, with every passerby crying, "Liar! Madman! Fool!" See how *you* hold up. O fans, it's been no picnic scratching out the truth here at Valhalla.

Or surviving those publishers down in New York. Let me share with you a representative sampling of their prose—and prudence, you might call it, if you were of a generous turn of mind.

Dear Mr. Smith:

I find what I have read of your novel thoroughly objectionable. It is a vicious and sadistic book of the most detestable sort, and your treatment of blacks, Jews, and women, not to mention the physically and mentally handicapped, is offensive in the extreme; in a word, sick.

Dear Mr. Smith:

We find your novel far-fetched and lacking authenticity and are returning it herewith.

Dear Mr. Smith:

Book blew my mind. Great put-down of Estab. Wild and zany black humor à la Bruce & Burroughs. The Yamms are a gas. I'd publish tomorrow if I was in charge here. But the Money Men tell me there's no filthy lucre in far-out novel by unknown ab't mythical baseball team. What can ya' do? Fallen world. I make what inroads I can but they are a CONGLOMERATE and I am just a "Smitty" to them. Anyhoo: let me buy you a lunch if you're ever down from Valhalla. And please let me see your next. Y'r 'umble.

Dear Mr. Smith:

I am returning your manuscript. Several people here found portions of it entertaining, but by and large the book seemed to most of us to strain for its effects and to simplify for the sake of facile satiric comment the complex realities of American political and cultural life.

Dear Mr. Smith:

Too long and a little old-hat. Sorry.

No need to quote from the other twenty-two filed here in my pocket, nor from my replies.

And now? Yet another year has passed—and I and the truth remain buried alive. Around me the other aged endear themselves to the doctor by playing checkers by day and dying by night. Weekly the incoming arrive on canes, the outgoing depart in polyethylene sacks. "Well," says the nurse to each

decrepit newcomer, "I think you're going to like it here,
Gramps. We look after you and you look after yourself, and
the world outside can just worry about its own problems for a
change." "Oh," comes the codger's reply, "sounds good to
me. No more teachers, no more books." "That's the spirit,"
chirps the slit, and sets him out in the sun to start in drying up
for the grave. "Some folks," she growls, as I hand her a letter
to post, "know how to enjoy the old age the good Lord has
been kind enough to grant them." To which *I* reply, "Tam-
pering with the mails is a federal offense. Be sure that goes
out tonight."

Yes, I fire off letter after letter—to Walter Cronkite, to
William Buckley, to David Susskind, to Senator Kennedy, to
Ralph Nader, to the Human Rights Commission of the UN, to
renowned American authors, to Ivy League professors, to
columnists, to political cartoonists, to candidates for public
office looking for an "issue"; alert to the danger of appearing
just another crank to the savvy secretaries of the great, I
employ in my correspondence a style as dignified as any an
investment banker or a funeral director might use on a pros-
pective client: I am respectful, I am thoughtful, I am restrained. I wrestle insistence into submission; I smother upper
case howls in the crib; exclamation points, those bloody dag-
gers, I drive back into my own innards; and I don't alliterate
(if I can help it). Yes, I forgo everything and anything smacking of seething, seething all the more so as I do so. And still I
never get a serious reply.

The latest and, admittedly, most desperate of my letters
follows. Beyond this there seems to me nowhere to go, except
to that undiscovered country from which no traveler returns.
Needless to say, when my fellows here learned of my letter's
destination, my reputation as resident laughingstock soared.
"There's the feller I tole you that writes them letters to
China," they inform the local do-gooders who bring us their
cakes and cookies once a week. "A real screwball, that one.
Imagination up and run away with him, and the two just never
come back. Cracked right down the middle, he is." "Well,"
say the good ladies of Valhalla, New York, "I myself feel
more pity than contempt for such a person," whereupon they
are informed that that is compassion misspent.

The plight of the artist, fans. Meanwhile, no answer from China as yet. But I will wait. I will wait, and I will wait, and I will wait. And need I tell you what that's like, for a man without the time for waiting, or the temperament?

Valhalla Home for the Aged
Valhalla, New York
January 15, 1973

Chairman Mao Tse-tung
Great Hall of the People
Peking, China

My dear Chairman Mao:

I am sure you are aware of the recent publication in the United States of a great historical novel by the Soviet writer and Nobel Prize winner for Literature, Alexander I. Solzhenitsyn. As you must know, Mr. Solzhenitsyn was not able to find a publisher for this work in the Soviet Union and subsequently has been vilified and traduced by his fellow Soviet writers for allowing his manuscript to be smuggled out to the West for publication. The reason Mr. Solzhenitsyn is despised in Russia is that his version of Russian history happens not to correspond with the version that is promulgated by the powers-that-be over there. In short, he refuses to accept lies for truth and myth for reality. For this he has been expelled from the Soviet writers' union and designated an enemy of the people by the Russian government. I understand that he lives now in isolation from society, virtually under arrest, in his apartment in Moscow.

If I have followed Mr. Solzhenitsyn's tragic circumstances with more than ordinary interest and concern during the months he has been in the news here, it is because I am an author who has for years lived in something like the same situation in America as he does in Soviet Russia. Presently I am as good as imprisoned in a county home for the destitute aged in upstate New York, where, by staff and inmates alike, I am considered deranged. Why? Because I have written a historical novel that does not accord with the American history with which they brainwash our little children in the schools. I say "historical," doubtless they would say "hysterical." Not a single American publisher dares to present the American people with the true story I have told, nor is there anyone here at Valhalla who considers me and my book anything but a joke. I have every reason to believe that upon my death, which like yours, Mr. Chairman, could occur any minute—I am nearing ninety, sir—the manuscript that is continually at my side for safekeeping will be destroyed, and with it all record of this heinous chapter in my country's history.

Now you may wonder why I am not addressing this letter to Party Chairman Brezhnev in Moscow. At first glance it might appear that he would pounce upon the opportunity for retaliation against the United States and the "traitor" Solzhenitsyn, by printing in Russia, and in Russian, a book that for all intents and purposes has been suppressed in America because it is at variance with the U.S. Government Officially Authorized Version of Reality. Once you have read the last chapter of my book, however, you will understand quickly enough why the Russians would find this work no less compromising than the Americans do. On the other hand, I would think that precisely what makes it so odious to these two fearful giants, is what would make it attractive to you.

I am writing to you, Chairman Mao, to propose the publication of my book in the People's Republic of China. I assure you that nobody knows better than I the difficulties of translation that are posed by a work like mine, particularly into Chinese. Still, I cannot believe that such obstacles would prove insurmountable to the people whose labor raised the Great Wall, or the leader whose determination has carried them on their Long March to Communism. I do not mean, by the way, to give the impression that I turn to you because I sympathize with your state and its methods, or feel a special kinship with your people or your system or yourself. I turn to Mao Tse-tung because I have no one else to turn to. Likewise, you should know that I am under no illusion about the devotion of politicians either to truth or to art, not even those like yourself who write poetry on the side. If you ran China on the side and wrote poetry in front, that would be another matter. But nations and leaders being what they are, I realize full well that if you publish my book, it will be because you consider it in the interest of your revolution to do so.

Mr. Chairman, we are two very old men who have survived great adversity and travail. In our own ways, on our own continents, with our own people, each has led an embattled life, and each continues to survive on the strength of an impassioned belief: yours is China, mine is art—an art, sir, not for its own sake, or the sake of national pride or personal renown, but art for the sake of the record, an art that reclaims what is and was from those whose every word is a falsification and a betrayal of the truth. "In battle with the lie," said Alexander I. Solzhenitsyn, "art has always been victorious, always wins out, visibly, incontrovertibly for all! The lie can stand against much in the world—but not against art.'' Thus my defiant Russian colleague in a Nobel Prize lecture that he was prevented from delivering in Stockholm by the falsifiers who govern in his land. O would that I might draw upon his courage, his strength, and his wisdom in the days and months to come, if they come. For I will need all that and more to survive in upstate New York when (and if) *The Great American Novel* is published in Peking.

Respectfully yours,
Word Smith
(Author of ''One
Man's Opinion'')